Susan H

Cold Kill

Published by Sunningdale Books

All rights reserved
© Susan Handley, 2023

Susan Handley has asserted her right under the Copyright, Designs and
Patents Act 1988 to be identified as the author of this work.

This book is a work of fiction and any resemblance to actual persons, living or
dead, is purely coincidental.

1.

'So, Mr Rudd, you just happened to be parked outside the jeweller's and the two men jumped into the back of your car?' DI Matt Fisher asked the man sitting opposite.

'That's right.'

'Why were you parked there?'

'Why shouldn't I be parked there?' Rudd grumbled.

'It's double yellows.'

'Yeah well, I couldn't find a space anywhere else, could I? Hey, are you really blind?'

Fisher felt a waft of air cross his face. He shot his hand out and snatched hold of the other man's wrist.

'What'ya doing? Let go!' Rudd tried to yank his hand away.

Fisher released his grip and heard Rudd clatter back into his seat.

'Try something like that again and you'll find assault of a police officer added to your charge sheet.'

'You assaulted me. What sort of scam are you running, making out you can't see?'

Fisher wasn't about to let on that Rudd wasn't the first person to wave a hand in front of his face, nor that he'd simply struck lucky with his aim.

'I take it you've never heard how losing your sight sharpens the other senses?'

A look of disbelief must have crossed Rudd's face, as DC Beth Nightingale, sitting next to Fisher, said, 'It's true.'

'Take my sense of smell,' Fisher went on. 'As keen as a dog's. Which is why I know you're lying. You reek of guilt. It's oozing out of your pores like a bad case of B.O.'

'Yeah. Well sniff this,' Rudd said, snorting out a reedy laugh.

Fisher turned to Nightingale.

'He just stuck his middle finger up at me, didn't he?'

'Yes, sir, he did.'

Fisher swivelled his head back towards the other man.

'Glad to see you're taking the situation seriously.' He slammed his hands down on the desk. 'Enough of the fun and games. Aside from the fact you were caught attempting to flee the scene this afternoon, a man matching your description was also seen in a car outside Fremlin's jeweller's when that was hit last month. An ID parade is being arranged in which you will be—'

Rudd didn't wait for Fisher to finish.

'Bring it on.'

'You don't seem unduly worried.'

'Like I'd be stupid enough not to wear a hat and keep me head down. That is, if it was me. Which, of course, it wasn't.'

'Ah yes, a hat. Now that would be sensible. Though not if it was like the one we found in your car at the time of your arrest, which was a baseball cap with a logo that's as discreet as a whore at a vicar's tea party.' Fisher shook his head. 'You're an idiot. You know that?' He turned to Nightingale. 'Detective Constable, I think we've got everything we need. Would you do the honours, please?'

Nightingale cleared her throat and said, 'Interview suspended at fourteen hundred hours.'

Fisher and Nightingale left Rudd in the hands of the custody sergeant, and started back to the office.

'Do you think anyone will ever buy it... the superhuman senses bit?' she asked.

'Does it matter?' Fisher replied, swinging his white stick in front of him in a wide arc. 'It's not like they're going to plead guilty either way, but I like to think it puts the wind up them a bit.'

Fisher stopped speaking, aware of approaching footsteps — a woman's heel, short and clipped. He recognised the gait as belonging to DCI Anita Fallon.

'DI Fisher,' she said, curt as always.

'Ma'am.'

'Have you seen Dave Beswick? I was told he was down here interviewing.'

'He's taken one of the suspects to hospital, reckons his nose is broken. Me and Beth are free, if something's come up?'

'It's okay. It can wait,' she replied, before striding off in the direction she came from.

Luna greeted Fisher enthusiastically on his return to his desk. He'd left her there, opting to take advantage of the relatively safe confines of the station to practise with his white stick. He sat down and patted her flanks.

'You missed me, huh?'

'I'll just top her water up,' Nightingale said, brushing past him as she reached for the bowl.

As she walked away, Fisher reached into his pocket and pulled out his mobile, unmuting it with the flick of a switch. The phone gave a ping, signalling a new message. He deftly swiped his thumb across the screen, listening to the automated voice read out the icons as he scrolled through to voicemail. He hit play.

'Hi. It's Andy. Give us a call when you're free, will ya?'

He thumbed the screen to return the call.

'Andy, it's Matt. What's up?' Fisher listened until the sergeant had finished, then, after heaving out a sigh, said, 'I bloody knew it. Thanks for the tip-off.'

Ever since his return to work, after being blinded in an acid attack, the DCI shied away from giving him any major cases to work. Something he suspected was more to do with the fact he'd once made the mistake of blurring the lines between work and pleasure than because she lacked confidence in him now that he was blind; he was learning first-hand what lengths a woman scorned might go to. Thankfully, he could still count on the rest of his team.

He ended the call and reached for Luna's harness. A moment later, they were standing outside the glass box that was the DCI's office. Finding the door open, he rapped his knuckles on the frame.

There was a slight pause, perhaps as the Falcon considered feigning her absence, then after an audible sigh, she gave a half-hearted, 'Come in.'

'Ma'am, I just heard about the fatal stabbing,' Fisher said, crossing the short distance to her desk. 'I assume you want me to head over there straightaway, seeing as I'm the only DI available.'

'Thank you but that won't be necessary. DI Beswick will be heading over there as soon as he's finished at the hospital.'

'But why? Dave's got his hands full working the armed robbery and I don't currently have an active case.' When, after a second, she still hadn't said anything, he went on, 'What were you expecting? It's hardly like I wasn't going to find out about it.'

'You were busy.'

He gripped Luna's harness and clenched his teeth. Mustering all his self-control, he said, 'I'd just told you I was free.'

For a long moment, the DCI said nothing and Fisher pictured her tortured expression as she hastened to come up with a reason as to why she wouldn't be assigning him the case. Eventually, she replied, 'There's no point arguing. I'm not giving you the case. The scene of a gangland killing is not a safe place for someone with your disability. I'll make sure to log the health and safety assessment on your file.'

'You're kidding?'

'Not at all. I'm showing concern for your welfare.'

'The hell you are. I don't believe it. Is this how it's going to be every time something new comes in?'

'Watch your tone, detective,' she snapped. 'I shouldn't have to remind you who you're talking to.'

'Like I could forget. You're the person who keeps stopping me doing what I'm paid to do, despite the fact that, so far, I've proved to be perfectly capable. You know you're going to have to give in eventually. An employment tribunal could run into hundreds of thousands. And you won't win. I promise you that.' After a moment's standoff, he said, 'Me and Beth can be there in less than half an hour.'

'I've told you; I've already asked Dave to deal with it. Now if you don't mind...' He heard the clunk of the phone as she picked up the receiver, followed by the sound of her painted talons stabbing the keys. 'Oh... and close the door on your way out.'

By the time he reached the threshold she was in full conversation. Back at his desk, he slumped in his chair. He heard Nightingale's light tread approach and felt Luna stir at his feet as she put down the water bowl.

She must have noticed his ennui as she asked, 'What's happening?'

Fisher let his head sag back and stared blindly at the ceiling.

'Nothing. Absolutely fucking nothing.'

***

That evening after dinner, Fisher was enjoying a cup of tea in the garden when his mobile started to ring. An electronic voice informed him Amanda was calling. There had been a time when he would have let it bounce to voicemail, the prospect of talking to his soon-to-be ex-wife after the sort of day he'd had being too much to bear. Thankfully, more recently, they had made peace with one another… most of the time, at least.

He swiped to answer.

'Hi. How's it going?' he asked, trying to inject his voice with some levity.

'I haven't caught you at work, have I?'

'No. I'm home. Just finished my dinner.'

'Well I won't keep you long. I'm just calling to see if you could have Joshua on Saturday. I know I said I was taking him to the coast for the weekend but I've got the chance to pitch for a new job.' Amanda was an event planner, weddings a speciality. A job she took very seriously.

'You know I'm always happy to have him if I can. Just Saturday or…?'

'Saturday and Sunday. If that's okay? If it's a problem I can always make other arrangements. I wouldn't want to get in the way of you and…' She let the sentence hang.

'If you mean Ginny, she likes Josh. It's really not a problem.'

'She'll be there then, will she? I thought she might be working Saturday night.'

Fisher felt the hair on the back of his neck bristle.

'Would it be a problem if she was?'

'It depends. Will she be staying? I don't like the idea of the pair of you together with Joshua in the next room.'

'Frazer stayed over with you.'

'Yes, well, that was a mistake.'

6

'All the same…' He could virtually hear her defences going up. He'd won some hard-fought battles in order to be able to see Josh on a regular basis, he didn't plan on undoing that any time soon. 'Look, I don't want to fall out about it. As it happens Ginny is working this weekend.'

After a long pause, Amanda said, 'Okay. That's fine. I'll drop him off sometime around midday.' And with that she rang off.

Fisher sat for a moment, contemplating the exchange. It had been almost a year since they'd decided to go their separate ways. Or rather, since Amanda decided she no longer wanted to be the wife of a has-been footballer turned disabled detective. And she was still calling the shots, even now.

He took a swig of his cold tea and scrolled through his contacts until he got to Ginny's number.

'Hey you,' she said on answering. 'What's up?'

'Nothing. Just thought I'd give you a ring, see how you're doing.'

'Matt, we saw each other last night. I'm doing pretty much the same as I was then. So, come on, spit it out.'

She was far too clever for him.

'I just had a call from Amanda.'

'Oh right.'

'She asked if I could have Josh over on Saturday.'

'Great. We should do something. Go out for the day or maybe even go somewhere for the weekend.'

'I thought you were working.'

'I am but I'm sure Ben will be happy to cover. He's always up for extra shifts.'

'Ah, well, the thing is, I was thinking I might use the time for a bit of father-son bonding.'

There was a pause, then she said, 'What you mean is A-man-da,' she said with a put-on posh accent, 'doesn't want me near her precious son.'

'That's not it at all.'

'Come on Matt. You saw Josh last week. On your own. And two weeks before that. On your own. How much father and son bonding do you need? Please don't take me for a fool.'

'You know I'd never do that. It was just an idea. Of course we can do something together. I'd love that.'

After ending the call, he sat for a moment, phone in hand. Luna came over and gave him a nudge.

'Why does life have to be so difficult, eh?' he said, dropping an arm around her neck.

2.

The following morning, Fisher was shrugging out of his coat when DS Wickham called over, 'Matt! The DCI wants to see you asap.'

'Did she say what about?'

'What do you think?'

Fisher threw his coat over the back of his chair and picked up his white stick. Then slowly — more slowly than really necessary — made his way to Fallon's office. He found the door open.

'You wanted to see me?' he said.

For a moment, he thought she mustn't have been there as she didn't reply. It was only when he turned to leave that she spoke.

'Come in. Take a seat.' He crossed the room until he felt his stick hit something. He set a hand out and on feeling an empty chair, sat down.

'I've been giving some thought to our conversation yesterday,' she said. 'And I understand your frustration.'

'You do?' Whatever he'd expected her to say, it wasn't that.

'Yes. And to prove it's not personal I've got something for you to get your teeth into.'

Fisher felt the scar tissue snag as his eyebrows shot up in surprise.

'The fatal stabbing?'

'No. Forget that. This is much bigger. I want you to head up a whole new unit — the Major Crimes Review Unit.'

Fisher's face fell.

'Review Unit? Review what exactly?'

'Open-unsolved cases.'

'We've already got a cold case review team; Brian Carp runs it.'

'Brian retires next month. Plus, the Chief Constable wants a renewed push on improving our solve rate. I want you to go back over our cold cases and look at them afresh.'

'Have you offered the job to any of the other DIs?' When she didn't reply, he said, 'That'll be a no then, because you know none of them would want it.'

'That's not true. I haven't asked them because I think you're the best man for the job.'

'You're giving a job that requires going through someone else's case files and running matching exercises to a blind man?'

'You're the one who keeps telling me your disability doesn't get in the way of the job. Besides, you seem to get on perfectly well with a screen reader. Think about it — you could get some results, with all the advances in forensics and DNA evidence, and the fact you think outside the box and see connections where others can't. Think of it as an opportunity to make your name.'

'I don't want to make my name. I just want to be able to work the same cases as everyone else.'

'What does it matter if the cases are old?'

'It matters. The truth is you'll do anything to get me off the force. You'll give me shit job after shit job, until I fold. Come on, we're both adults, the door's closed, just tell it as it is.'

Fallon blew out a long breath.

'Why do you have to reduce everything to an argument? I told you at the start of this conversation, I understand your frustration. I really do. For a man of your age to have lost so much...' There was a pause and for a second Fisher almost bought the sympathetic boss act, but then she was back on form and said briskly, 'But you still have your job. Which is why you would be wise to avoid doing anything that might jeopardise that.' Fisher leaned forward and opened his mouth to speak, but if she noticed, it didn't stop her. 'I suggest you use the intervening period to familiarise yourself with the list of cold cases and quiz Brian before he leaves.'

Fisher knew Brian. Knew he'd been coasting for a few years, winding down towards retirement. Maybe it wouldn't be such a bad gig after all — with his attention to detail and Beth's ability to chase down information they really could make a difference.

'Apart from Beth, who else will be on the team?' he asked.

'Why would you need a team?'

'How else am I going to investigate new leads. I can't do it all myself.'

'You don't need to investigate anything. All you need to do is rerun the forensics against the databases. Report back any matches that get thrown up and I'll decide how to take it forward.'

Fisher threw his weight back in his seat and folded his arms. 'Forget it. You could get an admin to do that. Either I take the cases on lock stock or you can get someone else to do your donkey work.'

'Are you sure you want to go down this road? Even your union rep will find it hard to back you if you refuse. Just look at it as an opportunity to put your money where your mouth is. You're always telling everyone how you're still up to the job. Prove it.'

'I don't recall having to tell anyone I'm up to the job. Apart from you. Who I seem to have to constantly remind, despite the fact that I've closed every one of my cases since I returned to work.'

For a moment the silence hung heavy in the room.

'You can have Nightingale, but that's all. I've already asked Brian to send the latest cold case report to you this morning. Seeing as you've got nothing else on, you may as well start today.'

Fisher heard papers being shuffled. The meeting was over. He rose from his seat, turned and started for the door, swinging his white stick in front of him like a scythe.

'Should keep you busy for a while,' Fallon said under her breath as he reached the door.

For a second, Fisher considered turning around and telling her to stick the cold cases where the sun doesn't shine, but that would only play into her hands. Instead, he took a deep breath, crossed the threshold and slammed the door behind him.

A sudden hush came over the office.

'Was that me?' he said loudly. 'Sorry. Don't know my own strength sometimes.'

As he crossed the floor, heading back to his desk, the sounds of a busy office crept back to normal levels. He had just sat down when he heard a quiet tread approach.

'Is something up?' It was Nightingale.

He wiped his hands roughly over his face then blew out his cheeks.

'Depends on your point of view.' He heard the chair next to his desk emit a squeak as she sat down. 'We've got a new case. Well, cases.'

'Brilliant.'

Fisher heard the hope in her voice. A flash of rage shot through him. It was one thing for the Falcon to take her spiteful vindictiveness out on him, but to subject Beth to the same punishment wasn't fair. He fleetingly thought of returning to argue it out with her but knew it would be pointless. The only

12

thing he could do was to make sure Beth got the most out of the experience.

He cleared his throat and gave a smile.

'The DCI wants me to run the cold case unit after Brian Carp retires.'

'Sounds good. How many cases are we talking about?'

'Let's take a look, shall we? Brian should have emailed me the details.' He slipped his headphones on and tapped at his keyboard.

Nightingale heaved out a sigh.

'There's hundreds of them.'

And Fisher hadn't even finished scrolling.

'Don't go getting all negative on me,' he said. 'All we need to do at this stage is pull out any cases where DNA and fingerprints were found at the scene, then run them through the databases again and see if there are any matches.'

With Nightingale returning to her desk to start working her half of the list, Fisher slipped on his headphones, and turned his attention to his half. It was barely five minutes later, when he sensed a light touch to his shoulder. Turning, he pulled down his headphones.

'It's Beth. Sorry to interrupt.'

'You can't have got something already.'

'No. It's not that. I just thought you'd want to know…' The familiar scent of her apple shampoo wafted over Fisher as she leaned in close and whispered, 'I just overheard the DCI talking to Kami. She asked her which of the DIs are in today.' Her breath tickled his ear as she spoke and he had to fight the urge to rub it. 'I had a look at the incident log, turns out an elderly woman has been found murdered in her home.'

Fisher jolted upright. He grabbed Luna's harness. 'Come on.' He started towards the office door.

'Where are we going?'

'To offer our services.'

As he approached the Falcon's office he said, 'Is she in?'

'Yes.'

'On her own?'

'Yes.'

He gave a sharp rap at the door and walked straight in.

'I hear a new case has come in. I want to run with it. Before you say no, I'll save you the trouble. I know I'm the only DI in. Plus, the others have all got active cases running. I'm the only one who hasn't.'

'You seem to have forgotten that little project I gave you.'

He thought of Nightingale, standing by his side, uncomplaining, despite the fact her career opportunities were being limited with every case he was denied.

'I said *active* cases. There's nothing on our list that won't keep. Yesterday you refused to let me take the stabbing case on the grounds of health and safety. I'm sure we can both agree there's little risk to me investigating the death of a pensioner in her own home.' The Falcon said nothing. She started to drum her fingers on the desk. Maybe he could help make the decision for her. 'Of course, you could give it to one of the others. But they're already over-stretched. At some point they're going to start to ask why I'm having such an easy time of it. This case doesn't sound likely to attract much attention from the media or the bigwigs upstairs, but what happens if none of the other DIs are available when the next case comes in and it's bigger and more newsworthy? What will you do then?'

The drumming stopped. The room fell quiet.

Fisher waited.

Eventually the Falcon came to a decision.

'You'll need this.' Fisher heard the sound of something slide across the desk towards him. 'It's the address.'

He stepped forward and brushed the polished wooden surface with his fingers until he felt the edge of a sheet of paper. He picked it up and started for the door.

'And Fisher...' she called after him. 'Don't make me regret this.'

3.

Fisher and Nightingale had been on the road for just over half an hour when Fisher felt the car slow and come to a stop.

'Nice house,' Nightingale said, pulling on the handbrake.

'Nice area, if I remember rightly.' Fisher knew the address. They were in an older part of town where grand Edwardian properties sit proudly behind short walls on tree-lined streets. 'King's Avenue... sounds familiar. I wonder if I've dealt with something here before.'

Leaving Luna in the car, Fisher donned his scene suit without incident — the hours of practising at home paying off — and set a hand on Nightingale's shoulder, letting her lead the way to the crime scene.

'Who else is here?' Fisher asked the officer standing guard at the front door after he'd taken their details.

'The CSIs, the pathologist and one of your lot.'

'Our lot?'

'Serious Crime.'

Fisher gave a nod and a tight smile. Had the Falcon changed her mind and sent one of the other DIs after all?

'If you're ready Beth...'

'You might want to go around the back,' the uniform said. 'It's a bit of a squeeze in the hallway.'

At the back door they slipped plastic covers over their shoes. Broken glass crunched underfoot as they stepped into the kitchen.

Fisher's nose twitched as the sickly sweet, cabbage-like aroma of death filled his nostrils.

'Hello! DI Fisher here. Anyone available to fill me in on what we've got?'

'Hey, Matt...'

'Andy? What are you doing here?' Fisher heard the crackle of polypropylene as the sergeant walked towards them.

'The DCI sent me. Wanted me to make a start while she looked for a deputy SIO. So, you got the gig then?' Wickham lowered his voice, 'How come?'

'Let's just say I managed to convince her that I'm not just a pretty face. So, what've we got?'

'The victim is Margery Walker. Eighty-two years old. Caucasian. Lived alone. Alarm was raised by a neighbour. Body was found in the hallway with a plastic bag over her head, tied with a length of electrical cord. She was lying face down, feet towards the front door, head towards the kitchen.'

'A bag *and* a ligature? Talk about overkill. Was she strangled or smothered to death?'

'What are you asking him for?' came a familiar voice.

'Bernie! Long time, no see.'

'Still with the jokes, eh Matt?' Fisher heard the clip of heels on the tiled floor as the pathologist, Dr Bernadette Cooper, entered the kitchen. 'But you're right, it's been a while. I keep telling you, you should pop by for cuppa. You know where I am.'

'No offence but I'll pass, thanks.'

Since losing his sight in the acid attack, Fisher had a valid excuse not to attend post mortems. Not many people could say they enjoyed watching what was once a living, breathing person get sliced open, and even fewer would claim not to mind the smell, but for Fisher it wasn't the stench of death that turned his stomach — he'd long got used to that — it was the fact that the combination of disinfectant and decay took him right back to his time in hospital when the medics fought to save his sight. The mere memory of it set his heart racing and his stomach churning.

Forcing the images from his head, he said, 'So doc, what can you tell us?'

'The victim appears to have suffered very few injuries, suggesting she succumbed to her attacker relatively easily. I think the bag over her head probably disorientated her, caused her to panic and resulted in an immediate shortage of oxygen.'

'What type of bag is it?'

'Black plastic. Not as big or flimsy as a bin bag, more heavy duty like a rubble sack.'

'And the electrical cord?'

'Just everyday electrical flex, the sort you get on appliances like a hairdryer or kettle, but with the plug cut off.'

'Odd choice, isn't it? I'd have thought it would be easier to get a decent grip with a rope.'

'Flex is less likely to trap fibres or any other microscopic evidence the CSIs seem adept at picking up. Maybe your murderer has picked up a few tips from the plethora of police and crime programmes that saturate our screens these days. Though why people want to watch them is beyond me. They should try working at the pointy end of crime. They'd soon change their minds.'

Fisher gave a lopsided smile.

'So, going back to my original question, was she smothered or strangled?'

'Shall I even bother with a post mortem? I suppose I could always take a stab in the dark now and spend tomorrow playing tennis.'

'It's only because I have such faith in your abilities.'

'Yeah, right,' the doctor said, with a heavy dose of humour. She continued, 'Based on a visual inspection of the marks on her neck from the flex, I think it's reasonable to assume the cause of death was ligature strangulation. I'll be able to confirm once I've completed a more thorough examination.'

'And would it be too impertinent of me to ask when this might have happened?'

'Ah, the million-dollar question. It's a tough one. The heating was on when we got here, which will have accelerated decomposition, but based on the fact that there is still some evidence of rigor, which in an older, inactive person tends to hang around, as well as some bloating to the abdomen and distinct marbling of the skin, I would estimate that life was extinguished between twenty-four and forty-eight hours ago.'

Fisher gave a soft whistle. 'A 24-four-hour window. You can't narrow it down any?'

'If I was pressed, I'd say it was probably closer to forty-eight hours than twenty-four. Maybe thirty-six to forty-two hours. But given how much time has passed and all the different variables, I wouldn't stake my pension on it.'

Fisher heard a buzzing moments before a fly settled on his cheek. He brushed it away.

'Sometime Tuesday then? Afternoon or early evening being most likely.'

'I'd say so, yes. Analysis of the stomach contents might be able to narrow it down a bit more, if you can find out when she last ate.'

'Any dirty dishes or half-eaten dinner around to indicate what her last meal was?'

'No,' Wickham replied.

'If that's everything?' Dr Cooper said. 'I'd like to get on.'

'Thank you,' Fisher said. 'You've been most helpful, as always.' He heard the doctor walk away and turned to Wickham. 'Andy, anything else we should be aware of?'

'A handbag, presumably the victim's, was found on the hallway floor, close to the body. A purse was next to it, empty of cash.'

'A petty robbery? First time I've heard of a burglar coming armed with a plastic bag and electrical flex. Was anything else taken?'

'Nothing obvious,' Wickham replied.

'Doc...' Fisher called.

'Yes?' Dr Cooper shouted back.

'Is the victim wearing any jewellery?'

He heard footsteps approach, though this time they didn't get as far as the tiled floor of the kitchen.

'No. But there is a pale band of skin on her ring finger that's smoother than the rest of her hand. It's possible she normally wears a ring or rings.'

With the doctor returning her attention to the deceased, Fisher said, 'Okay, so, we can't rule burglary out. Perhaps someone broke in, thinking the place empty and on finding the victim at home, panicked. Andy, I noticed there's some broken glass on the floor by the back door. Is that where the killer came in?'

'No. That was the responding unit. One of the uniforms broke a window in the kitchen door to get access. I've seen no sign of forced entry. Unfortunately, there's no doorbell camera, which would have been helpful.'

'Any sign of a struggle?'

'No. There's a hallway table with a lamp and a bowl of some dried flowers and stuff in it. None of that looks like it's been disturbed. But then, how much would you expect an old lady to struggle? Especially when she's got a bag over her head and a noose around her neck.'

'Yes, but unless the killer shoved the bag over her head at the doorstep — a bit tricky if you don't want the neighbours to see — there would have been a moment when she was face to face with her attacker.'

'She might have been too infirm to do anything,' Wickham said. 'Or maybe she knew them?'

Nightingale jumped in.

'Or maybe they pretended to be selling something or collecting for charity. She could have been looking in her purse for a donation when they pounced.'

'Maybe, maybe, maybe...' Fisher said. They were all good points. 'Right, okay. Andy, could you co-ordinate the house-to-house enquiries? Apart from the usual who saw what, find out if anyone's been canvassing the area or selling door-to-door recently. Beth, you and I will take a quick look around and then go and talk to whoever found the body. Andy, any idea who that was?'

'The uniform on the front door. Name's PC Greene.'

As Wickham left, Fisher turned to Nightingale. With one hand resting on her shoulder, Fisher matched her step for step as they moved forward. Stepping over the threshold into the hallway, he carefully felt his way onto a metal floor plate set down by the CSIs to avoid contamination and asked for a description of the scene.

'The victim is lying on the floor about a metre in front of us,' Nightingale started. 'A handbag and an open purse are lying next

21

to the body. As Andy said, there's a console table by the front door. On it is a small lamp, a bowl of potpourri and a phone — one of those ones you plug into the wall. Just to your left, there's a wooden chair, like a kitchen chair. There's a walking stick hanging over the back and a coat rack above it. There's no sign of any disturbance.'

'Okay. Let's move on to the next room.'

'The lounge is immediately to our right.' Nightingale started forward. After a few steps Fisher traded the hard floor pads for the welcoming caress of carpet. Even the air seemed fresher, with the foul stench of death having been masked by a reassuring bouquet — lily of the valley, if he wasn't mistaken.

'The smell of perfume's quite strong in here,' he said. 'Which suggests the door was closed. I wonder if the victim closed it before answering the door, or whether the killer pulled it to. Beth, could you go find one of the CSIs, make sure they check the door for prints, please?'

A minute later, Nightingale was back. She resumed her commentary, 'Okay, so this is the lounge. It's quite a big room. There's a three-seater sofa and an armchair. Looks like one of those riser-recliners. My nan's got one... she loves it. There's an open newspaper on one of the arms.' He heard her pad across the room. 'It's Tuesday's Telegraph. Looks like she'd nearly finished the crossword.'

'Is there a TV?'

'Yes.'

'Have a quick look, see if it's missing any cables. Though I can't imagine the killer had time to root around for a flex and a suitable plastic bag whilst making small talk with the victim. But you never know.'

'Might work if they were pretending to be a TV repair man,' Nightingale commented. 'Nothing missing as far as I can tell.

Both the TV and Sky box are wired up okay. Oh!' The note of surprise in her voice caused the hairs on the back of his neck to bristle.

'What is it?'

'There's a bookcase on the wall behind the sofa. There are some framed photographs on it. You're in one of them.'

'Me? Are you sure?'

'Yes. You look a lot younger but it's definitely you. You're with five other boys and an older guy who's holding a football. You're all in the same kit, apart from the older guy who's in a tracksuit.'

'How old would you say I am?'

Nightingale gave a groan.

'I don't know. Fourteen? Sixteen?'

'What does the older guy look like?'

'Short and stocky. He's got thick sandy hair, a flat nose and a wonky sort of mouth, though that might just be the way he's smiling.'

'Coach Walker.' Frowning, Fisher shook his head. 'What's the victim's name again?'

'Margery Walker. Same surname. Her husband maybe?'

'Oh my God, it's Em! Em Walker. I always thought Em was short for Emily or Emma, not Margery.' He wiped a hand over his face. 'You know, I owe a lot of my success to her and Coach Walker. A lot of the lads I used to hang around with do. They helped tame a group of unruly teenagers and turned us into half-decent adults with a fantastic future ahead of us. God...'

'So that's why you recognised the address. You've been here before.'

Fisher shook his head.

'Sadly, no.'

His shoulders sagged with the realisation that the woman who had once nurtured him like a second mother lay dead less than ten feet away. He blew out a sigh as a long-forgotten memory reared its ugly head. There he was, back in hospital with the bandages over his eyes, hearing a quiet tread crossing the room towards him, and then that delicate, floral fragrance enveloping him in its embrace.

'Hello Matthew,' she'd said, as she took his hand in her cool, papery clasp and explained how she'd seen the news of the acid attack on the television and felt compelled to visit. She'd even brought him some home-baked cake. Coffee and walnut. His favourite. She hadn't stayed long, not wanting to tire him, but gave him her address and an invitation to visit once he felt up to it. He remembered his parting words: a promise that he'd take her up on her offer as soon as he got out of hospital. He'd never got around to it and now it was too late. He clenched his jaw.

'You alright?' Nightingale asked softly, gently touching his arm.

He lifted a hand and said sharply, 'I'm fine.' After a moment's pause, he gave a short shake of the head. 'Sorry. The last thing I want to do is take it out on you. It's just… well, we really do come into contact with the cesspit of humanity in this job, don't we?'

They continued their tour of the house. Nightingale commented on the chain hanging loose from the front door frame as they passed on their way upstairs. With two of the three rooms empty, they focussed their attention on what had been the dead woman's bedroom.

'It's very tidy. There's a jewellery box on the dressing table.' Fisher heard a quiet snick as Nightingale took a look inside. 'There are necklaces, rings and a couple of brooches in here. I'm no expert, but they all look expensive.'

'I wonder if the killer was disturbed.'

After completing a cursory search of the rest of the room, followed by the bathroom, they made their way back downstairs, returning to the kitchen, which, according to Nightingale, was as spotless as the rest of the house.

'I wonder if she had a cleaner?' Fisher pondered out loud. 'If she had, they might know whether anything's been taken.'

For the following ten minutes, he listened to the sound of cupboard doors and drawers being pulled open as Nightingale looked for a cache of black bags. She found none.

'Is there a dishwasher?'

'Yes.' He heard a creak. 'It's about half-full. Can't tell what or when her last meal might have been; looks like she rinses everything before putting it in the dishwasher.'

'I've never understood the point of having a dishwasher if you're going to do that.' Nightingale said nothing. 'Anything else you want to mention before we head out?'

'Only that there's a calendar on the wall. She had something in for Tuesday. It says: 10 a.m. RW.' He heard her flicking through the pages. 'It's in every Tuesday.'

'We need to get hold of this RW. Find out whether they saw Mrs Walker this week and what time they were together until. Bag it up. We'll take it with us.'

With their rudimentary survey of the house completed, Fisher and Nightingale headed outside to speak with the uniformed officer who had discovered the body.

'A neighbour called triple-nine requesting an ambulance for a woman who had fallen in her home and was immobile,' PC Greene explained. 'On attending, the paramedics put in a call for a patrol car to help to gain access. When my partner and I arrived, the neighbour said she'd spotted the old lady on the floor in the hall, having looked through the letterbox when there was no answer to the doorbell. I took a look through the letterbox to confirm the situation. The victim was clearly visible. She was on the floor, facing away from the door, and didn't respond to my shouts. The front door appeared to be pretty sturdy, so I decided to go round the back, where I smashed a pane of glass in the door and unlocked it from the inside. I knew it was too late as soon as I stepped inside. The hallway was full of flies and, well... the smell. Wanting to be absolutely sure, I approached the hallway, which is when I saw the bag on her head. As soon as I touched her and felt how cold she was, I came straight out and called it in.'

'Where's the neighbour now?'

'At home; the house on the right. I asked her to stay there until someone had spoken to her.'

'Did she say what made her come around?'

'She noticed yesterday's milk on the doorstep. Said the old lady had had a fall not long ago and she was worried she might have had another.'

***

The neighbour, a woman called Abbie Greaves, invited them in.

'Sorry. Let me get that out of your way. I keep telling the kids to put their stuff away, but they never listen,' she complained. 'Is it okay if we talk in the kitchen? Only my four-year-old is in the lounge watching Peppa Pig. Careful! Watch that ball.' Nightingale took hold of Fisher's arm and steered him clear of the obstacles. 'Sorry,' Abbie Greaves said again.

As they made their way down the hallway to the kitchen, animated noises and a child's laughter could be heard coming from a room on the right. Shortly, Nightingale came to a stop.

'Would you like to sit down?' Mrs Greaves asked. 'There are a couple of stools by the breakfast bar.'

Fisher waved a hand. 'We're okay. Thank you.' After declining an offer of refreshments, he said, 'It must have been an enormous shock.'

'God, yes. I still can't believe it. This is a nice area. And Em was such a lovely lady. It doesn't make any sense.'

'I know you've already explained what happened once, but I'd appreciate it if you could go over it again.'

'There's not much to tell. I noticed Em hadn't taken yesterday's milk in when I took the kids to school this morning. I was in a bit of a hurry and didn't think anything of it at the time. It was only when I got back and it was still there, I thought she might have taken another tumble. She'd had a fall last Christmas and broke her hip. They fixed it up but she was never the same afterwards. I knew straight away something was wrong when she didn't answer the door. I tried calling through the letterbox; that's when I saw her lying on the floor. I thought she'd just fallen.'

'And that's when you called for an ambulance?'

'Yes.'

'Did you know Mrs Walker well?'

'Reasonably well. She used to babysit for me, obviously that was before she did her hip in. And I'd sometimes do a spot of shopping for her if there was something she couldn't get delivered. It was sad to see someone so independent become so reliant on others. Not that she ever complained.'

'Did she have her shopping delivered at the same time every week?'

'Yes. Usually Friday morning.'

Fisher's hopes took a nosedive. If it had been a Tuesday, they might have been able to learn something useful from the delivery driver.

'What about other deliveries? Anything on a Tuesday?'

27

'Tuesday? Why Tuesday?' She gave a gasp. 'Oh God! You mean she's been lying there for two days? That's terrible. I should have noticed the milk sooner.'

'Please don't blame yourself,' Fisher said. 'Short of catching the killer in the act, there would have been nothing you could have done.'

'But—'

'Honestly. So, going back to my question...'

'No,' she replied weakly. 'I don't think she had any deliveries on Tuesday. Though I don't spend my day staring out of the window.'

'That's fine. And what about money... did she keep much cash in the house?'

'She always had cash on her. I mean, she always paid me cash for the shopping. But I don't know how much.'

'I know Mrs Walker's husband died some years back but do you know whether she still wore her wedding ring?'

'Yes. She always had all her rings on: wedding ring, engagement ring and eternity ring. Is that what it was then... a robbery?'

'We're just gathering the facts at the moment.' Before she could ask anything else, Fisher said, 'On her calendar, every Tuesday it says ten o'clock RW. Does that mean anything to you?'

'RW? No.'

'Do you know if she had any friends who visited her regularly?'

'She did have a lot of friends. People were always popping in, especially after her husband died. But every Tuesday? I don't think I... Actually, thinking about it, she always went out on a Tuesday. She used to play bridge at that over-60s place in town. You know, the one with the community café.'

'Do you know the name of it?'

'It's something like Memory Lane or The Good Old Days. Sorry. I can't remember.'

'It doesn't matter. We can find out. Did you happen to see Mrs Walker this Tuesday?'

'No. I was out most of the day. I went shopping in the morning and then took my youngest swimming in the afternoon. To be honest, I haven't seen her for a while. I've been so busy.'

'Did she have any help around the house, a cleaner maybe?' Fisher asked.

'No. She insisted on doing everything herself. I imagine she found it quite difficult, what with her hip, but she insisted she could cope.'

'What about run-ins or arguments? Did Mrs Walker fall out with anyone recently?'

It was a routine question and knowing how mild-mannered and generous of spirit Em Walker was, Fisher expected an answer in the negative, so when Abbie Greaves said, 'maybe', and asked what he meant by recent, he bit back his surprise, replying, 'I'll take anything recent enough for you to remember.'

'I'm not sure it's the sort of thing you're after but, back in the spring, Em had a bit of bother with the bloke in the house behind her. There was a plant — a clematis, if memory serves — growing on Em's side of the fence. It had been there years and used to have a mass of gorgeous flowers in the Spring. Anyway, he complained, saying she'd let it grow too big. Before she could do anything about it, he took a hedge trimmer to it and accidentally — or so he said — cut the main stem down to the ground. Em was livid. Even talked about taking him to court, though I'm not sure it ever got that far.' A moment later, she said, 'Surely no one would kill someone over an argument about a plant?'

Fisher had known of more outlandish reasons.

Ignoring her question, he said, 'One last thing, then we'll get out of your hair. Have you seen anyone acting suspiciously recently?'

'No.'

'Anyone been knocking on doors, collecting for charity or selling stuff?'

'No. There hasn't been anyone doing that sort of thing around here for years. We used to get them a lot, but not any more. Thankfully. They used to be a real pain in the rear. You could never get rid of them.'

Fisher smiled and gave a nod. He pulled a business card from his pocket and held it towards her. 'If you think of anything else, please, don't hesitate to call.'

4.

On leaving Abbie Greaves, instead of returning to the crime scene, Fisher asked Nightingale to take him to the car.

'Let's go see if Mrs Walker's not-so-neighbourly neighbour is at home.'

After a quick check that Luna was okay, he climbed into the passenger seat and was fastening his seatbelt when Nightingale said, 'Remember When.'

'Remember when what?'

'That's the name of the over-60s club. Remember When. RW. The ten o'clock appointment in Mrs Walker's calendar. I just searched for it on my phone. Shall I call them and see if Mrs Walker was there on Tuesday?'

'No. We'll pop in on our way back to the station. Let's go see the clematis killer first.'

Five minutes later, Fisher gave a sharp rap at the door of what Nightingale called a bit of a dump. Inside, a dog issued a frenzied torrent of barks and started scratching at the door. Someone bellowed at it to shut up. Then came the sound of doors slamming, followed by the click of a latch. Fisher felt a push of stale air escape from the house.

'Yeah?' came a deep, gruff voice.

They informed the man, a builder called Pete Bridger, of his neighbour's tragic demise.

'So? What's it to do with me?'

'We wondered whether you saw anything,' Fisher said.

'No. How could I? You can't see her house from here.'

'You can't see it from any of your upstairs windows?' Nightingale asked, in a tone that suggested you ought to be able to.

'I've never tried.'

'I understand you and Mrs Walker had fallen out recently,' Fisher said. 'Something to do with you having killed one of her plants.'

'I don't know who you've been talking to but whoever it was is talking out of their arse. I didn't kill her precious plant. I only cleared it from my side of the fence. If the thing died it was nothing to do with me.'

'Mrs Walker must have thought it had something to do with you... given she talked about taking legal action.'

'First I've heard of it. Problem with people like her is they've got nowt to do apart from cause trouble for everyone else.'

'People like her?'

'Posh folk who think it's their job to sit and judge everyone else.'

'Could I remind you that the person you're talking about is dead; brutally murdered in her own home.'

'Yeah, well, I didn't do it. So what, you want me to make out she was some sweet old lady? Well that sweet old lady didn't half have a sharp tongue on her when she didn't get her own way.'

'Sounds like you had a lot of anger towards her.'

'No more than she deserved.'

'Where you were on Tuesday from midday to midnight?'

'What? Are you accusing me of murder? You must be stupid as well as blind if you think I'd risk going to prison over some poxy plant.'

'Then you won't mind telling us where you were.'

'I'm saying nothing without a lawyer. I know my rights.'

Fisher felt the sudden movement of air in front of him and on impulse stuck his out foot. The door bounced off its side, giving his little toe a sharp bang. He bit back the pain.

'Get out of my house,' Bridger snarled.

'I'm not in your house. Only my foot is. And if you won't cooperate, we'll continue this conversation at the station.' The seconds ticked by. Fisher gave one more push. 'Mr Bridger, just answer the question.'

'Tuesday, eh?' Bridger grumbled. Fisher could hear the sound of fingers rubbing against bristle and in his mind's eye saw a meaty hand scrub at an unshaved chin. 'I was here all day till five, then I went to the pub. Had a few jars with a couple of mates. Got home about eleven.'

'You weren't at work?'

'Got the day off, hadn't I?'

Fisher eased himself back and removed his foot from the doorway.

'Is there anybody who can—' The door slammed shut. Fisher's shoulders slumped. He turned to Nightingale. 'Schoolboy error… taking my foot out before I'd finished. Looks like we're done here. For now, at least.' As they made their way back to the car, he asked, 'So, Beth, what do your instincts tell you about Bridger?'

'I'm not sure. I appreciate people get upset about things to do with their homes, especially boundary issues, and I could easily see him hacking through a plant and killing it, but to murder someone in cold blood…'

'I agree. That said, Bridger was around most of Tuesday afternoon. If he'd gone around to Em's and made out he wanted to apologise it's pretty likely she'd have let him in. I don't think we can rule him out just yet.'

***

Back at the crime scene, Fisher and Nightingale stood alone in the hallway. The body was gone, the CSIs were finishing up and Wickham was still out knocking on doors.

'Beth, do me a favour. Guide me from the front door to where the body was.' After she had done as asked, he said, 'So, she was far enough from the door to suggest she had let her assailant in.'

'Or they barged their way in and she was trying to run away.'

Fisher nodded.

'Could be.' He stood thinking for a moment. 'You mentioned a chain on the door. I wonder if she used to use it?'

'My nan uses hers all the time. She says there's a lot to be said for a bit of old-fashioned suspiciousness.'

'Your nan sounds like a sensible woman. And from what I remember, Em Walker was too. I can't see her letting a stranger in, which makes me think she knew them, or at least recognised them.'

'What if they said they were collecting for charity? Maybe she didn't invite them in, but did open the door. They could have pushed their way in when she went to fetch her purse.'

'So the killer steps inside and then what… throws the bag and flex over her head? But why? For a handful of change and a few rings? If it was valuables they were after surely they'd have had a quick look around for anything else worth taking, wouldn't they?'

'Unless something spooked them.'

Fisher blew out a sigh.

'All this speculating is getting us nowhere. Let's head over to that over-60s place. See if they can shed some light on Mrs Walker's final hours.'

***

Later that afternoon, Fisher was with Nightingale and Wickham, filling DCI Fallon in on the investigation so far.

'We spoke to the organiser of the bridge club Mrs Walker was a member of,' he said. 'They confirmed their minibus picked her up at quarter to ten and dropped her back home at three. We talked to a couple of other members of the club as well as the minibus driver but learned nothing new.'

'Any mention of a fancy man?' Fallon asked. 'Maybe her regular bridge partner?'

'She didn't have a regular partner,' Fisher replied. 'Besides, she was in her eighties and still devoted to her dead husband.'

'When did being a devoted spouse ever stop anybody?' Fallon said with a sharp edge to her voice Fisher hoped the others didn't pick up on. 'Anyway, hadn't her husband been dead for years? How do you know she was still devoted to him?'

Fisher knew because of how tenderly she had talked about Coach Walker when she'd visited him in hospital; knew by the fact she still wore her rings some eight years after he'd died; and because of the photographs that, according to Nightingale, adorned every room of the house. He opened his mouth to answer but stopped himself just in time. If the Falcon knew that he and the victim had counted each other as friends, it would give her the perfect excuse to take him off the case.

'All I know is there's been no mention of a male friend and there was nothing in the house to suggest one.'

'What about family?'

'None, as far as we know. The couple never had children.'

'So that brings us back to the neighbour she'd had trouble with. What was your first impression of him… Nightingale?'

'Oh… Erm…' Nightingale stammered. 'I'm not sure. I—'

'Did he look guilty? Was he nervous or agitated by the questioning?'

'Not really, no. Though he did shut the door on us.'

'Did he now?'

'I'm not sure that's any indicator of guilt,' Fisher said.

'We didn't find any paperwork to do with any legal action at the house, ma'am,' Wickham added.

'What about a will?' the DCI asked, sounding keen.

'No.'

She blew out a sigh.

'So, no fancy man, no family, and no current dispute with anyone, as far as we are aware. Does that about sum it up?' Fallon asked.

'Yes, ma'am,' came the consensus.

'So, no personal motive as far as we can tell, which leaves us with an opportunist thief. Someone who happened at her door, maybe took in the rings on her fingers and decided to help themselves.'

'Why *her* door?' Fisher asked. 'From the house-to-house enquiries undertaken so far, it looks like no one else had any unexpected visitors on Tuesday. Or any time recently. Are you suggesting the killer selected Mrs Walker's house randomly? If that's the case, they were pretty bloody lucky to find themselves coming face-to-face with an elderly lady rather than some young bloke who's handy with his fists.'

'The killer could have recced the area first.'

But Fisher wasn't buying it.

'If the primary goal was robbery, why didn't they take the jewellery from the bedroom? There was a box full of it on her dressing table.'

'Could have been a junkie,' Fallon replied. 'They panicked, grabbed what they could and ran.'

'A junkie who happened to go equipped with a plastic bag and flex; who killed first, then panicked? Just for a few rings and bit of cash. It doesn't make sense.'

'Drug addicts rarely make sense. How many times do you hear about a junkie having done something stupid to fund their next fix? Who knows what goes on in their heads?'

'A junkie would have ransacked the house.'

'Matt! Don't make this more difficult than it needs to be. Her purse had been emptied out. With that and the rings, they might have thought they'd got enough. In any case, I'm not going to sit here arguing with you. I want enquiries made of all the pawn shops and cash-for-gold traders. Her stuff's going to show up sooner or later.'

'I've already sent out a communication to all the known dealers in the area, ma'am,' Wickham said.

'Good work, Andy.'

He cleared his throat and said, 'Actually, it was Matt's idea.'

The silence that followed stretched uncomfortably until eventually Fisher rose from his seat. Luna, sitting beside him, clambered to her feet.

'If that's all, ma'am?'

'Yes. Don't forget to keep me updated. Oh, and Matt, nothing gets said to the press without my go ahead.'

'Wouldn't dream of it, ma'am.'

5.

The Falcon was wrong. The rings didn't turn up. In fact, no new evidence did. The post mortem only confirmed what they already knew and their enquiries continued to draw a blank. There were no reports of anyone collecting for charity, genuine or otherwise. No gaunt, haunted-eyed junkies seen roaming the streets, looking for someone to turn over for a quick fix. In fact, no one reported seeing anything or anybody the slightest bit suspicious in the area. It was no surprise then that, despite his feelings on the matter, with no fresh leads and new cases coming in at an unprecedented rate, Fisher found himself with less and less time to spend on what looked set to become just another cold case.

It was one week after Mrs Walker's body was discovered and he and Nightingale were on their way back to the station having spent the morning at the hospital interviewing a tearful young woman following an attempted sexual assault, when Fisher said, 'What if she had something they wanted... something specific and the rest was just whitewash?'

'Who? Sasha Latham?' Nightingale replied, referring to the young woman whose bedside they had just left.

'No. Em Walker.' As had often been the case in recent days, his thoughts had returned to the murder of his old friend for which they had still so few answers. 'I keep asking myself why her? There have been no other burglaries in the area since and no other murders with the same MO. There has to be a reason she was targeted. I don't believe for a second it was just a case of bad luck.'

'What sort of thing are you thinking of?' Nightingale asked.

'I don't know. Maybe she was selling something on an online market place? Someone could have said they were interested and she gave them her address.'

'I thought she only had a Facebook account and Andy's already looked at that.'

'Hmm. Let's see, shall we?' Fisher replied, pulled his phone out of his pocket. A second later, 'Andy. It's Matt. The Walker case... You checked her social media accounts. Had she posted anything on any of the online marketplaces recently? What? Why the hell not? Go do it now.'

On their return to the office, Fisher had only just taken his seat when he heard Andy's steady tread.

'Sorry about that. Didn't occur to me.'

'It's okay. So?'

'Nothing.' Fisher gave a sigh, prompting Wickham to add, 'I take it you were you expecting something.'

After Fisher explained his thinking, Wickham said, 'You're not going to like what I'm going to say, but I agree with the DCI. I think the woman was the unlucky victim of some random burglar, probably a junkie. Maybe they put the bag over her head to subdue her, while they robbed her, only she collapsed and they panicked.'

'You're right. I don't like it. I don't agree with it. A junkie would have hit more houses. They're desperate and stupid. That did not look like the work of a desperate and stupid person.'

'Maybe they got enough from her so they didn't need to do any other places. Besides, having accidentally killed her, they'd

39

have been running scared. They're probably keeping their head down while the dust settles.'

'The last thing a junkie desperate for a fix is going to do is keep his head down. He'd want to shift the stuff as fast as possible, *then* he might disappear down a drug-induced rabbit hole, not before.'

The fact Fisher was sure he was right and Wickham was wrong gave him no comfort. Not when he had no viable alternative to offer. So, when, two days later, news of another woman found murdered in her home came in, his guilt at not having made an arrest for Em Walker's murder was matched only by his excitement that this might be the break they were waiting for.

He grabbed Luna's harness and made straight for the DCI's office. He was standing in front of her desk before she'd even finished saying come in.

'I've just heard there's a second victim. I take it you want me and Beth to head straight over there.'

'Second victim?'

'The woman found dead in her home.'

'Ah, that. No need. I've already asked Jen and Aaron to attend.'

'You've asked Jen to be deputy SIO? Why would you do that? She doesn't know the first thing about the Walker case.'

'So?'

'Two cases with the same MO and you don't think it makes sense to have the same detectives working both?'

'It may not be the same MO.'

'Elderly woman, bag over her head — how similar does it need to be? Jen will be starting from scratch. It should be me, Beth and Andy working the case.' The silence stretched like Fisher's nerves. 'I know everything there is to know about Mrs Walker's life, her habits and acquaintances. If there are any correlations between her death and this other woman's, Jen won't see them. I will. We owe it to the dead women to bring their killer to justice.' He gripped Luna's harness tight and gave it one more shot. 'Please, speak to Jen, explain it to her and pull her off the case. I know she's got enough on her plate already without the extra workload. She'll probably be grateful.' It was true. Due to the Falcon's reticence to allocate him his fair share of cases, the workloads of the other DIs were as packed as the cells when England lose a match during the world cup.

Eventually Fallon said, 'Fine,' in a tone suggesting it was anything but.

Fisher didn't hang around for her to change her mind.

***

'This time we're going to nail the bastard,' Fisher said, jerking sideways in his seat as Nightingale took a tight corner at speed.

'I hope so.'

From memory, Fisher conjured up an image of the area they were racing to. Seven miles from where the first murder had taken place, on the opposite side of the river, the estate where Ms Constance Lloyd's body had been discovered comprised a mixture of old and new terrace houses interspersed with industrial units and redundant office buildings converted into a tatty assembly of bedsits.

Not exactly rich pickings.

Shortly Nightingale announced their arrival at what she described as a characterless orange-brick block of a house, one of a long line of similar properties on a street jammed nose to tail with parked cars. Thankfully the cordon set up outside the crime scene allowed them to pull up directly outside the house.

Nightingale guided Fisher through the front door and into a small lounge-cum-dining room. At the back of the room, on the left, was the door to the kitchen.

'Twice in one week,' a friendly voice called out. 'You'll have people talking.'

'Morning Doc,' Fisher replied. 'I'd like to say it was a pleasure, but… Is the victim nearby?'

'About eight foot away from you. Near to the sink.'

'Actually in the kitchen then, huh. So… is it the same killer?'

'I'd say that was a reasonable assumption. Unless there happen to be two murderers with a penchant for sticking a black plastic bag and electrical flex over their victims' heads.'

An image of a woman, face shrouded in black plastic, flashed through Matt's mind. Each gasping breath drawing the bag into her mouth until there was no more breath to give.

A shiver ran through him. What had these women done to deserve such a cruel fate?

'What do we know about the latest victim?' he asked.

'White female. Late fifties, early sixties. From a cursory examination, the presentation of her injuries is consistent with ligature strangulation. Estimated time of death between 3 p.m. and 7 p.m. yesterday.'

Fisher thought back to the scene at Mrs Walker's.

'What about rings on her fingers?'

'No rings. No jewellery at all, that I can see,' she replied. 'Now, if that's everything?' Fisher heard the clasps on a bag snapping shut. 'PM will be tomorrow. I'll let you know if I find anything of interest.'

Fisher nodded. He sensed her walk past and turned to Nightingale.

'Observations, Beth?'

'There's a plate with some crumbs by the side of the sink plus a chopping board and dirty knife. In the corner, there's a couple of mugs by the kettle. They look clean. There's a spoon next to them and a jar of coffee. Maybe she was expecting someone?'

'Maybe. What else?'

'There's a handbag on the breakfast bar. Looks like it's been tipped up. There's a purse next to it.'

'It's empty,' said someone whose voice Fisher didn't recognise. 'Don't touch it. We haven't dusted for prints yet.'

'No worries,' Fisher replied. 'Anything else, Beth?'

'There's a calendar on the wall by the back door.' Fisher heard her walk away. A moment later, 'There's nothing for yesterday. Against today's date, there's a note that says: 9 a.m. Take Jen to hosp.' Fisher knew the alarm had been raised by a friend — Jen perhaps? 'Shall I bag it up?'

'Yeah, but wait until we're ready to go. I want to take a look around first.'

Nightingale led him back through into lounge-diner, over a veritable obstacle course of footplates that never seemed big enough for his size 11 feet.

'It's a nice room,' Nightingale said. 'Small but cosy. There are some framed photographs of the victim. She's with a man in a couple of them. He looks a bit older than her, though from the way they're standing, they could be an item.'

Fisher sent Nightingale upstairs on her own. Five minutes later, her light step came skipping back down.

'Only one set of clothes in the wardrobe and no men's toiletries in the bathroom. Perhaps they'd split up?'

'And still left the photos on display?'

'He could have died.'

Fisher nodded

'Any jewellery?'

'Some. Though none of it looks particularly expensive.'

He let out a sigh. It was slowly dawning on him that unless the killer had made a mistake and left some vital incriminating evidence, maybe a fingerprint or scrape of skin under the dead woman's nails, the chances of them making a quick arrest didn't look promising.

***

Leaving the crime scene to the CSIs, Fisher and Nightingale headed off to talk to the woman who had raised the alarm; the victim's friend, Jennifer Keeley. He decided to cover the short distance to her house on foot, taking the opportunity to practise with his white stick while he had the chance. Having Nightingale there, guarding against him doing anything stupid, like wandering into the road, gave him a much-needed confidence boost. All the same, it took them nearly fifteen minutes to negotiate the two streets, as opposed to the five minutes it would have taken had he all of his faculties. On arriving at their destination, he wiped his brow with the heel of his hand — the concentration needed to walk with his stick having raised a light sweat — then rapped on the door.

Mrs Keeley sounded older than Fisher had expected. Her voice had a delicate air to it and she sniffled intermittently as she spoke.

'I wondered when you would get here. Not that I've got anywhere to go. I just thought... well, I... I'm sorry, I don't know why I'm wittering on like this. Please come in.'

She led them through the hallway into the lounge. The air was redolent of sickness and Fisher was seized with a sudden, powerful urge to turn and run as memories of the bleak, dark thoughts — his bedfellows during the long dark days in the ophthalmic ward — came flooding back.

Nightingale, perhaps sensing something was wrong, took his arm and guided him to a sofa. Once everyone was seated, and when Fisher still hadn't spoken, she took the lead, and in a kindly voice said, 'Mrs Keeley, perhaps you could talk us through this morning... how did you come to find your friend?'

'I should have known something was wrong as soon as she didn't turn up. She was supposed to be taking me for my chemo session. She normally gets here by nine. When it got to quarter past and she still hadn't shown I tried calling her. When she didn't answer, I assumed she was on her way — she never uses her mobile when she's driving. Well, by twenty-five past I was getting worried. I tried calling again but still got no answer so I decided to walk around. I don't know what I was expecting to find. It never occurred to me that...' She started to cry. 'I'm sorry. I just...'

'You're doing very well,' Fisher said, on the back of a sympathetic smile. He waited a few minutes, until she had regained her composure, then asked, 'When did you last see your friend?'

'Friday. She came round for a cup of tea and a natter.'

'How did she seem?'

'Happy. Really happy. Things were finally working out for her. She'd recently got engaged. They were going shopping for rings on Saturday. She was really excited.'

'I noticed some framed photographs in Ms Lloyd's lounge,' Nightingale said. 'Of Ms Lloyd with a man — was that her fiancé?'

'That's right. Warren. I'm sorry, the surname's slipped my memory.'

Fisher heard the scratch of Nightingale's pen.

'Had they been seeing each other long?' she asked.

45

'Not really. Just a few months. It was something of a whirlwind romance. They met at the hospital. Connie had noticed him coming and going a few times, while she'd been waiting for me. Then one day they got chatting and he asked her on a date. She said no at first, not knowing anything about him. I told her she was an idiot and should seize the day. After all, none of us know how long we've got.' Perhaps the aptness of her words hit her, as she heaved a large sigh, then said, 'To be honest, it was a bit of a surprise when she changed her mind. I thought she was off men forever. But by God, she deserved some happiness, after all she'd been through.'

'What exactly had she been through?' Fisher asked.

'Connie was one of life's victims. She was a saint, yet for whatever reason, she always got taken advantage of. Her ex-husband cheated on her and then lied about his finances so she only got a fraction of what she was due. And then, to make matters worse, a so-called financial advisor duped her out of what little money she did have. Last I heard he's somewhere in South America living the high life. Mind you, that might have been about to change. Connie had joined some group legal action thing. Although there was talk of her getting her money back, it was by no means certain.'

Fisher could hear Nightingale scribbling away. He paused to give her time to catch up, then asked, 'Did Ms Lloyd still see her ex-husband?'

'Not as far as I know. Not since the divorce.'

'How long ago was that?'

'I'm not sure exactly. Maybe five years ago? Something like that.'

'No mention of having seen him recently?'

'No.'

'Has she mentioned seeing or meeting anyone recently, someone she wasn't expecting to see? Or maybe something happened that seemed unusual or odd in some way?'

'No.'

'What about her social life? Was she a member of any clubs or societies?'

'I don't think so. She used to volunteer but she stopped that a while ago.'

'What about Remember When, the over-60s club in town — do you know whether Connie ever went there?'

'She never mentioned it but I doubt it. She only turned sixty last month and she was always saying how she didn't feel her age.'

'Okay, well, I think we've covered everything.' Fisher felt about in his coat pocket and pulled out a business card. 'In case you remember anything...' He held it out and felt it slip from his fingers. After rising to leave, he said, 'Any idea how we might get hold of Ms Lloyd's fiancé?'

'You could try the hospital's oncology unit.'

'Is he a doctor there?'

'No. He's a patient.'

'He has cancer?'

'Yes.' She gave a sigh. 'Poor Connie. Even when her luck turned, it couldn't help but come with a sting in the tail.'

6.

There was only one Warren listed as receiving treatment at the hospital's cancer unit: Warren Newman, a sixty-six-year-old widower. Hospital records had him down as living some eleven miles away from the dead woman. Fisher decided to break the news himself.

When the front door opened, Fisher had got as far as saying 'Kent Police' when the homeowner said sharply, 'What's happened? Is he okay? I warned him about that bloody car.'

'Are you Mr Warren Newman?' Fisher asked.

'I am,' came a cautious reply.

'Would it be okay if we talked inside?'

'You must have made a mistake,' Newman insisted after Fisher had broken the news.

'No mistake, I'm afraid.'

'There must be,' Newman pressed. 'There's no way Connie would let a stranger into the house.'

'Her purse was found nearby, emptied of cash. It's possible her killer pretended to be collecting for charity or selling something.' As he said it, Fisher found himself wondering why then was the body found in the kitchen as, in order to get there, presumably she would have had to take them through the lounge. Wouldn't it be more likely that she would have made them wait at the door?

'I'm telling you she would not have let them in the house. She's been taken advantage of too many times. It was ingrained in her not to trust people.'

Fisher heard the insistence in the other man's voice. There was no point arguing. Instead, he changed the subject, 'When did you last see Ms Lloyd?'

'Sunday lunchtime. We spent Saturday night together here.' His voice cracked. 'We'd spent the day shopping for an engagement ring.'

The memory of the woman's bare fingers came to mind. What if the killer knew they were going ring shopping and expected to be richly rewarded when they confronted Ms Lloyd?

Fisher asked, 'Did you get one?'

'Yes. It's at the jeweller's. It needed adjusting.'

'Who knew that's what you were doing on the weekend?'

'No one. Well, apart from my son and I suppose I might have said something in passing to some of my staff.'

'What about Ms Lloyd? We know she'd told her friend Mrs Keeley. Is there anybody else she's likely to have mentioned it to?'

'No... I don't know. Does it matter? The only people likely to have known are friends and relatives.'

Fisher didn't want to disabuse him as to how many murders were committed by so-called friends and money-grabbing relatives.

'I'm simply exploring all of the bases Mr Newman. What about while you were shopping... did you see or talk to anyone? Bump into anyone as you were coming out of a jewellery store?'

'No.' There was a stretch of silence, then Newman said, 'Wasn't another woman murdered recently, something to do with a robbery? I remember seeing something on the news. She was found strangled with... Oh my God! Please don't tell me that's how it happened.' He gave a choked gasp which soon descended into a wheezing coughing fit.

'Mr Newman, would you like me to get you a glass of water?' Nightingale asked.

'I'll be alright. Just give me a minute.'

Fisher heard footsteps rush out of the room, followed by the sound of running water.

'He's gone as white as a sheet,' Nightingale whispered.

'That'll be the shock. It's starting to sink in.'

A minute later he was back.

'Sorry about that.'

'It's perfectly alright, sir,' Fisher replied. 'I realise it must be extremely distressing for you. Are you okay to continue?'

'He just nodded, sir,' Nightingale said.

'Sorry,' Newman said. 'Yes, I'm fine. Please carry on.'

For the following forty minutes, they probed Constance Lloyd's life. They discussed disagreements, recent and not so recent; membership of clubs or associations, particularly Remember When; issues arising from the class action taken against the absconded financial advisor; and the possibility of a will or life insurance policy. All lines of enquiry drew a blank, which left the question of the erstwhile husband.

'Long gone. And bloody good riddance too,' Newman growled, 'because if I ever got my hands on him…' There was a momentary silence, then he continued, 'You know he shafted Connie on the divorce settlement? The bastard cheated on her with his secretary then siphoned off all their savings into a secret account. What sort of man does that? One that deserves to be taught a lesson if you ask me. I tell you, if he'd dared show his face I'd have…'

He paused at the sound of a key in the door.

'Only me,' came a call from the hallway. Fisher heard footsteps approach. 'Just come to see if you wanted... Oh, sorry. I didn't realise you had company.'

'It's my son, Rob,' Warren Newman explained.

'Is everything alright? You look a bit—'

'It's Connie. She's been...' He stalled, then in a strangled voice said, 'I just can't...'

'She's been what?' Rob Newman asked. 'Who are these people?' Fisher imagined him taking in the scene, two suited strangers and a dog settled at their feet.

'I'm Detective Inspector Matt Fisher from Kent Police. I'm sorry to tell you but Ms Lloyd has been found dead,' Fisher replied.

'What, like in a car accident or something?'

'Not exactly. She was murdered in her home yesterday.'

Fisher heard the younger man cross the room to where his father was. 'Dad, I'm so sorry.' After a short pause, he said, 'Who would do such a thing?'

'That's what we're trying to find out,' Fisher said.

'Connie was always saying how she was a bad luck magnet,' Rob Newman said.

'Don't say such a thing,' his father snapped. 'The only thing wrong with Connie was she was too kind. People took advantage.'

'I was just saying how—'

'I don't care! I don't want to hear any more.'

'Okay. I'm sorry.' After a beat, Rob Newman asked, 'Is it okay to ask what happened? I mean why her?'

'I'm afraid I can't go into details,' Fisher replied. 'And as to why her, that's something we're trying to figure out.'

'It's the same as that other woman,' his father added.

'What other woman?' Rob Newman asked.

'The one the papers said had been strangled.'

'It's too early in the investigation to say whether the two are linked,' Fisher cautioned; though he was pretty sure they were.

'What are you talking about, man?' Warren Newman replied, clearly not one to be fobbed off. 'They must be. Anybody with half a brain can see that.'

Ignoring the slight, Fisher said, 'The previous victim was Mrs Margery Walker, Em to her friends. Does the name ring a bell?'

'Only from the news. We talked about it — Connie and me. Said how awful it was, not being safe in your own home.'

'Connie didn't say anything about having known the woman?'

'No.'

'Okay, well, I think that's everything, for now,' Fisher said, rising to his feet.

As he and Nightingale made their way out, Warren Newman asked, 'I take it the proper detectives will want to talk to me at some point?'

Fisher froze.

'The *proper* detectives?'

'The ones doing the investigation.'

'That would be us, Mr Newman. We're running the investigation.'

There was a long pause, then Newman said, 'Nothing personal but how can you investigate anything when you're blind? Don't you have to look for evidence and check things like CCTV? All you can do is sit and chat with the likes of me, clutching at straws as to what might have happened. I mean, first you suggest it might have been a robbery, then you think it could be something to do with that club you mentioned. Strikes me you don't have a clue what you're doing, which is why you keep taking stabs in the dark. I want Connie's killer brought to justice so don't think you'll get any sympathy from me if you're not up to the job.'

7.

That night, Warren Newman's caustic words bubbled away in Fisher's mind like a bad case of cerebral indigestion. The following morning, he knew the only remedy to the bad taste it had left was to prove to Newman and anyone else who doubted him that he was more than up to the job. Which is how he came to find himself trying his damndest to focus on Dr Cooper's running commentary, to a backing track of drilling and sawing sounds, whilst fighting a rising tide of nausea induced by the malodorous combination of death and industrial-strength detergent.

He listened intently as the pathologist detailed the victim's injuries, drawing attention to the bruising around the neck and the petechial haemorrhages present in the eyes.

'And she was definitely strangled with the cord, rather than suffocated with the bag, the same as Mrs Walker?'

'Yes. Although the evidence suggests substantially greater force was applied than in the case of Mrs Walker. That may be due to the fact that Mrs Walker was older and more infirm and didn't offer as much resistance, so the killer didn't need to put as much effort in.'

'A minute ago, you mentioned other marks on her neck. Any idea what caused them?'

While dissecting the flesh around Ms Lloyd's neck, Dr Cooper had drawn their attention to an inch-long strip running parallel to her jaw bone below the left ear, where something other than the rope appeared to have chafed the skin.

'Let's have a look, shall we?'

Fisher heard the pathologist move around the autopsy table. The soft clanging of metal on metal followed.

'What are you doing?' Fisher asked.

'I've removed a section of tissue from her neck. I'll pop it under the microscope so we can get more definition of the wound.' After a short while, she mumbled, 'Interesting...'

'What is?' he asked impatiently.

'The damage is consistent with a fine metal chain having been pulled tight against the skin. I suspect there was a necklace that either got caught and came off or was removed afterwards but unnecessarily forcibly, given the lady was in no position to stop its removal.'

'A necklace? She didn't wear any rings, so they took a necklace instead? Are we talking about a trophy?' Fisher's gut lurched at the thought of a serial killer.

Perhaps the question had the same impact on everyone else in the room, as no one answered.

Nightingale, who had been standing quietly at his side throughout, said, 'Can I ask a question?'

'Fire away,' the doctor replied.

'If they strangled her, why bother with the bag? It must have made it much more awkward having to slip a bag over, then the flex.'

'Your guess is as good as mine.'

'And if you were to guess...?' Fisher prompted.

'It could have been to limit the amount of forensic evidence taken from the scene. The murderer might have been worried some of the victim's saliva or hair might find its way onto his clothing. Or perhaps it was to disorientate the victims and make them more pliable. Or maybe the killer is a thoughtful soul and did it to expedite their deaths; suffocation combined with strangulation will finish anyone off pretty quickly. Take your pick.'

Fisher had already come to the same conclusions. Sadly, none of the answers helped in their search for the killer. Though news of the necklace was a definite plus.

'Anything else worth knowing?' he asked.

'I think that's everything. I'll send the flex and bag over to the lab for testing as soon as I finish up here.'

'I won't hold my breath.' The same items retrieved from Mrs Walker's person had yielded nothing.

They left the pathologist and her assistant stitching the body back together and collected Luna from Dr Cooper's dog-loving clerk, who had been more than happy to keep an eye on her during the post mortem. Back at the car, Fisher put his mobile on speakerphone and called Warren Newman.

'Mr Newman, it's DI Fisher. I'm sorry to trouble you again. I know you said Ms Lloyd didn't wear any rings, but did she wear any other jewellery?'

'Yes. A necklace. I gave it to her. If you've found fingerprints on it other than hers, they're probably mine.'

'Could you describe it for me?'

Newman blew out a long stream of air.

'Now you're asking. Connie chose it. There's a heart on a silver chain, with some other bits hanging off. I remember it was silver, because, well, I thought gold might be a bit classier, but Connie insisted that was what she wanted.'

'Can you remember where you got it from?'

'It was that trendy jewellery store where everything looks the same… to my eye, at least.'

Fisher wished he'd asked for a more detailed description of the jewellery Nightingale had found in Ms Lloyd's bedroom.

'You can't remember the name of the store?'

'It's a woman's name, something like Doreen or Dora or...'

'Pandora?' Nightingale suggested.

'That's the one. Pandora. I don't suppose it would be possible for me to have it back, would it? It would be something to remember her by.'

'We're not sure where the necklace is at the moment,' Fisher replied. 'Though we haven't finished looking through the contents of her house. When we find it, I'll pass your request on to whoever is dealing with Ms Lloyd's estate.'

'But she always wore it,' Newman said, with an optimistic tilt to his voice. Fisher knew exactly what was coming. 'Maybe it wasn't Connie? Maybe it was someone else? Maybe Connie's still alive?'

Fisher knew his next words would be like a blow to the back of the legs, sending the man crashing down, but there was no avoiding it.

'I'm sorry sir, but a close friend identified her. There's no doubt, the victim was definitely Ms Lloyd.'

'But the necklace?'

'She might have taken it off. As I said, we haven't finished searching the house.'

Or her attacker might have taken it, Fisher thought as he thanked the other man for his time. He hung up and turned to Nightingale.

'I don't suppose you remember seeing anything matching the necklace's description in the victim's bedroom?'

'No, but there was a bowl with some necklaces and a couple of bracelets in it. It could have been amongst them.'

Fisher nodded and got back on the phone, calling DS Wickham, who was undertaking a detailed search of Connie Lloyd's home.

'Andy, it's Matt. How's it going?'

'Nothing so far. What's up?'

Fisher told him about the necklace.

'I haven't seen it. I'll check with Kami.' Fisher heard Wickham shout the question out. A second later, he was back on the line. 'No sign of it yet.'

'Have you done her bedroom?'

'I think Kami's just finished in there. Do you want me to call you if we find it?'

'That would be good, thanks. Speak to you—'

'Hang on... Kami's gesturing. One sec... She wants to speak to you.'

'Hi Matt. I've just found some documents you might be interested in. They were in a drawer along with the victim's passport and other personal stuff. One of them gives the details of the executor to her will. The other is a letter from a law firm; something to do with a review of her divorce settlement. I don't know if it's relevant but they were both written about a month ago, within a few days of each other.'

'Really?' Fisher knew the dead woman was divorced years ago. 'Does it give her husband's name?'

'Yeah. Lewis Hunt.'

'Should be easy enough to track down. What about the executor?'

'A Mrs Jennifer Keeley. Address is—'

'That's alright. I know where she lives.' Fisher hung up and brought Nightingale up to speed. 'Sounds like the divorce wasn't ancient history, after all.'

8.

Lewis Hunt sounded surprised when Fisher called to inform him of his ex-wife's demise.

Surprised, yet not unduly upset.

'Come round if you must, but I don't see how you think I can help. I haven't seen Connie in years.'

They arranged to call on him at home but as Nightingale started the engine Fisher set out a hand.

'Hang on. Can you dig out the number for Jennifer Keeley and punch it into my phone, please?' He handed her his mobile.

A second later, she passed it back and soon Mrs Keeley's voice sang through the speaker.

'Hello?'

'Mrs Keeley. It's DI Fisher. We met the other day. I'm sorry to bother you again, but I have a question.'

'That's okay. What do you want to know?'

'I understand you're the executor of Ms Lloyd's will. Is that right?'

'Yes. I've been in touch with the solicitors, who've given me a copy. I was just looking at what I have to do, whether I need to apply for probate. It seems so complicated.'

'It tends to depend on how much her estate is worth,' Fisher said. 'Did she have much to leave?'

'Not as far as I know. Just a few bits of furniture and her car… oh, and whatever cash there is in her bank account, which I don't expect amounts to much.'

'And the house?'

'It's rented. She had hoped to buy her own place but that idea went down the pan when that fraudster ran off with her divorce settlement.'

'Who are her beneficiaries?'

'There are only two. I'm one of them. Connie was good enough to leave me her TV — it's much better than the one I've got now – plus a few bits of jewellery. I honestly wasn't expecting anything. Everything else goes to her fiancé, Warren Newman. Oh dear… I should have called to let you know his surname. I'm so sorry. I forgot.'

'That's okay. We found it ourselves. She must have written the will recently then?'

'Yes. She asked me to be executor about a month ago. She said she couldn't stand the idea of that no-good ex-husband of hers getting his hands on anything after she was dead. I said I didn't think he could, not now they're divorced, but she didn't want to chance it.'

'Why now? Why do you think she didn't write a will years ago, after she got divorced?'

'I don't know. Perhaps it was being in close contact with people with cancer… it has a tendency to make people aware of their own mortality.'

'Strange how Mr Newman didn't know she had left a will,' Nightingale said after the call with Mrs Keeley had ended.

'She might not have told him.'

'Or she had and that was why he killed her.'

'I don't think Warren Newman is short of a penny or two. I did a bit of digging last night. Turns out he owns Newman's

Autos. You know, that big second-hand car dealership on the other side of Ashford. I took a look at the accounts. Looks to be doing pretty well. At the moment, I'm more interested in the ex-husband — the *no-good* ex-husband. I quite fancy hearing what he thought about the review into their divorce settlement after all these years.'

***

When he greeted them at his home, Lewis Hunt didn't sound like a man worried about anything. On the contrary, he came across as a laid-back, smooth-talking kind of guy. He made a fuss of Luna, despite being asked not to, then showed them into the lounge.

'Can I get any drinks? Tea, coffee... something stronger?'

'We're fine, thank you, sir,' Fisher said. He half expected the man to excuse himself while he fetched himself a drink, but instead came the sound of something heavy sinking into what he assumed was a leather chair.

'Sit yourselves down.' As Fisher and Nightingale took a seat on an ample leather sofa, Hunt said, 'Hey, you're Matt Fisher the footballer.'

'I was. Now I'm Matt Fisher, the detective inspector.'

'Didn't you get stabbed in the head by some terrorist on the underground or something?'

'Or something.' Fisher couldn't be bothered to put him straight and tell him it was a face full of acid at Liverpool Street Station. Instead, he asked, 'What do you do for a living, Mr Hunt?'

'I run a property development company. We develop small to medium new build sites. If you're in the market for a nice des res,

I'm about to release four lovely executive family homes near Faversham.'

'I'll bear that in mind. So, going back to the reason for our visit, when did you last see your ex-wife?'

'Hmm… Let me think…' After what Fisher suspected was an unnecessarily long pause, Hunt said, 'It was probably just after we'd divorced. So, that's what… four, five years ago.'

'And under what circumstances did you meet?'

'I can't recall.'

'I'm sure you can. Think about it. Where were you?'

'It must have been when Connie came to the office to talk about the divorce. I remember, she didn't stay long.'

Fisher recalled what Jennifer Keeley had said about Ms Lloyd's reaction to the outcome of the settlement.

'Was she upset when you saw her?'

'I can't remember.'

'Try.'

'She might have been. A little,' Hunt replied, sounding flippant. 'She thought the settlement was unfair. I told her to take it up with the judge.'

'Unfair because you'd withheld details of some of your financial holdings?' Fisher said.

'What?'

'Rumour has it you transferred assets into an undisclosed bank account prior to informing your wife you were leaving her. Is that true?'

'I'm sorry but why are we even discussing this?' Hunt snapped. 'I thought you were here to talk about Connie's murder, not the events leading up to our divorce.'

'Perhaps they're related?'

'I don't know what you're insinuating but I don't like the way this is heading.'

'You do know she was appealing the divorce settlement?' Fisher said. 'She must have had a good reason for thinking it would go in her favour, seeing as she'd already gone as far as to instruct solicitors. Were you worried about what a review might uncover? I would have thought the courts would come down quite hard on anyone who was found to have lied.'

Fisher heard the squeak of leather, conjuring up an imagine of the other man squirming in his seat. Then came the sound of soft footfall pacing on the carpet.

'Everything I did was legal and above board.'

'But was it moral?'

'Who are you to judge?'

'Me? Nobody. But it wouldn't have been me doing the judging. If it had gone back to the courts, I imagine the fact you moved assets shortly before filing for divorce wouldn't have boded well.'

'I guess we'll never know, will we?'

'No. We won't. But you've just given yourself a perfect motive for murder, Mr Hunt.' Fisher waited a minute for his words to sink in, then said, 'Earlier, you said you hadn't seen your ex-wife since the time she came to your office.'

'That's correct.'

'Not at all?'

'We lived fifteen miles apart. It's hardly like we were going to bump into each other.'

'You know where she lived then? I was under the impression she moved there after the divorce.'

'I don't know how I came to know it, but yes, I knew.'

'Did you ever visit her at home?'

'No. I already told you we never saw each other. Besides, why would I?'

'It's small… the house. Not in the best of areas, either. But I understand it was the only thing she could afford. Did you know it was rented? She didn't have enough money to buy a place seeing as someone conned her out of what little money she got from the divorce.'

'Look, you can't pin that one on me. What Charlie Bamford did was inexcusable. I would never have dreamt of pointing him in Connie's direction if I'd known what he was planning. I lost money too, you know. He promised me an introduction fee for giving him her details. Never saw a penny of it.'

'You gave your ex-wife's details to a bent financial advisor?'

'I didn't know he was a crook. Not then, at least.'

'But you did later?'

'Let's just say, I suspected as much.'

'Did you have any money invested with him at the point he disappeared?'

'No.'

'Why not?'

'Like I said, I suspected he was up to something, so I terminated my investments with him.'

'And you didn't think to warn your wife?'

'*Ex*-wife.'

'Not ex enough when it came to the introduction fee though, was she?' When Hunt didn't reply, Fisher said, 'Bit of a bitch, was she, your ex-wife? The sort to drive you mad?'

'What?'

'Well, was she?'

'Why are you even asking? We divorced years ago.'

'I'm just wondering why you treated her so badly? It sounds like you well and truly stitched her up.'

'It was my money. My company generated it. It was right that I got to keep it.'

'Your wife didn't work hard too, then?'

'She didn't work at all for twelve years of our marriage.'

'Why was that?'

'She stayed at home to look after our son.'

'You have a son?' Fisher was shocked. This was the first he'd heard of it.

'Had. Finlay died. Cancer. He was eleven.' Fisher thought he detected the tiniest trace of sadness in the other man's voice. 'Connie found it difficult to move on. After a while we realised it wasn't working.' He huffed out a sigh and then his hard tone returned. 'So there you have it. Ancient history.'

'So you left the woman who bore your child, raised your child and buried your child, for your secretary, taking as much money as you could legally get away with.' Before Hunt could comment, Fisher asked, 'Where were you Tuesday afternoon and evening?'

Fisher heard footsteps cross the room.

'Get out!' Hunt growled.

Fisher remained seated.

'If you prefer, we can always continue the conversation at the station. That would give you time to sort out some legal representation. Is that what you want?'

The room fell quiet. The silence stretched, until eventually, Hunt folded. 'I was in a business meeting all afternoon until late that evening.'

'Can anyone corroborate that?'

'Are you calling me a liar?'

'This is a murder investigation. It shouldn't come as too much of a surprise that we need someone to confirm you were where you say you were.'

'My business trades on confidence. I am not prepared to throw away a potentially valuable contract because of some flight of fancy you might have that I somehow killed my ex-wife. If you want that information, you'll have to arrest me first.' Hunt's pugilistic attitude was back.

Fisher sat, saying nothing, letting the seconds tick by. There were no real grounds on which to arrest Hunt. Perhaps Hunt knew this, as he said nothing, seeming happy to let the silence stretch. Stalemate.

Changing tack, Fisher asked, 'Do you know a woman called Margery Walker? Em to her friends.'

'No. So, is that everything?'

Fisher stemmed a sigh and felt for Luna's harness. Gripping it, he rose to his feet.

'For now. Luna, the door.' He felt the gentle pull as the dog started for the hallway. 'Tosser,' he said, as soon as they were in the car. 'I knew there was a reason I don't like property developers, they're no better than bankers. All in it for their own selfish, money-grubbing needs.'

'My uncle's a property developer,' Nightingale said.

'I'm sure he's the exception to the rule.'

'He's okay... sort of.'

'How did Hunt look when we were talking about the appeal against the divorce settlement? Did he seem nervous or worried?'

'Not really.'

'All the same, I imagine he was worried when he first found out about it. Question is, would he have been worried enough to make sure it never happened?'

'How does Mrs Walker's murder fit in?'

Fisher sighed.

'Good question. I wish I had the answer.'

'So, what now?'

'Back to the station. Time for a bit more digging.'

9.

On the journey back to the station, Fisher's thoughts turned to the victims. Both women had been sociable, community-spirited people. Both over sixty. Both lived alone. Other than those basic facts there were no obvious cross-overs in their lives; no joint friends, no common interests. But if there was one thing Fisher was sure of, it was that the same pair of hands had snuffed the light out of both their lives.

In a strange quirk of synchronicity, Nightingale said, 'I've been thinking about the killer. If the same person killed both women, how did they know them? The victims didn't live close together and, as far as we know, they didn't go to the same places. And why? Why kill two random women? No one benefits from Mrs Walker's death, apart from the football trust and a handful of charities, and the people in Ms Lloyd's will don't appear to have any connection to Mrs Walker.'

'Don't forget Hunt,' Fisher said. 'He benefits in that his ex-wife isn't around to push for a review of their divorce settlement anymore.'

'There's still no link to Mrs Walker.'

'As far as we know.'

Nightingale went on, 'You know earlier, at the PM, you said something about the jewellery being taken as a trophy. Does that mean... well, do you think we really could be dealing with a serial killer? I had wondered. I mean, the way they were killed, it's not exactly your run of the mill MO, is it?'

'No. It isn't. But as for whether we're dealing with a serial killer… all I know is they exist, which means they have to practise their shit on someone's watch. Why not ours?'

What he didn't tell Beth was how much the prospect excited him in a perverse kind of way.

And frightened him… and not just because it might mean the loss of more innocent women's lives, but also because it would raise the stakes and give the Falcon even more cause to hand the investigation over to someone else.

But they weren't there yet.

Besides he still had his doubts, as he explained, 'Despite what I just said, it's way too soon to be launching a hunt for a serial killer. While the missing jewellery might fit, the fact they took the cash jars.' After a beat, he said, 'Anyway, it's by the by. The questions you just posed are as relevant, serial killer or not. The key to finding the killer has got to be in figuring out how they selected their victims. What links them?'

'But serial killers kill for the sake of it, don't they? In which case, couldn't the victims have been chosen at random?'

'You mean they would have killed whoever answered the door… male, female, old or young?'

'Yes.'

'Presumably they'd only want people who were alone in the house. If a woman of forty-five answered and her two teenage sons and husband were home, the killer wouldn't have had the same success. They must be applying some method of selection. Besides, I'm no expert, but I don't think serial killers do kill arbitrarily. Usually there's some characteristic or trait they're drawn to.' He shook his head. 'No. Something led the killer to their doors. We just don't know what.'

'What about their age, the fact they were both old?'

'How do you quantify old? They might seem old to you — you're barely out of your teens — but they weren't that old. Well, maybe Em was, but Connie Lloyd had only just turned sixty. It's almost ten years off retirement age.'

'Maybe the killer is more my age? What if they think anyone over sixty has outlived their usefulness? I remember at school, some idiot said they reckoned people should be euthanised at sixty to avoid being a drain on the health service and save the country a fortune in pensions. That was until the teacher pointed out the boy's grandparents would soon be falling into that category. He changed his tune pretty quickly after that.'

Fisher let slip a smirk, then said, 'Going back to the question then, how did the killer know enough about both women to select them?'

'What if they both went to the same doctors? Someone could have hacked the patient database.'

'They didn't. I checked.'

'Dentists?'

'Ditto. And before you ask, there is no record of Mrs Walker, or Coach Walker, ever having been seen by the oncology unit.'

Nightingale gave a groan.

'Then I don't know.' A second later, sounding hopeful, she said, 'What about a phone poll? I had someone call and ask me to do a lifestyle survey the other day. They asked me all sorts of stuff.'

'That's a thought. Congratulations! You've just got yourself the job of going through the victims' phone records to see whether they had any calls from the same number in the last few months.' A thought occurred to him: 'If it was a serial killer why use a black bag? Serial killers tend to kill because they enjoy the feeling of power. Surely they'd want to watch their victim, see the fear, their pleading expressions, as they pulled the cord tight and watch the light fade from their eyes. Where's the fun in putting a black bag over their head?'

'Maybe they thought it would frighten the victims even more if they couldn't see anything.'

'More frightening than having your windpipe crushed and feeling your lungs burst as they cry out for oxygen? Nah. It doesn't fit. And the other anomaly, which might seem trivial, is why was Connie Lloyd in her kitchen? Would she have led a stranger through the house into the kitchen and then get her purse out? You'd get them to wait at the door while you fetched your purse, wouldn't you?'

'Maybe she tried to run away and they chased her.'

'Without leaving any sign of a struggle? It seems to me neither woman was expecting anything when the bag went over her head. Which makes me think they trusted their assailant enough to let them get close while their back was turned. Would you turn your back on a total stranger who came to your house unexpectedly?'

'To be honest, I wouldn't let a stranger into my house in the first place.'

'But many serial killers are known to be cunning, manipulative charmers, which is how they manage to befriend their victims. Though if they were already known to their victims, why haven't the people we've talked to mentioned anyone new in the victims' lives?'

Nightingale quickly replied, 'Ms Lloyd hadn't known Warren Newman very long.' But before Fisher could respond, he heard the indicator click and felt the car start to slow as she announced, 'We're here.'

They were making their way across the station's tarmacked car park, when Nightingale asked, 'Apart from checking the phone records, what do we do next?'

'For starters, we need to do a search of HOLMES; see if the database contains any records of deaths or serious assaults with a similar MO in the last few years. If that comes up empty, we extend the search to cover animal abuse cases with a similar set-up. Then there's the ongoing task of finding a link between victims. We need to go back over their routines. Double check their circle of friends, look for any overlap. I also want to see if I can get a handle on Mr Hunt's financial position. If he's got money troubles, the last thing he'd want is the divorce settlement being reviewed.' Fisher upped his pace. 'Plenty to be getting on with.'

10.

With Nightingale off doing the checks on the victims' phone records, Fisher set about searching the police database for deaths and assaults involving a plastic bag and strangulation. He was sitting comfortably at his computer, concentrating on the staccato voice that was reading out the search results, when his headphones were abruptly yanked away from his ears.

'Fisher!' It was DCI Fallon. 'How loud do you have that thing? I've been standing here literally shouting your name and you still couldn't hear me.'

'They're noise cancelling headphones. They're designed to block out annoying background sounds.'

'Ha bloody ha.'

He held out his hand and she thrust the foam and leather headset into his palm.

He was tempted to tell her he wasn't joking. Instead, he said, 'Did you want something?'

'I take it you got nowhere with the ex-husband.'

'What makes you say that?'

'Because you would have let me know if you had, of course.'

'You want a blow-by-blow account? Fine. We arrived at 10:23, whereupon Mr Hunt escorted us into his lounge. I asked him when he last saw his ex-wife. He thought about it for a few minutes. Eventually he said four to five years ago, shortly after the divorce. I then asked him—'

'Don't be so facetious. You know exactly what I meant. Is he a suspect or isn't he?'

'Let's just say he's a person of interest. He told us he was in a business meeting when Ms Lloyd was attacked but refused to provide details of who he was with, thereby giving us no way of corroborating it.'

'Why wouldn't he say?'

'Some bullshit about not wanting confidence in his business to be undermined.'

'Doesn't sound unreasonable. Especially if there are no real grounds on which to suspect him. Are there?'

Fisher recounted what they'd learned about Connie Lloyd's efforts to challenge the divorce settlement.

'And what's his link to Mrs Walker?'

'That's next on my list. I figure—'

'In other words, there's no link.'

'Not that we are aware of, yet, but—'

'You need to stop wasting your time on wild goose chases. I've been in touch with DCI Waites, the lead on the Safer Streets project. He's going to pull together a list of known drug offenders worth interviewing. He's also agreed to get us details of pawn brokers and traders who aren't above fencing stolen goods. We're dealing with a desperate, and therefore dangerous, opportunist. Most probably a drug addict. That's where you should be focussing your efforts.'

'We've already been over this. If it was all about the cash, why not take the other valuables? Both women had stuff that could have easily been sold that the killer left behind. You could argue they were interrupted, but on both occasions?'

'Perhaps they didn't want to risk being seen taking things out of the house. It was broad daylight after all.'

'We're talking about jewellery, which would have fitted in a pocket.'

'Only Mrs Walker had anything worth stealing.'

'Would a drug-addled burglar know that?'

'I would imagine you get an eye for what sells over the years.'

It was clear she wasn't going to budge.

Back at his desk, slumped in his seat, Fisher called Nightingale over. On hearing the light trip of her footsteps, he pushed an empty chair from the side of his desk towards her.

'Take a pew.'

'Has something happened?'

'The Falcon has landed.'

'What?'

He shook his head.

'The DCI wants us to stop what we're doing and go back to looking at the crazed junkie theory.'

'On what basis?'

'On the basis that it's her idea and she happens to be singularly lacking in imagination.'

'But we went down that route after Mrs Walker died and found nothing. What are we supposed to do, run the same enquiries all over again?'

'Pretty much. The DCI has been in touch with someone in vice who's going to give us some leads, apparently.'

'Oh.' He could hear the deflation in her voice. 'So what do I do about the victims' phone details, not bother?'

'Have you got them?'

'No. I was promised later today.'

'No harm in taking a look once you've got them. I still plan on taking a look at our records to see if I can find any similar cases.'

'You might want to start with the death of a guitar teacher.'

'What?'

'I was about to come and tell you when you called me over. While I was on the phone to the telecoms companies, I started flicking through the list of cold cases the DCI wanted us to review. There's this one case, a fifty-three-year-old guy, a guitar teacher, found dead in his flat with a bag over his head and a belt around his neck.' Matt stiffened in his seat. 'It was five years ago, so it might not be related. Also, the MO wasn't exactly the same. Whoever killed him tried to make it look like auto-erotic asphyxiation gone wrong. The victim was naked, plus they found some dubious porn on the bed.'

'What was found at the scene that made it look suspicious?'

'The belt had been fastened to a light fitting above the bed. It looked as though he must have put too much downward pressure on the belt and the metal prong had slipped into the hole, meaning he couldn't unfasten it. It would have been put down as an accidental death if it wasn't for the fact the light fitting had come away from the ceiling. The view was that that would have released the pressure and made it possible for him to unfasten the belt. The pathologist also made some comment about the trauma around the neck not quite fitting with what you typically see in cases of auto-erotic asphyxiation. Though they did say that could have been due to rotational forces exerted on the neck by the light fitting as it came away from the ceiling.'

'Did they make much progress with the investigation?'

'Not really. Most of the effort was focussed on tracing the teacher's last appointment. According to his phone, he was scheduled to give someone called Mark a guitar lesson around the time he died. An appeal was run, asking this Mark to come forward, but no one ever did.'

'Any indication the guitar lesson thing was a front for something seedier?'

'Not explicitly, though they did find a snapshot of a boy on the floor near to the body. They traced the lad from his school uniform. Turns out that as well as being a guitar teacher, the dead guy had also been choirmaster at the local church.'

'And let me guess… the boy used to be in the choir.'

'You got it. Anyway, the boy had been around eight when the photo was taken and would have been coming up for sixteen when the teacher died, only it turns out he committed suicide six months earlier.'

'Did the investigation team talk to the boy's family?'

'Yes. Though there was never any question of them having had anything to do with the teacher's death. They moved to Ireland a few months after their son had died and there was no evidence they'd been back since. They were reported as being shocked to hear of the teacher's death but dismissed suggestions he might have had anything to do with their son's suicide.'

'Was there anything on file to indicate whether the guy was a suspected paedo?'

'No. Though he had filed a crime report following the boy's suicide, claiming to have received a number of telephone threats implying that was the case. All anonymous, of course.'

'I take it suicide was considered? If he was up to no good with the choir boys, maybe he was full of remorse after hearing about the boy's death.'

'Considered and discounted — because of the sexual nature of the scene.'

Fisher took a moment to digest the new information. He'd heard of, and seen, some strange approaches to suicide. If the teacher's death had been suicide, then it would have been up there amongst the strangest. But no matter, whatever the cause of his death, it bore little semblance to the two recent murders.

He gave a short shake of his head.

'I think we can rule it out as being related. The differences are too great.'

'I appreciate the settings aren't the same,' Nightingale said tentatively. 'But say the suspicions about the choirmaster weren't true, and the photo of the boy and the porn were planted, then we've got what appears to be three community-spirited individuals found dead with a bag over their heads tied with some sort of ligature.'

Matt leaned back in his seat and let the suggestion sink in.

'Okay, let's go with that idea. What if the teacher was the killer's first? After which, they managed to rein in their urges, for a while at least, until they found themselves wanting to kill again. Only this time their intended victim was a woman. They could hardly set the scene up the same way, so they made it look like a robbery. Finding that all too easy, they were compelled to do it again.' He sat up abruptly. 'We need to take a closer look at this teacher, see if he really does fit the profile.'

'What about the checks the DCI wants us to do?'

'Shit. I'd forgotten those... too busy coming up with real leads.' Fisher's shoulders slumped. If he ignored the Falcon's instruction, she'd have him for insubordination, but if he failed to follow up more worthwhile leads then he'd have his own conscience to deal with. He owed it to Em Walker and Connie Lloyd to do the best by them. There was only one thing for it. 'What time is it?'

'Half-three.'

'Is it already? Fancy that. I've got a doctor's appointment I'd forgotten all about. We need to go'

'Have you really?'

'I have if the Falcon asks. Stick it on the board in case she wonders where we are. Then grab your coat. I just need to make a quick phone call.'

11.

The Reverend Abigail Cartwright met Fisher's request for a meeting to discuss the church's erstwhile choirmaster with polite curiosity. After welcoming them at the door, she saw them settled into a pair of comfortable armchairs then promptly scurried off with the promise of tea.

'What will happen if the DCI finds out we've come here?' Nightingale asked in a hushed whisper.

'How's she going to find out? Anyway, it's no big deal, we'll do what she wants us to do tomorrow. It won't take long to prove her junkie idea is a load of codswall—'

'Here we are,' the Reverend said, her return heralded by the sound of clattering cups. 'We'll leave that to stew a minute, shall we?' She set the tray down with a thump. Fisher heard her take a few steps, then a heavy whoosh of air as she sat down. 'I have to admit, your call certainly piqued my interest. I can't imagine why you would want to talk about Jim Hatton after all this time.'

Fisher gave what he hoped was an encouraging smile in her direction and asked, 'Are you aware of the circumstances behind Mr Hatton's death?'

'If you mean that he was found in his flat after having partaken in a somewhat unwholesome activity, then yes, the officers leading the case did share some of the details with me.'

'What were your first thoughts when you heard that?'

'I was saddened, naturally. The man was dead.'

'But were you surprised by the nature of his demise?'

'Detective, I have seen far too much of life and of people's frailties to be surprised by anything. The question I would put to you is, what do we really know about anybody? People are comprised of so many layers, each stratum developing as a result of some past event, shaped by their response to it and softened or sharpened by the effects of time. Sometimes even the individual doesn't know what lies within until something happens that pierces their defences and exposes the lower layers.'

Fisher flashed a tight smile and said, 'Yes, that's very true, but did the news shock you?'

She gave a long sigh and for a moment said nothing, then she replied, 'Yes and no. Yes, because there had been nothing in Jim's demeanour or conduct that would suggest any unusual sexual proclivities. No, because to err is human. I suspect there is many a man — or woman — who engages in behaviour that would surprise, or even shock, those close to them.' After a beat, she said, 'Oh, I nearly forgot... the tea.'

Fisher heard a series of rattles and clinks as she stirred the pot, then the soft burble of tea being poured.

'Were there ever any complaints or suggestions that Mr Hatton might have, shall we say, any unhealthy interests... perhaps regarding the choristers?'

A cup rattled violently.

Reverend Cartwright said firmly, 'Absolutely not.'

'There was nothing that roused your suspicions, even retrospectively, after he died? You never found yourself thinking, well that explains things?'

'No.' With barely disguised contempt she added, 'I can assure you I am not the type to sweep any sort of indiscretion under the carpet.'

'I wasn't suggesting you were. Only, as we all know, hindsight can be a wonderful thing.'

'Yes, well, whichever way you meant it, my answer remains the same.'

'So as far as you know, Mr Hatton was never the subject of any gossip?'

This time she didn't protest. In fact, she didn't reply at all.

'Reverend?'

'I take it you're talking about Callum Finchley, the boy who killed himself?' Now it was Fisher's turn to stay silent. Obligingly, she went on to fill the gap. 'Naturally when something like that happens, tongues wag. Everyone wants an answer as to why things turned out the way they did. Jim wasn't the only person to come under the spotlight. There were a lot of different rumours doing the rounds if I recollect.'

Fisher felt a tug at his brow riding on the back of a frown as a question entered his head, but he knew better than to interrupt and kept his mouth shut.

The Reverend went on, 'When Callum first joined the choir, he was a lovely tempered boy. Angelic even. He stayed that way for four, maybe five years, and then one day that all changed. He became moody and withdrawn. Not that that set alarm bells ringing... you see it a lot with teenage boys. Eventually he decided to leave the choir — I think he gave school commitments or some such as the reason. I rarely saw him after that, despite the fact his parents and his sister regularly attended church. I recall asking after him once and seeing their faces grow ashen. They told me he was having trouble finding his feet in high school. It was obvious they were worried about him. I tried to reassure them that he would find his way, eventually. Like I said, mood swings and anxiety are all too common in teenagers. After that, I didn't hear anything for a while. By the time I did, it appeared things had escalated somewhat. Callum's behaviour had gone from being erratic to verging on delinquent. He had been suspended and was facing expulsion. One day I saw Mr and Mrs Finchley leaving the church and made a point of catching up with them to ask if there was anything I could do to help. They didn't say much, but it was clear they were at their wits' end, but even then, not entirely without hope. It seemed they had managed to get Callum referred to a psychologist who they hoped might be able to help. But it was not to be and sadly the child took his own life six months later.'

'And his parents never knew what was behind the change in personality?' Fisher asked.

'If they did, they didn't share it with me.'

12.

Fisher spent a troubled night, with Jim Hatton's death and the recent murders of the two women filling his head, leaving no room for dreams. The more he thought about them the more the differences between them began to grow like shadows cast by the rising moon. By morning, what had only yesterday seemed like a reasonable hypothesis now felt as unlikely as the Falcon letting him run the investigation his own way. As soon as they arrived at the office, Fisher had Nightingale sit at his computer and call up Jim Hatton's original case file.

'Find Callum Finchley's parents' details for me, will you? I think I'm going to give them a call.'

'Is that a good idea, after all this time?' Nightingale replied. 'We don't even know if Hatton's death had anything to do with their son.'

'But we need to know, which is why I want to talk to them,' he replied.

'And if it isn't related?'

'Then we leave Hatton's case languishing amongst the cold cases where we found it and stop wasting time chasing ghosts.'

'But what if...' Suddenly she dropped her voice to a whisper, 'The DCI's on her way over. She doesn't look happy.'

'Fisher!' Fallon shouted, sounding like she was reprimanding an unruly dog.

He spun in his seat to face her and pulled his lips into a smile that would make any ventriloquist proud.

'Ma'am.'

'How are you getting on with that list DCI Waites sent you?'

'Working through it, ma'am. I'll let you know as soon as we get anything.'

'Really?' The timbre of her voice sounded almost human, taking Fisher by surprise. It actually sounded like a genuine question rather than her usual sarcastic sneer.

He was about to respond when Nightingale said, 'Yes ma'am. We're going through them now.'

He should have realised the change in tone was down to the Falcon having addressed Nightingale, not him.

'Good,' she said briskly. 'But don't make the mistake of thinking this is a desk-based job. You need to go and talk people. Even if they didn't do it, they might know who did. Remember, there's no honour amongst thieves.'

Fisher waited until the solid tread of the DCI had faded away then said, 'Thanks Beth. You saved my bacon.'

'She won't fall for it a second time. We've got to do something about that list.'

'Print it out. And the one with the pawn shops and jeweller's. We'll fit them in somehow. Anyway, where were we?'

Twenty minutes later, Fisher replaced the phone's handset on the cradle. He slipped on his headset, about to dictate a new document, when Luna stirred at his feet. He felt a gentle tap on his shoulder and slipped the earphones off.

'Matt, it's Beth. I brought Luna some fresh water.' He heard the sound of water being poured into the dog's bowl. 'How did you get on with Mr and Mrs Finchley?'

'I may have got something. I'm not sure. From what they said, Callum used to be a carefree and happy lad, then one day

83

something changed. He became withdrawn and nervy. He was having problems at school, so when he said he wanted to quit the choir and spend more time on his studies, they didn't think anything of it. Though you'd think alarm bells might have gone off when he told them he was worried Mr Hatton would be upset and asked them to say it had been their decision. After that, things continued to go downhill and he got in with a bad crowd. It came to a head after he thumped another kid when an argument got out of hand and he was suspended. Out of ideas, his parents took him to see a psychologist, and for a short while he seemed happier and his studies improved. Needless to say, it came as one hell of a blow to discover him hanging from the banister one day.' An involuntary shiver coursed through him as the image of Josh, swinging, tongue lolling, flashed uninvited through his mind.

'And they didn't suspect anything, I mean in relation to Jim Hatton?'

'No. I even mentioned the rumours; said I'd heard that after Callum died there'd been talk that Hatton had an unhealthy relationship with his choir boys. I asked whether it was possible that was the reason for Callum's sudden change in behaviour. They were horrified; said they'd have known if that was the case. I wanted to tell them it was because people thought like that that paedos get away with it, that and the fact they scare the kids into silence. Only I figured they've been through enough. They did tell me one thing that might be worth following up. Callum had a friend, a bit older than him, might have been from the choir, they couldn't remember. Anyway, this friend, a lad called Petey, was something of a trouble-maker. It sounded like they partly blamed him for Callum's change in behaviour. It made me think... what if Hatton was abusing some of the kids, including this Petey, who instead of killing himself, decided to kill their tormentor?'

'Ok—ay,' Nightingale said. 'That's a big what if. And even if you're right, how does it fit with the latest murders?'

'I know it's a stretch, but what if Petey kills Hatton then finds he gets a kick out of delivering some vigilante justice? Don't forget, he might have already had behavioural or drug issues. Maybe he was able to control his urges for a few years but something happened and set Mrs Walker in his sights.' He rubbed his chin, the hairs rasping loudly, then shook his head. 'Did that sound as stupid to you as it did to me? If I'd been talking about Coach Walker, then it might make more sense. Not much more sense, I grant you. It's not like the coach ever did anything inappropriate with the kids he trained. Although someone looking for a victim that fit some skewed code might not have known that.' He stopped speaking for a moment, giving this latest hypothesis some thought, then said, 'What if the killer had planned on killing Coach Walker?'

'Mr Walker's been dead for years.'

'Maybe he didn't know that. The Academy still carries his name. I wouldn't be surprised if his photo's on the cover of the annual report. It always used to be.'

'What about Ms Lloyd? Why her?'

'Didn't someone say something about her volunteering with the Sunshine Club?'

'You think the killer's targeting people who do community work? I'm not really seeing it.'

Nor was Fisher, truth be told. All the same, whilst the idea of an angel of death handing out their own form of retribution seemed more at home in a work of fiction than in a real-life police investigation, he couldn't help but think it more plausible than the Falcon's half-baked idea of it being the work of some drug-crazed burglar.

13.

'Her name's Professor Martha Woolf, with a double O,' Fisher said, as Nightingale accelerated away from the station. They were heading for the university, having arranged to call on Callum Finchley's psychologist after his parents had called to endorse the meeting.

'Same as Virginia Woolf,' Nightingale said.

'Who?'

'The author.'

'Never heard of her. What sort of books does she write?'

'Wrote... she died in 1941. It was all stream of consciousness and feminism stuff. She had an affair with Vita Sackville-West, who was another novelist, though these days she's better known for her garden designs.'

'How come you know so much about her?'

'I did my thesis on feminism in twentieth-century literature as part of my degree.'

'You're kidding right? What did you study?'

'English literature.'

'Bit of a far cry from what you do now, isn't it? What made you join the police?'

After the smallest of pauses Nightingale said, 'I wanted to make a difference.'

If he could have, Fisher would have turned and taken a long, hard look at her, because although he was sure she did — want to make a difference, that is — her words rang hollow. He couldn't help but feel there was something she wasn't telling him.

Before he could probe any further, she said, 'Do you think she'll give us any details? I thought there were rules around client confidentiality.'

'It'll depend on the terms of their arrangement. If the kid agreed to share his therapy notes with his parents, then I guess they're entitled to share them with who they like.'

'And if he didn't?'

'Look, the kid's dead and it is a murder investigation. We've just got to hope she'll do the right thing.'

They found Professor Woolf's office on the fourth floor of the Psychology Faculty. Fisher knocked then waited, expecting someone to shout 'enter' from within. Instead, the door opened and a waft of perfume, floral with spicy undertones, swept over him.

'You must be the detectives.' She had a distinctive American accent and a voice as deep as one of Carl Jung's theories. 'Please, come in. Oh, what a beautiful dog. Is it a boy or a girl?'

'A girl,' Fisher said.

'Isn't she adorable? I take it you'd rather I don't pet her? I have a friend who has a service dog. I know how upset she gets when people try to stroke him when he's working.' Woolf's voice was drawing subtly quieter and Fisher guessed she was already retreating into her office. He instructed Luna to take him to a chair. Nightingale followed them in, closing the door behind her.

'Are you partially sighted or totally blind?'

Fisher found her level of directness refreshing. Most people pretended they hadn't noticed he couldn't see.

'I can make out the difference between light and dark. That's about it.'

88

'I can't say that I've heard of a blind detective before. Is it common in the UK?'

'No. I'm the first.' And probably the last, if I don't start getting some answers soon, he thought.

'You must have to rely a lot on those around you to give you visual cues. How does that make you feel, having to put your trust in others in order to do your job?'

Fisher went to answer then paused. He leaned back in his seat and smiled.

'As I explained on the phone, we'd like to talk to you about Callum Finchley, a patient of yours some six years ago.'

Woolf barked out a deep and throaty laugh.

'I'm sorry. I'm so used to asking the questions. I must admit, your psychological make-up fascinates me — to be able to do the job you do, with your particular disability. But consider my wrist appropriately slapped,' she said, with a playful lilt to her voice. 'So you want to know about Callum Finchley? I must warn you, although his parents contacted me, giving permission to share his therapy notes, that was never part of the arrangement. But if there's anything I can tell you that I don't feel breaches that confidentiality, then I'll happily share.'

'Thank you,' Fisher said. 'Just so you know, this is in relation to a murder enquiry. *Three* murders, actually. If that has any bearing on your decision as to what to disclose.'

'Three? Really? How awful. Are you able to tell me anything about them?'

'The first victim was a choirmaster at the church where Callum was a chorister. A man named Jim Hatton. He was found dead a few months after Callum committed suicide. We understand Callum went from a happy go lucky boy to a very troubled teen who got in with a bad crowd. We wondered

89

whether his change of attitude had anything to do with the choirmaster.'

'What makes you think the two might be connected?' Woolf asked.

'Mr Hatton was the subject of a number of accusations following Callum's suicide. Rumour had it he took advantage of the children in his charge, one of whom was Callum.'

'Did he ever face charges?'

'It appears no one notified the police of their concerns. The only reason we're aware of the rumours is because Mr Hatton himself filed a harassment complaint not long before he died.'

'All this took place years ago, yet you're only investigating it now?'

'Reinvestigating. The case remains open.'

'Oh, I see. Well, it's very interesting but I'm not sure what you want from me.'

'We were hoping you could tell us whether the allegations against Mr Hatton were true. If they were, it's possible he abused other children, one of whom could have gone on to kill him, either to end their own torment or perhaps in retaliation for Callum's death.'

'And that's all you need to know?'

'That and a name. When I spoke to Callum's mother, Mrs Finchley, she told me Callum had a close friend, someone who had been quite an influence on him, and not in a good way. We would like to speak with this individual. Perhaps Callum mentioned him to you? All Mrs Finchley knew is that Callum referred to him as Petey. She thought the two boys might have known each other from the choir but I've since spoken to the vicar who has no recollection of anyone of that name being there at the same time as Callum.'

'And you think this Petey is responsible for killing the choirmaster?'

'No. We just want to talk to him.'

'What about the other two?'

'Other two?'

'You said there were three victims. So far you've only talked about the choirmaster.'

'It's complicated.'

'That's okay. I have two degrees, a masters and a PhD. I can do complicated.'

Fisher couldn't help but smile.

'Let's just say, there are some similarities, particularly around the crime scene itself.'

'They shared the same modus operandi?'

'To an extent. Although Mr Hatton was murdered, his death had all the hallmarks of being an accident, whereas there's no doubt the two recent deaths were murder.'

'In which case, I'm puzzled as to why would you assume they are related. To kill someone and attempt to make it look like something other than murder is very different to blatantly murdering someone. It suggests a totally different psychology.' After a moment's pause, she asked, 'Can I ask, how could you tell Mr Hatton's death wasn't an accident?'

'The victim was supposedly engaged in an auto-erotic sex act. He was found with a noose fashioned from a belt tied to a light fitting above the bed. Presumably unbeknown to his killer, the light fitting came away from the ceiling. Hatton dropped to the bed and the resulting drop in tension on the belt meant, had he still been alive, he should have been able to free himself. On top of which, he had a plastic bag over his head — an almost suicidal act for someone practising the already dangerous pastime alone.'

'He wouldn't be the first person to have died in similar circumstances. Couldn't the light fitting have come away once he was dead... a case of too little too late?'

Fisher didn't want to waste time labouring the details of the cold case. He waved a hand.

'I think we're straying from the point. The fact is there are enough similarities to the recent murders for us to want to take another look at the Hatton case.'

'Can I ask, were the other two men found in a similar compromising position?'

'The latest victims were women. And no, the similarities are in the method by which they died, not the setting. I'm sorry but I can't be any more specific than that.'

'Then I don't think I can help you. It wouldn't be ethical of me to furnish you with the name of someone when I think it's highly unlikely that they are responsible for the deaths you've just outlined.'

'I don't understand.'

'I don't agree with your assessment that the deaths are related. I can't see why you would think they were committed by the same person.'

'What if, in Mr Hatton's case, the killer was motivated by something other than the desire to kill, then, having found they enjoyed the experience, took a more direct approach, not bothering trying to disguise what they'd done?'

Woolf again gave a throaty laugh.

'I take it you've had little experience of serial killers, Inspector? The thrill of the kill is there long before they take their first life. They learn how to control their emotions, their desires, to take their time so they can better savour the experience. Over time they build in subtleties as they finesse their technique. I don't think I've ever come across one where their method becomes blunter. The violence maybe, but the lead up, never.'

'You have experience in this area?'

'Serial killers are a particular interest of mine. Obviously, you can't see, but if you could, you might have figured that out from the contents of my somewhat overloaded bookcases, where in amongst the plethora of texts on the topic are several by one Martha Woolf.'

'Then I bow down to your superior knowledge on the matter. But isn't it possible in this case that the killer grew tired of operating under the radar? What if they wanted to flaunt what they're doing... a case of wanting their fifteen minutes of fame?'

'I think you've been watching too much TV. If someone is intent on killing, they're hardly going to want to get caught and put an end to it, are they? The serial killers who have been caught have usually made a costly mistake, or law enforcement got lucky.'

'I'm not saying they want to get caught, rather they are showing off what they've done while thinking they'll still get away with it. And to be honest, they're doing a good job of it so far.' Sensing his comments were having little impact other than to antagonise the professor, Fisher admitted defeat. 'Okay, what if they're not linked? We're still interested in speaking with Callum Finchley's friend. He might know something that could help our investigation into the choirmaster's death.'

'If the choirmaster was guilty of what you suspect, presumably there would have been plenty of people happy to see him six feet under. Will you be investigating all of the boys from the choir too?' While Fisher was considering his response, she went on, 'My point is, you have no reason to suspect this individual and I don't want to be responsible for making someone's life a misery because you don't have any other leads.'

Fisher gave a grim nod.

'I sincerely hope you're correct in your assessments, Professor Woolf. If you're not and there's another murder, I wonder whether you'll still feel justified in the stance you have taken.' He gripped Luna's harness and stood up. 'Beth, we're leaving.'

'Wait...' Woolf said. Fisher tilted his chin, turning his face in her direction. 'You said you thought this friend of Callum's may have killed the choirmaster out of revenge.'

'Yes.'

'One thing I will tell you is that at the time Callum died they were no longer friends. From what Callum told me, Petey was little more than a lazy, greedy delinquent who lost interest in him as soon as he realised Callum was a clever and honest boy who had simply lost his way. If you had told me the choirmaster had died after having been struck over the head and his flat ransacked, then I might be more inclined to think you are on the right lines. But engineering a murder to look like an accident, that takes some planning, some skill, don't you think?' Without giving Fisher a chance to answer, she went on, 'On that basis, a teenage delinquent wouldn't be my choice of potential suspect.'

Fisher thought back to Hatton's case notes. She was right. It had been expertly set up. If it hadn't been for the bodged light fitting, the noose would have held and no one would have been any the wiser. A very different scenario to the recent murders.

He gave a nod and said, 'Noted. Thank you for your time, Professor.'

'You're welcome. I'm only sorry I couldn't have been more help. But if you really are dealing with a serial killer, never forget Inspector, the drive to kill is a hungry beast that is always demanding fresh meat.'

14.

'She sounded just like Kathleen Turner, don't you think?' Fisher said to Nightingale as they crossed the car park on the way back to her car.

'Who's Kathleen Turner?'

'American actress. Tall, long blonde hair and a voice that makes the hairs on your head…. Never mind. She was in *Romancing the Stone* and *The Man with Two Brains*.'

'Nope.'

'How about the voice of Jessica Rabbit? You must have seen *Who Frame• Roger Rabbit?*'

'I've heard of it… I think.'

'Actually, forget it. I can barely remember it from when I was a kid. So, what do you reckon?'

'I liked her,' Nightingale said.

'I didn't mean what do you think of her. What do you think about what she said?'

'I think she had a point about Hatton. The way he was killed was totally different to the other two. On that basis, it seems unlikely the same person killed all three.'

He gave a long, worn-out sigh. 'I wish I thought you were both wrong. Sadly, it looks like we're back to square one… *again*. I guess there's nothing else for it, better make a start on those lists the DCI wants us to look at.'

Fisher heard a blip as Nightingale unlocked her car; Luna came to a stop at the same time. He secured the dog in the back then made his way to the passenger seat.

'Shall I head to the first address on the list?' Nightingale asked, starting the engine.

Fisher turned towards her.

'You really want to go and talk to a junkie with potential anger issues with a blind man in tow?'

'You think it might be too dangerous?'

'Damn right I do. Sorry but it's a no-go. Take me back to the station. You and Andy can go and do the visits, seeing as you can both handle yourselves, and I'll start phoning around the fences.'

In the office Fisher briefed DS Wickham and reluctantly sent him and Nightingale to shake down the addicts thought to be the most violent or prone to unpredictable outbursts — reluctantly, because every inch of his sadly expanding gut told him it was a non-starter. Though at least it would keep the DCI off their backs for a while.

Frustrated at his own shortcomings and the fact they'd made no progress, he settled at his desk, Luna at his feet, and started to plough through the names of fences known to deal in stolen jewellery. They had already circulated details of the stolen items to all of the bona fide outlets and visited as many of the off-the-radar places they could. All to no avail. Nevertheless, it needed doing again; not least because it was possible the perpetrator had waited for the dust to settle before cashing in the goods. Fisher had barely started when he got a result he hadn't been expecting. A small, estate-based trader said yes, he had recently bought a necklace with a heart pendant, though he claimed he was unable to recall who had sold it to him, despite having purchased it only the day before.

'You're seriously telling me you can't remember whether it was a man or a woman who brought it in?' Fisher grumbled.

'What can I say guv? My memory ain't what it used to be.'

'This is in relation to a murder investigation. Can you remember me saying that, at least?'

'Sure.'

'And you still won't give me a description.'

'It's not that I won't, guv. Like I said, can't remember, can I?'

'Fine,' Fisher snapped. 'Can you send me a photo of it? I need to check to see if it's the one that was stolen.' He recited his mobile number. 'And don't go flogging it till I get back to you.'

He hung up and immediately called Warren Newman.

'Mr Newman, it's DI Fisher.'

'Any news?'

'Possibly. I have a photograph I'd like you to look at. If I text it to you, could you tell me if the necklace is the same one you gave Ms Lloyd?' Fisher ended the call and pinged the photo over.

'It's nothing like it,' Newman said when Fisher rang back. 'I told you, the one I gave Connie was silver with a heart and other stuff hanging off it. The one in the photo is a tacky gold colour with a single heart that looks like cheap shit.'

'I apologise for the mix-up. At least we can rule the necklace out.'

'Is that all you can say? Jesus, if it's down to you it's going to be a bloody long investigation when you can't even identify a sodding necklace.'

Fisher took a calming breath and said, 'While I've got you on the phone, perhaps you can help me with another matter... Ms Lloyd's will.'

'What about it?'

'When we spoke before you said she didn't have a will.'

'I didn't know she had. Her friend called me yesterday and told me. First I knew about it.'

'She never talked about writing one after the two of you got engaged?'

'No.' There was a slight pause, then he said, 'I hope you're not suggesting I made her write one, because if you are—'

'Do you how much you'll be getting?' Fisher interrupted.

'Not much I shouldn't think. It sounds like her friend gets the lion's share.'

'Really? I thought she only got the TV and some jewellery.'

'Exactly. That's pretty much all Connie had to leave. Most of her money ended up in the Caribbean, lining the pockets of that cheating bastard who was supposed to be investing it for her.'

'Which was in the process of being recovered.'

'Yes, but… look, you can't go accusing someone of something you have no evidence for.'

'I wasn't accusing anyone of anything. These are routine questions. Is there a reason why they upset you so much?'

Fisher heard Newman mumble something he took to be a no. After ending the call, he hung up and slumped back in his seat as another bundle of straws he'd been clutching slipped from his grasp.

***

That evening, at home, Fisher cried off an invitation to join Ginny for dinner, opting instead for a night in with Luna and a microwave curry. During the day, a decision had been made to run a fresh appeal for information relating to the murders of the two women. He listened to the late-night news, a can of lager by his side.

By the time the news item finished, Fisher's mood was almost as black as his sight. In the 'good old days' he'd have set a roll of paper out on the dining table and used it to map out the facts of the case, organising his thoughts and making any gaps in his knowledge obvious. Now it all had to be done in his head — a hit and miss affair, given his thoughts had a habit of jumping around like an overzealous puppy. But like it or not, it was the only option available now, so he set aside his drink, settled into his chair and let his mind roam.

He thought about the final minutes of the two women's lives. Tried to imagine the moment the bag was thrown over their heads; how the feeling of disorientation gave way to terror as the ligature tightened around their necks. Em Walker, her warm, smiling eyes darting around as she gasped for air, the noose snuffing out what little fight she might have had. Why bother with the bag when they had the flex? It must have complicated things, having to slip it over their heads before wrapping the flex around. More time for the victims to fight back. Or did its effect — confusing and debilitating — make the job of killing easier? He thought back to Jim Hatton. Although the circumstances were different, the method was broadly the same. Someone had slipped a bag over his head and fastened a belt around his neck. Hatton had been a lot younger and fitter than the recent victims, and male. He was bound to have put up a fight, yet there had been no signs of a struggle. Had he aided in his own demise, donning the bag and belt willingly? Had his killer lured him to his death by persuading him to enter into some sort of sex game? What about Em Walker and Connie Lloyd's killer? How had he — assuming it was a he — convinced them to open their doors and let a total stranger in? Unless, of course, they weren't strangers.

15.

While Fisher was dining solo, chasing chunks of chicken around his shop-bought tikka masala, ten miles away a man parked his black hatchback on the dirt track outside a solitary house shrouded in darkness. He climbed out of the car and made his way up a path overgrown with weeds. Turning the key in the lock, the front door swung open silently on well-oiled hinges. He stepped over the threshold and stood for a moment, listening.

Nothing. Not that he expected to hear anything, but such cautious behaviour was ingrained in him after having spent years covering his tracks.

He closed the door. Throwing his keys down on the narrow shelf above the radiator, he made his way into the tiny but clean kitchen, where he grabbed a bottle of lager from the fridge. He raised the bottle in salute at his reflection in the stainless-steel door before padding through to the lounge. After a quick swig, he kicked off his shoes and flopped onto the sofa, setting the beer down on the coffee table. Condensation dribbled down the bottle's side and pooled onto a pine table already stained and scarred by years of abuse. He grabbed the TV remote, jabbed the on button and settled back.

A photograph of a woman appeared on the screen: grey hair, dyed blonde, framed a face lined with wrinkles; crows-feet around a pair of lively eyes.

Just like his mother. God bless her.

He turned the volume up and listened as the news anchor described the latest murder and relayed the police request for information into the woman's death.

16.

The following morning Fisher took a taxi to the office, Nightingale being unavailable, having to spend a second day tracking down possible suspects with DS Wickham.

He climbed out of the cab. The roar of traffic and the scuffle of commuters hastening to their desks threatened to overwhelm him. He tightened his grip on Luna's harness and took a deep breath. Using the retreating cab to orientate himself to the road, he instructed Luna to take him to the office and gave himself over to her slow and sure step.

He had barely sat down when he heard footsteps walking towards him. Recognising the short step and firm heel strike, he twisted in his seat and surreptitiously pulled out his mobile. Putting it to his ear, he started to mumble. He wasn't in the mood to talk to the Falcon most days but especially not today when he had so little to say. He continued with the pretence until he heard the footsteps pause and then retreat. Slowly, he lowered the phone.

DCI Fallon cleared her throat loudly. She sounded close. What the hell had she done, circle back on tiptoe? Despite knowing who it was, Fisher turned his head back and forth and said, 'Is someone there?'

'Don't bullshit me, Matt. I know you were only pretending to be on the phone. I saw you pull it out of your pocket when you heard me coming.'

'That's not true. I was talking to Beth; checking how they're getting on. So, how can I help?'

'Give me some good news. I'm getting pressure from upstairs.'

'What can I say? We're nearly done working through the checks you wanted doing. Nothing's come of them so far. We've also gone back over the lives of the two women, trying to find a common link, but again, nothing. No shared church, doctor, dentist, social club, hospital, you name it. Not even a delivery on the same day, which is a shame seeing as one of Mrs Walker's neighbours saw what they thought was a delivery driver at her door the afternoon of her death. I've also been looking into one of our cold cases with the same MO, though there are as many differences as there are similarities.'

'You call that progress? It's not good enough Matt. Not by a long chalk. '

'If you can think of anything we've missed, then tell me. I'm all ears.'

'Sounds like you're struggling. Perhaps it's time to hand the investigation over to someone else.'

'And what exactly will they be able to do that I can't?'

'It's all about fresh eyes, Matt. If we can't get answers your way, perhaps we need a new perspective. Keep me informed.'

As she strode away, he could feel the heat radiating from his cheeks and cursed himself for giving her the satisfaction of seeing the frustration written all over his face. He picked up his phone and tried Nightingale's number.

She answered immediately, 'Hi Matt. What's up?'

'How are you getting on?'

'We're almost done. Just two to go. So far, it's been a total waste of time. While I'm sure some of them would cut their own mothers' throat for a quick fix, I can't see any of them managing to con their way into someone's home. Plus, most couldn't even tie their own shoe laces, let alone handle a plastic bag and flex at the same time.'

'Okay, well, see you back here when you're done.' Fisher hung up and was about to return his phone to the desk when it started to ring. An automated voice began to recite a number he didn't recognise.

He put it to his ear and said, 'DI Fisher.'

'Detective, it's Martha Woolf, from the university.'

'Professor, how can I help you?'

'I wanted to apologise. I'm so used to having to protect my clients, the seriousness of the situation didn't sink in until afterwards. On reflection, it seems churlish not to have given you what you asked for, or at least help you to get it.'

Fisher felt his excitement grow. And then he remembered they'd all but concluded that the cases weren't linked. Any investigation into Jim Hatton would just be a distraction.

Woolf was still talking, 'I had a look at my case notes last night. What I can tell you is the boy you are looking for was at the same school as Callum, a year higher I believe. And he isn't actually called Petey or Peter or Pete. P. T. refers to his initials. Though I'm afraid I don't know what that stands for. The friendship only started after Callum left the choir, when he started to hang around with P.T. and some other delinquents. But as I said yesterday, the two had parted ways by the time Callum killed himself.'

'Thank you. I'll make a note. Though we might not be following it up for a while now. I've also had time to reflect and I think you were right; it's unlikely the cases are connected.'

'Actually, that was the other reason I called. It occurred to me that although it would be highly unusual, there is a chance it's the same perpetrator. You see, I failed to take into account the stage in the killer's development when the different crimes were committed. If Mr Hatton was their first victim, and they did it to stop the abuse from continuing, they'd hardly want to draw attention to themselves, hence they made it look like an accident. Many victims hide their abuse, hoping that in doing so, they can eventually forget it ever happened. Only they never can. Instead, it festers and grows, creating all manner of psychological problems. Years of suppressed anger and shame can do terrible things to a person. I gave it considerable thought last night and have a theory. What if the original abuse only happened because someone turned a blind eye? That someone being a female family member. The abuse victim might have spent years fantasising about revenge. Should this female family member have died without the victim having enacted any retaliation it's possible they experienced a transference, redirecting their feelings — often unconsciously — onto someone else. Most likely someone who reminds them of the original object of their attention. If that happens, and the abuse victim still harbours a mountain of pent-up hatred, it's not difficult to imagine them going a step further and taking their murderous desires out on a stranger.'

'You seriously think that's possible?'

'I do. Though I'm not saying this P.T. is your man. On the contrary, I still think that's highly unlikely.'

Fisher thought she may well be right, especially if this P.T. was as thuggish as he'd been led to believe, but seeing how close he and Callum had been, P.T. might at least be able to furnish them with some names.

'Anyway,' Woolf continued, 'I hope that helps and you find your man soon. If I can be of any further assistance, don't hesitate to call. I've spent most of my life studying the behaviour of serial killers. If there's information you need... well, you know where I am.'

17.

At the same time that Fisher was talking to the professor, Harry Moore, a bearded, bald-headed fifty-something pulled his van into the kerb on a quiet residential street. He climbed out and walked jauntily to the rear of the vehicle, where he retrieved a small foil tray from a large insulated box. Crossing the pavement, he started up a path to a flaking green door and pressed the bell. The air was warm and a bird trilled from the branches of a nearby tree. Spring was on its way.

While waiting, Harry surveyed the haphazard array of pots scattered over the cracked concrete that covered the front of the house. They sported a bedraggled collection of plants, most of which had died since the house's occupant had become too frail to tend them herself. He turned his head, taking in the neat and tidy fronts of the neighbouring houses. No paint to flake on their double-glazed uPVC windows and doors.

He pressed the bell again. A trill ring sounded in the hallway beyond.

A minute later, he squatted down and pushed open the letterbox.

'Mrs Choudhury! It's Harry, with your dinner.'

He put his ear to the flap.

Nothing.

With a puzzled frown, he crouched down and peered into the hallway. He gave a gasp and let the flap drop back before hurrying back to his van.

18.

By the time Fisher arrived at the scene his stomach was doing somersaults, and not just because of DC Kami Aptil's driving. Another murder meant another chance to catch the killer.

'Andy and Beth have just arrived,' Aptil said, as they climbed out of the car.

Fisher opened the rear window a couple of inches and gave Luna a squeaky toy to keep her occupied. He heard the familiar rustle of a protective suit being pulled from a bag.

'Here…' Aptil pressed the light plastic coverall into his hand. 'Do you need a hand?'

'I'm good thanks.' He sat on the edge of the passenger seat and slipped the suit over his feet. He was doing up the zip when two sets of footsteps approached, accompanied by a lot of rustling.

'Matt.' It was DS Wickham.

'Andy.' Fisher gave a nod. 'You there too, Beth?'

'Yes.'

'What do we know so far?' Wickham asked.

'Victim is believed to be seventy-two-year-old Meera Choudhury. Lived alone. Body was discovered by the guy delivering meals-on-wheels a couple of hours ago. According to the attending officers she was found with a black plastic bag over her head and flex around her neck.'

'Bin man strikes again.'

'What's that?'

'It's what the papers are calling the killer.'

'For God's sake, Andy. Think about what you're saying. If he's the bin man, what does that make his victims... rubbish? I don't want to hear that term again.'

'Sorry. You know I didn't mean it like that.'

'I know, but... well, just engage your brain next time.'

He let the scowl melt from his brow and asked Nightingale to lead the way to the house.

'I understand the victim was found in the hallway,' Fisher said to the uniformed officer on the door.

'That's right.'

'Then we'll go in by the back door. Lead the way, Beth.'

Fisher took hold of Nightingale's arm at the elbow.

'There's a gate ahead,' she said, steering him around to the back of the property.

The path underfoot was full of cracks and crevices and Fisher caught his foot on its uneven surface and stumbled forward. His hand briefly flailed in empty air until he regained his balance, his heart thumping a rapid tattoo in his chest. He blew out a thin stream of breath.

'Are you okay?' Nightingale asked.

'I'm fine. Come on, let's carry on.'

They entered the kitchen and crossed to the hallway. Fisher zoned out the background noises and focussed on Nightingale's commentary.

'The victim is lying on her side, about a metre from the front door. Doctor Cooper is currently examining the body.'

'Morning,' came the pathologist's chipper voice.

Nightingale continued, 'Next to the dead woman is a walking frame one of those metal ones with little rubber feet and something else. I can't see what it is. She's lying on top of it.'

'It's a calendar,' Dr Cooper supplied.

'Like a normal calendar you have on your kitchen wall?' Fisher asked.

'Yes.'

'There's an empty hook on the wall,' Nightingale said. 'Maybe it normally hung there.'

'What? Now the killer comes by appointment?' Fisher shook his head. 'Beth, make sure to grab it as soon as Bernie's finished with the body. Okay, so what else?'

'I can't see a handbag or purse.'

'Anyone seen a bag or purse anywhere?' Fisher shouted.

'There's a bag in the lounge,' someone called back.

'Andy, go take a look, would you?'

A minute later, Wickham was back.

'There's a handbag down the side of an armchair. There's a purse inside. Cash is still in it.'

'Is there another bag anywhere?' Fisher asked. 'Maybe in a cupboard in the hallway?' It was soon confirmed that the woman's only handbag was that in the lounge. 'Why did they leave the cash this time?' Fisher wondered out loud. 'Okay, well, Andy, Kami, go take a look around.'

As they left, Doctor Cooper joined Fisher and Nightingale in the kitchen.

'I'm done,' she said.

'Any obvious differences to the previous two?'

'Not that I can see, from a cursory examination at least. I should be able to fit the PM in tomorrow afternoon. That do for you?'

'Thanks. I appreciate it.' Fisher knew she was pulling out all the stops, the wait time for a post mortem usually being a lot longer.

After the pathologist took her leave, Fisher stood for a moment thinking about what to do next. It seemed the killer had, once again, acted slickly. Already his hopes for a breakthrough were disappearing like warm days in the advance of autumn.

'What now?' Nightingale asked.

Good question. What were they going to do?

'I'm not sure there's any benefit in wandering blindly around the house — no pun intended. Let's go and talk to some of neighbours. Somebody's got to have seen something.'

But first, Fisher had Nightingale take him back to the car.

Slumping onto the passenger seat, he pulled off his coverall, thinking how easy life would be if only he could slough off his feelings of failure as easily. Next, he let Luna out, gave her some water, then spent five minutes waiting for her to relieve herself. Then, all three of them made their way to the house to the right of the victim's property.

The door was opened by a young woman. She sounded harassed and interrupted the introductions to issue a series of yelled threats to what sounded like a hoard of dementors. Fisher declined the invitation to go inside and proceeded to quiz the woman whilst standing at the threshold.

'This morning? No. I didn't see anything. I had my hands full looking after that lot in there. I've got my own two plus another couple I mind for friends. My husband reckons I must be mad, but it pays for our holidays.' A series of loud bangs came from inside the house. 'Hang on a sec…' The woman hurried down the hallway. A minute later she was back. 'Sorry about that. Where was I?'

'This morning…' Fisher prompted.

'Oh yeah. Well, like I said, I didn't see anything but then I've barely opened the door.'

'What time did your friend drop her children off?'

'Friends — one kid each. They came around eight, about ten minutes apart. I didn't see anyone hanging around or going into Meera's then.'

'When your friends come to pick up their kids, could you let them know what's happened and ask them to call if they saw anything, no matter how trivial.'

'Sure.'

'You didn't hear any noises through the wall?' Nightingale asked.

'You're joking. With the amount of racket this lot make?' As if to underline her point, a hullabaloo of shouts and screams erupted from the house. 'They're even worse first thing in morning. They tend to run out of steam as the day wears on. Thank God.' From the noises emanating from inside the house it sounded like they still had plenty of life in them.

Fisher turned the conversation to the murdered woman.

'How well did you know Mrs Choudhury?'

'Not very, to be honest. I don't really know any of the neighbours. I don't have the time.'

'Do you know whether she had any relatives?'

'There's a son. He comes around most days since her husband died.'

'So she was married then? I don't suppose you know whether she still wore a wedding ring or any other jewellery?' Fisher asked. None had been found on the body.

'I can't say as I noticed. Sorry.'

With their questions complete, Fisher and Nightingale left the neighbour and her screaming charges and moved on to the next house in the row. When their knocks failed to get a response, they moved on to the next, and then the next, followed by the houses on the opposite side of the road and then those on the other side of the victim's home. Of the handful of residents that were in, none claimed to have seen anything or anyone out of the ordinary. Only a few admitted to knowing the victim and even then, only by sight. By the time they returned to the dead woman's house Wickham and Aptil had almost finished their cursory look around.

'Anything?' Fisher asked.

'Not really,' Wickham replied. 'We found a hospital appointment card — looks like she was being treated for dementia.'

'Would that be at the same hospital that Connie Lloyd used to take her friend?' A sliver of optimism peeped out from beneath the usual mantle of doubt Fisher carried with him.

'No. Canterbury.'

Fisher stemmed a sigh as his hope shrank back into the gloom.

'Anything else?'

'There was a charged mobile on the table in the lounge. I've bagged it up.'

'Is it locked?'

'No.'

'Can someone get it? We might be able to find a number for her son on it.' As Aptil went to fetch the phone, Fisher asked, 'What happened to the calendar that was under the body?'

'Bagged and ready to go,' Wickham replied.

'Beth, when we get back, could you go through it. See if any entries correlate to anything on the other women's calendars.'

'Will do.'

Fisher heard Aptil return.

'Kami, could you have a look, see if there's a contact that could be her son. Try her recent calls first. His is probably the most frequent.'

After a minute, she confirmed Fisher's assumption.

'She only ever called one number and most of the incoming calls came from there. The name given is Rakesh.'

Fisher passed her his own mobile. 'Could you put the number in for me, please?'

'There you go,' she said, handing it back.

'No time like the present to ruin someone's day,' Fisher said, as he waited for the call to connect.

A moment later, a man's voice answered, 'Hello?'

'Mr Rakesh Choudhury?'

'Yes.'

'This is Detective Inspector Fisher. I'm sorry but I've got some bad news regarding your mother.'

The other man gave an exasperated sigh.

'What's she done now? Whatever it is, please accept my apologies. She has dementia and isn't supposed to leave the house.'

'I'm so sorry to have to tell you, but your mother is dead.'

'Dead? There must be some mistake. I saw her a couple of days ago. She was fine then.'

'There's no mistake. I'm afraid she was attacked in her home earlier this morning.'

'Who did you say you were?'

'Detective Inspector Fisher, Kent Police. We don't yet know who is responsible but please take it from me, we will do everything we can to find them.'

'My mum is in her seventies. She's harmless. Who would want to attack her? Are you sure you're talking about the right person?'

'As sure as we can be. We will, of course, need you to undertake a formal identification. A family liaison officer will be in touch shortly. They will make arrangements for you to see your mother, and also answer any questions you may have.'

'I was going to go round last night, but something came up. I thought I'd go tonight instead. But... dead? How did... you said attacked... how did they...?'

'I'm sorry, I can't give you any details at the moment. Could you tell me whether your mother wore any jewellery?'

'Jewellery? No. She hardly ever left the house.'

'Not even a necklace or a wedding ring?' Fisher knew he shouldn't be prompting, but often it was the day-to-day items in people's lives that got overlooked.

And sure enough, Mr Choudhury had a change of heart.

'Oh, well, yes, she always wore her wedding ring. Dad died years ago, but she used to say she would always be married to him.'

Fisher heard a stifled sob and knew it was time to wind up the conversation. There would be time enough to talk another day. With there being little more he could usefully do on site, Fisher asked Wickham and Aptil to complete the search, while he, Nightingale and Luna returned to the station.

'I take it you and Andy didn't get anywhere this morning?' he said, as soon as he felt the car pull away.

'The whole exercise was pointless,' Nightingale replied. 'None of the people we talked to are the type to target old biddies in their home for a handful of change. If they needed cash, they'd either mug someone outside a cash machine or hold up an offie.' After a moment's pause, she said, 'How about you? How was your morning?'

Fisher told her about the phone call from Professor Woolf.

'So what... she reckons this is a result of an outpouring of anger against someone's mother or other female figure in their life? It sounds a bit out-there.'

'I'm only repeating what she said.'

'If this is all because Jim Hatton used to abuse kids, why isn't the killer targeting middle-aged blokes who remind them of him?'

'I don't know. Maybe because our man has already killed the real Jim Hatton? Professor Woolf said if the female family member is already dead, but not at the killer's hands, there's something called transference — I think that's what she said — which causes them to turn their attention onto other women.'

'So why didn't he stop after Mrs Walker? How many more victims does he need?'

A shiver of dread travelled up Fisher's spine.

'I don't know. Maybe he's developed a liking for it?' He couldn't deny it was looking increasingly likely that they were dealing with a psychopath. 'Anyway, that's all speculation. What I'm interested in is why didn't they empty her purse of cash? Why deviate from their pattern?'

'Her bag was tucked between a chair and the wall. Maybe they couldn't find it.'

'Or they were interrupted. When you get a chance, give the meals-on-wheels guy a call. Ask him if he heard any noise from inside the house, doors closing, anything like that. Also call the uniforms who were first on the scene; find out if the back door was locked. If the perp was interrupted, maybe they ran out the back. While you're busy doing that, I'll see if I can track this P.T. down. If nothing else, he might be able to tell us if we're on the right lines about Hatton abusing kids.'

'You really think Hatton's death is connected?'

The truth was he didn't, but to admit it would mean admitting he hadn't a clue where to look next.

Instead, he said, 'It doesn't matter what I think, Beth. It's what I know that counts, and at this stage, I don't know that it isn't.' Despondent and fast running out of ideas, he couldn't help but wonder if the DCI was right — maybe what the case needed was a new perspective.

19.

It was mid-afternoon by the time they reached the station. A fact Fisher knew by the rumbling of his stomach. He grabbed a granola bar from the vending machine and took up Nightingale's offer of a coffee, then settled down to chase down the delinquent P.T.

The deputy headmistress of Callum Finchley's school had no difficulty in furnishing Fisher with a name. Paul Tanner. Two years Callum Finchley's senior and, according to the deputy, an all-round bad boy. Tanner had left school at sixteen — a case of good riddance to bad rubbish — and that was the last they had heard of him.

Fisher spent the short journey to Tanner's last known address pondering the wisdom of their current line of enquiry. He knew the area from his days in uniform — row upon row of ugly, orange brick boxes topped with red roofs, built in the eighties. Not exactly a crime hotspot, but certainly an area with more than its fair share of problems. He rapped loudly on Tanner's door. The rabid barks of a dog were followed by the sounds of the animal scratching frantically at the thin wood, which was all that was between it and freedom. In the midst of the dog's assault on the door came a man's shouts. The dog fell silent. A moment later a door latch clicked. Fisher was grateful he'd left Luna in the car.

'What do you want?' The man had a lazy, mumbling sort of voice, like everything was too much bother.

'Police,' Fisher replied. 'We want to talk to Paul Tanner. Is that you?' There was a pause. Fisher knew he had his answer. 'Mr Tanner, we'd like to talk to you about an old friend. Perhaps we could come inside?'

Nightingale had been standing on Fisher's left. He felt her arm begin to slip from his grasp and knew they were being admitted. He reinstated his grip and followed her across the threshold. A few steps later they turned a sharp right, into a room where the air was a fusty mix of stale cigarettes laced with the sour scent of last night's alcohol overlaid with wet dog.

Which reminded Fisher…

'I take it we're safe from the dog in here?'

'You're fine. So, who's this friend then?'

'Callum Finchley.'

'Callum's been dead years. Killed himself. Looks like you had a wasted trip.'

'Why did he kill himself?' Fisher asked.

'Why you asking me?'

'We were told you were mates.'

'Then you were told wrong. He hung around with us for a bit. Until some shrink turned him into a mummy's boy. Total sap.'

'Before that, did he ever talk to you about what happened?'

'What do you mean, happened?'

'Why he was so angry? Why he'd started to kick off at school?'

'Why would I care?'

'Did he ever mention the name Jim Hatton? He was the choirmaster at the church Callum used to sing in.'

'No. Why? Was he a paedo? Did he *do* stuff to Callum? If anyone ever tried that on me I'd cut his bollocks off.'

What little hope Fisher had that Tanner was somehow involved in Hatton's death evaporated. Unlike the room's foul, stagnant air.

'You working at the moment?' Fisher asked.

'I was. Got a job stacking shelves at Morrison's until the bastards sacked me. I only missed a few shifts. Wankers need to chill more.'

'Do you live here alone?'

'Nah. I live with me mum.'

'Was she here with you yesterday morning?'

'Only till half-six. Her shift starts at seven.'

'So you were here on your own?'

'Why?'

'Just answer the question.'

Tanner barked out a laugh.

'You're out of luck if you were planning on framing me for something. You'll need to find yourselves another scapegoat. I was with my probation officer yesterday morning. Got there at eight. Though I don't know why I bothered. The bastard kept me waiting over half an hour. Didn't get out till half-ten.'

'What time did you leave here?'

'Got the five to seven bus. Takes forever.'

If his probation officer corroborated his alibi then Tanner was in the clear. Not that Fisher was surprised. Only disappointed. Yet another lead taking them down the path and straight into a brick wall.

***

The following morning, Fisher fed Luna before making himself a couple of slices of buttered toast and a pot of strong coffee in the hope it might go some way to lift his spirits after yet another restless night. After loading the dishwasher, he let Luna out of the back door. As he stood there, contemplating the day ahead, a light breeze stirred the leaves of a nearby daphne bush, filling the air with its heady aroma. He took a deep breath in and let out a long sigh.

Was he being selfish insisting on running the investigation himself?

He'd be the first to admit it if he thought someone else could have made more progress. But how could anyone have done anything different? Not that it mattered what he thought. In a job based on results, he knew if he didn't get a breakthrough soon, the Falcon would pull the case and his future from under his feet by tying him to his desk looking at cases as cold as her heart. The prospect hung heavy on his shoulders.

He threw what was left of his coffee onto the lawn and called Luna inside. By the time Nightingale arrived he had already composed a long list of tasks to drive the investigation forward.

'When we get in, I want you to track down Tanner's probation officer. See if they confirm his whereabouts yesterday morning. While you do that, I'll give Doctor Cooper a call, make sure there's no wriggle room on the time of death. I don't want to rule Tanner out if there's a chance he could have done it.' The pathologist had given them an estimated time of death at the crime scene and although it was rare for estimates given in the field to be wrong, it wasn't unheard of.

An hour later, Tanner was in the clear.

'Does that mean we're ruling Hatton out as having been killed by the same perp?' Nightingale asked.

'I'm not ruling anything out, but our focus needs to shift onto the latest victims. Which reminds me, how did you get on with the meals-on-wheels guy?'

'He heard nothing and the attending patrol said back door was locked.'

Fisher leaned back in his seat and started to stroke Luna's crown.

'Okay, let's run through what we know. Both Em Walker and Mrs Choudhury had mobility issues. Ms Lloyd on the other hand was, by all accounts, fit and healthy. Em Walker regularly went to the over-60s club, whereas neither of the other two did. Only Mrs Choudhury and Ms Lloyd attended hospital regularly, but different hospitals for different reasons.' Fisher shook his head. 'There's got to be something linking them. What are we missing?'

'What about meals-on-wheels? I know we don't know whether Mrs Walker used to have them and I can't see Connie Lloyd bothering — she was far too independent — but she did volunteer with the Sunshine Club as a driver at some point. What if she also delivered dinners? If the other women received them, that could be a link.'

It was certainly an angle Fisher hadn't previously thought of.

'I can check it out if you like?' Nightingale offered.

After Nightingale left, Fisher sat for a moment thinking over the developments. How was it possible that every line of enquiry drew a blank? He felt his scalp prickle as an unwelcome thought tiptoed into his mind: what if the Falcon was right and the case needed someone with more imagination, more ingenuity? Fisher had a lot of time for his colleagues; respected and trusted them. The only problem was they, like him, tended to think along the same lines. Maybe an injection of new thinking was just what they needed?

In a moment of serendipity, his mobile started to ring. He hit answer and cleared his throat.

'Hello?'

'Detective Fisher, it's Martha Woolf.'

'Hello Professor. How can I help you?'

'I wondered if it was convenient to talk, and please... call me Martha.'

'Now's fine... Martha.'

'I just heard the news about the latest victim. The Asian lady. They're saying her death is linked to the other two.'

'It looks that way.'

'In which case, I wanted to offer you a word of warning. I'm not sure whether I'm over-dramatising things. You know what it's like, when you've spent so much of your life studying something, there's a tendency to see it everywhere... serial killers are no different.' She gave a nervous, throaty laugh. 'But, anyway, it's the timeline. It's escalating. If this is the work of a serial killer, you need to find them soon as I don't think it'll be long before there's a fourth murder.'

'Believe me, we're doing everything we can.'

'I'm sure you are. I wondered whether you might be interested in a seminar I'm giving at the university this afternoon. It's on the psychology of serial killers. I'm sure you cover most of the basics at police college but I've been studying the topic for many years and you might be surprised at some of the things I've learned... things that might challenge your perception. You never know, it might spark an idea that could open up a new line of enquiry. Worth a shot, maybe?'

'Where is it and what time does it start?'

20.

Fisher tightened his grip on Luna's harness in response to the thunder of footfall around him. It felt like he was being swept along in a rip tide of bodies surging down the corridor.

'You alright?' Nightingale asked.

'Just about,' he said, with a grim smile.

'I think everyone's heading to the same place as us. The lecture theatre's just ahead.'

Fisher felt Luna steer him to the right. There was a subtle drop in temperature.

'Detective Inspector!' Professor Woolf's voice rang out through the PA system, making it impossible to place her location. 'Down here. I've reserved seats for you and your colleague at the front. Everyone, please let Detective Fisher through. And don't pet his adorable dog; as you can see, she's clearly working.'

'Best seats in the house,' Nightingale whispered as they made their way down a series of steps.

Fisher slipped his jacket off and placed it on the empty chair next to him. Slowly the surrounding chatter dropped to a murmur.

'Here we go,' he said. 'Sounds like the show's about to start.'

'Forget everything you've ever heard, read or seen about serial killers,' Woolf said to the room. 'Books, TV and movies are there to entertain. They are not made with the intention of educating you on how to recognise a serial killer. That's where I come in. And even I don't have all of the answers all of the time.' After a short pause, she added, '...only most of the time.'

On cue, the audience tittered politely, then settled in their seats as Professor Woolf went on to outline the most useful psychological assessment tools when trying to put together a profile for a suspected serial killer.

Forty minutes later, the lecture ended and the professor opened the floor to questions.

'Professor Woolf,' a man called from the crowd. Fisher felt Nightingale turn in her seat.

'Yes Dominic,' Woolf replied.

'Isn't it true to say psychological studies are simply another means of feeding people's obvious fascination with serial killers? Surely, when it comes to identifying potential killers, profiling is a numbers game. Every text book states that over 90% of serial killers are men and 86% are heterosexual; the majority wet their bed as adolescents, had extensive head injuries as children, exhibited tendencies towards animal cruelty and fire-setting... I could go on, but my point is that by looking into the characteristics displayed by serial killers, a computer could easily narrow down any manhunt to a handful of names in a matter of hours.'

A loud husky laugh reverberated around the room.

'If I had a dollar for every time one of my students has said that...' Fisher could hear the professor start to pace, her heels ringing out across the auditorium as she crossed the wooden floor. 'Of course, that's one approach. Though not one I would recommend. You see, if we were to use those same metrics then some of the most notorious serial killers in history would have slipped through the net. Think Harold Shipman, Myra Hindley, Dennis Nilson. To use your turn of phrase, I could go on. Now if you had suggested an analysis of key psychological characteristics and experiences born of their childhood, you'd be closer to the mark. But the main reason I think database-matching exercises don't work, and the one factor that makes all of your statistics worthless, is that they are based on serial killers who have been *caught.*' She emphasised the last word and then paused, presumably to let it sink in. Fisher heard a burble of assenting murmurs. Woolf went on, 'You see Dominic, you have to remember what it is we're trying to do. We're trying to catch those who have so far evaded detection. And maybe the reason they're still at large is because they don't have so much in common with their convicted counterparts.'

Before Dominic could launch a counter-challenge, Woolf said, 'Sarah Banner, I noticed you put your hand up a moment ago. You have a question?'

A young woman replied, 'Yes, thank you Professor. I just wondered how many serial killers are thought to be out there at any one time?'

'Where exactly? Worldwide or here in the UK?'

'In the UK.'

'Well, with an average of sixty unsolved murders each year, experts…' she said, loading her last word with a thick coating of cynicism, 'estimate there are at least two serial killers in operation at any one time. Now where I'm from, in the US, that figure jumps substantially. Estimates calculated in a similar manner give a figure of around thirty to fifty operating at any one time, though some say the actual number could be as high as 2,000. Sounds ridiculous to have such a big margin, right? But not when you realise the lower figure has been calculated based on the number of *known* murders. I personally think the upper figure is more accurate, as it credits some serial killers with enough intelligence to hide their crimes.'

Fisher cleared his throat and thrust his hand up.

'Detective Inspector, you have a question?'

'Yes. Thank you. Two questions really. You say there are serial killers out there continually evading detection. How do you know and how do they do it?'

'I'll answer the second question first, if I may.' Fisher gave a nod and Woolf went on, 'A serial killer wishing to remain at liberty must be prepared to forgo recognition for their crimes. The killers who get caught are the ones whose vanity outweighs their desire to kill. They want the world to marvel at their handiwork, which means they leave their kills for all to see. Which gives law enforcement agencies something to work with and ultimately leads to the killer's capture. A serial killer who wishes to remain anonymous, and therefore free to continue to kill, must put aside their desire for notoriety. They must conduct the killing expertly enough that the death is attributed to other means or do it in such a way that their victims aren't ever linked. No link, no serial killer — an approach that is particularly effective if the killer is able to move around the country, so even if murder is suspected, it will be different detectives in different forces dealing with them. Which is how Peter Sutcliffe, the Yorkshire Ripper, got away with it for so long. Despite your computers and databases, most successful detection still comes down to the right person having access to the right information at the right time. Which brings me back to where I started. The idea of these types of murderers leaving calling cards, of wanting to be caught, wanting the infamy and kudos of being labelled a notorious serial killer as shown on TV is bullshit... if you'll pardon my French. For whatever reason they do what they do, it's certainly not to give you or me something to read about over your great British breakfast. And how do I know this? Because I study the psychology of people, especially people who like to kill.

I've interviewed several serial killers who were caught because they made a mistake. They had made every attempt to cover up their crimes but for some reason or another — usually something unforeseen and therefore unavoidable — they got caught. It stands to reason there will be others who haven't had any bad luck and remain under the radar, getting away with murder. So, there you have it, an introduction to the world of serial killers. Next week we will be looking in detail at some of the world's most notorious killers and try to understand the psychology behind their crimes.'

Fisher listened to the small stampede as the students vacated the auditorium. In contrast to the crowd, one set of footsteps grew steadily louder.

'How did you find the lecture?' Woolf asked.

'It was very informative, thank you,' Fisher replied. 'Though I'm not sure it had much relevance to our cases. Our killer has made little effort to disguise the women's murders or the fact they're linked. Though, so far, their deaths are the only thing we can find that links them.'

'In which case, you should be very hopeful of catching him. He's either out to get his fifteen minutes of fame or he thinks he can outsmart you. Either way, unless he really is smarter, it won't be long before he makes a mistake. When serial killers have been in the public eye for a while and are still getting away with it, the thrill of the kill can be replaced by the thrill of the chase. Once the game changes, they start to be driven more by the need to be applauded for their cunning than they do by the act of killing.'

'Great. So how many more women will have to die while we wait for him to cock up?'

'Perhaps none. It's possible he has already told you more about himself than you realise. The murder scenes left by a serial killer usually say an awful lot about their psychology... if you know what you're looking for.' After a beat, she added, 'I'd be happy to help. If you want me to?'

Fisher hesitated. The force's use of external expertise was strictly controlled and subject to a mountain of red tape. Yet, with the investigation having drawn a blank, should he really be turning his back on offers of assistance? He thought of DCI Fallon. He knew if he so much as broached the subject with her she'd take it as a sign of his incompetence. It would be the equivalent of handing her his resignation. But then, what she didn't know about couldn't hurt her — or him — could it?

He flashed the professor a warm smile.

'Is there somewhere more private we can talk?'

21.

In the professor's fourth floor office, Fisher and Nightingale settled into a pair of easy chairs nestled around a low table whilst Woolf rustled up a pot of coffee. With the welcoming aroma filling the air, Fisher sat back and outlined their efforts to date.

'So far, the investigation has centred around chasing down known drug addicts with a history of violence. More at the insistence of my DCI than my own personal view, I should add.'

'Why is that?' Woolf asked. Fisher heard the rattle of crockery as she poured the drinks.

'The women didn't live very near to one another so I think it's unlikely they were targeted by the same drugged-up junkie, the likes of which don't tend to roam too far from their home turf. Also, the method of killing doesn't fit. If they'd been stabbed or hit over the head with a baseball bat or even throttled with bare hands, I might have been more inclined to believe it. But to have gone equipped with a plastic bag and flex and all for a handful of cash and a few bits of jewellery they'll have a hard time selling, it just doesn't fit.'

'I agree,' Woolf replied. After a short pause, she said, 'You didn't mention the choirmaster? Did you manage to get anywhere with the information I gave you?'

'Yes. And we've more or less ruled it out as being linked. We spoke to Paul Tanner, the friend Callum referred to as P.T. He's off the hook for the latest murders. And on reflection, the differences between the scenes are too big to ignore, including the fact that there had been an attempt to cover Hatton's murder up, which is definitely not the case with the latest crimes.'

'All good reasoning,' Woolf commented.

'So, going back to the current cases. You said before that we ought to be worried about the escalating timeline. I take it you think the shortening of the time between murders indicates an increasing instability.'

'That is usually the case, yes. Though it depends on so many factors. The gaps between killing could be random; they might simply reflect how frequently the killer is able to find someone who fits their criteria. You mentioned you observed some changes to the crime scenes. There may be some clues there. Ordinarily you would expect any change to the MO to be a result of either venting of frustration or because of an increasing desensitisation which drives up the desire for violence to maintain the same kill-thrill levels. But in this case, that's not what's happening. I admit, that puzzles me.' Woolf fell quiet for a few minutes. Fisher was on the verge of asking if everything was okay, when she said, 'An obvious explanation for them not taking the cash from the third victim is because her bag, and therefore purse, was in the lounge and not visible from the hallway. Which suggests it was taken in the first two cases simply because it was there. Although the profile of your typical serial killer is that every crime scene is planned with meticulous detail like some macabre tableau, it's not always the case. Perhaps the killer is short of cash. Or perhaps they were disturbed and didn't have time to look for the victim's bag.'

'There's no evidence of them being disturbed,' Fisher offered.

'All the same, I'm not sure we can read too much into whether the cash was taken or not. As regards the other change — the

131

siting of the calendar under the body of the third victim — did you find calendars in any of the other crime scenes?'

'Yes,' Nightingale replied. 'In both cases.'

'Both times under the body?'

'No. They were hanging up in the kitchen.'

'Ah,' Woolf sounded optimistic. 'Could be something there. Perhaps the killer left a clue in the first two, then with it not having been picked up, decided to be less subtle this time round. Have you analysed them thoroughly?'

'I went through all of the appointments,' Nightingale replied. 'I couldn't see any that appeared in all three.'

'Did you check for any hidden messages?'

'How would I see them if they were hidden?'

'I didn't mean literally hidden, more like a coded or cryptic clue.'

'No. I didn't—'

'Beth only looked for what I asked her to,' Fisher intervened. 'It's my fault if we missed anything. But it's a good point. We can take another look when we get back to the station.' He reached a hand out towards the table, feeling for the warm ceramic of his cup. He picked it up and took a swig of coffee then asked, 'What about the bags? Do you think the fact they're black has any significance?'

'I think it's of great significance,' Woolf said. 'In fact, I'd say it's the most singularly interesting aspect of the crime scene.'

'In what way?'

'Why wouldn't the killer want to see his victims' faces?'

'We wondered if it might be so they couldn't see his face, to make them more afraid.'

'If the point of the bag was to heighten the victims' fear, surely the killer would want to observe that. For many serial killers it's the act of inflicting suffering, the control and finally the power of taking a life that is so exhilarating. Why then would they cover their victim's face in those final moments? Why not simply cover their eyes? Are you sure the bag was placed on the head before the flex was used to strangle them… it couldn't have been slipped over afterwards?'

'The pathologist is certain both the flex and the bag were in place at the time of death,' Fisher said.

'In which case, I must admit what you've described interests me greatly. It is full of idiosyncrasies which I'm struggling to understand.'

'Glad it's not just us, eh, Beth?' Fisher said.

'I can see now why you have been having problems,' Woolf said. 'The one thing I will say is, not all serial killers kill purely for pleasure. The history books are full of examples of where they have been motivated by something else entirely.'

'Such as?'

'Money, fear, power, revenge, hate… all sorts of reasons. Maybe your killer gets their kicks by instilling panic in the community. Perhaps they want all elderly women to tremble in fear behind their net curtains.' Woolf must have noticed Fisher screw his face up as she quickly added, 'I'm not saying that's the case here, only that you need to look beyond the obvious. And while we're on that topic, don't forget, not all serial killers are men. I know I keep referring to the killer as he, but you could just as easily be looking for a woman. They can be just as ruthless as men. More so, depending on what their motivation for the murder is. There was one. Juana Barraza. She operated in Mexico in the 1990s. She became known as Little Old Lady Killer after she murdered around fifty women, strangling or beating them before stealing from them. You know, that could explain the flex. A woman might not have the physical strength to manually strangle her victims, especially if they put up a struggle.'

'Believe me Professor, we're ruling no one out. I'll consider anyone that comes under our radar, but at the moment we have no one. How do we flush them out?' Before she could reply, Fisher said, 'Do you think the fact the media keeps reporting on our lack of progress is making it worse? What if it's feeding the killer's desire for his, or *her*, fifteen minutes of fame? Would we be better off denying them the exposure?'

'Good question. One I'd love to be able to answer. But, as with everything, it's not that simple. Your killer might not actually want the publicity.'

'How does that fit with the fact they've made no effort to cover up the murders?'

'Perhaps they've found a method that works for them, one that allows them to do what they want whilst still evading detection. If that's the case, you'd be helping them if you blocked media coverage. As it is, you're putting the killer's target demographic on their guard.'

Fisher leaned back in his seat and folded his hands behind his head, blowing out a sigh that rasped loudly on his lips.

'We're damned if we do and damned if we don't.'

'I can see how frustrated you are, Matt… I hope I can call you Matt?' Fisher nodded. Woolf went on, 'I don't know if it will help but I can give you some general characteristics the killer is likely to possess. They may help you to assess potential suspects.'

Fisher straightened up. 'I'm listening.'

'For one thing they will have a very strong sense of self.'

'You mean conceited?'

'Yes, but not necessarily how you might think. They might not be a flash dresser or come over all that showy but they will have an overinflated opinion of their own abilities. They will genuinely believe they can turn their hand to anything with great success. With each murder that belief will strengthen. They will also have a high level of intellect to be able to plan an approach that is effective, that avoids them getting their hands dirty and that, so far, has allowed them to get away with it.'

Fisher started to nod.

'Makes sense.'

'Good.' Woolf started to gather up the cups and Fisher felt a surge of disappointment. There were still so many unanswered questions.

'Before we go...' he said. 'In your lecture you talked about the serial killers who forgo the limelight and do everything they can to keep their killing under the radar.'

There was a rattle of crockery. He heard the professor resume her seat.

'Yes?'

'While you talked about a serial killer's qualities, like being intelligent enough to cover up any psychopathic tendencies and emulate compassion, you didn't say how we can use that information to identify them. These killers need taking off the streets. How do we do it?'

'You remember what else I said about them?'

'Erm...'

'You said some are driven by the need to feel what they are doing is somehow vindicated,' Nightingale replied.

'Top of the class, Beth. That's exactly what I said.'

'How does that help us?' Fisher asked.

'Maybe they select their victims because they see them as a burden to society,' Woolf replied. 'Or perhaps their target has criminal tendencies of their own, so they see it as a form of rough justice. I'm not talking about those serial killers who kill in a religious fervour. I mean more subtle reasons. They feel compelled to kill, but also know that any obvious pattern by which they choose their victims is as good as putting a signpost to themselves. You need to have an open mind. Every time you investigate the death of someone people had a reason to hate, even if the cause of death doesn't initially appear to be out of the ordinary, ask yourself if it really is what it appears to be. Suicides, accidental deaths, fires… they can all be used to cover up murder.'

'So if we take the choirmaster for example. If he really did have a penchant for young boys, his death would fit the bill?'

'Maybe, though who's to say it wasn't really an accident? He wouldn't have been the first middle-aged man to have died as a result of an autoerotic asphyxiation.'

'True. Though there was enough doubt for the inquest to conclude an open verdict and for it to remain on our files.'

'In which case, if it was murder, it sounds like the killer was lucky to get away with it. But as to whether he — Mr Hatton — was killed by a serial killer, who knows. It's just as likely to have been one of his abuse victims or even the parent of a victim, don't you think?'

'It's a rather extreme way to exact revenge,' Fisher said.

'An eye for an eye, Inspector.'

'That might fit if Hatton had actually abused the children under his tutelage. Had he?'

'I'm not sure why you're asking me,' Woolf said, suddenly sounding defensive.

'You counselled Callum Finchley for some months. I would have thought if anyone knew whether he was being abused, you would.'

After a long pause, Woolf said on the back of a sigh, 'Callum was a typical teenage boy. He was never open about what was troubling him, preferring to skirt around the issue. You have to realise, I wasn't there to investigate the cause of his problems, my remit was to help him become a better version of himself by building his resilience.'

The explanation tripped off her tongue, yet Fisher didn't believe her. The professor had already shown herself skilled at asking probing questions. A teenage boy would be no match for her, especially one as vulnerable as Callum Finchley. It was a shame. He'd really started to like her.

22.

On returning to the office, Fisher called for DS Wickham to join him and Nightingale in the incident room.

'Andy, take a seat.' Fisher waited for the scrape of chair legs, then said, 'We need to redouble our efforts to find a link between the three women.'

'The serial killer lecture didn't pan out then?'

'The lecture was okay, but we got a lot more out of the conversation we had with the professor afterwards. She said a couple of things that got me thinking, especially that a serial killer in it for the thrill would want to see the whites of his victim's eyes. So why a black bag? Why not a clear plastic bag? It suggests they could be motivated by something other than the act of killing.'

'Such as?' Wickham asked.

'Apparently there are lots of reasons. It could be the desire to control, though in our case he didn't really make them do anything, as far as we know. Then there's jealousy... I can't see it myself. Revenge.'

'Revenge for what? All of the victims were harmless old biddies,' Wickham said,

'First off, sixty is not old,' Fisher said. 'I've got friends who are Connie Lloyd's age. Plus, it might not be revenge for something they did themselves.' He gave Wickham a brief rundown of the theory of transference as had been explained to him by the professor.

'So our perp might have killed them because they reminded him of someone who hurt him way back in the past?'

'Or turned a blind eye, allowing him to be abused. But yes, that's the theory.'

'Sounds to me like an excuse to get away with murder. It's almost as bad as God made me do it.' Wickham wasn't known for his liberalism.

'It's just one train of thought. Money is also a possible motive.'

'How? Apart from Mrs Walker none of them had anything worth killing for.'

'That's not necessarily true. Connie Lloyd was hoping to relieve her ex-husband of some of his wealth, plus she was taking legal action against the financial advisor who's sunning himself in the Caribbean. Talking of which, we need to check to see if any of the other victims were clients of his. Andy, can you take care of that?'

'Look Matt, you know I'll do what I can to help, but I'm kind of busy at the moment. The DCI's got me trawling the ANPR cameras looking for cars in the vicinity of the victims' homes around the times of their murder.'

Fisher let out a groan.

'How is that going to help? None of the streets they lived on had cameras on them. The killer could have easily chosen a route that avoided the main roads. And anyway, why hasn't she asked Gary to do that?'

DC Gary Sully had recently returned from a skiing holiday with a broken ankle and was consequently confined to desk duties.

'She has. And Kami. I'm covering the cameras nearest to victims one and two, Kami's doing those near victims two and three and Gary's got victims one and three. If any of us see the same car in two of the areas we're to look for it in the other area we're not covering.'

'She's got three officers tied up doing the same thing?'

'Pretty much. I did try to explain that to her. But you know how she is when she's gets an idea.'

Fisher shook his head.

'You couldn't make it up, could you? Don't waste any more time on it. I'll go talk to her. See if I can get her to agree to Gary doing the camera work on his own.'

'If you can, you won't hear me complaining. So, apart from checking up on the financial investor, is there anything else you want me to do?'

'Have a dig into Em Walker's financial affairs. We already know she left virtually everything to the Academy. Find out who manages the trust, who looks after their finances and whether it's in any difficulty. Familiarise yourself with the names of everyone we've talked to as part of the investigation and keep an eye open in case any of them appear in relation to Em Walker or the trust.'

'Will do.'

'What do you want me to do?' Nightingale asked.

'Take another look at Connie Lloyd's finances. Talk to the solicitors who she'd engaged to challenge the divorce settlement; find out what her chances were of getting more money out of Hunt and how much we're talking about. Was it enough to get him rattled? Also, see what you can learn about the financial advisor who absconded with her cash and the lawsuit against him. How close is it to being settled and what happens to Ms Lloyd's share now... does it go to her estate or is her part of the claim dropped? Meanwhile, I'll take Mrs Choudhury. We know her son inherited everything, including the house. I'll see if I can find out how badly he needed the cash. I'll also have another look at Warren Newman's finances. The accounts for his business checked out okay, but who's to say the guy himself isn't up to his neck in debt?'

'I thought you said he wasn't expecting to get anything,' Wickham said.

'That's what he told us. He might have been lying. Or maybe she lied to him. She could have told him she had more money than she had, not wanting him to think she was only interested in his money. We need to keep digging and pray that somewhere amongst all the crap there's a nugget of gold.'

With Wickham and Nightingale returning to their desks, Fisher turned to his computer for Mr Choudhury's contact details. He had no sooner reached for the phone when it began to ring.

'My office. Now.' It was the Falcon.

Fisher let out a sigh, tussled Luna's crown before grabbing hold of her harness.

'Luna, take me to the Falcon's nest.'

He gave a single knock and pushed the door open.

He was a few steps into the room when an icy voice said, 'Don't bother to shut it. This won't take long. I just saw Andy, asked him how he was getting on with the task I set him this morning. I'm sure I don't need to tell you what his reply was. You undermined me. Why?'

Fisher gave a groan.

'I was about to come and talk to you.'

'Like hell you were.'

'I was. I had no intention of doing anything without your agreement.'

'That's what you always say. Is it too much to talk to me *before* you go behind my back and override my instructions? You seem to forget who's in charge here.'

141

Like he could.

He gritted his teeth and said, 'Like you seem to forget who's supposed to be leading the investigation. Me. On your request.' He let out a sigh. 'Look, all I did was ask him to run some checks for me. We have a very small group of potential suspects. I think it will be better to focus on them than spend God knows how many hours staring at camera footage in the hope of seeing the same car three times.'

'Since when—'

'Please, just hear me out. You know as well as I do how patchy the CCTV coverage is. All three women lived in residential areas where the roads are like rabbit warrens. The killer could have approached in any number of ways without going anywhere near a camera. If we had nothing else to go on, then fine, tie up an experienced detective on something so mundane, but there are leads emerging all the time that need looking into.'

'What leads? And why am I the last to know about them?' Her voice had gone up an octave.

'There are still questions we haven't got answers to in relation to some of the people we interviewed originally. We need to go back and clarify those points and see if we can find a link between any of the victims' families and acquaintances.'

'You think one of them is a serial killer?' Fallon huffed out a laugh.

'Maybe not the sort of serial killer portrayed by the media. The expert I spoke to said not every serial killer is a deranged lunatic.' As soon as the words were out of his mouth, he knew he'd made a mistake. He hadn't said anything to the Falcon about going to Professor Woolf's lecture, let alone about the conversation that followed.

And she was on it like a hound on a cornered fox.

'What expert? I don't recall giving you permission to speak about this operation to an outsider.'

'We only talked in hypotheticals. I didn't give her any details.' He hoped the Falcon wouldn't think to check with Beth. He'd hate for her to have to lie for him… or worse, to tell the truth.

'I don't give a damn if all you did was talk about the weather. You had no authority to seek out the opinion of an expert.'

'It didn't cost anything, if you're worried about the budget. And if it's not that you're worried about, then what is it? Because from where I'm standing, if anyone can shed any light on who's killing innocent and vulnerable women, I'm prepared to give them a shot.'

The room fell quiet. Fisher waited it out. Eventually Fallon spoke, 'What's the name of this expert?'

'Professor Martha Woolf. She's lectures in psychology at Canterbury University, specialising in serial killers.'

Fallon didn't respond at first. The silence stretched.

After a while, Fisher said, 'Ma'am?'

He heard her issue a loud sigh and knew he'd won the battle, even if the war was still raging.

23.

It was an hour later when Fisher finally left the DCI's office. She insisted on hearing every detail of his proposed plan before grudgingly giving her approval. He had just sat down when he heard footsteps approach.

'Matt. It's Andy.'

Fisher held up both hands.

'I know. I'm sorry. I hadn't had chance to talk to her. I should have done it the second you and Beth left.'

'It's not that. I figured you hadn't got round to it. No. I came to update you on Lewis Hunt.'

'You found something?' Fisher asked, his voice alive with hope.

'Maybe. I'm not sure how relevant it is but there's a link between him and the football academy. Turns out he's been a big contributor to their fund-raising efforts in the past. And I mean big — his donations include a brand-new minibus. I also found out his son is on the junior programme. I spoke to one of the academy's trustees. Although she didn't come right out and say it, I got the distinct impression the two weren't unrelated.'

'Hunt bought his son a place on the programme?'

'That's what it looks like.'

'That is interesting. I don't know if it's still the case, but the academy used to be all about giving disadvantaged kids an opportunity to make something of themselves. We checked

Hunt's financial situation after Connie Lloyd died so I know he's not short of a bob or two, so how come his lad got on a programme?'

'You're not the only one to wonder. Apparently, it caused quite a stir amongst the coaching team, some of whom complained to Mrs Walker. The trustee said Mrs Walker was less than happy and was going to have a word with the person responsible.'

'And who was responsible?'

'The person she pointed me towards is a guy called Hugh Cowden.'

***

Hugh Cowden, chair of the Walker Football Academy, arranged to meet them at his home.

'There's not so much as a blade of grass out of place,' Nightingale said, as she pulled the car to a stop.

'What's the house like?' Fisher asked.

'A massive mock-Georgian thing with pillars either side of the door. Is that called a portico?'

'Don't ask me. You're the one with the university degree.'

'In English lit,' she reminded him.

As they navigated their way up the drive, Fisher heard a familiar ticking sound.

'Sounds like the engine's still warm. Must have just got here. Unless there's more than one car?'

'No, just the one. A silver Jag. My nan always calls them an old man's car.'

A smile curled on Fisher's lips. He'd bought himself an E-type Jaguar when he made the premier league at the grand old age of twenty. He'd felt like the dog's cojones in that car.

Cowden greeted them at the door with the sort of false jocularity Fisher associated with politicians, salesmen and, well, virtually anyone he distrusted. They were taken through to the garden — Cowden probably didn't want to get dog hair on his plush carpet, thought Fisher — where they were offered the choice of tea or coffee. Fisher declined on both their parts.

'We don't want to detain you any longer than necessary, Mr Cowden, so I'll get straight to the point.'

'Fine by me. You said on the phone you wanted to talk about a matter of concern to Mrs Walker. I confess, I don't recall her having any concerns.'

'Last year Mr Lewis Hunt gifted the academy a minibus. Is that correct?'

'Yes. We regularly get donations from local businesses.'

'A minibus seems like a very generous donation.'

'Yes. We're very fortunate.'

'Mr Hunt must be doing very well for himself, if he can afford to present you with a brand-new minibus.'

'I really couldn't say.'

'You surprise me. I assumed you'd have a pretty good handle on his financial situation.' When Cowden didn't respond, Fisher said, 'Perhaps you'd be more comfortable discussing Mr Hunt's son's performance on the pitch?'

'I'm sorry. I don't understand. What are you getting at?'

'I was trying to understand how Mr Hunt's son…' He paused for a moment, grappling to recall the name of the boy.

'Morgan,' Nightingale said, coming to his rescue.

Fisher darted a smile in her direction.

'Thank you. I was wondering how Morgan managed to get onto one of the academy's programmes. My understanding is that the academy was set up to help kids who can't afford to go elsewhere and for problem kids who are having difficulty at school or trouble with gangs. I would have assumed some sort of financial assessment is done on the parents before a child is accepted on a programme.'

'If you're asking about Morgan Hunt's application, I'm sorry but I'm not able to comment on a specific case.'

'Unable or unwilling?' Fisher waved a hand. 'Never mind. You see, I've seen details of Mr Hunt's finances and there's no way his kid should be on the programme.' Fisher took some pleasure imagining a ruddy flush suffusing Cowden's face, flagging up his embarrassment like a beacon. 'I also know Em Walker had intended on raising the matter with you.'

'She must have changed her mind, because she never mentioned it.'

'Or perhaps she was murdered before she had the chance.' Fisher waited a beat, then asked, 'How would you have responded, if she had?'

'What a ridiculous question. How can I answer if I don't know what her point would have been?'

'How about we take a guess? What if she wanted to know how come Lewis Hunt's son had been admitted onto the academy's leading programme when his father was clearly loaded? Which of the core criteria did the lad meet to warrant a place being given to him rather than some poor sod who needs a break?'

'This is farcical. Em had stepped down from an active role on the board. She stopped having a say in decision making when she ceased being chair.'

'You don't think she'd have taken an interest in a decision that went against everything that Coach Walker stood for? Because I do,' Fisher's tone hardened, 'But if it helps, forget Em Walker. It's me asking the question this time; and it will serve you well to remember this is a murder investigation. How did Morgan Hunt get a place on the academy's top programme when his father is loaded?'

'I can't remember,' Cowden said dismissively. Adding, 'Besides, I don't process the applications,' as if that might somehow let him off the hook.

'To say you can't remember suggests you did, at one point, know. But it doesn't matter. Just tell us who did process the lad's application and we'll talk to them.'

Cowden harrumphed.

'I would, but I—'

'Mr Cowden...' Fisher said with a steel edge to his voice. 'Please tell us or I'll have no choice but to charge you with obstruction.'

'This is preposterous. I've done nothing wrong. No rules were broken.'

Fisher clenched his teeth. He was going to lose his temper in a minute.

'How did Morgan Hunt get on the programme?'

Perhaps Cowden sensed Fisher's growing impatience, for the fight suddenly went out of him.

'The boy's mother completed the application. She claimed she and his father had separated and gave her income details, which were minimal.'

'I take it they hadn't really separated?'

'Lewis had just given the club a minibus for God's sake. Getting his lad onto the programme was a small price to pay.'

'But Em Walker didn't agree, did she?'

'Em Walker couldn't see beyond her loyalty to the memory of her husband. I told her the world moves on. We need sponsorship wherever we can get it. How else can we afford to cover our costs?'

'But what about the true cost… depriving some kid who really needed the support the academy offers?'

Cowden fell quiet, either shamed into silence or simply willing the argument to be over.

'So what was Mrs Walker planning on doing about it?' Fisher asked. 'And don't say nothing. I knew her well enough to know she wouldn't have let it rest.'

'She thought a compromise might be reached. She suggested the boy be taken off the main programme and put onto one of the summer courses.'

'The summer courses run for children with problems?'

'No. One of our basic skills courses. That way she said we could fulfil our promise to Lewis by giving Morgan access to an academy course, just not the main programme, which would at least put an end to the speculation he'd bought his way onto the team. I tried to dissuade her. Lewis would consider it an insult, an embarrassment even.' He gave a sigh. 'He has, shall we say, an over-inflated opinion of his son's talent.'

'You're telling me the kid can't play?'

'His lack of talent was the reason tongues started to wag in the first place.'

Fisher shook his head.

'So how did Mr Hunt take the news?'

'I never got as far as to speak to him about it. Em and I only discussed it the week before she died.'

'Did she ever speak to him about it directly?'

'If she did, neither of them said anything to me.'

'And now…?'

'Everyone was so shaken up by Em's murder, it seemed kinder to all involved to leave things as they were.'

'Kinder? What you mean is you don't have the backbone to honour your agreement with a dead woman.'

'Unbelievable!' Fisher said, as they crossed the short distance to their car. 'Em would have been livid, finding out the man trusted to oversee the work started by the coach was so easily bought.'

'What if she knew Cowden wouldn't do it?' Nightingale asked. 'Do you think she would have tried talking to Mr Hunt herself?'

'I wouldn't have put it past her.'

24.

'Yes?' It was a young boy's voice. The son, Morgan, Fisher assumed.

'Hi. Is your dad in?'

'Yeah.' A second later, 'Dad!'

Fisher stood with Luna at his feet and Nightingale to his left.

'Do I know you?' the boy asked.

Fisher shook his head.

'Not unless you've been in trouble.'

Footsteps approached.

'Detective Fisher, what's the problem this time?'

'Hey, you're Matt Fisher,' the boy piped up. 'Your picture's on the wall at the Walker Academy. I want to be a footballer one day. Is it true you can't see now?'

'Sadly, yes.'

'Hey, is that your guide dog?' Fisher felt Luna stir at his feet.

'Don't pet the dog,' Nightingale said. 'She shouldn't be disturbed while she's working.'

'Morgan, go inside. Tell your mother I'll be a few minutes.'

'But Dad...'

'Morgan, just do it.'

Fisher heard the boy run down the hallway, his feet slapping on the wooden floor, thinking, flatfooted by the sounds of it.

'You're not going to invite us in, Mr Hunt?' Fisher asked.

151

'I dislike dog hair on my carpets even more than I dislike dogs.'

'You should have said the last time we were here. It didn't seem to be a problem then. Perhaps you forgot your dislike for dogs the same way you forgot to mention you knew Mrs Margery Walker? By the way, we know about the disagreement.'

'What disagreement?'

'Don't pretend you don't know. I suspect Hugh Cowden was on the phone to you before we'd even pulled off his driveway.'

'Hugh's a good friend. Is it any surprise he thought I should know you're trying to make something out of nothing? He also told me that he explained the situation to you.'

'And now I want you to tell me. So, what happened when Mrs Walker spoke with you about moving your son from the main programme onto one of the summer courses?'

'We never had that conversation. I don't see why we would have.'

'You don't think after Mrs Walker had found out about your fraudulent application that she would—'

'Now hang on a minute! There was nothing fraudulent about that application.'

'Really? Your wife claimed you had separated and gave information about her limited income as part of the financial assessment. Yet you hadn't separated, had you? In my book that's fraud. Em Walker found out and wanted it put right.'

'Who's to say my wife and I haven't since reconciled?'

'Could you ask your wife to join us, please? Oh, and ask her to bring some evidence that at the time in question either you or she were living elsewhere.' Fisher gave a tight smile. 'We're happy to wait.'

Hunt huffed out a sigh.

'Look, it's no big deal. The truth is, we were advised to fill the application out the way we did. I had made a very generous donation to the trust and they obviously thought it would be a fitting gesture to give something back.'

'You mean your friend Mr Cowden did.' Before Hunt could give him any more flannel, Fisher asked, 'When was the last time you and Mrs Walker spoke?'

'I can't remember. At least a year ago at some fund-raising event. Are we done with the questions now?'

'Not quite. Did you know a Mrs Meera Choudhury? And I suggest you spend a minute thinking about it. We wouldn't want you forgetting anything else, would we?'

'I don't need a minute. Yes, I've heard the name.' For a second Fisher's optimism came out of its shell, until Hunt sent it scurrying back. 'That's the name of the latest victim. I do watch the news, Inspector.'

'Did you know the woman?'

'What are you suggesting? Of course I didn't. You think for some reason I go around knocking off women in their own homes? You know what I think? If the police force is serious about catching the killer, they should assign a detective capable of leading the case rather than leave it to some has-been footballer who's only been kept on the books to meet some disability target. Now, I'm going to return to my wife and son. If you have any more questions for me, then you'll have to ask them in the presence of my solicitor. I'm done playing nice.'

25.

On leaving Hunt's, Fisher told Nightingale to take him straight home. It was growing late and the thought of going back to the office and having to face telling the Falcon they'd made no progress depressed him more than he cared to admit. A feeling compounded by the self-reproach generated by Hunt's accusations of incompetence. Though why he let that bother him was anyone's guess. It wasn't like it was the first time he'd heard it. He ought to have anticipated it. He'd backed Hunt into a corner where his only defence was to attack.

All the same, it didn't stop him wondering if Hunt was right. Would a different detective have got a result by now? How? It wasn't as though the killer had written their name in two-foot letters in the dead women's homes and nobody thought to mention it. But still...

'You don't think we missed something at the crime scenes, do you?' he asked as Nightingale drove.

'If we missed it, how would I know?' Nightingale replied. After a moment's pause, she added, 'Seriously though, no, I can't see how we could have. If we had that means a lot of people didn't do their job properly.'

Fisher ought to have felt relieved at her assessment, only instead it worried him even more. What if the crime scenes had held clues that would point them in the direction of their killer? Perhaps if he'd witnessed them first hand, he might have noticed something the others hadn't. He shook his head. It was pointless speculating about such things.

Once he got home, he let Luna out into the garden. The air was still and warm and for a moment he stood at the back door, sheltered from the breeze, letting the sun soothe his tormented mood. Apart from the occasional burst of birdsong and a distant cooing of a collared dove, or perhaps it was a pigeon, all was quiet. Shortly, the warmth started to feel stifling. He slipped off his jacket, made his way into the house and ditched the suit.

Sporting jeans and a t-shirt, he was making his way back downstairs when the phone started to ring. He heard the sound of his own voice as the answer machine kicked in. Arriving in the kitchen he instructed Alexa to play the message as he padded over to the fridge and grabbed himself a beer.

'Hey Dad. It's Josh. About tonight...'

His stomach lurched. He'd forgotten his son was supposed to be coming over for the night. That was the problem with accommodating his estranged wife. The demands of Amanda's job meant she often asked him to have Josh outside of their agreed schedule. With his head full of work, it was hard to keep track. He'd long promised himself he'd get better at using the calendar on his phone, but that was easier said than done. His thoughts flitted to the contents of his fridge. He'd have to send out for pizza. Again.

He tuned back into the message.

'...next week then.'

Fisher instructed Alexa to play the message again, this time making sure to listen. His shoulders sagged with relief on hearing that Josh was unwell and wasn't coming. He was off the hook. After a quick slug of beer, he crossed to the back door, sat on the step and pulled out his mobile.

Josh picked up with a lively, 'Yo!'

'Josh, it's Dad. I just got your message.'

'Oh, hi. I didn't think you'd be in yet. I…' There was a sudden eruption of coughing. 'Sorry about that.' Another small cough followed. 'I really wanted to come over but…'

'It's okay. I understand. If you're not well, bed's the best place for you.'

'That's what Mum said.'

'Is your mum there?'

'What?'

'Your mum… I'd like a quick word.'

'She's just nipped out.'

'She should be at home if you're not well.'

'She's only gone to the corner shop, for some cough mixture.'

'Her standards must be slipping. The bathroom cabinet is usually better stocked than Boots.'

'Yeah, well, I finished the last bottle earlier, so…' More coughing.

'It's okay. Get yourself to bed. I'll catch up with you when you're feeling better.'

After ending the call, Fisher felt a wave of disappointment wash over him. He loved having Josh over, even if he didn't always remember exactly when that was going to be. He remembered his ambivalence when Amanda — or Mandy as her fun-loving alter-ego used to be called, back in the day — said she wanted to start a family. But after Josh was born, his love for his son knew no bounds. It was the strongest emotion he'd ever experienced and now, fourteen years on, it was still as strong as ever.

He thought back to the conversation with Lewis Hunt. Was it so terrible that he did what he could to help his own son realise his ambition? If the lad had been kicked off the academy's top course it would have been a big blow to the boy's confidence.

Switching him to one of the summer courses, usually filled with kids with little or no talent who just needed a distraction to keep them off the streets, would have felt like a punishment rather than a reward. No father would want that to happen to their child. The question was, exactly how far would Hunt go to protect his son?

26.

In the office the following morning, Fisher sent Nightingale to review Em Walker's phone records, asking her to look for calls coming from any of the numbers listed for Lewis Hunt or his business. Once alone, Fisher reached for his phone and called the third victim's son.

'Mr Choudhury, it's DI Fisher. We spoke shortly after your mother's death.'

'Hello Inspector.' There was a slight catch in the other man's voice. 'Is there any news?'

'No, but we are making good progress. I have a couple of questions, if that's okay?'

'Go ahead. Anything I can do to help.'

'Do you know a man called Lewis Hunt?'

'*Lewis* Hunt?'

'Yes.'

'No, I'm sorry. I don't.'

The way the other man had emphasised the name Lewis wasn't lost on Fisher.

'But you do know somebody by the name of Hunt?'

'Not exactly. It's just my son plays football with a boy of the same surname.'

'Would that be Morgan Hunt?'

'That's right.'

'Your son goes to the Walker Academy?'

'Yes.'

'Are the two boys friends?' Fisher asked. 'Only you recognised the name quite quickly.'

'That's because there's been a lot of talk about him and how he got his place on the team.'

'I see.' Suddenly seized with an idea, Fisher asked, 'Did your mother ever watch your son play football?'

'Maybe a couple of years ago, but not recently. She barely left the house this last year.' After the shortest of pauses, he asked, 'Does Mr Hunt have something to do with my mother's death?'

'There's no evidence to suggest that. We're just trying to find a link between the victims. Mr Hunt's ex-wife was the second victim.'

'And Mrs Walker was the first. I heard she wasn't happy about Morgan Hunt being on the programme. Are you sure his father had nothing to do with it?'

'As I said, there's no evidence to suggest that. Unless you know something we don't?'

'Me? No.'

'If you do know of anything, I urge you to tell us. Surely you want the killer caught as much as we do?'

But Mr Choudhury refused to be drawn, and Fisher had little choice other than to end the call and move on to the next.

Hugh Cowden sounded cagey when he first answered the phone, though his response changed to unctuous compliance once he knew why Fisher was calling.

'No problem at all, Inspector. I'll arrange to have Mr Choudhury's application emailed over to you post haste. Would you also like the supporting documents — copy bank statements, utility bills and the like — that were submitted as evidence?'

'Send whatever you've got,' Fisher replied, realising just how much of a blind eye must have been turned to find in favour of Morgan Hunt's application. Em Walker must have been furious.

Afterwards, he sat for a moment, toying with his mobile. If Hunt really did have something to do with the murders, what motive did he have? Fisher could think of several, but none that applied across all three victims.

He scrolled to one of his recent numbers and hit dial. Professor Woolf answered on the second ring.

'Hello Inspector. I didn't expect to hear from you so soon. I hope you're not calling with the news of another murder.'

'No, nothing so dramatic. I need to pick your brain. We have a potential suspect. Someone with links to all three victims, albeit tenuous.'

'Of course. Anything I can do to help.'

Fisher filled the professor in on what they knew, though he didn't go as far as naming names.

'You weren't wrong about it being tenuous, were you?' she replied once he'd finished. 'And what were you hoping to get from me?'

'When we last met, you talked a lot about motives. You said that serial killers can be motivated by all manner of things and I wondered... is it possible for a killer to have multiple motives? Like with our guy... the first time could have been to do with protecting his son from embarrassment; the second time was to protect himself from financial loss.'

'I shouldn't think it's impossible, though it would be a first for me. Perhaps the answer lies with the third murder? Do you have any idea what the motive for that might be?'

Fisher's shoulders slumped. He shook his head, despite the fact she wouldn't see, and said, 'No. No, I don't.'

And there it was, the flaw in his thinking blown open with a single question. Fisher knew he needed to hear it but all the same, the fact he had nothing still stung.

27.

While Fisher was pondering where to take the investigation next, Lewis Hunt was standing in the middle of a wasteland of long-forgotten warehouses holding court among a small crowd of district councillors. Around them, bent and buckled steel frames wore fragments of flimsy wall panels, which peeled away like sloughed skin.

Hunt wore a smile worthy of any toothpaste ad while talking passionately about his plan to convert the derelict no man's land into an exciting out-of-town shopping experience servicing the surrounding areas. The proposal had attracted widespread opposition, with many calling it the final nail in the coffin for the local high street. As a result, Hunt had invited the members of the planning committee to a presentation, plied them with wine and a buffet lunch, before taking them on a tour of the site, hoping to convince them of the merits of approving the application.

For two hours, he had schmoozed and charmed; quoting impressive levels of projected job growth; extra revenue for the council by way of business rates; and sizable numbers of residents expected to benefit from a wide range of services set to operate out of the proposed community hub.

Whilst winding up the event with a closing speech, Hunt scanned his audience, grateful to see most of them nodding. On spotting a full-head of long blonde hair his eyes lingered. Angela, the council's planning officer, met his gaze. Hunt subtly flashed his eyes, causing the trace of a smile to flit across her lips. He continued to scan his audience, looking each and every person squarely in the eye. By the time he finished it was obvious he had them eating out of his hand.

Afterwards, Hunt started to usher the gathering back to their cars, laying on the charm as he engaged in small talk. Angela strode out in front. On reaching her vehicle, she pulled open the door, then turned to look back, waiting to catch Hunt's eye. He noticed her looking and gave a slight nod before turning his attention back to the grey-haired woman held captive by his conversation. Angela slipped into her car and a minute later drove away.

Once the last hand had been shaken, Hunt made his way to his own vehicle, a navy Range Rover Sport complete with Hawke Harrier black alloys and double tinted windows. He started the engine with a wolfish smile on his lips. Too preoccupied with what was to come, he didn't notice the black hatchback parked on the roadside nearby — five-years old with no distinguishing features. He pulled away and didn't notice it follow after a suitably short gap, always keeping a couple of cars behind to avoid being spotted. Didn't even notice when it stopped a short distance from him, pulling in tight behind a parked van, when he reached his destination: a small semi-detached house in an unremarkable residential road. He hopped out with a spring in his step and crossed to the front door, looking about him as he pressed the bell. A minute later he stepped inside and the door closed behind him.

28.

As the working day drew to a close, Fisher called the team together for a debrief.

'Andy, do you want to start?'

'Sure. For what it's worth.' Fisher heard a mug being thumped down on the table. 'As far as Mrs Walker's beneficiaries go, six charities benefited, but the lion's share went to the Walker Academy. Unless someone has a twisted sense of altruism and killed her so their cause was better funded, I can't see money being the motive. All the same, I took a quick look at the accounts for all of the beneficiaries and they seem to be doing okay financially. As far as the CCTV checks go, we got diddly-squat; the cameras aren't in the right places to be of any use.'

'What a surprise,' Fisher said drily. 'Okay. How about you, Beth?'

'I spoke to the lawyer leading the group litigation against Connie Lloyd's financial advisor. All they could tell me was that it was being progressed. As nothing has been settled yet, with Ms Lloyd's demise the right to continue with the claim passes to her estate.'

'So if successful, whatever money comes out of it will go to Warren Newman,' Fisher said. 'Is that what you're saying?'

'Actually, it'll be split fifty-fifty between him and Jennifer Keeley.'

'I thought Mrs Keeley said she only got the TV and a few bits of jewellery.'

'Yes,' Nightingale replied. 'That's what she said, but I checked the will and it's quite clear. The financial assets, i.e. all Ms Lloyd's money, is divided equally between the two. Newman gets all the non-financial assets, apart from the TV and jewellery, which doesn't amount to much, judging from what was at the house. Though I suppose it does include her car.'

'So Mrs Keeley lied,' Fisher said, not disguising his surprise.

'I did challenge her on that,' Nightingale said. 'She told me she didn't mention it seeing as Ms Lloyd only had a few hundred quid… if that.'

'So how much are we talking about, should this claim ever get settled?'

'Two hundred grand. Pretty much the sum total of her divorce settlement.'

The cumulative gasp of the room's occupants sounded like the hiss of an air pump at a garage.

'Well, that's one hell of a motive. Good job for Mrs Keeley and Warren Newman that Ms Lloyd isn't the only victim,' Fisher said. 'Anything else, Beth?'

'The solicitors for the group action confirmed neither of the other victims were parties to the claim.'

'I can't say as I'm surprised, but at least we know. So, who wants to go next?'

'I hadn't finished,' Nightingale said quickly.

'Sorry. Go on.'

'You asked me to check Mrs Walker's phone records. I did and there's no record of a call to or from any of the numbers we've got for Lewis Hunt. So, unless he's got a phone we don't know about — which is possible, I suppose — it doesn't look like they were in touch any time in the lead up to her death.'

'If he was planning on murdering her, would he have been dumb enough to leave such an obvious trail?' Wickham asked.

'Might not have intended on killing her to begin with,' Fisher replied. 'He might have hoped to persuade her to let his kid stay on at the academy. All the same, if he did try and talk to her, doesn't look like he did it over the phone.'

Fisher nodded and reached into his pocket, pulling out his mobile. Holding it out in front of him, he said, 'Could someone punch in the number for the chairman of Walker's Academy please?'

'Here… I'll do it.' Wickham relieved him of the phone and a minute later handed it back. 'It's ringing.'

Fisher heard the familiar click as the call was picked up.

'Hello?'

'Mr Cowden. It's DI Fisher. We spoke recently.'

'I remember,' he replied drily.

'Mr Cowden, could you tell me whether Mrs Walker's home address is in any of the academy's documents or the trust's paperwork?'

'I don't think so. No.'

'I'm looking for a way someone might have learned of her address — if anyone contacted the academy's admin team, would they have given it out?

'Absolutely not.' Cowden sounded outraged.

'So if the academy was contacted by someone wishing to speak to Mrs Walker, how would they advise them to go about it?'

'I don't know.' After a small pause, he went on, 'I suppose one might suggest they come to the academy building just before a trust meeting and catch Em on the way in.'

'She used to come to the meetings? I thought she was no longer on the board.'

'She wasn't, but she was an honorary lifetime member, which allowed her access to the meetings. She never missed one as far as I know.'

'Do you know whether anyone asked to be put in touch with Mrs Walker in the months leading up to her death?'

'Of course I don't. I don't personally answer every phone call. There are staff who do that.'

'Fine. I'll arrange for someone to attend the academy later today and talk to the staff. What about CCTV — do you have cameras on the building where the trust meets?'

'Some. Although the coverage is limited. There's a camera inside the reception and one covering the car park.'

'We'll need a copy of the footage from both. The officer can collect it when they visit later today.'

Fisher ended the call then said, 'Andy, could you take that one? Have a look and see if you can spot anyone, Hunt in particular, talking with Mrs Walker on the dates of the trust's meetings.'

'Will do.'

After giving the floor over to the rest of the gathered team members, learning nothing new in the process, Fisher called an end to the briefing. Once they were alone, he turned to Nightingale and said, 'So Beth, what the hell are we going to do now?'

'You don't know?'

'I haven't got a scooby.'

'Oh.'

'If Andy manages to get some footage that shows Lewis Hunt talking to Em Walker shortly before she was killed, then I'd be happy to caution him and force his hand in giving up his alibi. That is if he really has got one. But at the moment, we don't have enough to bring him in.'

'You really think he did it… killed all three women? He'd have to be a total psycho to kill them just to keep his son happy and stop his ex-wife challenging the divorce settlement.'

Fisher's thoughts drifted to Hunt: to his confident, bolshy tone; his refusal to provide them with an alibi; the ruthless way he had deprived his ex-wife of what she was due.

There were no two ways about it. The man was a bastard. But was he a psychotic bastard?

He'd come up clean on the police database, but Fisher knew most cases of domestic violence go unreported. But unreported doesn't always mean kept under wraps.

'Beth, grab your coat.'

29.

Standing outside Warren Newman's home, Nightingale pressed the bell for a second time. A minute later, Fisher balled his hand into a fist and gave the door a hearty bang.

'Perhaps we should have called ahead,' Nightingale suggested unhelpfully.

'Have we got a mobile number for him?'

'I don't think so.'

Fisher shook his head and started back down the drive towards the car.

'We'll give it half an hour. You never know, he might come back.' Almost before he'd finished speaking, a vehicle pulled up nearby.

He paused. Moments later came the sound of a car door opening.

'We're in luck. He's just pulled up in a taxi,' Nightingale said.

They waited for Newman to join them on the drive.

'Is there news?' he asked.

'Not at the moment.'

'Oh.'

Fisher heard footsteps moving towards the house.

'Mr Newman...' he called. 'We need some information about Ms Lloyd — about her past.'

'You'd better come in then.'

All three were sitting in Warren Newman's lounge, mugs of tea on the table in front of them, Luna settled at Fisher's feet, when they heard the sound of a door opening. A second later, footsteps came hurrying down the hallway.

'Sorry Dad. I completely forgot. I was...' Rob Newman stopped speaking after having pushed open the door into the lounge. 'Is everything okay?'

'We just came by to ask your dad a few more questions,' Fisher said.

'Oh. Okay.'

'Don't let us keep you,' Warren Newman said. 'I'm sure you've got somewhere more important to be.'

'Look, I'm sorry. Something came up. Next time I promise I—'

'Don't bother,' his father snapped. 'At least a taxi driver doesn't make me feel like they're doing me a favour.'

'You don't drive, Mr Newman?' Fisher asked, hoping to defuse the argument before it started.

'I do. It's just I don't like to drive after chemo. It makes me feel so exhausted. But anyway, you didn't come here to hear my woes, what did you want to know?'

'Did Ms Lloyd talk much about her ex-husband and their relationship?'

'Sometimes. Not so much about the relationship, more about what a bastard he was.'

'Did he ever physically abuse her?'

'If he did, he'd have me to answer to.'

'She never mentioned anything?' Fisher pressed.

'No. She said plenty about him being a liar and a cheat, but as for anything else... To be honest, from what she told me, I can't see him wanting to get his hands dirty. He's far too slick for that. More of a con artist than a wife-beater.'

'Is he under suspicion then?' Rob Newman asked. Fisher pictured him leaning forward in his seat. 'Only I thought it was some random sicko targeting old women.'

'Connie wasn't old,' his father said sharply.

'Yeah, but, well... she wasn't young, was she?'

Ignoring the bickering, Fisher went on, 'We're just trying to build up a picture of Ms Lloyd's previous relationships, that's all.'

'I remember Connie telling me how her ex raised his fist to her once,' Rob Newman offered.

'She never told me,' Warren Newman said, sounding shocked.

'Maybe she didn't want you to know, in case you went and had a word with him.'

'I would have too.'

'Well, there you go then.'

Fisher interrupted the father-son double-act and asked. 'Did she say when that was?'

'No. I got the impression it wasn't recently,' Rob Newman replied. 'She reckoned it was only because someone walked in on them that he didn't hit her.'

Whilst the comment didn't paint Hunt in a good light, it wasn't exactly the ground-breaking revelation Fisher had hoped for. The conversation soon came to a close and Fisher and Nightingale took their leave. Fisher, figuring it too late to return to the office, had Nightingale take him straight home. They'd been on the road barely five minutes when his phone began to vibrate. He pulled it from his pocket, switched it from silent and swiped the screen.

'Today. Messages. Now,' came a stilted automated voice. 'Wickham. Checked academy CCTV. Nothing.'

'Another dead end,' Fisher said. He was about to return the phone to his pocket when it chimed with the arrival of another new text. His fingers tapped the screen and set it to play.

'Today. Messages. Now. The Falcon. Briefing. Nine am. My office. Expecting progress.'

Fisher closed the message and thrust the phone back into his pocket.

Nightingale said, 'Aren't you ever worried the DCI will hear what you call her?'

Fisher couldn't help but smile.

'You mean the fact I've got her in my contacts as The Falcon?'

'Yes.'

'I'll just tell her voice-to-text mistook what I said when I entered her details.'

'What if she asks why you've never changed it?'

'I'll say I don't need to, seeing as I know who it is.'

They lapsed into silence and it wasn't until they pulled up outside Fisher's house, Nightingale asked, 'What are you going to tell the DCI in the morning?'

'The truth. The links to Lewis Hunt. His unsubstantiated alibi. The fact we don't have much else.'

'Do you think she'll agree to a warrant for his arrest?'

'I doubt it. If he was some benefit-scrounging junkie she'd have no qualms in dragging him in off the street. But he's not. To be fair, if it was down to me, I probably wouldn't agree to a warrant either. There isn't enough evidence against him.'

Later that evening, after finishing dinner, Fisher opened his laptop and began to trawl the net for information about Lewis Hunt. Alongside references to an impressive schedule of property developments, there were plenty of mentions of Hunt's philanthropy. Not only did he regularly delve deep into his pockets for whatever the cause of the day was, but he could also list marathon running, abseiling, even rough sleeping, amongst his charitable endeavours. Despite trying, Fisher couldn't find a bad word said about the man.

30.

At the time Fisher was finding out what he could about Lewis Hunt, the man himself arrived home. He closed the front door on the rapidly failing light, dropped his briefcase by the door and made his way through to the kitchen.

His wife was sitting at the breakfast bar, an almost empty glass of white wine at her elbow. She looked up from the magazine that was open on the worktop in front of her and cocked an eyebrow.

'You're late. Again.'

'I told you. Those bloody councillors are like a load of old women. They just love the sound of their own voices. Plus, there's always a handful who have to be difficult, so they can tell their constituents they gave me a tough time.'

His wife rose from her seat and started towards the range oven.

'Still… you could have called.' She bent over and opened one of the oven's four doors. A waft of warm air escaped as she pulled out a foil-covered plate. 'It's probably ruined. If I'd have known, I could have made dinner later.'

'I'm sure it'll be fine.'

She carried the warm plate out of the kitchen and into a vast dining room and set it down on the table laid for one. Hunt followed, stripping off his tie and slipping out of his jacket as he walked. He flung both onto the back of a neighbouring chair and took his seat.

'Where's Morgan?' he asked, applying a liberal sprinkling of salt to his dinner.

'Upstairs, doing his homework.' She was already at the door on her way out.

'Shannon…' She turned and looked back at him, her face devoid of emotion. 'Be a love and get me something to wash this down with, will you?'

***

Outside, in the dying light of day, a figure clothed in black lithely climbed the fence at the rear of Hunt's home. Hugging the borders, which surrounded a large lawn, he traced a path to the house. Light spilled from the windows, clothing the grass in long shadows. Upstairs a single pendant illuminated what he took to be a bedroom. Downstairs, in what was clearly the kitchen, a woman — Mrs Hunt presumably — was standing next to a breakfast bar. He watched her lift a glass to her lips and knock the contents back before placing the empty glass in the dishwasher and walking out. Lewis Hunt could be seen, sitting alone at a substantial dining table, his back to a set of French windows.

Camouflaged against the large shrubs that filled the beds, the interloper skirted the house, switching his attention to the detached triple garage that loomed ahead. As he crept along the lawn's edge, he patted his pocket, reassuring himself of the lock pick's presence. Spotting a camera, he paused. Its position rendered it impossible to enter the house from the rear without being seen. Dressed top-to-toe in black, he had little reason to fear should his shadowy form be caught on camera. His real concern was the alarm. He had already noted the large yellow box perched under the eaves at the front of the house; the question was, was it real and if so, was it on? He knew most households rarely activate their security systems until they retire to bed, and often not even then, but was this one of them?

He stepped closer, squinting through the gathering gloom, looking for more cameras or a bead of light belying the presence of a laser. Out of the corner of his eye, he saw Hunt reach for a wine bottle.

Suddenly the lawn was illuminated like a prison yard after a breakout.

He raced to the border and dived into the leafy embrace of a large bush. Chancing a look back towards the dining room, his heart raced when he saw Hunt rise and approach the French doors.

Keeping himself pressed into the bushes, he forced his breathing to slow.

Hunt now had his face pressed against the glass; hands cupped around his eyes.

'Turn around and sit back down,' the man in the shadows said under his breath, as he watched and waited.

Hunt reached down, turned a key and twisted the handle. The doors swung open.

The man emerged from the bushes, sprinted down the garden and launched himself over the fence. Landing lightly on his feet, he quickly retraced his steps through the neighbouring gardens to emerge on a pavement one street away from Hunt's, where his car awaited him. He climbed into the back of the vehicle, locked the door and hunkered down in the footwell, out of sight, where he remained until the risk of someone noticing a car leaving the scene had long passed.

31.

The following morning, Fisher and Nightingale arrived at the office just before eight, giving Fisher at least an hour to prepare for his session with the Falcon. Or so he thought.

He was on his way to his desk when he heard her door click open. The strong scent of her perfume permeated the air.

'Fisher! My office, please.' The DCI retreated back into the room.

'I'll catch up with you later, Beth.' Fisher followed the DCI into her office. 'Your text said nine,' he said, pressing the door closed behind him.

'Sit down.' He heard a chair squeak as the DCI took a seat behind her desk.

Luna led the way to a chair on the opposite side.

'Has something happened?' he asked.

'Like you don't know.'

Fisher waited for her to elaborate. When she didn't, he said, 'Honestly, I have no idea.'

'Lewis Hunt was on the phone to me before I'd even got my coat off. He's already talking about complaining to the commissioner. And who'd blame him? So, which of them was it, Beth or Andy?'

'I have no idea what you're talking about. What are they supposed to have done?'

'Someone illegally gained entry into Mr Hunt's garden and was spying on him last night.'

'Why would anyone do that?'

'Perhaps because they're trying to find some evidence against him to place him as our killer.'

'And you think I knew something about it?'

'Mr Hunt certainly does. And I think it's not beyond the realms of possibility that he's right. If you admit it now and agree to take the full rap, I'll go easy on whichever of your cronies did it.'

'Cronies? You have a strange way of talking about my colleagues…. your team. And if you think Andy or Beth would do something like that, just on my say-so, then you really have no idea. They are both good, law-abiding officers. And what would be the point anyway? It'd be a total waste of time. Anything they found would be inadmissible. Why would anyone risk their job for that?' When DCI Fallon didn't reply, Fisher asked, 'Did the intruder damage or take anything?'

'No. Hunt spotted them before they had the chance.'

'I assume you've arranged for a CSI to pay him a visit and take a look around. Whoever did it might have left some evidence. There's been a fair amount of rain recently, could be they left a shoe print.' Again, she didn't reply, which Fisher took to mean he'd assumed wrongly. 'I'll organise that then, shall I?'

Eventually she broke her silence, 'If I find out you or any of your team had anything to do with it, heads will roll, believe me.'

Fisher stood up.

'Do you still want a briefing at nine, or shall I go and talk to Mr Hunt, reassure him that we're doing all that we can?'

'Just go.' As he reached the threshold to her office, she said, 'You've got until nine tomorrow morning. And you'd better have something good for me, else… well, you'll see.'

Lewis Hunt wasn't at home when Fisher and Nightingale arrived. Instead, his wife, Shannon answered the door. Fisher introduced themselves.

'If you're here to apologise, you're too late. My husband has already left for work.'

'We're not,' Fisher said. 'Your husband was mistaken. Whoever was here last night, it had nothing to do with us.'

'You would say that though, wouldn't you?'

'I can promise you, we don't have the resources to put everyone involved in a murder enquiry under surveillance.'

'What do you mean — involved in a murder enquiry? You can't possibly suspect Lewis?'

'We suspect anyone unwilling to provide an alibi for when one of the victims was killed.'

'If you mean his ex-wife, he was in a meeting when it happened.'

'With whom?'

'I don't know. Have you asked him?'

'Yes. He refuses to tell us.'

'Oh, for God's sake. Bloody men. I'll call him now. Tell him to talk to you.'

'That would be helpful, though maybe it could wait until we've finished talking to you about last night.' After being shown into the lounge, taking a seat on a large sofa, with Luna by his feet, Fisher said, 'One of the forensics team should be along shortly. They'll take a look around, see whether the intruder left anything behind.'

'Lewis already did that. He said he couldn't see anything.'

'Well, that does complicate things. We'll need the shoes he was wearing so we can rule out any prints we find. It would have been better if he hadn't contaminated the scene.' She made no

179

comment, so Fisher went on, 'Why don't you start by telling us what happened?'

'My husband had just finished his dinner. It was around seven thirty and was getting dark. He went to close the dining room curtains when the garden lights came on. They're on a timer. He thought he saw something move so went out to take a closer look. He's convinced he saw someone run to the bottom of the garden, but by the time he got there they'd escaped over the fence. He went out and walked around for a while but couldn't see anyone.'

'Did he get a look at this person?'

'Not really. He said they were wearing dark clothes and possibly a mask or balaclava.'

'Male? Female?'

'He couldn't tell.'

'Tall? Short? Fat? Thin?'

'I don't know. He didn't say.'

'Do you have a home security system?'

'Yes. We have an alarm, as well as cameras on the house and the garage.'

'Have you checked the footage?'

'Lewis did last night. He couldn't see anything.'

'Well, it sounds like an opportunist burglar. Hopefully they saw the cameras and will go elsewhere next time.'

'You definitely think it was a burglar?'

'It's the most obvious explanation. Unless you know of anyone else it might have been?' The pause that followed gave Fisher cause to think she had someone else in mind. 'Mrs Hunt, is there something you'd like to tell us?'

'No. It's only... well, my husband is involved in a lot of property developments, which don't always go down well with people. There have been threats in the past and recently he's been putting in a lot of extra hours on the project he's working on because of planning problems. Perhaps it's something to do with that.'

'We'll bear that in mind,' Fisher said. Just then the doorbell rang. 'That'll probably be the CSI officer. We can let them in on our way out, if you'd be kind enough to show them through to the garden.' He got to his feet and started for the front door.

'Bit of a coincidence, don't you think?' Nightingale said, once they were on the road. 'An attempted break-in so soon after we've been around asking questions.'

'You think he made it up?' Fisher had already had the same idea. 'Bit of a half-baked strategy if he thought it would get us to back off.'

'I guess, only that wasn't what I was thinking. I wondered if it might have been someone bent on revenge.'

'If you mean Warren Newman, I don't peg him as the vigilante type. I think for all his talk about making Hunt pay, he doesn't have it in him. Not these days, at least.' His thoughts flitted to his conversation with Mrs Choudhury's son. He'd specifically mentioned Lewis Hunt, but that couldn't be related... could it? He shook his head. 'This investigation gets worse by the day.'

And it was about to get a whole deal worse.

They were still en route to the station when the call they'd been dreading came in. Another woman had been found dead with a bag over her head and an electrical cable around her neck. Nightingale executed a hasty U-turn.

Fisher leant against the window, the cold glass vibrating against his face, and prayed that this one would give them the break they so sorely needed. Fifteen minutes later, he felt the car slow.

'We're here,' Nightingale said.

181

'Where is here?' Fisher asked.

'It's a bungalow at the end of a cul-de-sac of half a dozen similar houses. There's a small front garden and a ramp up to the front door and a rail on the wall. There are ramps and rails on a lot of the neighbouring properties.'

'So why this particular house and this particular victim? Why not any of the others?'

'Maybe it's the location? It's at the end of the road, set back a little. Less easy for prying eyes to see in.'

32.

The scene turned out to be virtually identical to the previous three. The victim, an eighty-five-year-old woman named Mrs Betty French, had been found on the floor in the doorway between the hallway and tiny lounge. The characteristic black plastic bag over her head was fixed with the same electrical flex and although there was no upturned handbag or empty purse nearby, when later interviewed, the neighbour who raised the alarm said one of the first things she noticed was the medical bracelet the dead woman usually wore was gone.

The atmosphere inside the house was subdued. Apart from the occasional murmured comment, the crime scene officers worked silently. Fisher and Nightingale waited in the kitchen while Dr Cooper conducted her examination. In the silence, Fisher's ears pricked up on hearing voices from the direction of the front door. He recognised the deep baritone of the PC tasked with guarding the scene but the second voice — another man's — was unfamiliar to him.

'Beth, take me to the front door, will you?' After skirting around the victim, dancing across the stepping plates that lined the hallway floor, he opened the door only to find the conversation had ended.

'Anyone we should know about?' he said, hoping the uniformed officer was still there.

'Sorry?' came the reply.

'I heard you talking to someone. When they didn't come in, I wondered who it was,' Fisher explained.

'It was a guy from the fire service. Said he'd come to install a smoke detector.'

'Is he still around?'

'No. He left after I told him what had happened.'

'Was he in uniform?

'He was wearing a navy polo-shirt with a badge on it. Does that count?'

'Did he show you any ID?'

'No.'

'Then how do you know he was who he said he was? It could have been the killer come back to gloat over the scene.'

'He was driving a bright red van with the Kent fire service logo plastered all over it.'

Fisher fell quiet. That would be pretty hard to fake.

He gave a nod.

'Fine. But anyone else turns up, come and get me.'

Ten minutes later, Fisher and Nightingale were in the kitchen, talking with Dr Cooper, when they heard raised voices. A loud bang resonated through the house as the front door was flung open.

'DI Fisher!' called the uniformed officer, his voice an octave higher than usual.

'Get out of my way!' barked a voice that caused Fisher to groan. The clank of the footplates travelled through the house almost as fast as the sharp cloying scent of her perfume.

'Ma'am,' Fisher said. 'I didn't realise we were expecting you.'

'Really? A serial killer on my patch and you don't think as SIO I'd be interested?'

'I didn't say you wouldn't be interested, only that I didn't think you would…' be bothered to leave the comfort of your office, was what he wanted to say; instead, he said, 'feel it necessary to come to the scene.'

Outside there was a volley of slamming car doors, shortly followed by a barrage of shouted questions. Fisher would have rolled his eyes if he could.

'Sounds like the media have arrived,' he said to no one in particular.

'Good job I came then,' Fallon said. 'I need updating and quickly. Doctor: what have we got?'

After the pathologist had outlined her initial findings, the DCI wasted no time in holding an impromptu doorstep press conference. Once the media circus had disbanded and the body had been dispatched to the morgue, Fisher had Nightingale take him back to the car. Luna greeted him with her usual enthusiasm when he opened the door to let her out.

'Why the hell is he doing this?' Fisher asked, leaning sideways on the passenger seat as he lifted his legs out of the plastic pantsuit.

'He?'

'The killer.'

'You don't think it's a woman then? Professor Woolf said—'

'I know what she said, but my gut says it's a bloke. According to Woolf, if it was a woman, money would be the most likely motive and we know there's no single beneficiary. The killer didn't take much to begin with and he's taken no cash at all in the last two cases. And if he isn't motivated by money, then what? Dahmer killed for company and liked to control, Sutcliffe said it was a message from God, Bundy... well, he was just a sadist. None of those things fit here. The killer comes in, kills quickly and efficiently, then leaves.'

'What about what the professor said about transference... killing them because they remind the killer of someone else?'

Fisher curled his lip cynically.

'Is it just me or does that sound like a loud of hokum?'

'Hokum?'

'You know... nonsense. None of the women resemble one another, and if what they look like is immaterial, then wouldn't we be knee deep in bodies?' After a beat, he added drily, 'Mind you, the way it's going, we soon will be.'

'What if it's the thrill of getting away with it?' Nightingale offered, as she took Fisher's balled-up scene suit from him.

'If that is the case, they must be having a bloody ball.'

Nightingale encouraged Luna back into the car, fastening her harness before climbing in behind the wheel. She waited until Fisher was buckled up, then said, 'What I don't get is why the victims let him, or her, into the house. I spoke to my nan the other day. Since the murders started, she's had the chain on the door permanently and won't open the door to anyone other than friends and family. Absolutely no one. She said the local Age UK place have sent leaflets to everyone telling them to be extra careful.'

'Not everyone reads those things, plus most people think it's not going to affect them,' Fisher replied. 'On top of which, there are a load of bona fide reasons for someone to turn up on the doorstep: delivery driver, meals-on-wheels; bloke come to fit a smoke detector.'

'But all of those will have been expected. Why would anyone open their door to someone who turns up out of the blue?'

'I don't know Beth.' Fisher rubbed his hands over his face and shook his head. 'I just don't know.'

33.

Fisher arrived home that evening with one single objective: to spend the evening researching serial killers, focussing specifically on what motivates them. So when the doorbell rang within half an hour of Nightingale having dropped him off, he shushed Luna to keep her quiet and sat tight. It rang again. He stayed where he was. After a few minutes, he continued his slow preparations for dinner, chopping onions for a chilli con carne.

When the back door opened the onion wasn't the only thing the knife sliced.

'Shit!' He stuck his bleeding finger into his mouth, wincing at the stinging wound.

'Hiya!' Ginny called as she came in. 'Sorry. Did I make you jump? I did try the doorbell. It mustn't be working.' She planted a kiss on his cheek.

Matt walked over to the sink and stuck his finger under the cold-water tap.

'I didn't think you were coming over tonight.'

'Chen recovered from his man-flu thing, which means I get the night off.' Fisher could hear her take over chopping the veg. 'I thought we might spend it, well... however we fancy.' Perhaps she noticed his expression — not exactly one of disappointment but not far off it — as, after a slight pause, she said, 'If I'm interrupting something, just say. We can always reschedule.'

'No. I'm sorry. It's… to be honest, I'm not exactly the best of company at the moment. There was another murder today.'

'Another woman?' Fisher nodded. 'How awful. Then it's a good thing I came over. Maybe I can help improve your mood.' She slipped her arms around his waist and pressed her cheek against his.

He eased himself free of her grip and said, 'I'm sure you could, it's just that, well… I was planning on spending the evening working. I need to get a handle on whoever's doing this, before anyone else gets killed.'

'That's okay. I can keep myself occupied. Why don't we have a bite to eat, then you can get on with some work while I watch the telly. How does that sound?' Her heels clipped across the tiled floor. Seconds later, he heard her start to fill a pan with water from the tap.

A huge distraction is what it sounded like; made worse by the fact he knew she wasn't going to take no for an answer.

An hour later, after enjoying a dinner of spaghetti bolognaise — Ginny not being a fan of spicy food — they loaded the dishwasher, then took what was left of a bottle of wine into the lounge. Fisher sat in his usual chair, while Ginny made herself comfortable on the sofa and turned on the TV.

He pulled out his laptop, pressed the on-button and was about to slip on his headphones when he felt Ginny's warm touch on his fingers.

'Why don't you leave it for tonight? Come and sit here with me. We can—'

As the grip of her hand intensified, his mobile rang. He snatched it off the arm of his chair and swiped to answer.

'DI Fisher.'

'Detective, it's Martha Woolf. I've just seen the news. Is it the same as the others?'

Fisher paused. By rights he ought to suggest she talk to the force's comms team for the official stance. But this wasn't an ordinary case and Professor Woolf wasn't an ordinary member of the public.

'It looks that way,' he said, standing up and starting towards the kitchen.

'The same MO? The same sorts of items taken?'

'Yes and yes. Well, more or less. No cash this time, again'

'And the MO was exactly the same? No change at all?'

'No.'

'Also, am I right in thinking the gap between this latest murder and the previous one is the longest of the lot?'

'Yes.'

'How very strange. Do you think you could have missed one? Perhaps there's an elderly lady lying dead undiscovered somewhere?'

'I'm not sure how to answer that. If they're undiscovered, how would I know?'

'True. That was a stupid question. But I do think there could be another victim, someone who has yet to be missed. From the timing I would have expected the killer to have been active in the intervening period.'

'Shit,' Fisher said under his breath, putting a hand to his eyes and rubbing. 'I thought you said in your lecture that it was a myth that all serial killers' crimes escalated.'

'I did. But if you recall, I was referring to those who have some sort of control over themselves. The ones who were smart enough to vary their routine to evade detection.'

'Well this one is certainly evading detection. Four murders in and we haven't got a clue.'

'I take it you've ruled out the man you suspected.'

'Not exactly. He's still a person of interest, though I think it's only a matter of time before he provides us with an alibi.'

'For what it's worth, I don't think he's your man. If you do find a link between him and the latest victim I would go as far as to suggest he's being set up. Anyone clever enough to gain entry to the women's homes without being seen or suspected isn't going to be so stupid as to have an obvious motive to point you in their direction.'

Was that it? Was someone setting Hunt up to take the fall? Perhaps his mysterious intruder had intended on planting some evidence. Or maybe Hunt was cleverer than they gave him credit for. After all, the intruder meant he was supposedly patrolling the streets around his home at the time Mrs French, the latest victim, was being garrotted. Who's to say he didn't hop in his car and head straight to her home, a mere five-minute drive away?

With that in mind, Fisher said, 'What if it's a double bluff and he set it up to make it look like he's too obvious a suspect so that we'd rule him out?'

'I honestly don't think he's your man. I'm not saying what you're suggesting isn't possible, only when we spoke before you seemed to think his motivation stemmed from the need to secure his assets or his son's happiness. There are four women dead now. He can't have had reason to kill them all, can he?'

'Then why won't he give us an alibi for the time his ex-wife was murdered?'

'I can think of several reasons, the simplest being he's hiding a different secret.'

'Hmm.' Fisher knew she was right but where did that leave them?

After the call ended, he returned to the lounge. Slumping down in his seat, he felt ten years older than when he left it.

Reaching for his wine, he took a gulp before returning the glass to the table with a bang.

'Everything okay?' Ginny asked.

'Yeah.'

'Was that one of your detectives?'

'No. Just someone who's helping with the investigation.'

'Just a random someone?' When Fisher didn't reply, after a moment of uncomfortable silence, she said, 'I know it was a woman. I heard her voice.'

'I never pegged you as the jealous type,' he replied. A second later, he felt the warm flush of shame colour his cheeks. Why did he have to be so confrontational?

'Sorry. That was uncalled for. That was a professor of psychology who happens to be an expert in serial killers.' After a moment's pause, he added, 'I told you I wasn't good company.'

'It's okay.' But he could tell from her voice that it wasn't and knew for certain she'd got the hump when she didn't say anything when he reached for his laptop. When his phone rang a second time, Fisher was sure the gods were conspiring against him.

An irate-sounding Amanda came on the line.

'I hope you've got a good explanation for the other night. You're going to need it for the custody hearing I'm going to demand.'

He'd only had the couple of glasses of wine, right? So how come everything Amanda just said made absolutely no sense?

'What have I done now?'

'Don't even think about denying it. I've seen the photos.'

'What photos?'

'Josh, drunk and with that slut.'

Whatever he'd expected her to say, it wasn't that.

'What are you on about? What slut?' He sensed Ginny stiffen in her seat.

'Is she talking about me?' she said in an angry whisper.

Fisher shook his head.

'You're going to have to spell it out for me, Mandy. I have no idea what you're talking about.'

'It's Amanda. And I'm talking about the photos your son — *our* son — posted on Instagram.'

'I don't know anything about any photos.'

'That's because you are an inadequate and irresponsible father. Who in their right mind takes a fourteen-year-old boy to somewhere like that in the first place, let alone someone who can't see? I assume it was something to do with *her*.'

'Whoa! Stop right there before you say something you regret. When was this supposed to have happened?'

He felt the chair arm dip as Ginny leaned towards him, trying to listen in to the conversation.

'She's definitely talking about me now.' She raised her voice, 'Well, you tell her—'

Fisher slapped a hand over the phone's mouthpiece and hissed, 'Shut up a minute.'

'Was it at her club?' Amanda continued unabated. 'Exactly how many nights out like that has he had? Well, you can forget it if you think...'

But Fisher wasn't listening. He was too busy thinking back to Josh's phone call. The cough. The sniffles. An Oscar winning performance. He hadn't been at home with a cold. Josh had played him off against Amanda and gone on a jolly with his mates. He'd bloody kill him when he got his hands on him. The problem was, if he told Amanda what Josh had done, she'd only want to restrict the boy's movements even more and they were already tighter than a teenager's trousers.

He barked out a laugh, making it as convincing as he could manage.

'Have you talked to Josh about this?'

'Not yet, no. He's not back from football practice.'

'Before you do, you might want to take another look at that photo. It'll have been photoshopped.'

'What?'

'Josh was here at home with me the whole time. I'd been telling him about a case I'd worked recently — a con artist who had convinced people he had friends in high places by photoshopping himself into scenes with all sorts of celebrities. Afterwards he spent the night playing on my computer. You know how quick he is to pick things up, especially anything to do with technology.'

Amanda fell quiet.

'It looked pretty real to me,' she said after a moment.

'It will do. All you have to do is select someone's face — someone of a similar build, but even that can be manipulated, if you know what you're doing — then switch a photo of your own face in its place. Sounds like Josh should pursue a career in IT; he's clearly got a talent for it.'

'Hmm. Well, all the same... I don't like the fact he's put it on Instagram for all the world to see. Everyone will think we let him run riot.'

'I agree. I'm disappointed too. Tell him to take it down and confiscate his computer and games consoles for the foreseeable. He needs to know he can't get away with that sort of stuff.'

Somewhat mollified by his explanation, Amanda ended the call, promising to inflict a suitably exacting punishment on Josh for the upset he'd caused.

Fisher immediately scrolled through his contacts and called his son's number. To say he was disappointed was an understatement. Josh could have sabotaged any chance he had of seeing him on a regular basis. If Amanda found out what he'd really done, Josh would be eligible to vote before she'd let him out of the house again.

It rang through to voicemail.

'Josh. It's Dad. Call me as soon as you pick this up. It's urgent.'

He ended the call but clung onto the phone, hoping he wouldn't have to wait too long for his son to call back.

'What the hell was that all about?' Ginny asked.

'Josh. Playing a dangerous game. He was supposed to be coming over the other night only he called and told me he was sick and would be staying home. Only he wasn't really ill. He went out with his mates when his mother thought he was here with me. He would have got away with it too, only the stupid git stuck a photo of himself with some girl on Instagram. Listening to Amanda it was a scene straight out of Sodom and Gomorrah. Though all that probably means is some girl had her cleavage on show. The point is, he lied and was stupid enough to post evidence of it.'

'And you just lied to Amanda, letting Josh off the hook.'

'Only because if she knew what he'd done, we'd all have to jump through hoops every time Josh wanted to come over.'

'As parents you should stick together. You're essentially letting Josh get away with what he did... and you're lying to Amanda, which makes you no better.'

'Hey, that's a bit harsh. I'm doing it because Amanda can never keep things in perspective.'

'I'm sure that's not true.'

'And also, I certainly won't be letting Josh get away with anything. By the time I've finished with him he'll wish—'

The phone rang, interrupting his tirade. He hit answer and held it up to his ear.

'Hey Dad, what's the emergency?'

Fisher filled Josh in, then listened to his excuses, followed by his embarrassed apologies. In the background he could hear Ginny moving around. Clearly she didn't agree with the course of action he'd taken. He'd win her over later. Or maybe he wouldn't. She had no children of her own, perhaps she'd never understand the lengths you're prepared to go to protect your own child… even if it was from the wrath of his own mother.

With Josh briefed on how to respond to his mother's interrogation when he got home, and a clear warning of what would happen should he pull the same stunt again, Fisher hung up.

'I hope Josh is as clever as I think he is and he pulls it off okay,' he said, setting the phone down on the table in front of him. 'If he doesn't, we're both in trouble.' When Ginny didn't reply, Fisher turned towards the sofa and gave a tentative smile. 'Come on. I don't want to fall out. Can't we at least agree to disagree?'

Still no reply.

Fisher slid off the chair, took a couple of steps sideways and sat on the sofa. He set out a hand. All he could feel was fresh air.

'Ginny…?' The room was quiet, apart from Luna who stirred nearby. 'Ginny!' he called.

Nothing.

He flopped back in his seat, wondering why life had to be so complicated.

34.

The media was full of speculation about the killer at large; talk of fears for the safety of women living alone was rife. On the television, the news presenter, against a background image of the four victims, reiterated the police appeal for anyone with information to come forward.

The man on the sofa stretched his arms across its back and stared at the screen. The images, taken from family snapshots, were full of smiles. He looked at the youngest of the women — the one who reminded him of his mother, though she would have been nearer the age of the latest victim had she still been alive — and memories of that fateful day came flooding back. Twenty-six years had passed and there hadn't been a single day when he hadn't thought of her. The black and blue bruises that her concealer failed to cover and her once-smiling brown eyes, glazed over, unseeing, as she lay on the floor at the bottom of the stairs while his father screamed at him to get out, sharp in his memory. He could still feel the grip of his old man's hand crushing his fingers when the police asked him what had happened.

Six months later his father had also died, too drunk to notice the cigarette drop onto the sofa, a cheap unregulated Chinese import that the flames consumed in record time.

Everyone proclaimed it a miracle that he, a nine-year old boy, was able to make it out unscathed with nothing more than the stench of smoke on his unwashed pyjamas.

He remembered so clearly how his heart had raced, how alive he had felt emerging from the inferno, when only an hour before he had been cowering on a chair in the lounge, afraid to speak, afraid to move, trying to be invisible for fear of enticing his father's wrath.

And it had paid off. His father had eventually succumbed to sleep, his snores filling the air with a whisky-drenched stench. For a while he sat there, watching... waiting.

Once he was satisfied that his father was enveloped in a deep slumber, he slipped off the chair and crept across the room to his father's side. With shaking fingers, he reached for his cigarettes. Pulling one out of the packet, he stuck it between his pursed lips and grabbed the matchbox. With a lit match pressed to the cigarette's end, he drew a long slow breath. His young lungs rebelled and sent a cough spasming through his chest and a plume of dirty smoke from his lips. He clamped a hand over his mouth as he tried to quieten his coughs. Through stinging eyes, he glanced at his father, expecting to see his saggy lidded eyes glowering at him. Oh, the relief when a thunderous breath rattled out.

The fire caught quickly. At first, he'd stood there, mesmerised by the canary yellow flames that raced up his father's shirt, then flirted with his face, tickling his unkempt beard before flickering over his greasy comb-over. If he closed his eyes, he could still smell the stench of burning hair, as sweet a smell as marshmallows on an open fire.

The heat soon reached an intolerable level. He moved to the door, but still couldn't tear his eyes away from his father, melting like a wax effigy. It was only when the room was engulfed in smoke, blocking his view of the most liberating spectacle of his short life, that he made good his escape.

He'd sworn on his mother's death he'd make him pay. And he did.

That was the day he changed from a boy to a man.

35.

'You okay?' Nightingale asked, as Fisher climbed in the passenger seat beside her, having secured Luna in the back.

'Yeah. I'm fine.'

The truth was he'd had a terrible night's sleep, probably not helped by the bottle of cheap red wine he'd polished off while listening to accounts of serial killers into the early hours.

Ten minutes into the journey, he said, 'Did you know, Ted Bundy used to make out he was injured, wore his arm in a sling or rocked up on crutches, to trick his victims into thinking he was harmless. What if our killer does something similar? Maybe he turns up at their door asking for help.'

'Hmm,' Nightingale said, a sure-fire sign she didn't agree.

'Why not?'

'What sort of help would anyone ask for from an elderly woman at the door to their own home? Bundy used to approach the women and ask for their help in loading his car or to carry something that was difficult to manage. He wasn't invading their space. He invited them to come to him. His injury got his victims off their guard, so they'd draw close enough for him to hit them over the head and bundle them into his car.'

'You've been doing some research too, huh?'

'Just a bit.'

Fisher smiled. A lot of detectives he knew left the job at the office at the end of the day. Clearly Beth wasn't one of them.

'What if he said his car had broken down and asked to use the phone?'

'What century are you in? Even my nan knows everyone has a mobile these days.'

'What if he said he'd run out of charge?'

'Then my nan would say he must have also run out of imagination. She'd slam the door on him and call the police.'

'I've said it before, your nan has got a wise head on her shoulders.' After a pause, he said, 'I still think it's worth thinking about. They were all kind, community-spirited women who would want to help. All the killer needed was a foot in the door.'

'I suppose, when you put it like that. But I still think it would be hard to come up with a plausible reason for needing help.'

They arrived at the office at 8:00 a.m. Crossing the threshold, Fisher immediately noticed the difference in atmosphere. A subdued hush pervaded the room, unlike the hum of chatter that usually greeted them. Ordinarily he'd put it down to four murders and no leads, but today Fisher was sure that concern for mothers and grandmothers, aunts and friends, in fact any woman over the age of sixty, had something to do with his colleagues' disquiet.

He crossed to his desk and had just sat down when his phone chimed with a reminder. His shoulders slumped. With everything that had happened the night before, he'd all but forgotten about his nine o'clock meeting with the DCI. He picked up his desk phone and punched in a number.

Wickham answered after two rings, 'Hey, Matt. What's up?'

'Got a minute?'

Wickham joined Fisher at his desk. It didn't take him long to run through what little they'd learned from the house-to-house enquiries undertaken around the home of the fourth victim.

'What happened to Britain being a nation of curtain-twitchers?' Fisher said. After a short pause, he added, 'What about CCTV?'

'We've got the same problem we had with the others. The house is on a quiet cul-de-sac on a small estate. There are cameras on the A road, about a mile away, but with the volume of traffic there's no way we'd be able to pin-point a particular vehicle, especially when we've got nothing to narrow it down with. On top of which, we don't even know the killer drove to his victims' homes.'

With Wickham retreating back to his desk, Fisher reached down, feeling for Luna's harness. Instead of the dog's soft pelt all he was met with was empty air. He leaned further over in his seat and found Luna lying on her side. Choosing not to disturb her, he found his white stick and made his way slowly across the office, only banging into a chair and a desk as he passed. Not bad going really.

He paused outside DCI Fallon's door, took a deep breath and raised his hand but before he could knock, her voice cut through the air, 'Come in and shut the door behind you.'

'Ma'am.' Fisher nodded, then did as asked before crossing the room until his stick hit something solid. He felt in front of him for an empty chair and sat down. 'You wanted an update...' He took a breath and started, 'The investigation is progressing as I would expect. Although nothing new has come to light, we are still running down a couple of previous leads and I've got a few ideas about where to go next.'

'When you say previous leads, I take it Lewis Hunt is in there somewhere?'

'Of course. We can link him to at least three of the victims and he still refuses to tell us where he was when Connie Lloyd was murdered.'

'Then why haven't you brought him in?'

'Because we've haven't got enough evidence against him.'

'Have you got *any* evidence against him?'

Fisher paused as his mind skipped over what they had got. It didn't take long. He shook his head.

'Nothing solid, but like I said, he's—'

'Nothing solid,' she interrupted. 'Yet you continue to badger him.'

'Badger? If you're referring to our visit yesterday, he called us, remember. Also, I just want to point out how convenient it is that he happened to be out looking for an intruder, which nobody but he saw, at the same time that Mrs French was killed.'

'You think he made it up?'

'It's not beyond the realms of possibility. No evidence of an intruder was found, though plenty of prints from Mr Hunt's shoes were; his explanation being that he took a good look around the garden the following morning.'

'You really have got it in for him, haven't you? Is that why you told his wife he was refusing to tell you where he was at the time of the second murder?'

'I didn't...' Fisher stopped — actually, he had. He cleared his throat and muttered, 'I might have said something in passing.'

'Why is it that everything you do ends up being a problem at my door?'

'I don't see—'

'No Matt. You don't see. That's the problem. I had Mr Hunt on the phone earlier. He was absolutely livid that you questioned his wife about his whereabouts. And given you have no evidence against the man I'd say he had cause to be.'

'Firstly, I didn't question his wife. I merely pointed out that his lack of alibi meant he was still considered a suspect. And secondly, don't you think the fact he's making such a song and dance about it is suspicious?'

'No. I don't.' Her voice had grown as hard as tempered steel. 'You just said yourself there's no evidence against the man.'

'No *hard* evidence. The guy's got a motive and no alibi for at least two of the murders.'

'Get real Matt. We're dealing with the next Peter Sutcliffe or Harold Shipman. Someone who kills for kicks, not because his son might get thrown off some stupid football programme. Unless you've got anything else on him, just leave the man alone.' Fisher opened his mouth, about to argue, but she cut him off before he had the chance. 'So, what are you going to do next?' He blew out a sigh. He felt so weary. 'Well?' the Falcon pressed.

'I plan on going back to Remember When, the over-60s place in town. We need to find out how the killer chooses their victims and we know that three of the women had been there before.'

It turned out the fourth victim, Mrs French, was an occasional visitor to the club and Mrs Choudhury had also been before, having attended a couple of events organised by a dementia charity, as her son later remembered.

'How will that help? Seeing as one of them had never been there.'

'We don't know that for sure. Connie Lloyd could have visited the café; it's open to anyone.'

'And if she did... how is any of this going to help you find their killer?'

It was a valid question. And one he didn't have an answer for. Good job he was good at blagging on his feet.

'If we can place all four women in a common location, we can start looking at who could have come into contact with them at that location,' he asserted. 'If it's okay with you, I'd like to talk to

Professor Woolf; see if she can give us any pointers about the murderer, seeing that she's an expert on serial killers.'

The Falcon fell quiet for a moment. Fisher waited for her to turn down his request, but she surprised him by saying, 'I think I'd like to meet this *expert*. Organise it, will you?'

'I'll ask her. No guarantee she'll say yes.'

'Of course she will. Talk to legal, see if we need to get her to sign any sort of confidentiality agreement. Don't want her selling the story to the highest bidder.'

'Anything else?'

'I want the house-to-house enquiries repeated.'

'But we've already—'

'Maybe you've missed something. I want to know every single person, every single vehicle that was seen in the vicinity of the victims' addresses around the time of their murder. Someone's got to have seen something. The killer didn't teleport themselves into their homes.'

'Fine.'

After leaving the DCI's office, Fisher sent Wickham off to lead a small group of constables to knock on doors. Again.

'Make sure you speak to someone in every single house on each of the streets. I don't want anyone accusing us of having only done half a job later down the line,' were his parting words.

Martha Woolf proved to be more elusive. Fisher tried her office and her mobile, getting her voicemail both times. He left a message, asking her to call back, before he and Nightingale headed out to visit Remember When.

The chief executive of the over-60s club ushered them into her office. Fisher placed her as being younger than the club's typical member. Her clear voice, brisk manner and firm handshake conjured up an image of a forty-year-old woman wearing a smart suit and polite smile.

'I understand the victims have all been more mature ladies but I don't quite see how you think we can help,' she said. 'Not all of them were regulars here.'

'As anyone can use your café, there's no way to be sure all four victims didn't come here at some point.' After a beat, Fisher asked, 'Do you have any cameras on the premises?'

'No. We've never seen the need. We don't keep anything of any value here.'

'Perhaps we could talk to the staff in the café?'

'You can try. It's largely run by volunteers, as are most of our activities. They all work different shifts, so not all of them will be in at the moment.'

'We'll take our chances.'

Over the course of the afternoon, Fisher and Nightingale talked to a selection of volunteers. Not that it helped them any. Although none of them recalled ever having seen Ms Lloyd, they all agreed it didn't necessarily mean she'd never visited.

'How did it go?' the chief executive asked, catching them in the foyer as they made their way out.

Fisher shook his head.

'Nothing. You were right. We always knew it was a bit of a long shot. But thank you anyway.'

He gripped Luna's harness and was about to make his way to the door when Nightingale said, 'Excuse me, this noticeboard... there's a poster for meals-on-wheels and one for Sunshine Coaches. Are they both run by your organisation?'

Fisher's ears pricked up. They knew Mrs Choudhury had meals-on-wheels and Connie Lloyd had once been a volunteer mini-bus driver for Sunshine Coaches, a company that operated a transport service for disabled children and invalided pensioners.

'Meals-on-wheels is. We don't have anything to do with Sunshine Coaches. Anyone is welcome to put posters on the board provided they're advertising something relevant to our members.'

With yet another avenue turning out to be a dead-end, they returned to the car. Fisher felt Luna come to a stop just as his mobile began to ring. 'Can you get Luna in the car, while I take this, please?' He handed the dog over then swiped to answer. 'DI Fisher.'

'Detective, it's Martha Woolf.'

'Professor. Thank you for calling back. I was talking to my DCI earlier today. She's very keen to meet you. We wondered whether you'd be willing to come in for a meeting. We're hoping you'll give us the benefit of your knowledge.'

'I'd love to help, only I'm not sure there's much more I can tell you, given how little I know about the cases.'

'It would be official this time. You would, of course, get full access to the investigation findings. Would that help?' The line fell silent. After a moment, Fisher said, 'Professor...?'

'I'm sorry. Yes. Of course. I'd be glad to help. When were you thinking of?'

36.

Fisher took the lift down to the ground floor and stepped out, his white stick leading the way.

'Detective Fisher!' Woolf's husky timbre sounded warm to his ears.

'Professor, thank you for coming.' He gave a smile and held out his hand.

The solid clack of heels came across the floor and then stopped in front of him. A firm hand took his in its grip.

'Have you signed in yet?'

'I have.'

'Good. We'll go straight up then.'

'Have you made any more progress?' Woolf asked, as Fisher led the way to the serious crimes office on the third floor.

'Not so as you'd notice.' He held his security pass to the pad on the door then pushed through into the main office. Keeping left he counted out eight steps, then stopped and turned. He set out a hand and felt for the door. Finding it ajar, he rapped on the doorframe and leaned in. 'Professor Woolf, ma'am.' He heard movement ahead and waited.

The strong scent of the DCI's perfume reached them before she did.

'Good to meet you. I'm DCI Anita Fallon. I hear you're something of an expert when it comes to serial killers.'

'I guess I'm an expert as much as anyone can be. Serial killers are an elusive breed,' Woolf said, as she was being ushered inside. 'Please, call me Martha.'

Fisher went to follow the pair, but the Falcon's brusque tone stopped him in his tracks.

'That will be all, DI Fisher.'

A cloud of a frown darkened his brow.

'But I thought—'

'Close the door behind you.'

He gritted his teeth, then turned on his heel and started to walk away. If she wanted the door closed, she could bloody well close it herself.

He was navigating his way through the warren of office furniture, back to his own desk, when he heard Woolf's raised voice.

'I'm sorry. There must be some misunderstanding. I was here at Detective Fisher's invitation. If he isn't present, then I won't be staying.'

Fisher heard footsteps approach.

'Detective!' Woolf called. He turned as she came over. 'If you still want that conversation, perhaps there's somewhere else we can talk?'

Fisher was about to respond when the DCI's voice cut in, 'Professor Woolf, please... Of course, Detective Fisher is welcome to join us.' Fisher started making his way back towards the two women. Fallon went on, 'I had no intention of excluding the DI from our conversation, it's only... I thought... well, he has rather a lot to be getting on with.'

'A busy man, huh?' Woolf replied. 'Well, Detective Inspector, I consider myself privileged that you're prepared to give up your time to talk to me.'

Despite Fisher's ire at being treated the way he had he couldn't help but smile. The professor had been in the building less than ten minutes and already she had the measure of the Falcon.

Once they were all seated, the DCI cleared her throat.

'As I'm sure you're aware, Professor, four women over the age of sixty have been murdered in exactly the same way. All picked at random.'

'How do you know it's random?'

'There are absolutely no links between the victims.'

'Just because you haven't found any links doesn't mean they don't exist.'

'I assure you. If there's a link, we would have found it. Detective Fisher and his team have scrutinised the victims' backgrounds and their lives. Which is why we need to shift our focus onto the killer. Hence why you're here. We'd like you to produce a profile of our killer. A picture of the type of person we should be looking for.'

'Like a photo-fit?' Woolf replied. Fisher sensed a rough edge to her voice.

'That would be perfect,' Fallon replied.

Woolf's throaty laugh filled the room.

'I'm afraid it doesn't work like that. I can take details of the victims and the scenes and draw a set of conclusions about your killer, such as how he might have selected his victims and some suggestions as to what motivations them, but anyone who says they can tell you how tall or fat or fair or dark they are, is lying.'

'We understand that,' Fisher said. 'At this stage, we'll take whatever help we can get.'

'Not that we're desperate,' Fallon jumped in. 'We have got several lines of enquiry open. We just need something to compare our suspects to.'

Woolf cleared her throat.

'Okay. So, first of all, I'll need to see the crime scene photos and whatever information you've got on the victims. You said a moment ago, all the crime scenes were the same. I thought there were some subtle differences between them?'

Fisher nodded and said, 'There were.'

'That's debatable,' Fallon said dismissively. 'The differences are so subtle as to be inconsequential.'

'That's not how I see it,' Fisher argued. 'There were differences in the position and location of the bodies, money was taken in some cases, but not in others. Likewise, a calendar was found under the body of one of the women and not the others.'

'But they were all broadly the same,' Fallon replied.

'Those differences could be incredibly important,' Woolf said. 'There could be a reason behind every discrepancy. The crime scene tells us an awful lot. Take the choice of bag, for example...'

'You're going to say it could be a woman, aren't you?' Fallon said. 'I thought that. That's why they used a bag as well as the flex.'

'I've given this matter a lot of thought and I'm not actually sure that the bag would subdue anyone. On the contrary, it would cause an immediate fight and flight response. The victim would be desperately trying to escape. So, no. I don't think it follows that the killer is female. I think the bag is more ritualistic. I have a few ideas, but I'd need to see the crime scene shots and perhaps talk to someone who attended the scenes before sharing them. Perhaps Detective Fisher and his partner, Beth, could accompany me while I looked through the files? It will save a considerable amount of time if he's able to answer any questions I may have.'

'I'd be happy to.' Fisher gripped his white stick and rose from his seat. 'If that's everything ma'am, we'll get right on to it?'

210

Fisher heard the door open. Woolf, it seemed, had got there first.

'I'll join you,' Fallon said.

Fisher's shoulders slumped.

'Of course, ma'am. Whatever you say.'

37.

The woman was arrogant, egotistical, narcissistic: everything he despised.

She ran her manicured fingers through her blonde hair, lips permanently pursed as she sat in judgement on everyone else, making their lives hell.

How he'd love to see that mouth wide open, screaming for mercy. And it wouldn't be a black plastic bag he'd use on her, that's for sure. No, he'd come up with something much more refined, much more special.

Maybe another sex game gone wrong scenario?

He wondered which would frighten her the most... the physical violence or the idea that she'd be left naked, exposed for all to see. He felt his predatory instincts stirring deliciously as the image played through his mind like a film reel.

But he mustn't. Now was not the time. He had other business to attend to first.

He watched as she lifted a mug to her mouth, lips pursing even more as she took a sip, then tore his gaze away, promising himself that one day he'd come back for her.

38.

Fisher tasked Nightingale with pulling together the crime scene photographs, post mortem reports and victims' particulars, including the inventories of items missing from their homes. While she was doing that, he sent for coffee, then went to check on Luna. A few minutes later, he arrived at the meeting room only to find it in silence.

He was standing at the threshold mentally retracing his steps, wondering if he'd somehow taken a wrong turning, when the Falcon called, 'Fisher! Are you coming in or are you going to stand there like a spare part all afternoon?'

'Just getting my bearings, ma'am.'

He shook his head and ambled over. At the table, he sat down and went to place his hands in front of him, but a large stack of files got in the way. He pushed them to one side.

'Did Beth put these here?'

'No,' Fallon replied. 'They were already here when we came in. There's paperwork all over the table. Probably why the investigation is in such a mess. You need to be better organised.'

'It's probably from the house-to-house enquiries. Of course, there'll be even more now you've instructed them to be repeated.' Fisher flashed a tight smile in her direction.

Just then, Nightingale arrived. She hurried over to the table and sat next to Fisher.

'Sorry I was so long. I made copies of some of the documents; thought it might make things easier.'

'Good thinking,' Fisher said. 'We'll start with the photos, shall we? Beth, could you talk us through what was found in each of the different crime scenes?'

For the following hour, Nightingale detailed the findings at each of the victim's homes.

Apart from the occasional 'interesting' or 'hmm,' the professor kept her thoughts to herself until the end, when she asked, 'The calendar that was found under the third victim's body, were there any appointments that day?'

'No,' Nightingale replied.

'Then why was it there?' Woolf said, as much to herself as to the others. After a moment's pause, she asked, 'Beth, you were going to look through the calendars for obscure messages or symbols. Did you find anything?'

'No. I couldn't see anything other than what looks like normal appointments.'

'What were you expecting?' DCI Fallon asked.

'If the placement of the calendar was deliberate, then clearly the killer wanted to draw attention to it,' Woolf replied. 'In which case it's possible he'd left a hidden message.'

'Why would he do that?'

'He might see it as a way to prove his cunning. But if that was the case, I would have expected such a message to be visible to anyone looking for it, otherwise there's no point.'

'I think the calendar has something to do with how the killer is getting in to the houses,' Fisher commented.

He heard the Falcon give an exasperated sigh. 'We know none of the women were expecting anyone the day they were attacked.'

'What if the killer made out he was there to book an appointment,' Fisher pressed. 'Say he pretended to be from some company, I don't know, selling boilers or double glazing, and said he was arranging sales visits for anyone interested in getting a quote.'

'Did the victims need a new boiler or double glazing?' Fallon asked.

'I was speaking hypothetically.'

'That's a good suggestion,' Woolf said. 'If the killer has one of those faces that people trust, that might be enough to open the door and start the conversation. Then he suggests stepping inside to find a suitable date and once he's in, it's game over. It could all be done and dusted in less than five minutes. You said earlier that you have yet to find a link between the women. Perhaps you need to look at services or products targeted to the over-60s that none of the women had.'

Fisher nodded.

'I like that idea. It might explain why Connie Lloyd was in the kitchen. Her calendar was on the kitchen wall. Beth, make a note. We can brainstorm some ideas later.'

'The calendar could be incidental,' DCI Fallon said. 'I mean, everyone has a calendar on their kitchen wall.'

Fisher was quick to respond. 'I don't.'

'Well it wouldn't be much use to you, would it?'

'I meant I didn't used to. I've always used the calendar on my phone.'

'Whatever. Can we move on?'

Sensing the Falcon was losing interest, Fisher said, 'If you need to go, we can carry on briefing Professor Woolf. We're only going over things you already know.'

He heard her chair scrape across the floor as she stood up.

'You're right. I'm too busy for this. I look forward to seeing the profile in due course.'

The room fell silent until the sound of Fallon's retreating footsteps were snuffed out by the closing door.

'Oh my God.' Woolf's American accent sounded even stronger than usual. 'Is she always like that?'

'Pretty much. You get used to it,' Fisher lied. 'So, what's next?'

'Nothing,' Nightingale said. 'We've covered everything.'

'It's been very interesting,' Woolf said. 'What would really help now is if I could talk to some of the folk who knew the dead women. Maybe they'll tell me something they didn't think worth mentioning to you.'

'You mean on your own?' Fisher said. 'Only I'm not sure we can—'

'Of course not. Obviously I'll need you to do the introductions.'

'But if we're there, won't they tell you exactly what they told us?'

'Not necessarily. I'll be asking different questions.'

Fisher thought about it for moment, then gave a nod.

'I assume first on the list is Lewis Hunt.'

'You've already spoken to him at length. I'm not sure I'll get anything new out of him.'

'Oh.'

'You sound disappointed, Inspector.'

'It's just... well, I thought it would be a good idea for you to see him. With your knowledge of serial killers, I'd be interested to see whether he sets any alarms ringing.'

'Like some sort of sixth sense? I'm afraid it doesn't work like that. Why are you so convinced he's your man?'

'I'm not. It's only there are a few loose ends with him.'

'You mean the fact he refuses to give you an alibi for when his ex-wife was killed.'

'Precisely. Says we'll have to arrest him first. Gave us some bull about not wanting the people he was meeting with getting dragged into a police investigation.'

'I think it's more likely he was somewhere he shouldn't have been,' Woolf replied. '…with someone he shouldn't have been with.'

'An affair?'

'That seems the most obvious explanation, don't you think? Anyway, if it helps, after we talked last time, I took the liberty of looking Mr Hunt up. From what I could see of him on social media and media reports he doesn't strike me as the sort of person you're looking for.'

'I thought you hadn't been able to do a profile… not enough information.'

'I don't need a profile to tell me he's not the type. If he was going to kill someone, I'm sure he'd do it very differently. Perhaps we could start by talking to someone who knew the first victim. She was the one found by a neighbour, yes?'

'That's right.'

'Did she have any children or close relatives?'

'No. No living relatives at all, as far as we know.'

'Who benefited from her death?'

Financially? That would be the football academy set up by her husband — apart from a few charitable bequests she left them everything.'

'And the guy in charge there, what's he like?'

'A pompous little prick. The sort that likes to feel important and have friends in high places. I would imagine he'd find murder beneath him. Besides, apart from the fact the grandson of the third victim goes to the academy, there's nothing to link him to any of the other victims.'

'What about Mrs Walker's friends?'

'From what we've been told, she occasionally received visitors at home, though recently the extent of her social life was the bridge club at the over-60s place in town.'

'Perhaps we'd be better starting with the second victim then. I think you said there's a boyfriend—'

'Fiancé,' Nightingale corrected.

'Yes,' Fisher said. 'Though they hadn't been together very long—'

'Four months.'

'Thank you, Beth. The point is, I'm not sure how well he knew Ms Lloyd. The woman who raised the alarm had known her for a lot longer.'

'The friend who was supposed to be getting a lift to the hospital?' Woolf asked.

'That's right.'

'In which case, I think I'd like to speak to both of them, if I may. Starting with the friend.'

39.

Jennifer Keeley met them at the door with a warm welcome. Indoors, Fisher sat knee-to-knee with Nightingale on a small sofa, while Professor Woolf made herself comfortable on a nearby armchair.

Fisher opened the conversation as soon as they were settled.

'Mrs Keeley, thank you for agreeing to see us at such short notice. As I explained on the phone, we have a few questions in relation to some new lines of enquiry.'

'You're no closer to finding out who did it then?'

Fisher felt a shiver of guilt course through him.

'We've made some progress,' he replied, hoping Beth and the professor had good poker faces. 'If it's okay, I'll hand straight over to Professor Woolf.' He turned his head in Woolf's direction.

'Thank you, Inspector. Jen… is it okay to call you Jen?' Her voice sounded even warmer and softer than usual.

'Of course. No need to be on ceremony here.'

'Jen, please call me Martha. Why don't you tell me about your friend Connie?'

'She was a lovely lady. Do anything for anybody. Which is amazing, given how badly she was treated by other people. First, there was her ex-husband. He cheated on her then lied about how much money he had, so she got hardly anything from the divorce. And if that wasn't bad enough, some sleazy con artist ran off with what little money she did get. That's why I don't understand how it could have happened... given her past, Connie was naturally suspicious. She wouldn't have let any Tom, Dick or Harry into her home.'

'I understand you raised the alarm when she didn't show up to take you to the hospital.'

'That's right.'

'Was that part of an organised transport arrangement... Sunshine Coaches, is it?'

'No. She stopped that ages ago. She just did it as a friend. I offered to pay her petrol money but she wouldn't hear of it.'

'Was this at the same hospital where she met her fiancé?'

'That's right. I'd gone in for my usual chemo session — the one thing you don't realise is how long it takes; the hours just drag by — anyway, Connie nipped out for a coffee and some fresh air. When she got back, she mentioned how she'd got chatting to a man. They bumped into each other again at my next session and he asked her out. She was clearly thrilled but turned him down, worried it would end badly. I told her it was time her luck changed and convinced her to give him a go. Of all the people who deserved some happiness, Connie did,' she said, with a distinct wobble to her voice.

'At least she was able to enjoy a few happy months, thanks to your advice,' Woolf said gently. Fisher heard a sniff then sensed the professor shift in her seat towards their upset host. 'Here...'

'Thank you,' Jen Keeley said, before blowing her nose.

'Warren sounds like a real gent. Do you know much about him?'

'Not really. From what Connie told me, he'd long since given up any idea of finding someone else after his wife died, what with having a young son to bring up as well as a business to run.'

'Were you surprised they got engaged so soon?'

220

'Yes. I imagine most people were. But it was lovely to see her so happy. I'd known her a long time and, well, although she hadn't had it easy, she always made the best of things. I can remember a time when…' Her three guests listened politely as she regaled them with memories of her friend.

Eventually, Woolf brought the conversation back to the investigation.

'It's been lovely talking to you, Jen. It's clear how much your friend meant to you and you to her.'

'Thank you.'

'That's what is so sad about what's happened, all of the victims sound so lovely. Did you know any of the others?'

'The other women that died? No.'

'I only ask because, well, it's a small world. I'm often surprised at how people's paths cross.'

'When you get to my age you don't get out very much. I dare say I'll be getting out even less now.'

'Well, that was a waste of time,' Fisher said, as soon as Mrs Keeley closed the door behind them.

'Really?' Woolf sounded surprised. 'I thought it was very informative. It sounds like the killer performed a miracle getting into Ms Lloyd's home unchallenged.' After a beat, she added, 'I must say, I am looking forward to meeting Mr Newman.'

As Nightingale called the dead woman's fiancé to let him know they were en route, Woolf asked, 'Do you know what sort of cancer he has and how advanced it is?'

'No and no,' Fisher replied. 'Based on the fact they were planning on getting married, I assume it isn't terminal.'

'I wouldn't assume anything of the sort, Inspector,' Woolf replied. 'Many people faced with the prospect of their own mortality feel the need to make up for a lifetime of missed opportunities. The fact he wanted to get married so soon might mean the exact opposite to what you think.'

Fisher sensed Luna slow and then stop.

'Are we at the car?' he asked.

'Yes,' Nightingale replied.

He heard the snap of the doors unlocking. Moving to the rear door, he unhooked Luna's harness and ushered her inside. Having conceded the passenger seat to their guest, he clambered in to sit alongside the dog, then asked, 'Is it relevant... Mr Newman's cancer?'

'Not necessarily,' Woolf replied. 'I only asked because dealing with a serious illness can impact a person's psychology. And not only in respect of the emotional strain. An aggressive or terminal cancer and its treatment can bring with it a whole host of chemical changes that can affect personality and behaviour. By the way, have you confirmed Mrs Keeley's whereabouts at the time of the murders?'

'Surely you don't suspect her?' Nightingale said.

'You mean because she appears to be old and infirm? She might not be as frail as she appears.'

'But what would be the motive?'

'Good old-fashioned cash. If Ms Lloyd's legal case gets settled her friend will do very well out of it. What do you think Inspector?'

'I prefer to save my suspicions for those who warrant it,' he said, as he buckled up. 'Beth, are we going or what?'

Nightingale started the engine.

40.

'So, they've brought you in to help, have they? I'm not surprised,' Warren Newman said to Professor Woolf after Fisher made the introductions. 'The murderer must have thought he'd won the lottery having a blind bloke run the investigation. How many women is it now? Four? Five?'

'Professor Woolf is acting as a consultant,' Fisher explained. 'She's here in an advisory capacity.'

'Wasting taxpayers' money you mean? What is it with you public sector—'

'Mr Newman…' Woolf interrupted, her voice firm but gentle. 'I can see how distressed you are. And no wonder, considering everything you've gone through. But I can assure you, we all want the same thing… which is to bring Connie's killer to justice. Please, could we come in? I only have a few questions.'

Grudgingly, Newman led them through into the lounge. Fisher had Luna guide him to an empty chair.

There was no offer of drinks and as soon as everyone was seated, Newman said, 'What do you want to know?'

Woolf explained how they were trying to learn more about Ms Lloyd's lifestyle and habits.

'Even details such as whether any work was needed on her house could be important.'

'Connie's place was rented. If anything needed doing, she'd have got the landlord to do it.'

'What if it wasn't a problem with the house. What if it was… I don't know, say her washing machine was playing up?'

'She would have told me. I know a lot of tradesfolk. I'd have got someone to do it mates-rates.'

'What if someone turned up at the door claiming to be from a company specialising in whatever it was needed doing,' Woolf replied. 'Would she have let them in, say to get a quote?'

'Only if she was a bloody idiot. And that's one thing Connie wasn't. I already said, she'd have told me if anything needed doing.'

'Are you sure?' Woolf coaxed. 'If she was anything like me — and I've lived alone for some years now — you get used to sorting things out for yourself.'

'She wasn't alone. She had me'

'Of course. I didn't mean…' Woolf decided to change tack. 'How long had you been together?'

'Five months. Best five months of my life. I still can't believe it…' His voice trailed off. A moment later he took a heaving breath in.

'Had you been on your own long before you met Connie?'

'Twenty-five years. Ever since my wife died.'

'I'm sorry to hear that. She must have been very young.'

'Thirty-one. Turns out she had a heart problem. We didn't know.'

'That must have been awful for you and your son. I assume he was just a child when it happened. I can see why the relationship with Connie meant so much to you.' Woolf's throaty voice was as soothing as a lozenge. 'Had you set a date?'

'We were hoping December. Connie said she'd always fancied a winter wedding.'

'December this year?' Fisher thought there was an up-tick of surprise in Woolf's voice.

'Yes. Though we hadn't ruled out doing it sooner, if we could find somewhere we liked that could fit us in. We'd both been on our own for far too long and it's not like we were getting any younger. We thought, why wait? Life's too short. That's what they say, isn't it?' Newman said in a strangled voice. 'Though I never thought it would be as short as it was, not for Connie at least. Me, on the other hand…'

'How is your cancer treatment going?' Woolf asked.

'They tell me it's working. Though I don't know why I don't just stop it now and give in to the inevitable.'

'Surely you don't mean that? What about your family?'

'Rob would be better off if I was dead.'

'I'm sure that's not true and I bet your little granddaughter wouldn't want that. Is that her in the photo?'

'Yes. Ava. She'll be five in January.'

'Then think of her. She's the reason you need to stay strong. You don't want to deprive her of lots of lovely memories with her granddaddy, do you?'

'You sound like Connie. She kept telling me to sell up and retire, so I'd have more time to spend with Ava.'

'Will you still retire?'

'What's the point? So I can sit around all day, twiddling my thumbs? No thank you. Once the chemo's done, and I've got my strength back, it'll be business as usual.'

'You're not working at the moment?'

'I try to go in at least a few hours a day. I've got a couple of lads who keep the place ticking over for me.'

'Your son isn't in the business?'

'No. He's in IT.' He gave a sigh. 'Selling cars never did interest him. He prefers to drive the merchandise than flog it.' He cleared his throat. 'So, is that everything?'

'I think so,' Woolf replied. 'Thank you for taking the time to talk to me.'

Fisher eased forward in his seat in what he hoped was the direction of their host.

'I know we've spoken a few times, Mr Newman. I wondered whether you've given any more thought as to why Ms Lloyd might have been targeted?'

'Good God, man, if you don't know the answer to that you're more bloody useless than I thought. It's blindingly obvious, isn't it? The killer's a psychopathic nutter with a beef against women of a certain age. Maybe they've got a complex against their mother, like in that film, Psycho. You should be out there, looking for someone who likes starting fires. They all start that way, so my lad tells me.'

For once, Woolf gave no hint of her views on the theories promulgated by the entertainment industry.

'Was that as enlightening as you expected, Professor?' Fisher asked, after the interview had ended and the three of them had returned to the car.

'Enlightening, no, but still fascinating, nonetheless. I think it's astounding how people believe something to be simply because they've been told it's true,' she replied. 'The power of suggestion is a topic that interests me enormously.'

'Hmm.' Fisher wondered whether the professor's interests were ever going to bear fruit and help them catch their killer. He heard Nightingale slip the key into the ignition and said, 'Would you like to speak with anyone else or have you heard enough?'

'I think I've got enough to go on, for now. Although there is one detail...'

'Yes?'

'The calendar found underneath the body of one of the women.'

'Mrs Choudhury, the third victim,' Nightingale supplied.

'Could it have been knocked off the wall during a struggle?'

'Beth?' Fisher prompted.

'It's unlikely,' she replied. 'The hook it usually hung on was nowhere near the body, plus, the pathologist said there wouldn't have been much of a struggle, given how frail she was.'

'And she had no appointments on the day she was attacked?'

'No.'

'That's why we thought the killer may have made out they were there to book an appointment,' Fisher said.

'Of course. Yes,' Woolf replied. 'I can see why you'd think that.'

'So what do you think?'

'I think I need a little more time to gather my thoughts.'

The professor's reticence caught Fisher by surprise. He was sure she had already started to compose a picture of their killer in her own mind. But if she didn't want to say, what could he do? He could hardly strong-arm the information out of her.

He slumped back in his seat and found himself wondering what Woolf was more interested in: bringing the killer to justice or bolstering her own knowledge on what was clearly her pet subject.

41.

'Our priority now is to find out whether the victims were having any work done or needed work doing that required a tradesperson or had bought anything that needed installing,' Fisher said, as they strode up the tarmac path to the station. 'Although Newman reckons he'd have known if Connie needed anything doing, like you said Professor, she'd been coping on her own for a long time.' A small groan escaped him as a thought sprang to mind. 'You know what we should have asked him? Whether she'd had any tradespeople in over the last few months. The killer might use the day job to identify possible future victims. If that's the case, they wouldn't be complete strangers. Maybe that's how they gain entry.'

'Do you want me to call him and find out?' Nightingale asked.

Fisher gave it a moment's thought, then shook his head. The last thing he wanted was give the antagonistic bastard even more reason to think him incompetent.

'No. We'll ask the other relatives and friends first. Newman was only on the scene for a few months, it's questionable how much he knows.'

Back at the station, Woolf asked to be pointed in the direction of the ladies. Nightingale obliged, showing her the way, as well as acting as chaperone, given the professor's lack of security clearance. Meanwhile, Luna led Fisher to his desk where he set about finding the contact details for Mr Choudhury, the third victim's son. From earlier conversations with the man, it was obvious he had a good handle on his mother's life. If anyone knew whether she had recently engaged the services of any tradespeople, he would. He was about to make the call when he heard footsteps approach. He paused and cocked his head.

'How did you get on?' It was DCI Fallon.

'Good. It's given us a few ideas to work on.'

'That's it... a few ideas? I don't know why I'm surprised. Anyone calling themselves an expert on anything usually knows a lot less than they profess. You know what they say, those that can do, those that can't—'

'Teach.' Woolf's voice sliced the air like a scalpel, and for a second it seemed like all the sound in the room had escaped through the cut. Fisher hadn't heard her return from the ladies.

The Falcon cleared her throat.

'Professor Woolf, I didn't realise you were still here.'

'Evidently,' Woolf replied, her tone as cold as the atmosphere between the two women.

'We were just talking about—'

'I know exactly what you were talking about. I could hardly have missed it... what with your foghorn mouth.'

'I beg your pardon?'

'Apology accepted.' Fisher sensed Woolf skirt around the DCI and take the vacant chair next to his desk. 'So, Inspector Fisher, you were going to—'

'Hang on a minute...' Fallon said. 'You can't talk to me like that here.'

'I think you'll find I just did.'

'And I think you should leave, right now.'

'And I think you should stop being so disrespectful.'

'Please!' Fisher set out his hands, palms out. 'This isn't helping. Ma'am, I've agreed with Professor Woolf that we—'

'I don't give a toss what you've agreed. You're not in charge here. I am.' Just then Fisher's phone started to ring. A robotic voice began to recite the number calling. Fallon continued full pelt, 'Now, I think we've had about as much outside help as we need, so—'

The phone continued to ring. Fisher again held out a hand and said, 'Ma'am, I really need to get this. It could be important.' And without waiting, answered the call. 'DI Fisher.'

He heard Fallon stomp off in the direction of her office and blew out a long stream of air, before turning his attention back to the caller.

'Hello. Sorry for the delay. How can I help?'

'Hi, this is Rob Newman. You saw my dad this morning.'

'Hello Mr Newman.'

'I hope it's okay to call, only Dad said you asked him whether Connie needed any work doing at her house.'

Fisher sensed Woolf moving closer, her spicy scent enveloping him. He moved his phone away from his ear a little, giving her access to the conversation.

'That's right.'

'I don't know if it helps but not long ago, Dad was moaning about the cost of heating. Connie said she'd had something through the post from a company doing free loft insulation for the over-sixties. I remember, because she made a joke about there being some benefits to getting older. She never mentioned it again, but I wondered, perhaps she decided to go ahead and get it done.'

'I thought she was in rented accommodation,' Fisher replied. 'Wouldn't that fall to her landlord to do?'

'Oh. I don't know. Would it?'

'I would have thought so but we'll check it out. Thanks for taking the time to call.'

After hanging up, Fisher turned to Woolf. 'Did you get all that?'

'Yes. Interesting he should phone, don't you think?'

'Yes, and I'm glad he did. He's given me an idea.'

'I think that was the point.'

'I take it you heard him mention a brochure for loft insulation. I wonder whether everyone in the neighbourhood got one or whether the company used consumer data to target customers in a certain demographic. I mean, how many times have you had a cold call or a letter from a company who seems to know all manner of personal stuff about you? Too many times, if you're anything like me. What if our killer works for a company that filters customers based on gender or age or number of people in the household? With a list like that, he could pick and choose his victims.' Fisher slumped back in his seat and rubbed his hands over his face, stubble rasping loudly. 'If that's the case, we're stuffed. There must be countless companies that could target our victims' demographic with God knows how many employees.'

'Say there was such a list,' Woolf said. Fisher could hear her turning the pages of some document on his desk. 'One that includes women over sixty who live alone within a certain radius of town. Does the killer select a name at random off that list or was there something else that attracted him to the victims? Because if there is, I can't see what it is. There's nothing in these investigation reports that jumps out. And why were there subtle differences, such as the cash being taken in some cases and not others?'

'Maybe the killer's hard up. Couldn't resist helping himself when it was in easy reach.'

Woolf gave a huff.

'A serial killer in the throes of doing what he's dreamed of and rehearsed in his head over and over again would not, in my opinion, succumb to pocketing a handful of change. Or if they did, they'd do it in every case.' Fisher heard her put the report down on the table. Shortly, she said, 'Perhaps they did it deliberately, to confuse the investigation.'

'They've certainly done that.' They fell quiet for a moment, then Fisher said, 'Where's Beth? I thought she went with you.'

'She did but then she went to fetch the calendars — you said you wanted us to take another look.'

He had said that. Only events had overtaken things and he wasn't sure there was any point now. Excited by his new train of thought, he said, 'What if we create our own database? Only not of potential victims but of possible killers. We start with men — seeing the killer's most likely to be male — who live in the county and work for companies that sell products aimed at women over a certain age. We can then add other criteria specific to serial killers as a filter.'

'Criteria such as…?'

'You tell me… a criminal record for animal abuse or arson or a history of being abused as a child—'

'And any other rubbish Hollywood has sold you,' Woolf said drily.

'Are they really that far off the mark? I know you said not all serial killers are considerate enough to fit the stereotypes but presumably some are?'

'And you think those sorts of details will be easy to come by?'

'I don't know, but I'm willing to find out.'

42.

He pressed the button for the ignition and was about to slip the car into gear when a sliver of black plastic poking out of the bag on the passenger seat caught his eye. He leaned over and pushed it down, out of sight. It was one thing to have his tools to hand, quite another for them to stick out like the gun bulge under an undercover cop's coat.

He took a circuitous route to avoid the roadside cameras and used the extra time to run through his plan of attack. He'd practised the moves on an upside-down mop so many times the action felt as natural as breathing. It was surprisingly easy if you'd got good reflexes and a timid victim.

Two streets away from his target, he found a gap amongst a long line of parked cars and pulled in. A thick blanket of concrete grey cloud cast the day in a dull half-light and rendered the air unseasonably chilly. He wrapped his coat around him, pulled up his hood and set off with a sure and steady tread, bag swinging from his shoulder.

Rounding a corner, his destination came into view. The compact terraced house might once have sat behind a pretty front garden. Now the small space was as weed-ridden as the cracks in the pavement. The gate squeaked as he pushed through, on his way to the flaking front door. He pasted on a warm smile and pressed a gloved finger to the bell.

Shortly, a scuffling sound could be heard in the hallway beyond. The door inched open and a papery, lined face peered out. The elderly lady's cheeks wrinkled as she broke into a welcoming smile.

'Hello again. Did you forget something?' she asked, reaching for the security chain. 'Sorry dear, you'll have to give me a minute. You've caught me on a bad day.' He watched her set one shaky foot in front of the other while attempting to manoeuvre an aluminium walking frame around in the small space. 'But, you know, mustn't grumble.'

And straight away, he knew it wasn't her.

The excuses tripped off his tongue with well-practised ease as he made a hasty departure.

43.

'Has Professor Woolf gone?' Nightingale asked, taking the empty chair next to Fisher's desk.

'Yes. She's lecturing this afternoon. Though I think that might have been an excuse. I get the impression she's beginning to realise how much of a slog detective work is.' After a short pause, he added, 'Plus, I might have offended her... a little.' He explained the discussion that had taken place just before Woolf had excused herself. 'I'm sure she'll get over it. If she doesn't, well... we might not need her help much longer. I've had an idea. Could be a game-changer.'

'What?' Nightingale asked eagerly.

'Don't get too excited.' He explained the call from Rob Newman and how it gave him the idea of creating a database of potential killers. 'I know it'll take a bit of doing but we can start by looking at companies who target older women using consumer records, then look to see who has access to those records. It might only throw up a handful of people in each company. Customer information's covered by the Data Protection Act, so not everyone in the organisation is going to be able to look up customer details. I thought we could email every company based in the county and ask them whether they use consumer data to target their customers. There are a number of business directories we can get the details from.'

'Or we could start with companies that fit smoke detectors.' Something in Beth's tone conjured up an image of her sitting there wearing a cheeky smile.

'You've found something?'

'Might have...' She was positively teasing him now. She went on, 'At least three of the women had appointments to have a smoke detector fitted. As soon as I saw the first appointment it reminded me of a poster I saw at Remember When, advertising free detectors for the over-60s. What if it's a scam... a way of getting through the door?'

'I don't know. A fire officer turned up at Mrs French's while we were there, remember?

'What if the guy who turned up wasn't really from the fire service?'

Fisher explained how he'd challenged the uniformed officer at the entrance to the crime scene and his subsequent reassurance of the man's authenticity.

But Nightingale wasn't easily deterred.

'What if it's him then? He turns up to fit their smoke detectors then garrotes them.'

A frown tugged at the scar tissue on Fisher's brow.

'There were no appointments to have fire alarms fitted on the days the victims died other than Mrs French and her appointment was hours after she'd been killed. And you just said one of them didn't have an appointment to have one fitted. Which one was it, by the way?'

'Connie Lloyd. Maybe she had an appointment but didn't write it down.'

'It's possible but it doesn't exactly fit our killer's profile. We know he's a clever little shit; how likely is he to make an appointment for something, turn up early, kill the victim, then leave the calendar there for all the world to see?' Fisher started to stroke the top of Luna's head. 'Mind you, I have to admit, it is something of a coincidence — three of them being due to have an alarm fitted. And you know I don't like coincidences. Also, everyone trusts a fireman. A damn sight more than they trust a policeman, that's for sure.' He froze. A frown crystallised on his brow. 'But why then would he turn up at Mrs French's when the place is crawling with police and CSIs?'

'Revisiting the scene?' Nightingale said.

'Hmm.' Fisher gave the question some thought. 'What if the killer isn't the fire officer, but someone who knew the victims were due to have a smoke detector fitted and turned up before the scheduled time? The fire service, or whoever does it, must have people booking the appointments as well as people fitting the alarms. Or maybe the work is divvied up across a team but they all get to see the whole schedule? Beth, find me the number for the fire service's main switchboard, will you please?'

Fifteen minutes later, Fisher slammed the phone handpiece down on its base.

'Honestly, I give up. Bloody Data Protection Act. We're trying to run a murder investigation here — *four* murder investigations — and they won't give us the information without a warrant because it would be a breach of data protection.'

'Oh,' Nightingale said, in a voice loaded with disappointment. Then, after a beat, added, 'I suppose though if they gave us the information and it turned out they shouldn't have, the evidence would be inadmissible anyway.'

'It's not evidence. It's just a list of names... a list of names we could investigate.'

'So let's get a warrant.'

'On what basis? We have no evidence the killer is a fire employee. No magistrate is going to give anyone a warrant based on what-ifs and maybes.' Fisher reached out a hand and hit the off switch on his computer. 'Come on. I'm done for today. I don't know about you but I could do with something to wash the frustration down with.'

The Pig and Pickle was a regular stop-off on the way to Fisher's. It was dog-friendly, plus there were plenty of quiet corners where they could discuss whatever aspect of a case was troubling them. Nightingale put their drinks and a couple of packets of crisps on the table and handed Fisher his change.

'Do you think Professor Woolf will be back in touch?' she asked after taking her seat.

Luna stirred at Fisher's feet.

'I don't know. I'd be surprised, given how the Falcon treated her.'

'And the fact that you upset her.'

'She was more disappointed than upset. To be honest, I don't understand what the fuss was about. I only suggested we use stereotypical traits of serial killers to narrow down the list of likely suspects.'

'What's wrong with that? She's never said they don't apply, only that it's not that black and white.'

'That's what I said. Sort of. Anyway, I'm sure she'll come round.'

'I hope so. I want to see what she does with her hair.'

'Her hair?'

'She's thinking about dyeing it. Said she wants to grow old disgracefully. She asked me what it's like being a redhead. I told her to go purple. Nobody looks twice at a ginger.'

'That's not true, is it?'

'As an adult it is. And when you're a kid it's the wrong sort of attention. I got a lot of stick at school.' She gave a light laugh. 'When I told the professor that, she said no one with any sense would think of bullying her.'

'I dare say, she's probably right.'

44.

An hour later, after being dropped off at home, Fisher followed Luna from the kerb to the front door, rewarding himself with a subtle fist pump on finding the keyhole at the first attempt. He pushed the door open and was about to step inside when a through-draught pulled the handle from his grip. The hairs on the back of his neck prickled. He wasn't in the habit of leaving windows open, so where was the draught coming from?

He tightened his grip on Luna's harness and felt her tail bang the side of his leg. He stood listening for a moment; from somewhere ahead came what sounded like men arguing. He took a step forward. And then another. The voices were louder now and underlaid by a monotonous, repetitive beat. Music? If you could call it that.

He walked slowly forward.

'Hello!?'

No reply.

After a few more steps, he tried again, 'Hello! Anyone there?'

The front door slammed shut behind him, causing him to jump and Luna to scurry into the kitchen. With his heart hammering in his chest, he felt for the wall and started after her. The music grew steadily louder. On entering the kitchen, the rectangle of patchy light he saw told him the back door was open.

He crossed the room and, holding on to the door jamb, stepped outside.

'Hello!' he yelled.

The music stopped.

'Dad!'

'Christ, Josh! You gave me a fright.' Fisher felt his adrenalin level begin to subside. 'What are you doing here?'

'We arranged it weeks ago. You forgot again?' His words took Fisher's breath from him like a knife to the chest.

'I've been a bit busy.'

'You haven't got to work tonight, have you?'

'No. Not tonight.' Fisher gave a tight smile; he really could have done with having some time to think through the latest developments. 'Besides, we need to talk.'

'Oh, yeah, about that...'

Fisher stepped out onto the patio. He crossed to the table and pulled out a chair.

'Want to tell me what happened?'

'We were just joking around. One of the sixth-formers was having a party. My mate Ben's brother said it was okay if I went with them.'

'And since when does Ben's brother call the shots where you're concerned?'

'I don't see what the problem is. It was just a stupid party. Nothing happened.'

'The photos didn't look that innocent by all accounts.'

'Mum would say that. You know what she's like.' He gave a giggle. 'The guys at school reckon you're awesome, convincing mum that I'd photoshopped it. I still can't believe she thought I'd fake it to look cool.'

'Is that what you thought you were being... cool?'

'Well, I...'

'How much did you have to drink?'

'Not much...'

241

'How much?'

'A couple of beers. Everyone was drinking.'

'And were they all fourteen?'

'I'm nearly fifteen.'

'And the legal age for alcohol is eighteen, so drop the back-chat.'

'I bet you used to drink when you were my age.'

'When I was your age I was too busy playing football to have time for parties. I thought you were getting into your sport. That's what your mum told me.'

'Relax Dad, it was only one party. It's not like I do it every weekend. I still plan on being a footballer. Anyway, Ben's brother says footballers are always out partying with really banging chicks.'

Fisher clenched his jaw. Forcing himself to be calm, he asked, 'Does Ben's brother know any footballers?'

'Dunno. I don't think so.'

'Well, I do and I'll tell you now, they don't spend their weekends partying. They're either playing or training. So I suggest you stop listening to Ben's brother and knuckle down with your training.'

'I bet they do if they're really good.'

'Argue it all you like son, your partying days are over. At least until you're eighteen. By then, hopefully, you'll have more sense.'

'I've got sense.'

'The photos beg to differ. If your mother knew they were genuine, you'd be grounded.'

'Yeah, well at least then I wouldn't have to sit here being lectured by you.'

Fisher opened his mouth, about to launch a full parent-powered retort when the music — some American homie stuttering out an irate rap to a thumping bass — resumed, only three times louder than before.

Fisher stood up and whistled Luna over. He grabbed her harness and started to make his way back into the kitchen. Pausing, he said over his shoulder, 'And you can turn that racket down. I might be blind but there's nothing wrong with my ears.' He waited. The music continued to thud. 'Josh, you're skating on thin ice,' he said, in a cold, steely voice. The volume halved. 'Thank you. Dinner's in half an hour.'

Josh spent the rest of the evening sulking. Hormones, Fisher thought, doing his best to ignore it, though not without a degree of sadness, as he wondered whether it marked the end of his son's unquestioning adoration.

By morning, some of the old Josh had resurfaced as he chatted about school and his impending exams over a bowl of coco pops. Fisher and Nightingale dropped him off at the school gates.

After Josh had climbed out of the car, slamming the door shut behind him, Fisher said, 'Wait a sec… I want to see what he does. Can you still see him?'

'Yes. He's just joined a group of lads.'

'His age?'

'I'd say so, yes.'

'What are they doing?'

'Just being lads. Looks like he's popular with his mates. They're walking away now.'

Fisher wondered what he'd been expecting. Was Josh really any different to other boys his age?

'Did you ever make out you were something you weren't?' he asked. 'At school, I mean.'

'Are you kidding? All the time.'

'You did?'

243

'How many gays do you think are comfortable being themselves at fourteen or fifteen? Or sixteen or seventeen, for that matter. Even if I hadn't been gay, I probably would have still put up some sort of front. You have to, to fit in, don't you?'

Fisher let his head rest against the cold window.

At Josh's age, he'd been so obsessed with kicking a ball around, he never had time to worry about what people thought of him. Or perhaps it was because people had told him how good he was at kicking a ball around, he hadn't needed to worry. Either way, he'd never had to pretend to be something he wasn't. It pained him that Josh felt the need to.

'By the way,' Nightingale said, as they stop-started through the school drop-off zone. 'I don't know if I mentioned it, but I called Warren Newman yesterday, to see whether Connie Lloyd had a smoke detector. He wasn't in, but I left a message. He returned my call last night. He said she definitely had. He knows because he helped change the battery in it once.'

When, after a minute, Fisher hadn't commented, she said, 'Did you hear what I said? Warren Newman—'

'I heard. What do you want me to say? Another dead end. Why am I not surprised?'

45.

As they entered the office, Nightingale let out a surprised, 'Oh!' Then, in a whisper, said, 'Professor Woolf's sitting by your desk.'

Fisher smiled and was about to instruct Luna to lead him to his seat when he heard a door click open and DCI Fallon said, with enough vinegar in her tone to supply the whole of Harry Ramsden's, 'Fisher, my office. Now.'

'Coming, ma'am. Beth, do me a favour, go keep the professor amused till the DCI's finished with me.'

Steeling himself, he instructed Luna to lead him into the dragon's den.

'Shall I sit down or is this going to be a quick bollocking?' he asked after closing the door. Just then someone cleared their throat and it wasn't the Falcon. 'Sorry. I didn't realise you had company, ma'am.'

'Just take a seat, will you.'

He settled Luna at his feet, then waited.

'I've got DCI Jack Whitlow with me, from the Met. Jack recently wrote an article for Policing Today on the profiling of serial killers. I thought it might help to tap into his extensive knowledge.'

'Anita, you flatter me,' DCI Whitlow said in a smooth baritone that oozed smugness. 'But I'll certainly do what I can to help.'

Fisher had, on occasion, read the magazine before being robbed of his sight. It was an easy read, coffee-break type of publication, full of sometimes amusing, sometimes tragic, true-life stories interspersed with dumbed-down articles on the latest changes to legislation likely to affect the police service. He didn't recall it being renowned for its ground-breaking articles.

'You've had some dealing with serial killers then? On the job, I mean.'

'I've read extensively on the topic. Articles on cases ranging from—'

'Yes, but actual experience...?'

'Jack has a whole world more experience than any academic,' Fallon interjected, making the word 'academic' sound like a vulgarity.

'It's okay, Anita,' Whitlow said. 'I'm happy to defend myself. I've long been a fan of true crime books and you can learn an awful lot from the internet.'

'The internet, huh? In which case, I'm not sure you're going to be able to help. Our guy doesn't exactly fit your typical serial killer mould, which is why—'

'I beg to differ,' Whitlow interrupted. 'From what your DCI has told me, it all sounds very run-of-the-mill... as far as serial killers go.' He gave a strange put-on sort of laugh. 'In fact, I would say from the choice of victims and the method used, it's quite simple to construct a profile of your killer.'

'Really?' Fisher said, not disguising his disdain.

'Absolutely,' Whitlow's confidence was abundant and Fisher felt it bear down on him in the confines of the small room. 'From the evidence, I would say you are looking for a white middle-class man, between the ages of forty and sixty, who has recently been subjected to a humiliating or demeaning event. Perhaps he's been passed over for promotion or made redundant or his wife

246

has divorced him after many years. As a result, he's taking his anger and his feeling of loss of power out on these women. It's his way of regaining control.'

'And what do you make of the fact the bags were black and cash was taken in some cases and not others?'

'Trivial details. The bags are probably the type the perpetrator uses at home. As for the cash, he might have felt he was owed it. After the first few murders, it became inconsequential as he got more out of the actual act of killing.'

'If that was the case, wouldn't you expect to see some sort of escalation? The gap before the last victim was the longest of all of them.'

'Perhaps he'd intended on going to ground but couldn't help himself.'

Fisher ran it all through in his head. Easy answers. None of them very convincing. And they certainly didn't fit with Professor Woolf's analysis.

'And how do you think he picked his victims?' he asked.

'This is all about power — he needed someone he could control. Old women living alone fit the bill perfectly.'

'Connie Lloyd was hardly old. She was barely sixty. And besides, with the bag and the belt, the killer was guaranteed to overpower them.'

'Sixty is old, if you're a younger, fitter guy. Besides, I hadn't finished. The other reason he focussed on older women is that they represent his mother; a figure of authority. As I said earlier, I expect he's recently had some sort of run-in with authority, or a falling out with his wife, so is channelling his resentment onto older females.'

Fisher thought back to Professor Woolf's explanation of transference. Was it possible, given how different all of the women were?

'Okay, accepting he's got a penchant for older women, what made him choose the ones he did? There are thousands of older women who live alone, why those four?'

'Easy. He spotted them when he was out and about, then followed them home, to make sure they lived alone, before attacking them.'

'So he just hangs around town, or wherever, sees a woman he likes and that's it?'

'Exactly.'

'Given that most of them either drove or used transport services how could he have followed them?'

'He could be a taxi driver or work for whatever transport services the victims used. Have you thought about that, eh?' Whitlow sounded particularly pleased with himself at that one.

'Good point,' Fallon fawned. 'Have you?'

Fisher thought it time to pour some cold reality over the glowing embers of their enthusiasm and give them some actual facts.

'None of the victims lived anywhere near each other. Connie Lloyd had her own car. Em Walker used the complimentary mini-bus service to get to the over-60s club and I don't know about the others, but I don't recall anyone mentioning them travelling by taxi. Two of them rarely ventured out at all. Their daily routines bore no similarities.'

'I'm sorry Jack, I should have warned you,' Fallon said. 'DI Fisher has a knack of finding fault with every suggestion that's not his own.'

'That's okay Anita. Fisher, I can see what you're saying, but they would only need to have travelled by taxi once. Just think about it — everyone chats to taxi drivers. It would be simplicity itself for a cabbie to learn who lives alone and, more importantly, where they live.'

'I couldn't have said it better myself, Jack,' Fallon said. 'So, Fisher, now you know the type of man you're looking for and where to find him. No excuses.'

'As easy as that, eh?' Rising, Fisher seized Luna's harness and started for the door.

Fallon called after him, 'And Matt...' He paused. 'Now we've got the profile sorted, I don't expect to see Professor Woolf again. Got it?'

Fisher continued through the door, pulling it shut behind him, but not before he heard Fallon say, 'See what I was talking about? He's impossible.'

46.

Fisher crossed the floor towards his desk, shoulders slumped. As he drew close, he heard someone move.

Nightingale said, 'Sorry... I was just keeping it warm for you.'

He set out a hand, feeling for the back of his chair and sat down. With his hands resting on the desk in front of him, he huffed out a sigh.

'I am so fed up with dealing with fucking idiots.'

'What's happened?' Professor Woolf asked.

'The Falcon has outdone herself this time. She's only gone and found her own pet profiler.'

'What?' Woolf's voice was sharp with surprise. 'Who?'

'Don't worry. The guy wouldn't know a serial killer if they walked up and beat him to death with one of his so-called expert articles.'

'But who is he?'

'Some DCI from London. Wrote an article for a magazine once and now thinks he's an authority on the subject. He reckons our perp's a middle-aged white guy, probably a taxi driver, with a penchant for killing old ladies to relieve some little-man syndrome he got as a result of being fired, or demoted, or told off by his wife... take your pick.' Fisher shook his head.

'Talk about clichéd.' Woolf said. 'If that was true, then the killer would have exercised some control over them. He'd have wanted them scared and begging him to spare them. He certainly wouldn't be sticking a bag over their head — a black bag, at that — and killing them as swiftly as possible. I'm sorry but the guy hasn't got a clue.'

'You don't need to tell me that,' Fisher replied. 'But that's not the worst of it. The DCI is so convinced he's given us our answer, she wants us to go and start looking at the town's taxi drivers.'

'How are we supposed to know who's been sacked or made redundant or had a row with his wife?' Nightingale complained. 'A profile like that might help if we had a suspect but—'

'Or if it was remotely accurate,' Woolf interjected.

'That too,' Nightingale replied. 'It doesn't help us one bit, does it?'

'Oh, and Professor...' Fisher said. 'I've been told to let you know your services are no longer required.'

'What a surprise. I know her type. She's afraid I might show her up. And she's right to be worried. Unlike your killer, I'm no wolf in sheep's clothing... just a wolf. I'd eat her for breakfast.'

'That I'd like to see.' Fisher broke out a smile, which froze on his face. Something the professor had said...

'What is it?' Nightingale asked.

He raised a hand.

'Give me a minute. I need to think.' He brought his hands together in front of his face, as though in prayer, and thought through all of the possibilities. Eventually, he lowered his hands. 'Your comment, wolf in sheep's clothing... it's funny, over the last few days, there have been several references to folk pretending to be something they're not. What if that's what the killer is doing? I don't mean pretending to be someone else in order to get into the victims' homes — I'm sure, they're doing that as well — I mean, what if the whole serial killer thing is a sham? And before anyone gets all pedantic and points out that technically anyone who kills more than three people is a serial

251

killer, I realise that. What I mean is, what if some of the murders were only committed to cover up one murder in particular?'

'Sounds like something out of a film,' Nightingale said.

'But so much of it does though, doesn't it?' Fisher replied. 'It's as though the killer has taken everything they've seen in countless true crime documentaries and TV detective dramas and put it all together for us, the hapless police, to ponder what it all means. When, in reality, it means nothing.'

'I'm not sure,' Woolf said, her American accent sharpening. 'If that was the case, I'd expect to see some sort of symbolism in play. Most TV and film portrayals of serial killers either paint them as demonic geniuses who leave cryptic clues in their wake or deranged, psychotic sadists who inflict all manner of violence on their victims before leaving them like a piece of butchered meat. These cases have none of those hallmarks.'

'Maybe our killer isn't smart enough to devise cryptic clues,' Fisher responded. 'And the fact they're not a sadistic killer could account for why they used black bags... because they haven't really got the stomach for killing. By blanking out the faces of his victims doesn't it somehow sanitise the act of murder?' Just then another thought occurred to him and he added excitedly, 'What if Em Walker was initially the only intended victim? The killer took a few bits of jewellery and some cash, hoping to make it look like an opportunist robbery. Then, having found it pretty easy, thought they'd get rid of another problem in the same way. Goodbye Connie Lloyd. The last two victims were red herrings, to make it look like the work of a serial killer and steer the investigation in the wrong direction.'

'You're thinking of Mr Hunt,' Woolf said.

'It could explain why Mrs Choudhury was next. Her grandson knows Hunt's son. Perhaps Hunt had met her before, or heard her grandson talk about her, and knew she lived alone.'

'If that's true, he must be pretty stupid,' Woolf said. 'And I didn't get the impression that was the case.'

'Why must he be?' Fisher asked.

'With such obvious motives you were bound to suspect him.'

'Maybe he thought no one would link him to Mrs Walker.' When Woolf and Nightingale didn't reply, he said, 'Come on folks, cut me some slack.'

'You're right in that the presentation of the crime scene doesn't exactly fit the psychology of your typical serial killer and as I'm always telling my students, the ones that get away with it aren't typical,' Woolf conceded. 'But what I am struggling with is the idea of someone killing four women in order to cover up the murder of one of them. If the killer is as clever as they seem then surely they could have found a better way of despatching their intended victim without any unnecessary loss of life. I mean, accidents happen all the time.'

'Maybe he's a sociopath and doesn't see killing elderly ladies as that big a deal if it gives him what he wants,' Fisher replied.

'What could anyone want so badly?' Nightingale asked. 'You don't kill someone just to keep your kid on a football programme.'

'Look — I don't have all the answers,' Fisher said, trying not to sound desperate. 'I only came up with the idea five minutes ago. Seeing as we keep going round in circles, I thought it was worth thinking outside the box.'

'Of course, you're right,' Woolf said. 'It always pays to keep an open mind. Though I think you might have a job telling that to your boss lady. I imagine she'll implode when you explain your new theory to her.'

Fisher sensed Nightingale turn in her seat.

'Talking of which…' she said, 'the DCI's just opened the door to her office. She's looking over and she doesn't look happy.'

253

47.

With no intention of sending Professor Woolf packing, Fisher reconvened the meeting at his house, inviting Wickham to join them. Mercifully, DCI Fallon had already left for a management meeting with the top brass and wasn't around when they started bagging up case files and ferrying them out of the office.

'It sounds a bit far-fetched if you ask me,' Wickham said, after Fisher had explained his latest thinking.

'I don't see what the big deal is. All I'm saying is, we might not be looking for a serial killer. So instead of going down a load of blind alleys — no pun intended — looking for some middle-aged taxi driver with an authority complex, we take another look at the victims' friends and family.'

'I suppose we've got nothing to lose,' Wickham said, grudgingly.

'Good.' Fisher clapped his hands together. 'Em Walker then. Shall we park Lewis Hunt for now? I think we've done him to death. Let's start with Hugh Cowden.'

'Which one's he again?' Woolf asked.

'The chairman of the academy.'

'What would be his motive?'

'Maybe Mrs Walker didn't like the way he was running things, like letting Lewis Hunt buy his son a place on the top squad.'

'Did she have any say in how the trust was run since she stepped down from the board?'

'Good question. I don't know is the answer. I imagine she could have made life difficult for him. Plus, with her dead, there'd be the added incentive of knowing her inheritance would seal the future of the academy for years to come.'

'Assuming he knew about her will,' Nightingale said.

'I can check that out, if you like,' Wickham said. 'My original contact at the academy isn't a fan of Cowden. If there's any dirt to dish, I reckon she'd be more than happy to oblige.'

'Just tread carefully,' Fisher cautioned. 'I get the impression Cowden's the sort to complain directly to the police commissioner.'

'Will do.'

'Moving on then,' Fisher said. 'What do we think about the neighbour? The one Mrs Walker fell out with about the plant at the end of the garden.'

'Neighbourly disputes, especially boundary issues, can be incredibly emotive,' Woolf replied. 'Though, that said, they're more likely to give rise to sudden outbursts of violence rather than a cleverly concocted murder.'

Fisher gave a nod.

'I agree. Beth, make a note of what the professor just said. Okay, anyone got any other suggestions or shall we move on to Connie Lloyd?'

Nightingale ran through what they knew of Ms Lloyd. Fisher could almost recite the details of her ex-husband's motive for wanting her dead and those of the claim being lodged against the fraudster who had left her virtually penniless. But instead, he sat quietly, listening to it all again, in the hope that it would reveal something new; some little gem of a fact that they could use in their armoury against Hunt.

It didn't.

'So unless this financial advisor is charged and made to recompense his victims, Connie Lloyd had virtually no assets to leave, is that right?' Woolf said, once all of the details had been gone through.

'Pretty much,' Nightingale replied.

'That rules the fiancé out then,' Wickham said.

'Not necessarily,' Fisher said. 'Money might not be the motive.'

'Can I have a look at his file?' Woolf asked. Fisher heard the sound of a folder being slid across the table top.

'I haven't met him,' Wickham said. 'What's he like?'

'Normal sort of bloke,' Fisher replied. 'Owns a big second-hand car place on the other side of town. They hadn't been seeing each other long… four, five months. They met at the hospital where he's having chemo.'

'Her death appears to have hit him quite hard,' Nightingale added.

'Appearances can be deceptive,' Woolf said.

'You say money might not be the motive, but what other reason would he want her dead?' Wickham asked.

Fisher went to answer, but was beaten to it by the professor.

'I can dream up a whole bunch of possible reasons,' Woolf replied. 'He could have discovered she was only marrying him for his money; or because she felt sorry for him, because of his cancer; or maybe he found her being a little too friendly with his son—'

'I don't think—' Nightingale started.

But Woolf wasn't to be deterred. 'I'm not saying that is the case, only… well, these things happen.'

'All I was going to say is that everyone we've spoken to has said what a lovely person Connie Lloyd was, always putting other people first. I personally don't think she'd have done any of those things,' Nightingale asserted.

'I don't mean to tell you how to do your job,' Woolf replied, 'but you've only had third-person accounts of the victims. How well did those people really know her?' After a beat, she added, 'Actually, I've just thought of another reason he might have wanted her dead.'

'Let's hear it,' Fisher said.

'Mr Newman comes across as very old school. I imagine he has some rather old-fashioned ideas about how a marriage should work. In contrast, the victim had spent years living on her own and would have been used to doing things for herself. That could have easily created some tension between them, especially if Connie wasn't as biddable as Newman would have liked.'

'Mmm... I'm not sure,' Fisher said. 'But it doesn't hurt to leave him on the table. For now, at least.'

After a brief discussion around other potential suspects for Ms Lloyd's murder, including her good friend, Mrs Keeley — who they all agreed they'd like to rule out but felt unable to, given she had means, motive and opportunity, in theory, at least — they moved on to Mrs Choudhury.

Nightingale outlined what they knew of the third victim, including the fact that her only son and heir had a watertight alibi for two of the murders.

'So that rules him out, right?' Nightingale said.

'Unless he had an accomplice?' Wickham countered.

Nightingale came back with, 'What would be his motive?'

'Money... he inherits the house and a reasonable amount of savings. His son got into the academy on a means-tested scholarship, don't forget.'

'Plus, his mother would have been an increasing burden, given her dementia,' Woolf chimed.

'I didn't get the impression he needed her money or saw her as a burden,' Nightingale said. 'I think he was genuinely worried about his mother's state of health. If he didn't care, he wouldn't have been going around there every other day. I'm really not sure—'

'It doesn't matter, Beth,' Fisher jumped in. 'The fact he has an alibi for two of the murders puts him at the bottom of our list. Given no one else appears to gain from her death, if my theory is right, Mrs Choudhury was killed to distract us from the real target.'

It was Woolf's turn to give a thoughtful, 'Hmm…' then, she said, '*If* — and I stress *if* — three of the murders were simply a red herring, then I agree. Mrs Choudhury is unlikely to be the original intended victim. The person behind this would most likely be someone who isn't a born killer. Psychologically speaking, the prospect of having to get away with two or three murders before you actually kill the one person you're desperate to see dead would be too much for most people. They wouldn't want to run the risk of being caught or having to stop before they achieved their goal. It makes sense for the real target to have been one of the first two victims.'

'I hear what you're saying, Professor,' Fisher replied. 'But for the sake of completeness, we need to look at all of the victims. Beth, could you tell us about Mrs French, please?'

Nightingale proceeded to recount the scant information they had on the fourth victim; an eighty-five-year-old widow who lived alone, looked after by a trio of home carers ever since the death of her husband some eight years ago. Although the couple had a son, William had sadly died of a heart attack two years earlier, aged fifty-five.

'You mentioned the medic-alert bracelet she usually wore was missing,' Woolf said. 'What condition did she have?'

Nightingale flicked through the file.

'Deep vein thrombosis. She was on warfarin.'

'Sounds like the killer did her a favour,' Woolf said, drily.

'What?' Nightingale sounded horrified.

'I'm thinking of it from the killer's point of view,' the professor replied. 'But her condition does fit with the idea that she wasn't the main target. It would have been easy enough to engineer an overdose of her medication and make her death look like an accident, without needing to resort to killing the others.'

'Good point,' Fisher said. 'So, that's the lot. I'm not sure we're any better off than we were when we started. I suppose we have managed to—'

'Sorry to interrupt,' Wickham said. 'You've missed a file.'

Fisher's scarred brow pulled into a frown.

'That's not related,' Nightingale said. 'I brought it by accident.'

'Which file is it?' Fisher asked.

'Jim Hatton's.'

'Who's he?' Wickham asked.

'He was the choirmaster-cum-guitar teacher murdered six years ago, who may or may not have been abusing boys. Early on we thought it might have been connected, seeing as the MO was similar.'

'And it's definitely not related?' Wickham asked.

'He doesn't fit the victim profile,' Fisher replied. 'Plus, it was six years ago and the killer attempted to cover it up, made it look like auto-erotic asphyxiation gone wrong.'

'Still... similar MO,' Wickham mused. 'What if our killer offed Hatton, then years later, someone else is making their life a misery. They got away with it once, why not do the same again? Warren Newman has a son. Do we know whether he was ever in a choir?'

'When Hatton died, Newman's son would have been in his twenties,' Woolf pointed out. 'The two are obviously unrelated.'

'Says you,' Wickham said more sharply than was warranted. 'Our job is to consider every angle, regardless of how unlikely.'

'You either want my expertise or you don't,' Woolf said, sounding like she couldn't care less.

'Let's not argue,' Fisher said. 'Andy, you're right. In these sessions nothing's off the table. But in this instance I think the professor is right. Rob Newman would have been too old when Hatton was killed.' He set his hands on his lap. 'Well, there we are. I think there are a number of things to take away from tonight. Andy, first thing tomorrow I want you to find out what you can about what's-his-name the chairman.'

'Hugh Cowden. I'll get straight onto it.'

'Beth, if you pick me up at, say, half-seven, we can go straight over to see Lewis Hunt. If he still doesn't want to give us his alibi, we'll take him in. I'm fed up with being messed around. And Professor, all that leaves me with is to say thank you for your assistance and I hope you won't consider me too discourteous if I say I hope we never have to call upon your services again.'

48.

On a quiet residential street in a leafy suburb, a white transit van sat innocuously amongst a long line of parked cars. Inside the van, a man pulled the zip on his fleece up to his chin. A thick blanket of cloud muffled the dawn's light and brought an unwelcome chill to the air. He rubbed his hands together and rolled his shoulders, setting off a volley of clicks and creaks in joints frozen stiff. Although a better choice of vehicle for surveillance than the black hatchback, once the engine was off the van's interior was about as comfortable as a shop doorway.

The dashboard clock showed 07:40.

He'd been there for almost an hour, eyes trained on the large Georgian villa on the opposite side of the road, some hundred metres away, waiting for the first stirrings of life.

A dog walker came striding down the road, a Labrador bouncing at his heel. Inside the van, the man reached for the clipboard on the passenger seat and made a show of consulting it; though he needn't have worried — the dog walker and his canine companion continued past without so much as a glance. Posing as a delivery driver was as good as a cloak of invisibility these days.

His gaze slid back to the house. In those few seconds he'd looked away, the upstairs curtains had opened. Two minutes later, an invisible hand flung open the downstairs ones too.

Another twenty-five minutes passed with no further action. And then he got what he was waiting for.

A dark blue BMW coupé slowed, then pulled up in front of the drive. The horn beeped twice. The front door swung open and a shortish man with a rounded belly and salt and pepper hair, sporting a pair of smart jeans and navy polo shirt, emerged. He pulled the door closed behind him, crossed to the car and climbed in. Moments later, the BMW disappeared in the direction it had come from.

The street was quiet once more.

Flinging the clipboard back onto the passenger seat, he slipped the car into gear and drove away. At the next junction he turned the van around and retraced his route, and came to a stop directly outside the house he'd been watching. He made his way to the back of the van and retrieved a box wrapped in brown paper. Slipping the parcel under his arm, he trotted up to the front door and rang the bell. The trill-ring echoed around the empty house. He rang the bell a second time then stepped back, making a play of looking at the windows. After darting a glance back to the road to check the coast was clear, he hurried around to the side of the house, dodging behind a large laurel bush that screened a pair of wheeled bins and a wooden gate leading to the rear of the property. A quick test of the gate's latch showed it to be locked. Wasting no time, he pitched the parcel over the fence into the garden, clambered onto a bin and followed it over. Landing lightly on his feet, he stepped over the parcel and began his appraisal of the entry points. A sturdy u-PVC door on the side of the property was do-able, but would take time. Instead, he made straight for a pair of wooden-framed patio doors. Noting the doors' cheap eurocylinder lock, a trace of a smile crossed his lips.

He reached into a pocket, pulled out a pair of latex gloves and slipped them on. Next, out came his lock pick set. He quickly selected the appropriate pick and set to work. Fifty seconds later, the doors stood open.

He set a black crepe-soled shoe over the threshold, stepping noiselessly onto the beige carpet. The room was dominated by a long mahogany dining table, its surface dull with dust. On the left-hand wall, a matching sideboard housed a collection of framed photographs. He stood for a moment, eyes roaming from picture to picture. Then, moving quickly, he opened the drawers and cupboards and scanned their contents. Finding nothing of interest, he moved on to the kitchen and repeated the exercise. In one cupboard, a cache of black plastic bin bags sat alongside a basket of cleaning products. He made a mental note and moved on to the lounge, a blandly decorated room furnished with a large three-piece suite in brown velour and teak coffee table. A small unit, also teak, housed an over-sized TV, a DVD player and a handful of discs, mostly old films. Across the hallway there was a small study into which had been squeezed a scarred but substantial oak desk, bolstered on either side by a pair of battered filing cabinets. A laptop lay open on the desk, half-obscured under a pile of paperwork. He quickly riffled through the papers, then started on the drawers. Dismissing their contents, most of which related to the homeowner's business affairs, he climbed the stairs and continued his search on the first floor.

Of the four bedrooms, two were furnished. The smaller of the two had clearly once been a boy's domain. Remnants of old posters — a decade-old mix of female pop stars and F1 drivers with their cars — still adorned the blue painted walls. A single bed, a tall wardrobe in white melamine and matching bedside cabinet all yielded nothing.

He moved on to the only bedroom currently in use.

A double bed had its head against the far wall, looking sadly lost in the generously proportioned room. He checked the contents of the wardrobe and chest of drawers before moving on to the two bedside cupboards. No surprises. No secrets. Nothing untoward. He dropped to his knees and checked under the bed, before casting his eye over the contents of the small en suite bathroom. Back on the landing, a noise outside caused him to stall. He crept stealthily over to the window, pressed himself against the wall and peered out from behind the curtains. A uniformed police officer, a young chubby guy with ruddy cheeks, stood on the drive. Next to him, an older man with a ring of grey hair around a largely bald head was saying something and pointing towards the bins. At that moment, the front door bell's shrill ring resonated through the house.

'Hello...?' A woman called through the letter box flap. 'Anyone home? Mr Newman...?'

He felt his heart rate climb and took a couple of calming breaths. Shortly the flap issued a squeak as it dropped closed. He moved to the front bedroom and chanced a look through the window. A second uniformed officer, a tall, slim woman with long dark hair, was walking from the direction of the front door, shaking her head. The old man spoke and pointed to the bins again. The female PC walked towards the gate and out of sight.

He eased away from the curtains and crept to the top of the stairs. Approaching the landing window at a crouch, he watched the PC set a foot against the bottom of the gate. She hauled herself up and peered into the garden at the paper-wrapped parcel lying on the grass, before lowering herself back down and joining the two men. After a few shared words and shaken heads, she and her colleague drove away. The old man shot a last worried look at the house then crossed the road and disappeared into the property opposite.

He backed away from the window. By rights he ought to get the hell out of there. The neighbour was probably calling the homeowner's mobile at that very moment. He glanced up at the ceiling, to the small hatch looming above him. The loft was the only place left. He raised a hand and pushed. The door clicked then dropped down to hang from its hinges, exposing an extendable ladder. A minute later, he was stooped in the dark, cramped space, staring at an artificial Christmas tree and collection of boxes with the words XMAS DECS written in a neat hand on their sides. A thick layer of dust lay undisturbed on their surfaces.

Confident that no one had been in the loft for some time, he called time on his search and exited the loft, closing the hatch behind him. Returning downstairs, he left the house by the French doors, locking them with the same technique he'd used to gain access. Hurrying across the lawn, he scooped up the brown paper parcel as he passed and dropped it over the gate before following it over. Taking cover behind the laurel bush, he pulled out his mobile, slipped in a pay-as-you-go sim and looked up the number for the house opposite in White Pages. He hit dial and waited.

He pictured the old man hearing the phone ring; imagined him making his way into the hallway, to where an old-fashioned handset sat on a small shelf or console table, next to an outdated phone book.

And then a man's clipped voice rang out, rousing him from his reverie.

He ended the call to a backdrop of repeated hellos, tucked the parcel under his arm and jogged down the drive to the roadside, where he climbed into the van and drove off.

49.

Lewis Hunt opened the door and groaned.

'What now?'

Fisher flashed him a tight smile.

'Mr Hunt. I'm so pleased we found you at home. If you wouldn't mind, we'd like you to accompany us to the station. We have some unfinished business.'

'Actually I do mind. Are you arresting me?'

'Not at this stage. We would prefer it to be a voluntary interview. However, if you refuse, then we'll have no choice.'

'If you'd like to get your coat…' Nightingale said.

'I don't know what you're up to, but your bully-boy tactics don't wash with me.'

'Fine.' Fisher shrugged. 'We can talk here. Perhaps your wife would like to join us for the conversation about where you were the evening your ex-wife was murdered?'

With perfect timing, somewhere inside a door clicked open and footsteps approached.

'Lewis, what's going on? Why are the police here again?'

'Good morning, Mrs Hunt. I was just explaining to your husband—'

'It's alright love. I won't be long.'

'Are they arresting you?'

'No. Routine questioning. That's right, isn't it, Inspector?'

'Absolutely.'

'I should be back in no time.'

'Depends on how satisfactory the answers to our questions are,' Fisher muttered as they escorted Hunt out of the door.

At the station, they found a free interview room, set the equipment to record, and once again asked the property developer to explain his whereabouts the evening Connie Lloyd was murdered.

'And please don't say in a business meeting,' Fisher said. 'I shouldn't need to remind you that we're investigating four murders for which you have no alibi.'

'What are you talking about? You know I was at home being stalked by some nutter when one of them happened. I reported it. You came out to the house.'

'Your wife told us she retired to bed and was asleep before you returned from looking for this so-called intruder. Who's to say you weren't out longer than you claim?'

'What? This is ridiculous.'

'Just tell us where you were and who you were with when your ex-wife died and you're in the clear,' Fisher pressed.

'I've already told you I'm not prepared to have my reputation ruined simply because you can't do your job and find who did it.'

'What will happen to your reputation if we arrest you?'

'You do that, then when you find the real killer you'll be forced to issue an apology and I'll have a story to dine out on for years.'

'I don't mean to disillusion you, but it doesn't work that way. From where I'm sitting, you have means, motive and opportunity. More than enough to get a warrant to search your home and office. We'll turn them upside down looking for evidence to tie you to the murders. Do you really want to put your wife and son through all that?'

Fisher crossed his arms and leaned back in his chair, content to let the silence stretch.

Eventually, Hunt gave a pained sigh.

'Fine,' he said, spitting the word out. 'I was with a council officer discussing a planning application from three in the afternoon until nine that night.'

'And this officer's name?'

'Her name is...' He paused. 'Look, promise me you'll be discreet. Only contact her at work. You mustn't turn up at her home.'

'Why's that?' Fisher asked, though he had a pretty good idea.

'She's married.'

'So? I would have though most council officers are.'

'Yes, well, we held the, erm, meeting at her house. I'm not sure her husband would be too happy if he found out.'

'You met a planning officer in her home for a six-hour meeting that ran into the evening? Was anyone else there with you?'

'No.'

'Presumably her colleagues would be aware of such a meeting? Maybe she took minutes?'

'What? No!' Fisher could hear the panic in his voice. 'It was more of a private thing.'

'Like an extra-marital type of private thing?'

'Call it what you like. Look, will you be discreet or not?'

Fisher let Hunt sweat for a moment, then said, 'We'll do what we can.'

50.

He parked a little further down the street than he had that morning, away from prying eyes. He only hoped he hadn't missed the old man's return during the short time he'd been swapping the white transit for the small black hatchback. He slipped down in his seat — his black outfit merging with the upholstery — and settled in for the wait.

Five hours later, stiff from lack of movement, his eye was caught by an approaching car. Dark, wide and low, the BMW came into focus. It continued past and pulled onto the drive of the house he was now as familiar with on the inside as he was from the outside. He twisted his rear-view mirror and watched.

The passenger door flung open and the man with the salt and pepper hair climbed out. He started to walk towards the house, then stopped and looked back towards the road. There, scurrying across the tarmac, was the watchful neighbour, talking and pointing — mostly in the direction of the bins and gate. The older man returned to the car, opened the passenger door and said something. The driver climbed out: a young blond-haired man, dressed in tight trousers, light blue shirt and navy tie. All three walked out of sight.

He could imagine them looking for the brown paper parcel. They'd be looking a long time, seeing as he'd taken it with him. No point in risking leaving any incriminating forensic evidence behind.

Shortly, all three reappeared. They stood by the car and spent a few minutes conversing. Eventually, the neighbour started down the drive and ambled across the road, back to where he'd come from.

The man with salt and pepper hair muttered something to the younger man, before heading for the front door. The young guy climbed back into the car, his sprayed-on trousers straining at the seams, and set off, passing the small, black hatchback without a second look.

The man in the hatchback turned the key in the ignition, firing the engine into life, and set off after the BMW. Shortly, both vehicles could be seen travelling a discreet distance apart, heading towards Ashford. Skirting south of the town centre, they continued east, past a parade of shops and then, a little further on, a Tesco local, which sat half hidden behind a scrubby hedge on a small roundabout. The BMW crossed straight over, but then, unlike the majority of traffic, which kept ahead, it slowed and indicated right.

The black hatchback slowed, and pulled in behind.

After taking the turn, the Beemer continued for a few hundred metres then slowed, before turning onto a drive that led to a wide concrete apron fronting a large brick building. Four floor-to-ceiling red doors took up the full width of the building, above which were the words: Kent Fire and Rescue Service.

51.

'So that's him in the clear,' Nightingale said, after the council's planning manager confirmed Hunt's alibi.

Fisher was sitting, tapping his fingers on his desk, with a face like a sat-out sofa.

She went on, 'It doesn't leave many suspects, does it? Not if we limit it to the victims' friends and family.'

'No.' He shook his head and blew out a sigh. 'But if it wasn't them, then we're back to it being a random psychopath. Which means we're back to the question, why those specific women and why did they let the killer into their homes?' After a beat, he said, 'Think about your nan. Who would she open the door to? More importantly, who would she actually let into the house?'

'She wouldn't let a doorstep collector in, that's for sure. Or a delivery man, especially not if she hadn't actually ordered anything. She'd probably let the gas or leccy man in, or someone else official-sounding, but only if they had ID.'

'Which can be forged.'

'True,' Nightingale said, sounding despondent. Then, more eagerly, 'Do you remember, at Ms Lloyd's place there were two mugs on the kitchen work top and a kettle full of water. What if she thought the killer would be there long enough to warrant offering them a cup of tea? Like the leccy man come to fit a new smart meter.'

'Or she knew him. Which would fit, if she was the intended victim.'

'If that's the case and it's not Lewis Hunt, then how did the killer choose the others, given they didn't have anything in common with each other?'

Fisher felt a surge of excitement.

'But they have.'

'They were getting a smoke detector!' they said in unison.

Fisher continued, 'All of the appointments were *after* the women were murdered. That would explain why Mrs Choudhury's calendar was found next to her. She was pointing out that they'd got the wrong day. Which brings us back to who would want Connie Lloyd dead, other than the people we've already ruled out?'

'What about a jealous ex-boyfriend who heard she was getting married?'

'Didn't her friend say she'd been on her own a long time?'

Nightingale heaved out a sigh. 'I don't know then.' A second later she said in a whisper, 'The DCI's just walked in. She's going to want to know how we're getting on looking for that taxi driver.'

'You mean the white, middle-aged, male taxi driver with a grudge against women who happened to have driven all four victims recently?'

'It's not funny. She'll have you for insubordination if you don't do it.'

'Who says I'm not doing it?'

'Matt, I'm serious.' He could hear the worry in her voice.

'It's alright. I'm not a total idiot. I've got Kami working on it. So, anyway, back to these smoke detectors. Remember the firefighter who turned up at Mrs French's? The uniform guarding the door didn't check his ID but did say he was driving what looked like a kosher fire brigade van.'

'I could call the fire brigade, find out if he was legit?' Nightingale offered.

'You could but what would that tell us? What's to say he didn't turn up earlier than scheduled to kill Mrs French and then came back later? He could have been there legitimately when we saw him.'

'What if he shouldn't have been there at all? If I call them, I could also ask whether the same person was due to fit the detectors for the other women.'

While Nightingale went off to make the call, Wickham approached Fisher.

'Cowden's a no go,' he said, taking a seat. 'He's got a stone-bonker alibi for when Mrs French was killed.'

'He told us he'd been at home on his own all morning.'

'He'd been test-driving a new car. He'd forgotten. I checked with the garage. He's in the clear.'

'It might not matter now.' He filled Wickham in on his and Nightingale's latest thinking.

'What about the night Connie Lloyd was killed? Is there any wriggle room with the timing? Could Hunt have done it after leaving the planning officer?'

'I wish, but no. He wouldn't have had enough time. His wife is adamant he got home at 9:15.' Wickham slumped back in his seat, causing Luna to stir. Fisher reached down and tousled the top of her head. 'It's alright. He didn't mean to make you jump.' Just then his mobile began to ring.

'I'll be at my desk if you need me,' Wickham said, rising from his seat.

Fisher touched the screen and listened as the robotic voice announced it was Amanda calling. He hit answer.

'Hi. Everything alright?'

'I'm alright. I'm not sure about Josh.'

'Oh?'

'I need you to talk to him. All he does is shut himself in his room, listening to some God-awful American rap rubbish that's all about guns and girls and drugs. On top of which, he's started to hang around with a group of boys who are considerably older than he is. I'm worried they're a bad influence. I've tried talking to him but I may as well be talking to the wall.'

'You're clearly not dope enough.'

'What?'

'Dope, you know, means you've got street cred.'

'Matt! This isn't funny.'

'Sorry. Of course I'll talk to him. At least, I'll try. I'm not sure he listens to me any more than he does you. I'm only an old has-been footballer. Is he there now or do you want me to come over?'

'I thought you could do it when you see him tonight.'

Fisher stiffened. Had he forgotten again? He recalled the last conversation he'd had with Josh. He was sure they'd agreed next week.

'I'm not seeing him tonight. I've got a big case on. We agreed to a rain check.'

'You must be mistaken. He definitely said he's going to yours. He took an overnight bag to school with him this morning.'

'Give me a minute just to make sure. I'll call you straight back.'

Fisher rang off and navigated to his diary. After the last mix-up he'd put all their planned get-togethers into his mobile.

'The lying little…'

He called Amanda back.

'Hi. I checked and—'

'Good. Well, look, I've got to go. I'm running late. You'll have that chat with him then, yes?'

Naturally she'd assumed he'd got it wrong.

'I can have a chat with him when I see him next but it won't be tonight.'

'What?'

'It looks like he's pulled a fast one.'

'What do you mean?'

'I think he's taking advantage of the fact I cancelled. He's probably arranged to stay at a mate's. It's the only explanation I can think of.'

Amanda gave a groan.

'Why does he always do this when I'm up to my neck in it? Well can you meet him after school and talk to him at least? It's nearly three. I'm not sure I can get there in time.'

'What time does he finish?'

'Quarter past.'

'Quarter past three?' he blurted. 'Are you sure? That's early, isn't it?'

'If you ever paid any attention to your son's schooling, you wouldn't need to ask.'

'I pay his fees, isn't that enough? I recall someone saying how a private education would make him a more mature, well-rounded person. Doesn't seem to be working, does it?'

'He's a teenager, Matt. And can we save the argument until later? Will you pick him up or shall I call the Head and get her to hold him back until I can get there?'

'No. I'll do it. But you'll need to call the Head anyway. I'm not sure I'll be able to get there in time either.'

***

Josh banged and thumped as he got into the back seat. The dog gave a whimper.

'Josh! Stop making such a song and dance about it. And mind Luna.'

'I can't believe you and Mum did that to me, embarrassing me in front of all my friends.'

'Embarrassing you how?'

'Making me wait behind. Like a child.'

'The way you're acting now, sounds about right.'

Fisher heard Josh throw himself back in his seat; imagined him angrily crossing his arms and wearing a dirty scowl. He turned in his seat to face his son.

'I trusted you to do the right thing after last time. You've let me down badly. What were you thinking? How can me or your mum ever trust you again? You lied and you—'

'I didn't lie,' Josh said, his voice cracking halfway through.

'You told your mum you were coming to mine tonight.'

'I didn't lie to you though.' Now he sounded sulky.

'Me, your mum, it doesn't matter who. I didn't raise you to be a liar.'

'Raise me? You don't even live in the same house as me. And before that, when you were sick, it was like…' He stopped abruptly.

'Like what?'

'Doesn't matter.'

'Say it.'

But Josh stayed silent.

'Is this about Ben's brother? Is he putting you under pressure to do things? Because I know how hard it is when—'

'You don't know anything,' Josh said, his pitch reaching heights only a fourteen-year-old boy's could. 'I hate you. And I hate Mum. I wish you'd both die and then I'd be rich and could do what I wanted.'

The words hit Fisher like a slap.

'Beth, please start the car. We're taking Josh home... to his mum's.'

'What?' Josh croaked. 'I thought—'

'You thought we'd go back to mine, so you could play at slamming doors all night? Well, not this time. You owe your mum an apology and I don't think it can wait.'

52.

Fisher closed the door on his old marital home and let out a deep, sorrowful sigh. Ordinarily he'd have felt sorry for Josh having to deal with the tsunami of anger and disappointment directed at him from Amanda, but not this time. The boy needed some tough love before it was too late and his dalliance with the older, more streetwise teens led him to do something he'd regret.

'You okay?' Nightingale asked as he pulled on his seat belt.

'Me? Yeah. I'm fine. I can't say the same for Josh. He's going to be on a tight lead for the foreseeable.'

'Kids say some horrible things, don't they,' she said, as they pulled away. 'I'm not sure I want any. If, you know, I ever meet someone.'

'You get used to it.'

'I'm not sure I'd ever get used my kid wishing I was dead.'

'That old chestnut. He's been rolling that out since he was about seven, whenever he can't get his own way. The bit about being rich was new...' A frown gathered on Fisher's brow as an idea slowly formed. He shook his head. 'I can't believe we missed it. It's so bleeding obvious.'

'What is?'

'We've been looking for reasons someone wanted one of the victims dead, yeah? Connie Lloyd in particular. Well, think about it... who gains the most from her murder?'

'Lewis Hunt?'

'No. At worst Hunt might have had to make up for what he diddled her out of on their divorce, but he can afford it. He's loaded.'

'So's Warren Newman.'

'But his son isn't.'

'Rob Newman? What does he gain?'

'Think about it.'

'He didn't want his dad to remarry?'

'Yes, but not just because of any loyalty to his dead mother. It was all about the money. His father marrying meant there's a good chance he'd lose his inheritance. And you just said it yourself, Warren Newman is loaded. Six months ago, Rob Newman was in line for a hefty pay-out should his dad die. Something he might have reasonably expected to get sooner rather than later, given his dad's cancer diagnosis. Then, Daddy dearest comes home and says, "Meet your soon-to-be stepmother".'

'But to have killed all those other women…'

'If Connie Lloyd was the only victim, we would have soon figured it out. Plus, he's a young guy. The other victims were elderly and infirm. He probably thought he was doing them a favour.'

'Like the professor said.'

'In a way, I suppose. So, what do we know about him?'

'Nothing,' Nightingale replied, taking a corner without so much as tickling the brake. Fisher held onto the side of his seat as he swayed sideways.

'Not true. We know he's an only child and that he's married with a young daughter. As soon as we get back, I need you to run his details through the databases, and while you're at it, take a look on social media. I want to know everything there is about him. While you're doing that, I'll call his father. Find out whether or not—' Fisher's phone started to ring. He pulled it out of his pocket and hit answer. 'DI Fisher.'

'Detective, it's Warren Newman.'

Fisher twitched his eyebrows, causing an uncomfortable tightness to pinch his brow.

'Mr Newman. How can I help?'

'Someone broke into my house earlier today when I was at my chemotherapy session.'

'I'm sorry to hear that. Was much taken?'

'No. Nothing was. At least as far as I know.'

'Did they damage anything?'

'No. You can't even see how they got in. I only know because my neighbour saw the man who did it. He pretended to be a delivery driver. Brian, my neighbour, said he got in over the back gate.'

'He saw him climb the gate?'

'Not exactly. There's a big bush covers the gate. He saw him go around it and not come back.'

'I'm not sure what I can do about it now. It would have been helpful if Brian had called 999 at the time.'

'He did. A couple of uniformed officers came out. They looked through the downstairs window and the letter box but couldn't see anyone. There was a parcel on the other side of the gate so they figured it was just a delivery driver and left.'

'And you think it wasn't a delivery driver because…?'

'The parcel was gone when I got home. The burglar must have taken it with him.'

'I take it your neighbour didn't see him leave.'

'The intruder was clever enough to phone my neighbour on his home phone, drawing him away from the window long enough to make his escape.'

Fisher shook his head. Turning to Nightingale, he mouthed, 'You couldn't make this stuff up.' More loudly, he said to Warren Newman, 'How did he get his number?'

'Don't ask me. I thought you'd know that sort of thing.'

'I'm sorry, but I still don't understand. What is it you want me to do about it?'

'I figured you'd want to find who did it. It must be related to what happened to Connie,' Newman said, as though it was blindingly obvious.

'Or it was a burglar who high-tailed it after the police turned up.'

'You're forgetting nothing was taken.'

Fisher was about to point out that's what happens when burglars are interrupted, when it dawned on him that there was another reason someone might break in and not take anything. Maybe they should go over there, take a look around?

'Have you told your son about the intruder?'

'He was there when Brian came over and told me what happened.'

Fisher's hopes stalled. He parked his optimism briefly and asked, 'Was he with you all afternoon?'

'No. He left work early to pick me up from the hospital. What's that got to do with anything?'

'Where does your son work?'

'At the fire headquarters. Why?'

Fisher's heart thumped excitedly.

'Does he fit smoke detectors?'

'No. He's in the IT department.'

'No doubt where he'd be able to access records of who was due to have a smoke detector fitted,' Fisher said to Nightingale after ending the call with Newman. 'I can see him now, flashing his brigade badge, detector in one hand, tool box in the other, complete with plastic bag and electrical flex.' Fisher lifted his phone and began to dial.

Five minutes later, Fisher swayed in his seat as the car rolled round a bend.

'How would he know the women lived alone?' Nightingale asked as they raced to Rob Newman's home address.

'Maybe their system flags it up. Could be people living alone are deemed higher risk and have some sort of marker against them to denote they should be put at the top of the list. I dare say we'll find out in due course.'

53.

The indicator ticked down the seconds while they waited for a gap in the traffic. Fisher tightened his grip on the handle above the window as the car lurched to the right. He clung on for a few more gentle corners and then the car started to decelerate as Nightingale announced their arrival.

'Any cars on the drive?' Fisher asked.

'Just the one. A Corsa. Oh, looks like we're being watched; there's a kid's head poking through the curtains.'

They climbed out. Fisher opted to take his white stick, leaving Luna in the car with the window cranked open a couple of inches. He heard the front door open as they started down the drive.

A woman's voice called, 'Can I help you?'

'Mrs Newman?' Fisher replied.

'Yes.'

'DI Fisher and DC Nightingale.' He pulled out his warrant card. 'We were hoping to talk to your husband.'

'He's not here.'

'Do you know when he'll be back?'

'Any time now. In fact I thought you were him. He's lost his keys so I came to let him in.' After a short pause, she asked, 'What do you want him for?'

'We're investigating the murder of Ms Connie Lloyd. Is it okay if we come in and wait for him?'

'Of course. I'm Lisa. Rob's wife. It's so awful, what happened to Connie... and the others, of course.'

She led them through to the lounge, directing them to a large corner sofa. As Fisher sat down, he felt something sink into the cushion alongside him.

'Ava, come here and leave the man alone,' Lisa Newman chided.

Fisher felt a gentle pull on his white stick that was resting on his lap.

'What's this for?' asked the young girl.

'It's so I know where I'm going,' Fisher said. 'My eyes don't work anymore.'

'Does it see for you, like the video on Mummy and Daddy's phones?'

Fisher smiled.

'No. I have a guide dog who does that for me.'

'Is your dog in the car?' He felt the little girl clamber onto the back of the sofa, presumably to peer out of the window.

'Ava, come here. Now!'

But the little girl didn't budge.

'Do you know where my daddy is?'

'No. Perhaps your Mummy could give him a call?'

'I'll get my phone,' Lisa Newman said, taking the hint. Her footsteps padded across the carpet and out of the room. A moment later she returned. 'It's ringing... Oh, it's gone straight through to voicemail. Hi darling, it's me. I was just wondering what time you're going to be in. There are a couple of police... erm, detectives here. They want to...'

'Ask a few routine questions,' Fisher supplied.

'They just want to ask you some routine questions. Call me back as soon as you can.' The room fell quiet. Mrs Newman eventually broke the silence. 'I don't know what could be keeping him.'

'He's not normally this late?' Fisher asked.

'No. He had to take his dad to the hospital earlier. He was going to work late to make up the time, but even so… It's lucky I don't have to work tonight, otherwise I'd have needed to arrange for someone to take Ava. Mind you, that wouldn't have helped. Rob wouldn't have been able to get in, seeing as he hasn't got a key.'

'The keys that he's lost… does that include the one for his father's house?' Fisher asked, thinking about the so-called break-in.

'Yes. All of his keys were on the same fob, including his car key. It's a complete pain. He reckons they'll turn up, but what if they don't? I'll have to get the locks changed, which will mean taking a day off to wait for a locksmith. He seems to forget, I get less leave than he does.'

'What do you do?'

'I'm a clerk at the district council.'

'And you have to work nights, doing that?'

'I have to take minutes at evening meetings. It's only a few times a month but it's not something I can easily get out of.'

'I like it when mummy goes to work,' chirped the little girl. 'Daddy gives me crisps when I have to wait in the car.'

'No, he does not,' her mother quickly replied. 'He doesn't make her wait in the car.'

'He does too.'

'Ava, don't tell fibs. She's saying that in the hope I'll let her have some crisps.'

'I'm not fibbing,' Ava yelled back. 'I did have to wait. And he did give me crisps.'

'Ava, shush,' Mrs Newman said. 'Can I get either of you a drink?'

'I'm okay, thanks,' Nightingale said.

'I'd love a cup of tea,' Fisher replied. 'Milk, no sugar. Thank you.' He heard her start to walk away.

As soon as they were on their own, Nightingale said, 'Shouldn't we be finding out where Mr Newman works and head over there?'

'All in due course,' Fisher replied. More softly he said, 'Ava, why don't you tell me about the time your daddy gave you crisps while you waited in the car? I bet you were a good girl while he left you.'

'She just nodded,' Nightingale supplied.

'Where were you when he asked you to wait?'

'Outside a lady's house. She was very old.'

'Do you know the lady?'

'No.'

'How do you know she was old?'

'I saw her open the door.'

'Did your daddy say why he was seeing the lady?'

'I think he was buying mummy a present.'

'Why do you think that?'

'He said it was a surprise. Said I had to keep it a secret. Daddy's always giving Mummy surprises. Do you like surprises?'

'Only good ones.' Fisher turned towards Nightingale and said, 'Now we can leave. Could you go and tell Mrs Newman we won't be stopping after all. And find out what car her husband drives. Get a number plate if you can.' Fisher felt the sofa shift beneath him as Nightingale rose to her feet.

'We've got the bastard, Beth. I'm sure it's him,' he said, feeling a rush of adrenalin as they crossed to the car. 'Can you believe the audacity of the man? Leaving his four-year-old daughter in the car while he goes and garrotes some poor bloody woman.'

'It's his wife I feel sorry for. I think you could be right about the motive, though. It's a pretty big house, full of what looks to me like expensive furniture. Plus, a BMW M3 can't have come cheap, even if he leases it. I don't know how much they earn between them but I can't see them being able to afford it all.'

'Let's not prejudge,' Fisher said, rounding the bonnet to the passenger door. 'Appearances can be deceptive; besides, a lot of people are up to their ears in debt and don't resort to murder. That said, not everybody expects a substantial inheritance when their father dies. I dare say that might have influenced their spending decisions.'

As Nightingale started the car, Fisher arranged for a patrol unit to go to fire service headquarters with instructions to bring Rob Newman in for questioning. Ten minutes later, when they were a mere five minutes away from the station, Fisher's phone rang.

After a short exchange, he hung up.

'Change of plan.'

'Newman's not there?'

'There's no sign of him. An alert's gone out for him and the car.'

'So what now? Do you still want to head for the station?'

Fisher thought through the options.

'No. Let's pay Warren Newman a surprise visit. See if he knows his son's whereabouts.'

'You think he might be there?'

'I don't know but if he is, we'll nab him. If he isn't, we'll take the opportunity to have a nose around.'

'A nose around for what?'

'The tokens taken from the crime scenes.'

'You think they're in it together?'

'No. I think Rob Newman broke in to his father's and hid the jewellery where there's less likelihood of a nosy wife or curious kid coming across them. At first I couldn't understand why he would have broken in, but if he's lost his keys, it makes perfect sense.'

54.

Warren Newman met them at the door. After Fisher explained the reason for their visit, he led them into the living room, huffing out a tirade of grumbles.

'See! He's not here.'

They had already assumed as much, given the absence of the navy BMW outside the house.

'Talk about the blind leading the blind. You must really be clutching at straws,' Newman protested as Nightingale disappeared upstairs to start her search. 'The whole idea that Rob had anything to do with those women's deaths is preposterous. For one thing, he didn't know any of them, apart from Connie. And as for Connie, he wouldn't have hurt a hair on her head. He knew how much she meant to me.'

'Have you ever given your son any financial support?' Fisher asked.

'Of course. I bought him his first computer when he needed one for school and a car when he was learning to drive, and I helped him with the deposit on his first house. Have you got kids?'

'Yes. A son.'

'Do you ever buy him anything?'

'Fair point. But what about more recently? Your son has a large house in a very desirable area. Did you help pay for that?'

'I didn't need to. Rob's got a good job. So has his wife.'

'No financial problems, as far as you're aware?'

'No. Look, why don't I try calling him? He might be at home now. The sooner you talk to him, the sooner this can all be cleared up.' After a short, futile call, Newman hung up. 'Perhaps he's still at the station. Have you tried there?'

'We tried his office. There was no one there.'

'He wasn't going back to the office. He was going to see if there was a desk free at Ashford station, save him driving all the way to Maidstone.'

Fisher curbed a groan and reached for his mobile.

DS Wickham called him back fifteen minutes later.

'And he was definitely there earlier?' Fisher replied.

'Yes. His car's still here but no one's seen him since six.'

'He can't have gone far then,' Fisher said, feeling a growing sense of excitement as the net closed in. 'Stick your car somewhere out of sight and keep an eye on the BMW. If Newman shows, hold him till we get there.'

Putting the house search on hold, Fisher and Nightingale set off on the short drive to the fire station. They found Wickham's Skoda tucked in a dark corner with the BMW in line of sight. After Nightingale parked alongside, Fisher knocked on the window and beckoned to the sergeant to join them.

Wickham climbed in the back, next to Luna.

'What do we do now?'

'Now we wait.'

After three hours and still no sign, Fisher's growing concern for Luna forced a break and he sent Nightingale to beg a bowl of water from the fire crew inside the station.

On her way back, a saucepan of fresh water in hand, she paused by the main door. On the wall was a large green button; a nearby sign stated that the button was to be depressed at the same time as the handle was turned. As the task needed both hands, Nightingale set the pan down and was about to press the button when she spotted movement through the door's glass panel. She peered into the dark and watched as a man emerged from the gloom and hurried across the car park, heading towards the building. A clear six inches taller than Rob Newman, he had short, almost shaved, dark hair, a far cry from Newman's trendy styled blond hair. Confident he wasn't their man Nightingale turned her attention back to the door. It was a complete shock then to see the BMW surge towards the road as she stepped outside.

She threw the saucepan to the ground and sprinted after it yelling, 'Police! Stop!'

The car swerved onto the carriageway, tyres squealing. By the time Nightingale reached the road, the car's rear lights were little more than a diminishing dot in the distance. Chest heaving, she shook her head. Behind her came a hurry of footsteps as Wickham rushed to join her. He came to a stop and stared down the empty road.

'He got away,' Wickham said, arriving back at the car to find Fisher leaning against the bonnet.

'I gathered that.' Warren Newman's comment about the blind leading the blind sprang to mind. 'The Falcon's going to have a bloody field day when she hears about this.'

'I should have got into the driver's seat after Beth got out,' Wickham said. 'I couldn't see anything from the back. The first thing I knew was when I heard the engine start.'

'It wasn't Rob Newman,' Nightingale said.

'What?' Fisher and Wickham replied in unison.

Fisher asked, 'Are you sure?'

'Yes. I watched him walk across the car park. Six foot; slim build; dark, close-cropped hair. I thought he was a firefighter, until I saw him drive off.'

'So who the hell is he?' Fisher asked, wondering if things could get any worse.

'A friend of Newman's sent to get his car?' Nightingale hazarded.

'Why didn't Newman take it when he left?' Wickham asked.

'I don't know but we've given the game away now, haven't we?' Fisher said. 'All those calls from his wife and dad telling him we're trying to get hold of him.' He blew out a sigh. For a moment, he stood there, feeling the cold metal against his legs, glad of the support.

The seconds ticked by as he grappled with what to do. Give up and go home or carry on with what was turning out to be a wild goose chase.

'Matt?' It was Beth.

What sort of example would he set if he threw the towel in now? It was a minor setback, that's all, he told himself.

He gave the bonnet a brisk tap.

'Right, well, no point hanging around here feeling sorry for ourselves. We've got until morning to find him. Are there any CCTV cameras out here?'

'I can see a couple,' Wickham replied.

'Good. Go in and see if you can get a copy of any footage covering this part of the car park. Oh, and if you come up with any good images of the guy, get them circulated, will you? After you've done that, get over to Warren Newman's place. Apart from being there in case Rob shows up, you can finish the search that Beth started.'

'You don't want me to do that?' Nightingale asked.

'No. We're going to pay Newman's wife another visit. See if she knows this mate of his. Might even get you to take a little look around there. If she'll let us.'

55.

Fisher heard the front door open before he'd even climbed out of the car.

'Any news?' Lisa Newman called.

Ignoring her obvious distress, Fisher said, 'Could we come in? There are some things we need to ask you.'

'This isn't like him,' she said as soon as they were all seated in the lounge. 'He always phones if he's going to be back late. Always.'

'We believe your husband may be with a friend. Around six-foot tall, slim built, short, almost shaved, dark hair. Sound familiar?'

'Not really. What makes you think he's a friend of Rob's?'

'He was seen driving away from Ashford fire station in your husband's car.'

'Then he must have stolen it — he must have taken Rob's keys. Rob's been using the spare.'

'Or your husband gave him the keys and got him to pick the car up for him.'

'Rob never lets anyone drive that car, not even me. It's his pride and joy.'

'Maybe he made an exception.'

'But why? And where is he? Why wouldn't he drive the car himself?'

'We were hoping you might have some ideas.'

'I already told you, he said he was going to be working late. That's all I know.'

'Perhaps he's lying low to avoid talking to us?'

'Why would he do that? It's not like he's a suspect or anything.' After a moment's pause, she said, 'He's not, is he?'

'Would it surprise you if he was?'

'Of course it would,' she snapped.

Fisher waited for the usual litany of denials: he wouldn't hurt a fly; he'd do anything for anybody; he'd never do anything to hurt me or our little girl. She said nothing.

'Was your husband happy to learn of his father's engagement?' he asked.

'Happy? I don't know. I suppose.'

'You suppose?'

'I mean, yes, of course he was. It's only, well, it happened so quickly.'

'How did he feel about losing his inheritance?'

'What do you mean?'

'You have a beautiful home, so I'm told. Would losing the inheritance have made things difficult for you financially, in the long run?'

'Why should it?'

'It might if you've bought a lot of things on credit in the expectation that you'll come into a lot of money one day.'

'So what if we have a lot on credit? Who doesn't? You can't think Rob killed Connie just to stop her getting his inheritance.'

That's exactly what Fisher thought. A man in his seventies, living on his own and already battling one bout of cancer… how many years could he reasonably be expected to live? From a young man's perspective, perhaps not that many. But Fisher needed Lisa Newman's help, so kept his thoughts to himself.

Instead, he said, 'It's our job to consider every possibility. I'd be just as happy as you to be able to rule your husband out of our enquiries.' Thankfully, his unseeing eyes and the scar tissue that bound his brow made for the best poker face. 'We're going to need to take a look around. If we find no evidence relating to the crimes, that will certainly help his case. If it's okay with you, Beth could take a quick look around now. She can be quick and won't disturb anything.'

'You're not serious? You want to search my home?'

'If it's a problem, I can arrange for a warrant and get a team out here first thing tomorrow. Of course, they'll go through everything a lot more thoroughly.'

He let the silence mount. Eventually, Lisa Newman replied, 'Go ahead,' spitting the word out. 'You won't find anything.'

'I'm sure you're right,' Fisher said, thinking back to the call from Warren Newman about the so-called burglar.

'Would you like to go and get your daughter?' Nightingale said. 'I wouldn't want to alarm her if she wakes up while I'm in her room.' Fisher heard the snap of a pair of latex gloves being pulled on.

'You're going to search her room too?' Mrs Newman said, sounding a little breathy.

It was all starting to sink in, Fisher thought.

'I need to look everywhere, but I'll be as careful as possible,' Nightingale replied.

While Mrs Newman roused her daughter, Fisher took the opportunity to call DS Wickham for an update. It wasn't good news.

'And you've checked everywhere?' Fisher asked.

'Yep. No jewellery or electrical flex. There was a roll of black bags in the kitchen, but not the same type as used on the victims.'

'Okay, well, thank Mr Newman and get out of there. Are you happy to hang around and keep an eye on the house from outside in case the suspect turns up, or do you want me to see if anyone else in the team is available?' he asked with a smile, knowing full well Wickham would bite his arm off for the overtime.

Lisa Newman returned to the lounge, settling a sleepy Ava down on the sofa. The presence of the child meant whatever angst her mother was feeling remained unspoken. Instead, she did what most people do when they don't want to talk: she put the TV on. It was almost an hour and a half later when Fisher heard the stairs creak.

Nightingale entered the room.

'DI Fisher, have you got a minute?'

'What is it? What have you found?' Lisa Newman asked urgently, causing the child beside her to stir.

Fisher rose from his seat and had Luna lead him to the door.

'Tell me what you've found!' Mrs Newman called after him. 'I've got a right to know. Whatever it is, it might be mine.'

He continued through to the hallway. Behind him, the indignant cries turned to harsh accusations.

'You brought it with you. You're trying to set my husband up. Do you have any idea what this will do to my family?'

Her anguished shouts roused her daughter, who started to cry. Fisher was grateful for the distraction. As Lisa Newman went from protective spouse to caring mother and tried to shush the child back to sleep, he slipped outside, joining Nightingale, and pulled the front door to. The air felt damp and noticeably cooler than when they'd first arrived, reminding him that time was ticking.

'So?'

'I found it... the jewellery,' Nightingale said, unable to hide her excitement. 'All of it.'

'Fucking knew it.' Fisher fist-pumped the air. He'd barely dared dream of such a result. 'Where was it?'

'Inside a pair of men's shoes in a box in the bottom of a wardrobe. And that's not all. I found a roll of black bags that look the same as the ones used and there's a small home office with a load of computer gear, including a box full of cables.'

'Well, if that isn't that the cherry on the cake.'

Having done all they could, Fisher arranged for an unmarked patrol car to keep watch on the house, should the wanted man return home, before having Nightingale drive him home.

'You sure you don't want anything?' Fisher asked, handing Nightingale a twenty-pound note. They had stopped off at a pizza place on their way back.

'No. I'll grab a bowl of cereal or something when I get in. I won't be able to sleep if I have anything too heavy.'

Sensible girl, Fisher reflected, as he lay awake in the early hours of the morning, having demolished a whole cheese and salami pizza before bed. He thought about the Falcon; about what she would do once she learned how they'd lost their man. She'd blame him, of course. Despite the fact that if it had been down to her, they'd still be looking for a malcontent middle-aged taxi driver with a pathological hatred of older women. A fact she'd conveniently forget when it came to it.

He threw himself onto his side and hauled the duvet up, huffing out a sigh.

Why did it have to be such a battle? They were all supposed to be on the same side. Sometimes the thought of taking ill health retirement had a real allure. What was it about the job that made it worth the fight anyway? Then he thought of Em Walker: the way she'd sat by his hospital bed, clasping his hand in her papery grip, while gently reassuring him that he would pull through and be as good a father, a husband, a detective, as he'd ever been. She said it with such certainty he never doubted her. If she could see him now, wallowing in self-pity, she'd have a few words to say.

But he was so very tired.

And he was only going to get more tired as, just then, his mobile started to ring.

Not bothering to find out who was calling, he swiped to accept the call and put the phone to his ear. Fifteen minutes later, he stood shivering on the pavement, listening for the sound of an approaching engine.

56.

'How did it happen?' Nightingale asked, as Fisher buckled up. He'd called her immediately after the force control room had rung to inform him that Rob Newman had been found. Dead.

'Hanged himself,' he replied. 'A group of firefighters found him at their station after they were called out to an incident. That's as much as I know.'

The quiet roads gave them a clear run and it wasn't long before Nightingale announced their arrival at the rural fire station located in a small village west of Ashford. Leaving Luna in the car, Fisher unfolded his white stick. Nightingale guided him around the station building to a large concreted parking area.

'Newman's BMW is over on our left,' she said as they rounded a corner. 'Directly ahead there's a tall metal tower.' They took a few more steps. 'I can see a body on the floor at the base of the tower.'

It was no surprise that Rob Newman had been cut down from his impromptu gallows. The fire crew would have wanted to make sure the man was definitely dead.

He cocked his ear. All he could hear was silence.

'Where is everyone?'

'There's no one here, apart from a couple of PCs sitting in a patrol car.'

'Let's go have a chat, shall we?'

As Nightingale guided him towards the car, Fisher heard the sound of car doors opening. After brief introductions, he asked for an account of what had happened.

A young-sounding woman answered, 'PC Dexter here, sir. At 3:24 a.m. firefighters were called out to an incident. The first officer to arrive at the station noticed the body of a man hanging from the tower they use to train on. The other officers arrived over the course of the following five minutes. One of the firefighters called an ambulance, while the others lowered the man down, hoping to be able to resuscitate him, although it soon became clear they were too late. They then called for a police attendance, as per protocol. On our arrival, the officer in charge approached us, concerned about the crew being kept longer than necessary — most have got day jobs to go to. There didn't seem any reason to keep them, so we took their details and let them go.' There was a rustle of paper. 'Here... The one at the top is the guy in charge.'

Assuming Nightingale had taken the proffered information, Fisher asked, 'Who requested serious crime's attendance?'

'We did.'

'On what grounds? What made you think it might not be suicide?'

'Nothing. It wasn't that. It was the car. We were aware of the alert out for the BMW. We compared the photo circulated yesterday of Mr Newman with the deceased, which is when we called it in.'

'Excellent work,' Fisher said. 'So, the scene then... did the crew describe how they found Newman?'

'Yes. They said he was hanging from the rail at the top of the first flight of steps with a plastic bag over his head.'

'A black plastic bag?'

'No. Clear plastic.'

'And the noose?'

'Electrical flex. That was black. We bagged both of them up, just in case.'

Fisher raised his hands to his face, steepled his fingers and blew through them, thinking desperately.

Why was the bag different this time? Had they got Newman all wrong? If so, then why did he have the jewellery?

'Did anyone see Newman or anyone else around here before it happened?'

'No. The station isn't staffed. The firefighters only turn up when they're called out.'

Fisher let out a despondent sigh and reached for his phone.

'I don't much fancy their chances of finding anything,' he commented on ending the call to control, having requested the services of a CSI unit. 'How did Newman get into the tower? Wasn't it secured?' He imagined the tall structure to be a health and safety nightmare.

'It was. There's a metal gate blocking the entrance,' came a male voice. 'The padlock has been cut through. A pair of bolt cutters were found on the floor next to it.'

'Must have been a boy scout.'

'What's that, sir?'

'Just saying, he came prepared.' After a moment, he said, 'A clear plastic bag, eh?'

'Yes sir.'

'No writing or anything on it?'

'No.'

'And the fire crew definitely said the bag was over the deceased's head when he was found?'

'Yes.'

Maybe it was the only bag he had with him. Maybe it was suicide, after all.

301

'What about the Beemer... any sign of the keys?'

'They're still in the ignition,' PC Dexter replied.

'You took a look inside?'

'Only through the window. Didn't want to risk contaminating it.'

Fisher flashed a smile in the PC's direction, then turned to Nightingale.

'Let's have a little look, shall we, Beth? Slip some gloves on and have a nose around. Be careful though, we don't want to upset the CSIs.'

As Nightingale walked off, Fisher set out his cane and started after her. Shortly, he heard a car door open.

'There's an envelope on the passenger seat,' Nightingale called over to him.

'And...?'

'There's no address and it doesn't look like it's sealed. Hang on...' Shortly, she continued, 'Inside there's a single sheet of paper...' After another short pause she went on, 'It's a signed confession. Rob Newman admits to killing all four women. He says he did it because he didn't want Connie Lloyd to marry his father and take what was his.'

Fisher blew out a sigh.

'Well, there we have it. Thank God for that. An end to all the killing. I'd be lying if I said there were times I thought we'd never get to the bottom of it. I'll call the Falcon, give her the good news.'

Just then his mobile started to ring.

'What's the betting this is her now?' He reached into his pocket and swiped to answer. 'DI Fisher.'

'Hi Matt. It's Andy. I think I've got the answer as to why we haven't been able to find Rob Newman. I took another look at the CCTV from the fire station. I wanted to see if Newman left with anyone.'

'Hold up! I'll stop you there. You're too late, mate. I'm standing less than twenty feet away from him as we speak.'

'Well, I wasn't expecting that. What about the guy who took him? Is he there as well?'

'What do you mean the guy that took him?'

'The one from last night.'

'You're going to have to explain.'

'Newman left the station building at six-thirty. He was opening his car door when this guy gets out of a hatchback parked next to him and says something to him. Newman says something back, then the pair of them walk around to the rear of this other guy's car. The guy opens the boot and, from what I can tell, shoves Newman inside. He then shuts the boot and drives off. I can't be a hundred per cent certain but he seemed a pretty good match to the guy who took the Beemer. He kept his head down, but the hair, the build, the way he moved, looked the same to me.'

'It was probably the same mate. Newman must have got him to pick him up, stow him somewhere, then fetch the car for him later.'

'It didn't look like they were mates. Newman was about to put his key into the car door when the other guy got out. He didn't even notice the other guy was there until he spoke to him. If it was a mate, wouldn't Newman have got in the passenger seat? But anyway, you're there with Newman, why don't you ask him what happened?' When Fisher didn't reply, Wickham said, 'Oh shit, don't tell me...'

'Stone cold.'

57.

'Matt!' DCI Fallon called from her office. She actually sounded pleased to see him for once.

'She won't sound so pleased if it turns out we've got the wrong guy,' Fisher muttered under his breath. Something in his gut told him there was still a chance all wasn't as it seemed.

'Do you want me to come in with you?' Nightingale asked.

'No. Run while you've got the chance.' He started towards the DCI's office, but paused and turned and said, 'Actually, if you want to help, go and see Andy, help him trace this mystery man. I want to talk to him asap.'

He knocked once and entered the Falcon's lair.

'Take a seat, Matt.'

He crossed the room in a few short steps and sat down, settling Luna at his feet.

'I hear you've had a result. I hope you'll remember to thank DCI Whitlow for his assistance.'

'Who? Oh, him. What am I thanking him for?'

'The lead he gave you — the perpetrator... thirty-year-old, white guy, works for an organisation providing services to the elderly. Matches the profile exactly.'

'Hardly,' Fisher said, disparagingly. 'Besides, Newman wasn't a serial killer he simply—'

She didn't give him time to finish.

'Don't ruin a great result by splitting hairs, Matt. I understand you found the items taken from the victims at the dead guy's house.'

'Yes. Plus some black plastic bags that look a good match. We'll know soon enough whether they're the same type used in the murders.'

'So, why do you look like someone's just killed your dog? Surely, you're not moping because he killed himself. Call it poetic justice.'

'I'll be celebrating along with everyone else, once his death is confirmed as suicide.' Fisher steeled himself for her reaction.

'What else could it be?'

'He was last seen alive being bundled into the boot of a car as he left the fire station. Most likely by the same person who later came back for the BMW. It's possible someone figured he was the killer and caught up with him before we did.'

'You not disputing that Newman killed the four women then?'

'Not at this stage.'

'I suppose I should be grateful for that, at least. So now we might have two killers? I should have known. You can't touch anything without it turning to shit. Anyway, what do you mean at this stage? You found the jewellery in his house. You were all set to arrest him.'

'The jewellery could have been planted by the killer to shift attention onto Newman. He then kills Newman, making it look like he hanged himself out of remorse. With Newman dead, the case is closed and the real killer escapes undetected.'

The room fell silent. Fisher waited. Eventually Fallon said, 'Or maybe you're looking at shadows and seeing monsters.'

'Meaning what?'

'Meaning you can't accept everything is as it appears.' Sounding chirpier, she said, 'Well, thankfully one of us can see clearly. Newman's our man and he hanged himself rather than face the consequences. Given there's no evidence to the contrary I'm closing the case.'

'What if we find some new evidence that—'

Fallon jumped in, 'You won't. The investigation is over. The case is closed. I swear, Matt, if it was down to you our solve rate would be in negative figures.' Fisher went to respond but the DCI beat him to it. 'You know where the door is.'

He hurried out of the room before he said something he regretted and made for Wickham's desk. As he drew close, the sergeant said, 'There's an empty chair right in front of you Matt. Beth's here too.'

Fisher waved a hand around until he made contact with the coarse seat fabric. He sat down and asked, 'How are you getting on?'

'No joy,' Wickham said. 'The hatchback had cloned plates.'

'What about the forensics from this morning's scene?'

'The BMW is still being worked on,' Nightingale replied. 'We do know there were no prints on the gate to the tower, the padlock or the bolt cutter and only Newman's prints were found on the plastic bag.'

'When you say no prints on the tower or the bolt cutters…'

'They were wiped clean.'

'We were just saying, why would Newman have done that?' Wickham said. 'Makes no sense, and if someone killed him and then cleaned up after themselves, they must have realised we'd suspect foul play when we couldn't find any prints.'

'Maybe the killer hoped the whole set-up plus the note would be enough to convince everyone that Newman had taken his own life,' Fisher replied. 'How many suicides end up with a CSI team checking for prints?'

'True,' Wickham agreed. 'So where does that leave us?'

'We need to find out whether Newman really did kill those four women or whether he's been set up.'

'How do we do that?' Wickham asked.

'Beth, what happened to the jewellery you found at Newman's last night?'

'It's on my desk. I was going to give it to Colin to log into evidence and get him to send it over to the lab, only I haven't had a chance, what with everything that's happened.'

'Okay, well do it now. Only once you've logged it, could you take it over to the lab yourself? Turn on the charm and see if you can get it bumped up the list. And while you're there, ask them if they can get a handwriting expert to look at that confession. You'll need to give Mrs Newman a call and get a sample of her husband's writing to compare it to.'

'Will do.'

'Meanwhile, I'm going to call the professor. I need to satisfy myself that we've not been blindsided by a clever son-of-a bitch serial killer.'

58.

The phone rang on. For a moment Fisher thought the professor wasn't going to answer, then the ring tone ended and he heard Woolf's honeyed voice.

'Detective Fisher. This is a nice surprise. I wasn't expecting to hear from you again.'

'I wish I could say it was a social call. Unfortunately, I'm in need of your professional expertise, once again,' Fisher replied, before running through the events of the previous night.

When he finished, Woolf said, 'I see. That is something of a puzzle.'

'Is it possible we've been dealing with a serial killer all this time and they set Rob Newman up to take the fall?'

'You think the killer planted the items you found at Mr Newman's house?'

'It's possible, isn't it?'

'Everything's possible, but a serial killer using trophies in that way... it doesn't feel right. They usually mean too much to discard them like that. Now, if they'd used something else to implicate him with, maybe.'

'But you said yourself, not all serial killers are the same.'

'If you recall, I was referring to the methods they use and how they evade detection.'

Fisher slumped back in his seat. Why was he the only one to feel something was amiss?

'What about the bag? It was clear plastic, unlike the others.'

'He didn't need to cover his own face,' Woolf parried.

'Or it was a serial killer and they wanted to see his fear before he pushed him off the tower.'

'But if the same person killed all four women, why didn't they use clear bags then?'

Fisher blew out a long stream of air.

'Why does none of this make sense?'

'The only thing stopping it from making sense is the video of him supposedly being bundled into the back of a stranger's car. Without that it's fairly straightforward — Mr Newman killed the four women, then committed suicide out of remorse. How sure are you it wasn't a friend who picked him up and stowed him in the boot of the car out of sight?'

'My team reassures me it didn't look like that on the video. And what about the fact there were no prints on the gate or bolt cutters?'

'He probably wiped the surfaces out of force of habit.'

'What about the false plates on the car he was taken in?'

'All that says is his friend is pretty clued-up. How long before you'd have picked him up if he hadn't had false plates on? Not very long, I imagine. Whereas the way things played out, Mr Newman was smuggled out, while his BMW stayed put until it was safe for his friend to retrieve it.'

'And then, after going to all that trouble, Newman just goes and hangs himself?'

'I imagine he spent a few desperate hours wondering what the hell he was going to do. It would have slowly dawned on him that he'd let his wife and daughter down, his father would never forgive him, on top of which he'd be facing the rest of his life in prison. Suicide might have seemed the only option.'

Fisher thought about Wickham's description of the scene as it played out on the CCTV footage at the station. Maybe Woolf was right. He thanked her for her time and after ending the call, sought Wickham out and gave him a rundown of the professor's theory.

'It didn't look like that to me,' the sergeant replied.

Fisher thought about DCI Fallon's comment — was Wickham seeing monsters where there were only shadows?

'Are you being a little biased? We're so used to seeing wrongdoing everywhere we look.'

'I don't think so. I can watch it again, if you want. See if I still think the same.'

'Get the film cued up. I'll get Beth to join us.'

59.

With Nightingale and Wickham watching the screen, Fisher listened as the pair took turns commentating.

'The footage is from a camera mounted on a post at the edge of the car park,' Wickham explained. 'You can just see the door to the station on the far left of the screen.' A few seconds later: 'Here we go. The door's opening… Rob Newman has come out. He's walking across the car park. He's looking pretty relaxed, wouldn't you say, Beth?'

'I guess. Though he might be trying to look casual.'

'Yeah well, wait a sec…' Shortly, Wickham continued, 'Watch it now… Newman rounds the car and gets his key out of his pocket. The indicators have flashed, so he's obviously unlocked it. Then he goes to the driver's door. He's about to reach for the handle… now look at the black hatchback. The unknown guy has got out and says something to Newman. It doesn't look to me like they know each other. It looks like Newman's puzzled or undecided over something.'

'I'm not sure,' Nightingale said. 'If it was a mate, he could have said something like, "What are you doing, you idiot? Get round the back of the car and out of sight of the cameras."'

'I don't agree, but…' Wickham said.

'Oh, he's moving now.' Nightingale took over the commentary. 'He's gone round to the back of the other guy's car. The unknown has opened the hatchback so you can't see either of them now.' She fell quiet for a moment, then said, 'The boot lid is down again. There's no sign of Newman. The unknown is in shot. He's just bent down. Looks like he picked something up.'

Fisher tensed in his seat.

'What was it?'

'Maybe Newman dropped his key,' Wickham suggested.

'Rewind it,' Fisher said impatiently.

A minute later, Nightingale said, 'Whatever it is was small enough for the guy to palm it when he picked it up.'

Fisher waved a hand.

'Okay, keep going. We'll get the technical IT team to blow it up later.'

'That's it really. After that the mystery guy gets back in the hatchback and drives off.'

'So, what do you both think? Andy, you go first, seeing as you've seen it twice.'

'I stand by what I said before. They could be mates but my gut says they're not.'

'Beth?'

'I'd agree apart from the fact there was no sign of a struggle. Rob Newman was reasonably fit and healthy. The other guy has a few inches on him, but he's no muscle man.'

'What if he stuck him with a sedative? Could it have been a hypodermic he picked up?' Fisher asked.

'If he did, it was pretty slick.' Beth said.

'Right. Andy, go and see what can be done with that footage. Find out what he picked up.'

'What do you want me to do?' Nightingale asked after Wickham had left.

'Call Dr Cooper. Find out what time the post mortem is and tell her to be on the lookout for any puncture wounds. Tell her we think it's possible Newman was sedated earlier in the day.

While you do that, I'll get onto the CSI team. They must have something for us by now.'

And they did. The jewellery found at Rob Newman's home had been tested for prints. Newman might have worn gloves when he'd taken them from his victims — as evidenced by the original owners' smudged prints — but he clearly hadn't worn any when stowing the items in the shoe box. His prints were all over them. Conclusive evidence that he'd played some part in the women's murders. The search of his car also paid off, revealing a small silver and crystal heart charm trapped at the back of the glove box — a match for one missing on Connie Lloyd's necklace retrieved from the shoebox. It placed the necklace in the BMW and gave the theory the jewellery had been planted in Newman's home much less credence.

Whilst it was looking increasingly likely that Newman had acted alone in the four women's murders, there was a growing bank of evidence to suggest the one death he hadn't had a hand in was his own. Thankfully, although the fire training tower, padlock and bolt cutters all came up clean, the CSIs did manage to find a print on the BMW's key... and it wasn't Newman's.

Fisher was deep in thought, trying to fit everything together, when he became aware of someone coming his way. He turned in their direction.

'Matt. It's Andy.'

'How did you get on?'

'They blew the footage up. No sign of any hypodermics, I'm afraid. We're pretty sure he picked up the key to the Beemer.'

'Yes!' Fisher thumped the table with the edge of his fist. 'You've just made my day.' He told him about the thumb print found on Newman's car key. 'They're running it through the system as we speak. Oh God, I hope they find something. We are so overdue a shot of luck.'

Fisher tilted his head, picking up a light tap of heels heading his way.

'Has something happened?' It was Nightingale. 'You looked like you were celebrating.'

'Pull up a pew.' Fisher heard her wheel a chair over to his desk. He told her about the key, then asked, 'How about you? Any news?'

'PM's scheduled for this afternoon. Luckily, Dr Cooper was at the morgue. She took a quick look at Mr Newman's neck. She said she could see what looks like at least one puncture wound, possibly two. She'll need to take a sample and look at it under the microscope to be sure.'

'Two?'

'That's what I said. Dr Cooper asked me how easy I thought it would be to convince a man to walk up a flight of steps, put his head in a noose and throw himself to his death.'

'Ahh, he was sedated before being thrown over. Makes sense. The killer must have got him to write the confession in between being picked up and strung up. Assuming Newman actually wrote it. Though I'll be surprised if he didn't. Seeing as his wife will end up with the letter, she'll know the second she sees it if he didn't write it.'

'Were there any prints on the note or envelope?' Nightingale asked.

'Just Newman's. But that's not surprising. The killer could have worn gloves when he wrote it, then pressed Newman's fingers on it after he was sedated.'

'If he was wearing gloves, why wipe the gate to the tower?'

'I don't know. If Newman was carried up the tower, maybe the killer thought the absence of his prints amongst a shed load of others would have been more suspicious than no prints at all.'

'So, the killer just asks Newman to write a suicide note, gets him to leave it on the seat of his car and then what...? Newman lets himself be sedated and carried to his death?' Nightingale said. 'It doesn't make sense. You'd put up a fight, wouldn't you? You certainly wouldn't help by writing your own confession.'

She had a point. Fisher thought about it for a moment.

'I don't suppose you took a copy of the letter before letting the CSIs have it?'

'Of course. I was going to type it up so you could read it yourself.'

'Beth, you're a star. Go grab it for me, will you?'

A few minutes later, after Nightingale finished reading the last sentence, Fisher said, 'That's it?'

Wickham cleared his throat.

'He confessed to all four murders and explained his motive. What else do you want?'

'Some expression of regret. A sorry, perhaps,' Fisher said.

'The guy killed in cold blood just to get his hands on his inheritance,' Wickham argued.

'Exactly, he killed in cold blood, yet think about his choice of words: "I didn't want Connie marrying my father and taking what I wrongly thought was mine." Why wrongly thought? Why not just thought? Or what I was due? It doesn't sound right.'

'I see what Matt's saying,' Nightingale said. 'If someone killed Newman to avenge the dead women, you'd expect the note to say how sorry he was for causing such suffering. But if everything's been done by a serial killer using Newman as a decoy, then the way it's written makes more sense — serial killers are renowned for having no remorse.'

'There is a third possibility,' Fisher said. 'Newman didn't know he was going to die and had no intention of killing himself. He wrote the note because he was instructed to confess.'

'You mean like to a priest?' Wickham asked.

'Not quite. Think about how it's worded. Doesn't it sound like the sort of thing drafted by a lawyer on behalf of a client… or a police officer, taking down a statement?'

'That's exactly what it sounds like.' Nightingale said.

'You're not suggesting someone on the force killed him?' Wickham sounded incredulous.

'No,' Fisher replied. 'But it could have been somebody impersonating a police officer.'

'How would they know Newman was a person of interest? We didn't know ourselves until last night.'

'Maybe we've got a leak?' Fisher rubbed the two-day old stubble on his chin, causing it to rasp loudly.

The thought of someone betraying the department like that was the sort of thing that gave him sleepless nights, but who would leak information like that, and why? It didn't make sense.

Trying to think of an alternative explanation, he was so lost in thought that when his mobile started to ring, he jumped, sending Luna to her feet, barking loudly. He reached for the phone, patting and stroking the dog's flanks.

Ten minutes later, he ended the call, let his head fall back and heaved out a loud sigh.

'Finally, a lead! We've got a match to the thumb print found on Newman's car key. It was lifted at the scene of a suspicious death a couple of years ago. The victim, a guy called Nigel Madden, was apparently known to us. Beth, can you do a search, see what you can find on him?' Fisher wheeled along a couple of feet to give her access to his computer.

For a few minutes all he could hear was keys clicking, then Nightingale said, 'Here we go… eight arrests for rape with violence, one resulting in a custodial sentence. He was actually awaiting trial when he died.'

'How come he was arrested so often, but only sentenced the once?'

'Let's see...' Fisher waited while Nightingale skimmed the reports. 'It looks like the alleged victims withdrew their allegations while Madden was out on bail.'

'Unconditional bail, I bet.' An angry scowl flashed across Fisher's face. 'When are the courts going to realise you can't give unconditional bail in cases like that. I don't understand what the problem is with putting a few bloody conditions in place. At least make the victims think someone cares about them. Would that be too much to ask?' He stopped and held up his hands in apology. 'Sorry. I know, I'm preaching to the converted. It just makes my blood boil.' He took a deep breath and refocussed. 'Going back to Madden then... how did he die?'

'Cause of death was a broken neck resulting from a fall,' Nightingale read. 'He was found at the bottom of an external flight of stairs at a block of flats on the Copthorne estate. Death was instantaneous.'

'What does the report say about prints?'

'Due to the circumstance of his death, police were called to the scene and a full forensic review undertaken... Blah blah blah.... Here we are... Prints were taken from the metal railings on the stairwell as well as from various items found in the vicinity of the body, including a Coke can and a pair of men's sunglasses. DNA was also taken from a couple of cigarette stubs found on the landing where it's thought Madden fell from. It was investigated and ruled accidental death.'

Wickham gave a snort.

'I can't imagine the investigating officers spent too much time looking for evidence of foul play, given Madden's history.' Fisher thought he was probably right. 'How does any of that help us?'

Wickham went on. 'Our killer could have lived on the estate. There's always all manner of crap lying around those places.'

'Two dead alleged offenders and the same person's prints found near both... that sounds like one hell of a coincidence. And you know how I don't like coincidences. We need to go through Madden's files and look for anything, anything whatsoever, no matter how vague, that could be a link to our mystery man. I'll focus on the investigation into Madden's death plus the rape case he was on bail for when he died; you two divvy up the other files between you.'

***

The investigation into Nigel Madden's death had been mired by a complete dearth of information. Fisher wasn't surprised. He knew the area where it had happened, having done his fair share of footwork there as a probationer. Concrete block sat aside concrete block, separated by enough alleyways and covered landings to keep a whole army of drug runners and muggers in business. The estate was as rough as they come and residents knew better than to open their mouths to the filth.

Madden was thought to have fallen from the first-floor landing. According to the report, no one witnessed him fall, though a pensioner living in a ground-floor flat opposite admitted to having seen the man topple down the last few steps before hitting the ground, where he lay immobile. It transpired the same pensioner had made the 999 call, hanging up before giving his name. He claimed not to have seen the dead man before, nor anyone in the vicinity at the time of the incident. Fisher knew it would have been easy enough for someone to have pushed Madden to his death or even broken his neck and sent him toppling down the stairs before slipping away unnoticed. As usual with unexplained deaths, the scene was quickly cordoned off and the crime scene investigation team brought in. It was during the routine search that followed that several items had been bagged as potential evidence and prints taken.

Fisher paused the screen reader on his computer and called the lab, interested in knowing which of the items found at the scene had the prints on that were a match to the one on Newman's car key. It turned out to have been a pair of men's Rayban sunglasses found near Nigel Madden's body.

Fisher mulled this over.

A pair of branded glasses wouldn't usually last five minutes on an estate like that before some light-fingered reprobate hot-footed it away with them. The only reason he could think of as to why they were still there was because of their proximity to the body, which no one wanted to admit having seen. That, and the paramedics' speedy response.

Parking the information for later, Fisher moved on to the alleged rape Madden was awaiting trial for. The victim was a twenty-two-year-old woman, assaulted on her way home from a shift as a trainee nurse at the local hospital. At 21:00, unable to afford a car and with no buses running at that time of night, she had been walking home, tired and looking forward to something to eat. It had been dark, drizzly and the streets were quiet. She was snatched while crossing an alleyway that led to a cluster of rundown garages, dragged at knife point to an empty unit, where her attacker did all manner of unspeakable things to her. A man had discovered her semi-conscious, battered and bloody body while taking his bin out the following morning.

Fisher closed the file and unclenched his fists. The whole thing made for unpleasant reading, but what made it worse was that he knew, had Madden lived to see trial, the likelihood was he would walk away a free man, as happened all too often — the conviction rate for rape being shockingly low, especially where there was so little forensic evidence to tie the perpetrator to the scene.

He took a moment, letting go of his anger and refocussing on the case in hand, then opened the next file. It was an unnecessarily wordy document, which presented the prosecution's case opposing bail. His concentration drifted in and out as the legalese washed over him, until he got to the supporting appendices. He bolted upright in his seat; heart racing, stomach churning. There it was... the answer he'd been looking for.

So, that's what it felt like, to be kicked in the gut.

60.

'You really think someone's selecting their victims based on information provided by Professor Woolf?' Nightingale asked.

'I can't think of any other explanation,' Fisher replied, letting out a long slow breath in an attempt to keep the contents of his stomach from decorating the interior of the car as they sped towards the university.

The last report in the investigation pack had been a psychological assessment of Madden, conducted by a renowned leader in the field of criminal psychology, a certain Professor Martha Woolf.

'But how?' Wickham asked, as he and Luna lurched around in the back seat as Nightingale took another tight turn. 'I thought you said she was a stickler for confidentiality. So much so, she held back information in a murder investigation.'

'I know.' Fisher said. 'I'm having a hard time believing it myself, but I can't think of any alternative. Best case scenario is someone's been helping themselves to her files. It's a university. It's hardly going to have the strongest security measures in place.'

'I'm sorry, but I still don't understand how this has anything to do with Rob Newman's death,' Nightingale said. 'How could she have known we suspected him? We'd only just figured it out ourselves.'

'I don't know. I don't have all the answers,' Fisher replied. 'She's a bright woman. Maybe she worked it out for herself.'

Fisher thought back to the call he'd got from Rob Newman, when Newman had told him how Connie Lloyd had talked about getting loft insulation after receiving a brochure — an obvious lie designed to send Fisher on a wild goose chase. Woolf had listened in to the conversation. He remembered them discussing it afterwards. Although they'd quickly ruled out the killer having masqueraded as a loft insulation salesman, as Connie Lloyd was renting her house, it had given Fisher an idea, and he'd said as much. And what was it Woolf had said? Something about that being the point. Fisher hadn't really understood what she meant at the time. Now he couldn't help wonder whether, even at that stage, Woolf had got the measure of Newman.

He reached into his pocket and fingered the warrant they'd brought with them to force Professor Woolf to surrender her files should she prove unwilling. Would it come to that? Yesterday he would have said definitely not. Today, he wasn't so sure.

At the university, Nightingale pulled up directly outside the psychology faculty. A man on reception informed them in a supercilious tone that the professor was delivering a lecture and couldn't be interrupted.

'This is an urgent police matter,' Fisher snapped. 'We need to speak to the professor now.'

After a moment's impasse, the man said, 'Lecture room six. The session is almost finished. Perhaps you could wait for her outside?'

Fisher turned to Nightingale and Wickham.

'You two go and get her. I'll only slow you down. I'll meet you at her office.'

The sound of their heels running across the foyer echoed hollowly around the space. Fisher thought about his last trip to the university. He reckoned he could just about remember his way to the professor's room. After asking Luna to lead him to the lift, they walked steadily forward. Shortly, Luna came to a stop and Fisher tentatively set out a hand. He swept his fingers over the surface of the wall until he felt the cold metal of the lift's control panel.

Behind him, the receptionist said in a quiet voice, 'This is a message for Professor Woolf. It's Peter on reception. I've just had three detectives here…'

The lift doors opened with a ping.

Fisher followed Luna inside. Turning, he set a hand out and located the control panel. His fingers skimmed its surface, feeling for the buttons. He quickly counted up from the bottom button and chose what he hoped was the fourth-floor. The doors stuttered shut and Fisher felt his stomach roll as the lift started its ascent. He continued to probe the control panel's steel surface, feeling the dots next to each button. His attempts to learn braille were progressing slowly, but from what he could tell, he'd made the right call. A ping heralded the lift's arrival. He softened his knees as it lurched to a stop then waited until the doors opened with a gentle rattle. Stepping out onto the corridor, he blew out a long breath. So far so good.

***

Nightingale and Wickham followed the signs to lecture room six.

'Haven't we been down this corridor already?' Nightingale asked, as Wickham pushed through yet another door in the building's labyrinthine maze of narrow windowless corridors.

Wickham stopped and looked around.

'I don't know. It all looks the same to me.'

They continued ahead a short distance to where a sign at a junction of corridors pointed the way. They set off at a jog.

At the end of that corridor, through another door was a short rise of steps, which led to a T-junction of corridors. They spun on their heels, looking for another sign. There wasn't one.

Wickham held out his hands and hitched up his shoulders.

'Where now?'

'I've no idea. We need to find someone and ask.'

'We could split up. I'll go left, you go right.'

'No. We need to stick together. Otherwise you could find it, while I'm still wandering the corridors.'

'Okay. Why don't we—'

'Wait. I can hear voices...'

A rising babble of conversation was heading their way.

'I'm going to ask someone.' Nightingale trotted up the stairs before Wickham could object. She approached the first student. 'Which way to lecture room six?'

The girl hooked a thumb over her shoulder and said, 'If you're here for the lecture, you're too late. It just finished.'

The pair started to push and weave their way through the crowd, fighting the swell.

Arriving at the lecture theatre as the last stragglers made their way out, they scanned the room. There was no sign of the professor.

Wickham stopped the last student as he was about to leave.

'Is Professor Woolf around?'

'She already left.'

'When was that?'

'A few minutes ago.'

Wickham looked at Nightingale and rolled his eyes.

'Let's just hope she's gone straight to her office.'

Fisher took his time, following his memorised route to the professor's office. After a couple of false turns, which would have seen him walking into walls if it wasn't for Luna, he stopped outside what he thought was the right room. He felt the door frame, and the closed door, then knocked. As expected, there was no answer. He found the door handle and pressed down. The door swung open. He entered the room, his nose twitching at the professor's familiar scent hanging heavy in the air, and stood for a moment, trying to recall the layout. The last time they had been there, he and Beth had sat on two chairs whose backs faced the door, while Woolf had taken a seat opposite. He issued Luna an instruction to find an empty chair. She started to walk forward. Then stopped. Fisher set a hand down, expecting to find Luna's head hovering over an empty chair, instead he found her head up, ears alert.

Then came the sound of movement in front of him.

'Is it customary for the British police force to enter a lady's room without an invitation?'

'Professor. I'm sorry. I didn't realise you were here. The guy on reception said you were lecturing. I came in to wait for you… I did knock,' he added as an afterthought.

'Yes, and I'm sorry I didn't answer. I didn't want any distractions. I'm in something of a hurry right now. Perhaps we could reschedule for later?'

Fisher felt her brush past him.

'I'm sorry. This can't wait. We need to talk.'

Woolf continued moving around the room.

'I'm listening.'

He took a couple of steps forward until he found a chair and sank down.

'You know I talked to you about Rob Newman's apparent suicide?'

'Apparent? You're still not sure then?'

'No. We're pretty sure. He was murdered... by a serial killer.'

'A serial killer. Really? You do surprise me. I was sure a serial killer wouldn't have used black bags.' She gave a throaty laugh. 'Maybe I should pay more attention to my own lectures. I'm always saying the ones that get away are those that don't stick to the script.'

'You misunderstand. We're pretty sure Newman murdered the four women — he didn't want Connie Lloyd cheating him out of his inheritance. I meant Rob Newman was the victim of the serial killer.'

'That sounds highly improbable.' A second later, he heard what sounded like a zip being pulled.

'Professor, would you please sit down. It's hard enough having a conversation when you're blind, but when the person you're talking to is moving around it's downright impossible.'

'I'm sorry Inspector but I really must go. I have an appointment I can't be late for. I'd be happy to carry on this conversation later at the station.'

'That's not an option, I'm afraid. Four women and one man are dead. I need answers now.'

'How sure are you he didn't commit suicide? You said yourself Rob Newman killed those women. Never underestimate the impact guilt can have on a man, Inspector.'

'We know someone else was with him at the time he died.'

'You have evidence someone was there at that precise moment?' The question hung in the air for a moment. Woolf added, 'If you're convinced it was murder, then I suggest you look at the friends and relatives of the dead women. If Mr Newman was responsible for their murders, any one of them might feel justified in wanting him dead, don't you think?'

Fisher sensed her move towards the door. He jabbed a finger in the air, hoping it was in Woolf's direction.

'Don't you go anywhere. I haven't finished. I didn't come here to ask for your expert advice. I want to know who you've shared information about the cases with.'

'How dare you? I'm a professional.'

'What about your files? Who has access other than you?'

'Nobody. They are always kept secure. Besides, there's nothing in my files in relation to your cases. Any notes I might have made I destroyed after we last met. What is this really about?'

'We found a fingerprint on Mr Newman's car key that was a match to one found at a crime scene a few years ago. A man was found dead with a broken neck at the bottom of a flight of stairs. He'd only recently appeared in court charged with serial rape. You might remember it... you recommended the accused be refused bail. I don't believe in coincidence at the best of times but that's three men, suspected of violent crimes, of whom you had knowledge in a professional context, who subsequently ended up dead. I think it's time you told me the truth.'

**

Wickham and Nightingale retraced their steps to the reception where they took the lift to the fourth floor. Wickham stood leaning against the back wall, hands thrust in his pockets, looking down at his feet, while Nightingale waited at the front of the lift, eyes fixed on the floor indicator. Shortly, a ping signalled their arrival.

'Be interesting to see what the professor has to say for herself,' Wickham said, as the doors started to slide open.

Nightingale glanced back at him.

'Doesn't look good, does it?' She stepped out of the lift and straight into the path of a man hurrying down the corridor. She held her hands up and stepped aside. 'Sorry.'

Something in the man's behaviour, a subtle drop of the chin, a sudden turn of the head, made Nightingale look back at him.

'It's him!' she called.

The man started to run.

'Stop! Police!' Wickham called, giving chase just as the man darted through the door to the stairs.

***

Fisher felt Luna reverse into his legs.

'Steady, girl.' He patted her flanks, settling her back down. 'So, Professor, why don't you sit down and tell me the whole story? And please don't underestimate me. I might be blind, but I'm not stupid. And just in case you plan on spouting some bollocks about client confidentiality, I should warn you, I've got a warrant to search all of your papers. The magistrate didn't need too much persuading, once we'd explained how this person has killed more than once.' Before Woolf could answer, a man's shouts could be heard in the corridor. Fisher recognised Wickham's hard-edged voice. He clambered to his feet. 'What's going on?'

A heavy silence clothed the room. 'Professor…?'

He turned his head, trying to sense her presence, only it soon became apparent that whilst her perfume lingered, the woman hadn't.

'Bloody hell!' Fisher cursed. 'Luna… the door.' He started forward, guided by the gentle pull of the harness. A moment later, his foot caught on a chair leg, sending him sprawling to the ground. It took him a few minutes to untangle himself and Luna's harness. He had just clambered to his feet when he heard footsteps hurrying down the corridor towards him.

'The guy was here — the one Beth saw at the station,' Wickham said, his breath coursing in and out. 'We went after him but he was too quick for us.'

Fisher shook his head.

'Shit.'

'We went as fast as we could,' Nightingale said. 'But it was like chasing Usain Bolt. The guy on reception said he flew through the doors and ran off up the road.'

'Shit,' Fisher repeated.

After a short pause, Wickham said, 'No Professor Woolf?'

'She was here but she left,' Fisher replied. He slumped against what he took to be the professor's desk. 'Seems she had something more important to attend to.'

'So what do we do now?' Nightingale asked.

Fisher roused himself.

'Right. Okay. This is what we're going to do. Andy, you're going to stay here and wait for a CSI to dust the place for prints. Once that's done, box up the files and get them over to the station. Beth, you and I are going to pay the professor a little visit at home.' Fisher felt Luna nudge his leg. His hand dropped to her crown. 'I know, girl. The Falcon's going to have my guts for garters. And for once, I don't blame her.'

'Did you manage to get anything out of Professor Woolf before she left?' Nightingale asked, as they made their way down to the ground floor.

'Not really. She assured me she never shares information with anyone, but the fact she did a runner speaks for itself. And she obviously knows this mystery guy, seeing he was here.'

'Who do you think he is?'

'One of her clients. Or a lecturer. Maybe even be a student. Who knows?'

'He'd have to be a mature student.'

'How old would you say he is? Roughly.' Nightingale always struggled with people's ages.

'Forty? Could be a bit older... or younger.'

The man on reception was adamant that Professor Woolf was still somewhere in the building, seeing as he hadn't seen her leave. Fisher quizzed him about fire exits and learned that there were several on the ground floor, as per regulations, though none of which were alarmed. Despite the irrefutable evidence that the professor could have made a discreet exit, the receptionist refused to supply the details of her home address or registration plate, and Fisher was forced to wait a frustrating twenty minutes before one of the university's HR officers came up with the goods.

61.

While Nightingale navigated the roads out of Canterbury, heading West towards the southern Kent coast to Woolf's home address, Fisher arranged for a local patrol car to attend, with instructions to detain anyone at the property.

On reaching their destination, Fisher couldn't get out of the car fast enough, after being thrown around in his seat as the car made its way along a winding route of twisty-turny country lanes at breakneck speed. According to Nightingale, the house was about as remote as you could get in the south east of England, located at the end of a quiet lane, with no nearby neighbours and no passing traffic.

'There's a patrol car outside,' Nightingale commented as she pulled on the handbrake. 'I can't see any other cars.'

Fisher climbed out. Picking up the sound of a car door opening he said, 'The uniforms getting out of their car?'

'Yes.'

He gave a nod then pulled out his warrant card and held it up.

'Detectives Fisher and Nightingale,' he called over. 'I take it there's no sign of the professor?'

'No,' came the reply. 'The place was empty by the time we got here.'

Fisher felt the scar tissue around his eyes tighten as his eyebrows hitched up.

'By the time you got here... you think she beat you to it?'

'Looks like it,' replied the patrol officer. 'There are empty hangers in the wardrobe and hardly any toiletries in the bathroom. No toothbrushes or toothpaste.'

'Nothing?' Fisher asked.

'Maybe a bit of make-up.'

Fisher's brow twitched. Perhaps Woolf hadn't packed her own bags? When he'd lived with Amanda, she'd have forgotten her passport before she forgot her make-up.

'The bins have been emptied too,' the officer added. 'Even the wheelie bin.'

The surprises were coming thick and fast. Fisher gave a nod and pulled out his phone summoning the services of the CSI team.

'Okay, well we'll go and take a look. Beth, go grab a couple of scene suits will you, please?'

Ten minutes later, Nightingale gave a muted 'wow' as she guided Fisher into the lounge.

'What is it?'

'It's so bare. There are no pictures or ornaments. In fact, there are no personal effects at all.'

'Maybe she took them with her?'

'I don't think so. The place is totally soulless. Apart from a cheap sofa, coffee table and a TV, there's nothing.'

'Maybe she hasn't been here long?'

'Maybe.'

The rest of the house was similarly barren. The kitchen was basic but spotlessly clean, the sparse contents of the fridge reminding Fisher of his own inadequate culinary expertise. Upstairs, the bathroom cabinet had been raided apart from a handful of items, all of them unopened. The bedroom was their last stop.

Fisher heard a dull scuffing at the carpet.

'Nothing under there,' Nightingale said.

The sound of wooden doors being opened came next. The wardrobe, Fisher presumed.

'Anything?' he asked.

'A few bits and pieces. There are some men's shirts and trousers.' He heard her inhale deeply. 'Everything smells freshly washed.'

A smile crept on Fisher's lips. Smart girl.

She closed the doors. Next came the sound of a drawer being tugged open. Then closed. Followed by another. 'There's some underwear in the drawers. Men's and women's.'

Matt felt a twinge in the pit of his stomach as his disappointment made itself felt. It was looking increasingly likely the professor was more involved with their killer than he imagined.

Back in the lounge, Nightingale asked, 'So what do we do now?'

Fisher was about to answer, when he heard a car door slam.

'Go see who that is,' he said urgently. He heard her footsteps trip quickly across the room.

'It's the CSI.'

'Good. I want this place dusted for prints asap.'

While Nightingale explained the situation to the crime scene investigator, Fisher put a call through to Wickham.

'How's it going?'

'Okay. I've started to box the files up. There's way too many of them for me to go through here. They go back eight years.'

'Anyone else at the university have access to them?'

'Not without the professor's permission. There's only one key to the filing room and Woolf's got it. I had to get the caretaker to take the door off its hinges. How about you? I take it she wasn't at the house.'

333

'No. It's weird. According to Beth the place looks hardly lived in. Plus, we found some men's clothing in the wardrobe in the bedroom... and only one bed.'

Wickham gave a groan. 'Shit... the DCI's going to go ballistic.'

'Thanks for pointing that out.'

It's not like Fisher needed to be told; he'd already worked that out for himself. This could well be his undoing, seeing as he was the one who insisted on bringing the professor into the investigation. He brushed the thought aside and asked, 'Has the CSI arrived yet?'

'Yes. She's dusting for prints as we speak.'

'Can I have a quick word?'

A woman called Kerry came to the phone.

'Your sergeant told me you were in something of a hurry. I'm still working on them. There are dozens. Apparently, this room is regularly used to meet students.'

'What about the filing room?'

'I only found one set of prints on the inside of the door and the files.'

Meaning Woolf couldn't claim that someone accessed the files without her knowledge — another nail in the professor's coffin.

'Has DS Wickham explained that we're particularly interested in seeing if any of the prints match the one we took from the BMW in the Rob Newman investigation?'

'Yes.'

'Okay. Well, call me on this number the second you get any results.' He hung up and leaned against the wall, blowing out a sigh.

62.

The following hour stretched Fisher's patience to its limit as he waited for the CSIs to do their thing. After checking in with force control for the umpteenth time, only to be told there were still no sightings of the professor's car, he turned to Nightingale.

'Beth, can you get hold of the CSI for me, please. I need to talk to him about fingerprints.'

'Hi. I'm Connor Murphy,' came a soft Irish voice. 'What do you want to know?'

Fisher's surprise must have been evident as Nightingale said, 'I thought you might want an update.'

Fisher nodded. 'Thanks.' He turned towards the scientist. 'How are you getting on Connor?'

'So far, the prints all look like they're from the same person. Though I'd say the house has been recently cleaned throughout.'

Fisher frowned.

'I wonder if the killer and the professor have parted ways?'

'Maybe he's gone somewhere else, to lie low,' Nightingale suggested. 'Professor Woolf could have gone to warn him, now she knows we're on to them.'

'He knows anyway, otherwise he wouldn't have run.'

'True, but Woolf doesn't know that, does she?'

She was right.

'We've got to find Woolf. We need her to lead us to him.'

The following morning, with still no news of the professor, Fisher gathered the team together.

'The university has agreed to send us Woolf's personnel file,' he told them. 'Hopefully it will tell us where she lived and worked before. You never know, she might have chosen somewhere familiar to go to ground.'

'Don't get your hopes up,' DC Kami Aptil said. 'I spoke to the letting agent the professor rented the house from. They told me she's been there eight years, having come straight over from the States.'

'She's been at the university the same amount of time,' Wickham said.

'She can't have lived in that house eight years,' Nightingale commented. 'It looked like she'd only just moved in.'

'Maybe she was in the process of moving out?' Wickham said.

Fisher nodded.

'That's not a bad suggestion.'

'If she was, she hadn't said anything to the letting agents,' Aptil advised.

An idea flashed into Fisher's head.

'Don't you need references to rent a house? Could be worth following up. She might be staying with friends.'

'I checked,' Aptil said. 'All her referees were American residents.'

'Call the agents and get their details anyway. Maybe one of them has since moved to the UK. Likewise, Andy, when you get the info from the university, see if you can trace the referees from when she applied for the job.'

'No problem,' Wickham replied. 'I could also check to see if any other cars have been registered to Woolf's address. If the killer lived there at some point, he might have registered his car there.'

'No need. I already checked,' Fisher said. 'The Seat's been the only car at that address for the last three years.'

'What about the white van?' Nightingale said.

'Good point, Beth,' Fisher replied. 'For anyone who doesn't know, a white transit was parked near Warren Newman's house while he was supposedly being broken in to. Beth, seeing as you raised it, maybe you could follow that up?'

'Will do.'

'And when you've done that, give the post office a call. Find out whether the same person usually delivers Woolf's post and see if they've seen a white van there, or any car other than the Seat, for that matter.' Fisher turned his head towards where he knew DS Wickham to be sitting. 'Andy, while you're waiting for Woolf's HR file to arrive, could you make a start reviewing the stuff you bought back from her office. Look for any leads to a possible bolthole. Maybe she did some counselling somewhere else in the country and there's a place she usually stays.' Fisher eased himself up off the desk he'd been perched on. 'Right, there's no time to waste.'

Everyone quickly dispersed, galvanized into action, and by the time Fisher was slowly making his way across the office, the tap of keyboards and urgent buzz of phone conversations were already filling the air.

And then came the icy tone of DCI Fallon, cutting through the hubbub.

'It's true then?'

Fisher stopped walking and spun on his heel.

'What is?'

'You, being hell-bent on destroying your career.'

'I haven't got time for this right now.' He started to walk away.

337

She hurried after him. Her talon-like fingers grabbed his arm, pinching the flesh.

'Don't you walk away from me when I'm talking to you.'

'Let go of me,' he said, keeping his voice low but the menace clear.

She released her grip and stepped closer, enveloping him in a cloud of cloyingly strong perfume. His nose wrinkled in distaste.

'You need to stop this now,' she hissed into his ear. 'Forget the professor. Forget the mystery man. Newman killed himself. End of.'

Fisher spun around.

'We can catch this guy or are you so obsessed with solve rates you're prepared to let a killer walk free?'

'This is nothing to do with targets, this is about keeping you in check. You should be grateful. If it gets out that someone you brought into the investigation was involved in the death of the prime suspect it won't be my head on the chopping block. I'll make it clear to any inquiry that I was against bringing an outsider onto the investigation from the start.'

'And I'll argue that if that was true, you would have stopped it. And you didn't.' He started to walk away.

'Fisher!' she called after him. 'I mean it.'

He returned to his desk and slumped in his seat. The Falcon's warning had a troubling edge to it. It was arse-covering in the extreme. Yet, despite that, he knew if he let it drop and it later got out that they'd failed to pursue a murderer, she'd be first to point the finger of blame in his direction.

He was damned if he did and damned if he didn't.

Which made it a very easy decision. There was a killer out there and he wasn't about to let them walk.

The sound of approaching footsteps roused him from his thoughts.

'Is everything okay?' It was Nightingale. 'I saw you talking to the DCI. I figured it's not good news. She had that look, you know.'

Fisher smiled.

'When is it ever good news with her? But no, we're fine.'

'Oh good. Well, you'll be pleased to hear I managed to talk to the postie whose round covers the professor's house. She said she's never seen a white transit, only the black Seat, but she has caught glimpses of a man. Description matches our guy. As there was never any post for him, she assumed he was a boyfriend who stopped over occasionally.'

'Boyfriend, eh?' he grumbled. Woolf really had pulled the wool over their eyes. 'She must have had an interesting take on pillow talk, sharing injustices she'd unearthed during her counselling sessions. I'd assumed she was single and married to the job.' He gave a derisory snort, adding, 'What am I saying? She was. In fact she was so dedicated, she even took her work home with her.' Fisher's face puckered into a frown. 'That's it!' He shook his head. 'How could we miss it?'

'Miss what? What are you on about?' Nightingale asked.

'Hang on a sec.' He leaned back in seat and called, 'Andy! Have you got a minute?'

Wickham came straight over.

'What is it?'

'Woolf's files hold the answer... our killer's in there somewhere. Think about it — where is a psychologist most likely to meet someone?'

'You think he was one of her clients?' Wickham said.

'Got to be. It would be hard for her to single out a student, especially a mature student, without raising a few eyebrows. And although it's possible she met serial killers in prison as part of her research, it's likely they're still locked up. But a patient, or client, whatever you want to call them, wouldn't draw any attention. If that's the case, you'd expect it to be a few sessions before they got it on, don't you think? Which means there's a good chance there'll be notes of their conversations in her files.'

Wickham groaned.

'Where the hell do we start? There's a mountain of files.'

'We need to look for words like murder or death or talk of someone getting what they deserved or rough justice or references to the urge to kill. Anything that gets your detective antennae twitching. And as for the amount of stuff, I'll get everyone to pitch in.'

'Okay.' Wickham didn't sound convinced. He started to walk away, but Fisher heard his footsteps stall. 'Actually, I was going to come and talk to you before you called me over. It might be a coincidence, but I know you always say there's no such thing, so...' Fisher felt his heart rate leap a little. Wickham went on, 'I started to look at the files, like you asked, looking for a clue of her whereabouts. Out of interest, I started with the one for the kid who killed himself, Callum Finchley. I wanted to see if there was any reference to the choirmaster. Although most of the sessions were spent talking about the boy's feelings and his behaviour, a couple of times she got him to open up about the abuse. Hatton's name is there in black and white, including the fact he also taught guitar from home.'

'Woolf told us the boy never admitted to being abused,' Nightingale said, sounding shocked.

'I wonder why?' Fisher replied in a tone heavy on the irony. 'Andy, go on.'

'After that, I pulled out her file on Nigel Madden, the rapist found with his neck broken. She'd produced a sound argument as to why he should be denied bail, citing a long list of arrests where the victims withdrew their accusations before it went to trial. The file contains a bundle of background information, including details of where the attacks had taken place and what time of day they happened as well as what the victims had been doing, wearing, that sort of thing.'

'Perfect for someone looking to either track or lure the rapist to his death,' Fisher commented.

'That's what I thought. After that, I started to pull files where the person being counselled had been a victim of any sort of crime. I've found a few. The first was a woman who'd been referred to Woolf by a domestic abuse shelter. She'd been beaten up by her husband on more than one occasion but kept going back to him. In their last session the woman said she wouldn't be needing any more counselling given the recent demise of her husband. Turns out he died after their house went up in flames due to a chip pan fire. His wife was back in the shelter after another beating when it happened and had a cast-iron alibi. The coroner ruled it as accidental death. It looked like the guy had fallen asleep after putting the chip pan on. The guy's habit of eating late at night after getting in from the pub was mentioned in Woolf's notes.'

'Interesting,' Fisher said.

'There's another case — a man whose GP referred him for counselling. He was suffering from anxiety and insomnia as a result of being bullied at work.'

'Don't tell me,' Fisher said. 'The bully turned up face down in the Medway?'

'Not quite. He's alive and well, as far as I can tell, but in her notes Woolf had written that the insomnia was actually down to a neighbour's dog crying through the night. She suggested her client speak to the neighbour, but he said that wasn't an option as the neighbour was the type to talk with his fists. Everyone in the neighbourhood knew he beat and starved the dog, but nobody dared do anything about it. What caught my eye was that Woolf had made a note of the neighbour's name and address. I did a quick check and got a hit straightaway. The neighbour died a couple of months after Woolf's final session with her client.'

'How?' Fisher asked.

'You'll like this. Cause of death was a suspected heart attack. Though the pathologist couldn't say with certainty as the body had been partially eaten by the guy's dog. There were no obvious signs of foul play, but we all know how easy it is to administer drugs that mimic the symptoms of a heart attack. It's got to be possible for somebody to have injected him with something and the dog ate the evidence… you can't find needle marks where the flesh doesn't exist.'

Fisher felt the colour drain from his face.

'Jesus. That's four suspicious deaths out of… how many files have you managed to get through?'

'Twenty-seven, so far.'

Fisher blew out his cheeks. The potential was mind-blowing.

'I can keep working my way through them if—'

Fisher's phone gave a trill ring.

'Hang on a sec.' He swiped to answer and put the phone to his ear. After a minute's nodding and the occasional 'uh-huh' he finally hung up.

'Beth, get your coat. Woolf's car's been found. Looks like someone tried to set it alight. And get this — a member of the public phoned treble nine, claiming there was a woman trapped inside.'

342

63.

Nightingale drove them to a barren tract of land on the outskirts of a rundown housing estate. Fisher climbed out, his nose twitching at the acrid smell of smoke hanging in the air. Nightingale guided him across the scrub; the rough ground snagged and grabbed at his feet, threatening to send him toppling, and he gave a sigh of relief when she finally drew to a stop.

'The area's been cordoned off,' she said. 'The car's just ahead. It doesn't look too bad from the outside, though from what I can tell the interior's badly burnt.'

'I can smell petrol,' Fisher said, sniffing at the air. Just then he heard voices nearby. 'Who's that?'

'The fire crew. Looks like they're packing up to go.'

'Anyone else around? Any medics?'

'Not that I can see.'

'See if you can find someone to come and talk to us.'

A moment later, one of the firefighters joined them.

'Hi. I'm Crew Manager Warwick,' a female voice said. 'How can I help?'

'What's the state of play with the casualty?' Fisher asked. 'I take it she's already on her way to hospital given the lack of an ambulance.'

'The casualty?'

'The woman trapped in the car,' he explained, trying not to sound irritable.

The fire officer gave a strange laugh, then said, 'Follow me.'

Fisher turned to Nightingale.

'You go. I'll wait here.'

A minute later she was back. She gave a weighty sigh and said, 'You're not going to believe it.'

***

'I swear you couldn't tell it wasn't her real hair,' Nightingale said, as she and Fisher returned to the car.

Fisher was still trying to make sense of it all. There had been no woman in the car, only a wig and some clothing discarded on the back seat. The person who discovered the fire smashed a window and pulled the wig and a coat out before retreating from the flames. Nightingale confirmed the coat was a match for one she had seen the professor wear. As for the wig…

'Wouldn't have been much of a disguise if you could, would it?' Fisher said, shaking his head dolefully. They'd been well and truly duped.

'What do you mean disguise?'

Fisher stopped and turned to her.

'Remember the guy who picked the Beemer up? You said he looked familiar.'

'Yeah. I still don't know where…' She gave a sharp intake of breath. 'Oh my God. I can't believe it. Are you sure?' Fisher kept his mouth shut, giving her time for it to sink in. Shortly she said, 'Even after seeing the wig I didn't make the connection.'

'You're not the only one. I should have figured it out a lot sooner,' Fisher admitted. 'When the lift doors opened and you and Andy saw him standing there, you said he took one look at you and ran. How did he know who you were? As far as we knew, he'd never seen you before. When he picked the BMW up you were inside the fire station and Andy was in the car with me. The only person who knew who either of you were was Woolf. All the time I was sitting there in her office, Woolf must have changed and cleaned off her make up before slipping out, leaving me holding my dick. A minute later, a bloke with a rucksack — no doubt full of women's clothes — is leading you and Andy a merry dance and Woolf's nowhere to be seen.' He let out a groan. 'And the house and the files — only one set of prints. It's all so bloody obvious now. No wonder Woolf claimed to have a profound insight into the mind of a serial killer. She, he, whatever they are, is one. She totally played us. We virtually handed her Rob Newman's head on a plate. And I tell you what, Lewis Hunt and anyone else Woolf eyed up as being the killer should count themselves lucky.'

'I don't understand.'

'I'll stake my reputation on Woolf being Hunt's intruder. I think Woolf decided to play vigilante right from the off. No wonder he, she, was so keen to help. He wanted the lowdown on the likely suspects, so he could do a bit of investigating of his own.' He gave a groan. 'If we're right about the people referred to in the university files who've since died and then factor in the files we haven't even got round to yet, this could turn into the biggest manhunt for a serial killer since the Yorkshire Ripper.'

The question was, would he still be in the job, let alone part of the investigation, once the powers that be realised who had brought Woolf inside the fold and the Falcon started wielding the blame? If she was going to throw him to the wolves, maybe he should leave it to her to track down Woolf. The DCI was certainly no Red Riding Hood but he had no doubt Woolf would make light work of her. Yet perhaps there was another way forward...?

He pulled his phone from his pocket and called Fallon.

'Ma'am. I wondered if you're free for a briefing this afternoon. Now the Newman case is closed I thought it would be a good idea if we—'

She didn't give him time to finish.

'You've finally seen sense then.'

'On reflection, I have to agree with your assessment; it was obviously suicide. So, anyway, I've switched mine and Beth's focus to the cold cases you wanted us to review. There's one — the suspected murder of a choirmaster a few years back that's caught my attention— we originally thought it might have been linked to the other murders. As it turns out the choirmaster is mentioned in one of the professor's files we seized from the university.'

'And?'

Fisher cleared his throat.

'Well, it turns out he's not the only person mentioned in the files who has since died. We were hoping to talk to the professor about it, only it seems she's disappeared.'

'What do you mean disappeared?'

'Gone. Done a bunk. Oh, and it turns out she is probably a he. Anyway, I can give you more details when we meet.'

The line went silent.

Fisher gave a wry smile. Who knew cold cases could be so much fun?

64.

He glanced in the rear-view mirror, checking out his new look. A pair of intelligent brown eyes peered out from underneath a thick fringe of black hair styled in a classic side parting. It was astounding what a difference a pair of coloured contacts and wig could make. He rubbed a hand over his chin, listened to it rasp, the designer stubble completing his transformation.

He drew the cuff of his expensive suit jacket up and glanced down at the Rolex that adorned his wrist — a fitting memento from his latest project.

18:22.

Another hour and he would reach his destination and his new life would begin.

He slipped his shirt cuff down to cover the face of the watch and smiled, the action feeling pleasingly symbolic. Perhaps he should have used a black bag on Newman... given him a taste of his own medicine. But then he would have missed that exquisite high on watching the life, and the hope of any reprieve, ebb from his eyes. Stupid boy. Thinking he could get away with it. His initial confusion as the sedative wore off, swiftly replaced by an irate scowl as he demanded to be let free, buoyed up on a raft of denials. Then the softening of his features and the blinking back of tears... the palpable relief at the offer of freedom in exchange for a written confession, no doubt one he would have reneged on the second he walked free. Not that that was ever going to happen. That had been a little white lie.

He'd known Newman had to die the very first time he'd seen Connie Lloyd's photo on the news. It had brought back so many painful memories of his mother's death at his father's sadistic hand.

Call it justice if you will. The universe got its karma and he got his thrills overpowering that arrogant little nobody who killed for something as trifling as money.

He turned his attention back to the road, moving the silver Audi Q8 into the right lane for the M6 toll, then easing back in his seat.

Above, the denim blue sky was beginning to brighten as the concrete-coloured clouds diminished in his rear-view mirror. He set the cruise control to a respectable 74 mph — not too fast to attract the attention of the cameras, not too slow to annoy fellow road users. Perfect for staying anonymous.

Just like him.

Acknowledgements

It's a small miracle that this book ever got finished, with the introduction of two rescue dogs into our household only a few months into its creation. Thankfully with help from my husband John, I managed to get my writing back on track and get it finished, albeit a little later than scheduled. John deserves a medal for his unswerving support, not to mention his pedantry — which ordinarily might be a source of tension, but is a wonderful asset when it comes to commenting on my first drafts.

As with my previous novels, I am extremely grateful to Julie Platt, for her brilliant editing skills, as well as her invaluable feedback that makes the book as true to life and readable as possible. And to Kath Middleton and Samantha Brownley for taking the time to read and feedback on the final draft and for continuing to provide encouragement and friendship, not just to me but to a whole community of crime fiction authors.

Also deserving of a mention is Andrew Nattrass for his insight into life as a visually impaired person, and for showing me how everything is possible provided you put your mind to it and are prepared to adapt to your environment.

Finally, I would like to thank all of my readers for their ongoing support and lovely feedback. It's what makes it all worthwhile.

And finally...

Thank you for reading Cold Kill, the second in the DI Matt Fisher series.

As so many readers rely on reviews to help them decide whether to try a new author, it would mean a great deal to me if you could spare five minutes and leave a review on Amazon or Goodreads.

And if you enjoyed this book, why not other books of mine, such as the DC Cat McKenzie series, which starts with A Confusion of Crows, available from Amazon.

If you'd like to know more about me and my work, then check out my website www.susanhandley.co.uk or follow me on Twitter @shandleyauthor or Facebook @SusanHandleyAuthor

Printed in Great Britain
by Amazon